LOVE

Great short stories
by women chosen by
Victoria Hislop

HEAD
of ZEUS

The paperback collection *Love* was first published within *The Story*,
a hardback published in the UK in 2013 by Head of Zeus Ltd.
This paperback edition published in the UK in 2014 by Head of Zeus Ltd.

Introduction Copyright © Victoria Hislop, 2013

9 7 5 3 1 2 4 6 8

A CIP catalogue record for this book is available from the British Library.

Paperback ISBN: 9781781856642
Ebook ISBN: 9781781857298

Print

CONTENTS

Introduction

Extended Copyright

THE
STORY

A GENERAL INTRODUCTION
TO LOVE, LIFE AND LOSS
BY VICTORIA HISLOP

While gathering the short stories for the anthology in which this volume *Love* originally appeared, I read some of the most brilliant and profound pieces of writing that I have ever come across.

The authors in the anthology range from a Nobel Prize winner, Doris Lessing, to the acknowledged queen of short stories, Alice Munro. There are Man Booker winners, Costa winners and Pulitzer winners. A few were born in the 19th century but the majority are more modern. Several of them are as yet unknown, others are household names, like Virginia Woolf. Many of the most vivid and passionate storytellers are young. And without doubt many of the most powerfully original are contemporary writers.

Apart from the writers all being female, the other guiding factor in the selection is that the stories have been written in English. The stories are varied and I am sure that no single reader will like them all. Perhaps I enjoyed certain stories because they meant something very personal to me. Others I think would be admired by any reader.

I discovered that it is possible for a short story (unlike a novel) to attain something close to perfection. Its brevity can mean that an author has the chance to produce a series of almost perfectly formed sentences, where every carefully chosen word contributes to its meaning. Occasionally the result is flawless, something a novel can never be.

Readers are allowed to be impatient with short stories. My own patience limit for a novel which I am not hugely enjoying may be three or four chapters. If it has not engaged me by then, it has lost me and is returned to the library or taken to a charity shop. With a short story, three or four pages are the maximum I allow (sometimes they are only five or six pages long in any case). A short story can entice us in without preamble or background information, and for that reason it has no excuse. It must not bore us even for a second.

If a short story has no excuse for being dull, it has even less reason to be bland. As I selected the stories for this anthology, I found myself reading stories that made me laugh out loud, gasp and often weep. If a story did not arouse a strong response in me, then I did not select it. Even if it is elegaic or whimsical, it must still stir something deep in the pit of the stomach or make the heart race.

Some stories had such a strong effect on me that I had to put a collection down and do something different with the rest of my day. I could read nothing else. I needed to ponder it, or possibly read it for a second time. Muriel Spark's 'The First Year of My Life' (Loss) dazzled me with its brilliance. That was a day when I didn't need to do anything other than reflect on her wisdom. For different reasons, Alice Munro's 'Miles City, Montana' (Loss) rendered me incapable of continuing to read. She moves seamlessly from a description of a drowned boy's funeral to an incident on a family outing where we believe that one of the children will drown. Even the relief I felt at the story's relatively happy conclusion was not enough to lift my mood.

Quite often an anthology is named after the author's favourite short story, and if that were the case I would read the eponymous story first. More often, there is no particular entry point into an anthology (unless you are happy to read them in the order they appear, something I usually resisted) and in that case, there was no better guide than simply whether the title intrigued me. Who, for example, would not go straight to a story entitled 'How I Finally Lost My Heart' (Doris Lessing, *Love*), 'A Weight Problem' (Elspeth Davie, *Life*), 'How Did I Get Away with Killing One of the Biggest Lawyers in the State? It Was Easy.' (Alice Walker, *Life*) or even the intriguingly named: 'The Life You Save May Be Your Own' (Flannery O'Connor, *Loss*)?

A short story can be more surreal than many readers might tolerate with a novel and, perhaps, less grounded in reality. Succinctness sometimes allows a writer to explore ideas that may not sustain over a greater length. An example of this is Nicola Barker's 'Inside Information' (*Loss*), a shiningly original story told through the voice of an unborn child who is considering the suitability of its soon-to-be mother. Personally, I love the slightly quirky in a short story, but I would probably not be so patient if I had to listen to the voice of a foetus over three hundred pages.

I think the short story can give a writer the opportunity to experiment and to try a style or a voice that they would not use in the novel form, so there is often an element of freshness and surprise for the reader – and perhaps for the writer too.

For me, the stories that make the greatest impact are those that are the most emotional. On a few occasions, when I was reading in the library, I noted curious glances from my neighbours. They gave me sympathetic looks, but tactfully chose to ignore my tears, the context probably reassuring them that I was weeping over the fate of a fictional character rather than some personal catastrophe. Perhaps a few hours later, I would be shaking with suppressed laughter. I think I must have been a very annoying person with whom to share a desk.

I have divided the stories into three categories – *Love, Loss* and *Life* – but these titles are loose. Love is, of course, a central preoccupation of literature, but a love story is so often a story of loss, or indeed a story of life. Many of these stories take an amusing and sardonic look at love, so the division, though slightly artificial, is designed to give a reader the chance to read according to her or his mood. Many of them could appear under more than one heading and, I will admit, some stories could probably fit happily into all three categories.

LOVE

In the volume entitled *Love*, love appears in all its guises and disguises. As Yiyun Li describes in 'Love in the Marketplace': 'A romance is more than a love story with a man.'

Perhaps maternal love is the most visceral of all loves. At least it felt so the first time I read the phenomenal 'My Son the Hero' by Clare Boylan. 'Reach' by Rachel Seiffert and 'The Turtle' by Roshi Fernando also powerfully evoke the strength of a mother's love, and 'Even Pretty Eyes Commit Crimes' by M. J. Hyland touches beautifully on the love between father and son.

In this section there is the painful poignancy of romantic love in Margaret Drabble's 'Faithful Lovers', love that is more like madness in 'Master' by Angela Carter and love that is unrecognised until it is too late in 'The Man from Mars' by Margaret Atwood. There is love that for some reason is not meant to be. Chimamanda Ngozi Adichie writes about this in 'The Thing Around your Neck'. There is love as infatuation, short-lived and potentially destructive, in Jennifer Egan's 'The Watch Trick', and the making of love, sometimes kinkily, as in Anne Enright's 'Revenge'.

Many readers will know the experience of being haunted by an ex, and Alison Lurie writes vividly about the effect of lost or past loves in her characters' lives ('In the Shadow' and also the even more extraordinary 'Ilse's House').

LOSS

Many of the stories in *Loss* are tragic, some are shocking. All of them are emotional.

From Katherine Mansfield's almost unbearably poignant 'The Canary', which is written with a feather-light touch, to Alice Munro's 'Gravel', which is blunt to the point of brutality, I think few of these stories will leave readers cold.

There are lost lives, lost loves, lost innocence, a lost mother (Colette Paul's 'Renaissance'), lost breasts (Ellen Gilchrist's 'Indignities'), loss of hearing (Helen Simpson's 'Sorry?') and even a lost leopard (Anna Kavan's extraordinary 'A Visit').

'The First Year of My Life' by Muriel Spark takes the idea that babies are born omniscient and gradually lose their power and their knowledge. In this story, a baby is born in 1913, 'in the very worst year that the world had ever seen so far', and watches, dismayed, unsmiling, sardonic: 'My teeth were coming through very nicely in my opinion, and well worth all the trouble I was put to in bringing them forth. I weighed twenty pounds. On all the world's fighting fronts the men killed in action or dead of wounds numbered 8,538,315 and the warriors wounded and maimed were 21,219,452. With these figures in mind I sat up in my high chair and banged my spoon on the table.'

It is a profound story – a curious companion piece to others in the anthology in which the story is also told by a wise, all-knowing baby: Nicola Barker's masterful 'Inside Information' and Ali Smith's 'The Child' (*Life*) are especially engaging and fresh.

Carol Shields' 'Fragility', with its hinterland story of a disabled child and a couple's lost happiness, shares much of the pathos of Yiyun Li's 'After a Life', in which a dying child lies incarcerated in a small apartment. Both stories are agonising to read. Lorrie Moore's 'Agnes of Iowa' is similarly tragic but even more open-ended, with a couple doomed to live in perpetuity with their woes.

Susan Hill's 'Father, Father', a story of two daughters 'losing' their father to a second wife, their step-mother, is insightful and real, a common situation faultlessly described.

LIFE

Life provides infinite shades of light and dark and in this section there are many curious tales and unusual settings. There is a handful of stories that made me ask: What on earth gave her this idea? Where did this come from? One example is 'The Axe' by Penelope Fitzgerald. It is a chilling horror story that takes place in the deceptively banal environment of an office and describes what happens when a man finds his job has been 'axed'. The narrator leaves us, as she should in such a story, with our hairs standing on end.

There is plenty of humour in this section and this is often provided by an unexpected or rather marvellous twist. 'How Did I Get Away with Killing One of the Biggest Lawyers in the State? It Was Easy.' by Alice Walker is flawless. And Penelope Lively's 'Corruption' is too, with the most brilliant visual image perhaps of any story – where a judge, involved in a pornography trial, takes some of his 'research papers' on holiday. A gust of wind sends copies of the offending magazines flying around the beach to be gathered by innocent children and even a woman who, until this moment, has been flirting with the judge. It is brilliantly comic. I felt I was watching the action unfold scene by scene, just as if I was watching a film.

There is a mildly pornographic element too in A. M. Homes' darkly comic 'A Real Doll'. It's almost about love, but more to do with sex. A boy uses his sister's Barbie as a sex toy and all sorts of jealousies ensue (Ken has an opinion, naturally). It's funny, outrageous and totally original.

Alison Lurie's 'Fat People' is once again funny, dark and unique. One could say it is about dieting, but that would only be one per cent of it. But, for me, Nicola Barker is the wittiest and often the most original. I chose three of her stories for the anthology but had to restrain myself from selecting so many more. In 'G-String', her powers of description had me laughing out loud: 'It felt like her G-string was making headway from between her buttocks up into her throat... now she knew how a horse felt when offered a new bit and bridle for the first time.' Most women will know how accurate this is. Needless to say, this is a hilarious tale right to the very end, where the woman ends up 'knickerless... a truly modern female'.

Ali Smith's 'The Child' is also comic and surreal. A baby with the voice of an adult is placed in a woman's supermarket trolley. It's the reverse of a baby-snatching drama, and is both farcical and strangely daring. It was one of my favourites, and visits to the supermarket have not been the same since...

Elspeth Davie's 'Change of Face' about a street artist is haunting as is her story 'A Weight Problem'. The situations she describes seem to have been magicked from thin air.

Other stories are slightly more shocking: a death may take place, but the loss is not, in itself, a focal point. It is perhaps more to do with learning. Margaret Atwood's very clever story, 'Betty', is about this. Over a small number of pages, one gets a strong sense of the narrator's identity, her stages of growing up and how she reinterprets the past in the light of her age and experience. It is full of wisdom.

Helen Simpson's story 'Ahead of the Pack' is brief but brilliant. The central notion is that we should have a quota of carbon points each day (in the same way that people on diets allow themselves a certain number of calories). It is such a clever idea that I wondered if it should not become a reality. What better way to ensure that we do not get 'in terms of [our] planetary profile... an absolutely vast arse'.

I happily included the slightly self-referential 'A Society' by Virginia Woolf, where the character of Poll is left a fortune by her father on condition that she reads all the books in the London Library. She declares them 'for the most part unutterably bad!' Having done most of my research for this anthology there, I can confirm that Poll is wrong.

I have had interesting discussions about whether there is a female 'voice' and whether women write differently from men. I believe there are some quintessentially feminine writers – and some whose writing provides no clues as to their identity. Angela Carter's 'The Bloody Chamber' (*Love*), for example, is neither masculine nor feminine. It is simply one of the most powerful, imaginative and sensual pieces of writing that I have ever come across. If I did not have the knowledge, I would certainly not be able to identify that A. M. Homes' stories are from a woman's pen. Her male protagonists are totally convincing and their 'voices' provocative and disturbing.

Some stories are so vivid that it is hard to imagine them as anything other than autobiography – even when the writer is female and the narrator is male. 'Before He Left the Family' by Carrie Tiffany (*Loss*) is a very matter-of-fact, no-blame narration of parental separation, but in subtle ways leaves the reader with little doubt over the effect this had on the sons. It is masterful storytelling. The male voice is very real.

I believe that many of the writers in this volume have the

ability to leave their gender behind in their writing, whether through deliberately disguising themselves behind a male narrator, or adopting a masculine sensibility. Once again, this is something that would be more difficult to sustain over the duration of an entire novel.

Short stories seem ideally suited to how many of us are reading now. They are perfect to read on an iPad, even on a phone. They can last as long as a short bus or train journey. They are complete in themselves – though from time to time they leave us hanging in mid-air with some kind of twist or ambiguity, as if this story we have in our hands is merely a beginning.

This is a very personal selection of my favourite stories. There will definitely be omissions (some of them accidental, some of them deliberate). Many of these writers were suggested by friends and colleagues. It seems that everyone has a favourite writer of short stories – and whenever I mentioned to people what I was doing they all insisted that I must read one author or another. I always followed up on recommendations, but I did not always find that I shared their taste.

It's been a glorious adventure putting this book together. I hope readers will share some of my excitement and enthusiasm and use it as a starting point for their own explorations into this extraordinary genre.

Victoria Hislop
June 2014

Adapted from the introduction to *The Story: Love Loss and The Lives of Women* (Head of Zeus, 2013)

A MARRIED MAN'S STORY

Katherine Mansfield

Katherine Mansfield (1888–1923) was born in Wellington, New Zealand. After moving to England at nineteen, Mansfield secured her reputation as a writer with the story collection *Bliss*, published in 1920. She reached the height of her powers with her 1922 collection *The Garden Party*. Her last five years were shadowed by tuberculosis; she died from the disease at the age of thirty-four.

It is evening. Supper is over. We have left the small, cold dining room; we have come back to the sitting room where there is a fire. All is as usual. I am sitting at my writing table which is placed across a corner so that I am behind it, as it were, and facing the room. The lamp with the green shade is alight; I have before me two large books of reference, both open, a pile of papers. ... All the paraphernalia, in fact, of an extremely occupied man. My wife, with our little boy on her lap, is in a low chair before the fire. She is about to put him to bed before she clears away the dishes and piles them up in the kitchen for the servant girl to-morrow morning. But the warmth, the quiet, and the sleepy baby have made her dreamy. One of his red woollen boots is off; one is on. She sits, bent forward, clasping the little bare foot, staring into the glow, and as the fire quickens, falls, flares again, her shadow – an immense *Mother and Child* – is here and gone again upon the wall. ...

Outside it is raining. I like to think of that cold drenched window behind the blind, and beyond, the dark bushes in the garden, their broad leaves bright with rain, and beyond the fence, the gleaming road with the two hoarse little gutters singing against each other, and the wavering reflections of the lamps, like fishes' tails. ... While I am here, I am there, lifting my face to the dim sky, and it seems to me it must be raining all over the world – that the whole earth is drenched, is sounding with a soft quick patter or hard steady drumming, or gurgling and something that is like sobbing and laughing mingled together, and that light playful splashing that is of water falling into still lakes and flowing rivers. And all at one and the same moment I am arriving in a strange city, slipping under the hood of the cab while the driver whips the cover off the breathing horse, running from shelter to shelter, dodging someone, swerving by someone else. I am conscious of tall houses, their doors and shutters sealed against the night, of dripping balconies and sodden flower pots, I am brushing through deserted gardens and peering into moist smelling summer-houses (you know how soft and almost crumbling the wood of a summer-house is in the rain), I am standing on the dark quayside, giving my ticket into the wet red hand of the old sailor in an oilskin – How strong the sea smells! How loudly those tied-up boats knock against one another! I am crossing the wet stackyard, hooded in an old sack, carrying a lantern, while the house-dog, like a soaking doormat, springs, shakes himself over me. And now I am walking along a deserted road – it is impossible to miss the puddles and the trees are stirring – stirring. ...

But one could go on with such a catalogue for ever – on and on – until one lifted the single arum lily leaf and discovered the tiny snails clinging, until one counted ... and what then? Aren't those just the signs, the traces of my feeling? The bright green streaks made by someone who walks over the dewy grass? Not the feeling itself. And as I think that, a mournful glorious voice begins to sing in my bosom. Yes, perhaps that is nearer what I mean. What a voice! What power! What velvety softness! Marvellous!

Suddenly my wife turns round quickly. She knows – how long has she known? – that I am not 'working'! It is strange that with her full, open gaze, she should smile so timidly – and that she should say in such a hesitating voice: 'What are you thinking?'

I smile and draw two fingers across my forehead in the way I have. 'Nothing,' I answer softly.

At that she stirs, and still trying not to make it sound important, she says: 'Oh, but you must have been thinking of something!'

Then I really meet her gaze, meet it fully, and I fancy her face quivers. Will she never grow accustomed to these simple – one might say – everyday little lies? Will she never learn not to expose herself – or to build up defences?

'Truly, I was thinking of nothing!'

There! I seem to see it dart at her. She turns away, pulls the other red sock off the baby – sits him up, and begins to unbutton him behind. I wonder if that little soft rolling bundle sees anything, feels anything? Now she turns him over on her knee, and in this light, his soft arms and legs waving, he is extraordinarily like a young crab. A queer thing is I can't connect him with my wife and myself; I've never accepted him as ours. Each time when I come into the hall and see the perambulator, I catch myself thinking: 'H'm, someone has brought a baby.' Or, when his crying wakes me at night, I feel inclined to blame my wife for having brought the baby in from outside. The truth is, that though one might suspect her of strong maternal feelings, my wife doesn't seem to me the type of woman who bears children in her own body. There's an immense difference! Where is that ... animal ease and playfulness, that quick kissing and cuddling one has been taught to expect of young mothers? She hasn't a sign of it. I believe that when she ties its bonnet she feels like an aunt and not a mother. But of course I may be wrong; she may be passionately devoted. ... I don't think so. At any rate, isn't it a trifle indecent to feel like this about one's own wife? Indecent or not, one has these feelings. And one other thing. How can I reasonably expect my wife, *a broken-hearted woman*, to spend her time tossing the baby? But that is beside the mark. She never even began to toss when her heart was whole.

And now she has carried the baby to bed. I hear her soft deliberate steps moving between the dining room and the kitchen, there and back again, to the tune of the clattering dishes. And now all is quiet. What is happening now? Oh, I know just as surely as if I'd gone to see – she is standing in the middle of the kitchen, facing the rainy window. Her head is bent, with one finger she is tracing something – nothing – on the table. It is cold in the kitchen; the gas jumps; the tap drips; it's a forlorn picture. And nobody is going to come behind her, to take her in his arms, to kiss her soft hair, to lead her to the fire and to rub her hands warm again. Nobody is going to call her or to wonder what she is doing out there. And she knows it. And yet, being a woman, deep down, deep down, she really does expect the miracle to happen; she really could embrace that dark, dark deceit, rather than live – like this.

To live like this … I write those words, very carefully, very beautifully. For some reason I feel inclined to sign them, or to write underneath – Trying a New Pen. But seriously, isn't it staggering to think what may be contained in one innocent-looking little phrase? It tempts me – it tempts me terribly. Scene. The supper-table. My wife has just handed me my tea. I stir it, lift the spoon, idly chase and then carefully capture a speck of tea-leaf, and having brought it ashore, I murmur, quite gently, 'How long shall we continue to live – like – this?' And immediately there is that famous 'blinding flash and deafening roar. Huge pieces of débris (I must say I like débris) are flung into the air … and when the dark clouds of smoke have drifted away … ' But this will never happen; I shall never know it. It will be found upon me 'intact' as they say. 'Open my heart and you will see … '

Why? Ah, there you have me! There is the most difficult question of all to answer. Why do people stay together? Putting aside 'for the sake of the children', and 'the habit of years' and 'economic reasons' as lawyers' nonsense – it's not much more – if one really does try to find out why it is that people don't leave each other, one discovers a mystery. It is because they can't; they are bound. And nobody on earth knows what are the bands that bind them except those two. Am I being obscure? Well, the thing itself isn't so frightfully crystal clear, is it? Let me put it like this. Supposing you are taken, absolutely, first into his confidence and then into hers. Supposing you know all there is to know about the situation. And having given it not only your deepest sympathy but your most honest impartial criticism, you declare, very calmly (but not without the slightest suggestion of relish – for there is – I swear there is – in the very best of us – something that leaps up and cries 'A-ahh!' for joy at the thought of destroying), 'Well, my opinion is that you two people ought to part. You'll do no earthly good together. Indeed, it seems to me, it's the duty of either to set the other free.' What happens then? He – and she – agree. It is their conviction too. You are only saying what they have been thinking all last night. And away they go to act on your advice, immediately … And the next time you hear of them they are still together. You see – you've reckoned without the unknown quantity – which is their secret relation to each other – and that they can't disclose even if they want to. Thus far you may tell and no further. Oh, don't misunderstand me! It need not necessarily have anything to do with their sleeping together ... But this brings me to a thought I've often half entertained. Which is, that human beings, as we know them, don't choose each other at all. It is the owner, the second self inhabiting them, who makes the choice for his own particular purposes, and – this may sound absurdly far-fetched – it's the second self in the other which responds. Dimly – dimly – or so it has seemed to me – we realise this, at any rate to the extent that we realise the hopelessness of trying to escape. So that, what it all amounts to is – if the impermanent selves of my wife and me are happy – *tant mieux pour nous* – if miserable – *tant pis*. ... But I don't know, I don't know. And it may be that it's something entirely individual in me – this sensation (yes, it is even a sensation) of how extraordinarily *shell-like* we are as we are – little creatures, peering out of the sentry-box at the gate, ogling through our glass case at the entry, wan little servants, who never can say for certain, even, if the master is out or in ...

The door opens ... My wife. She says: 'I am going to bed.'

And I look up vaguely, and vaguely say: 'You are going to bed.'

'Yes.' A tiny pause. 'Don't forget – will you? – to turn out the gas in the hall.'

And again I repeat: 'The gas in the hall.'

There was a time – the time before – when this habit of mine (it really has become a habit now – it wasn't one then) was one of our sweetest jokes together. It began, of course, when, on several occasions, I really was deeply engaged and I didn't hear. I emerged only to see her shaking her head and laughing at me, 'You haven't heard a word!'

'No. What did you say?'

Why should she think that so funny and charming? She did; it delighted her. 'Oh, my darling, it's so like you! It's so – so – .' And I knew she loved me for it – knew she positively looked forward to coming in and disturbing me, and so – as one does – I played up. I was guaranteed to be wrapped away every evening at 10.30 p.m. But now? For some reason I feel it would be crude to stop my performance. It's simplest to play on. But what is she waiting for to-night? Why doesn't she go? Why prolong this? She is going. No, her hand on the door-knob, she turns round again, and she says in the most curious, small, breathless voice, 'You're not cold?'

Oh, it's not fair to be as pathetic as that! That was simply damnable, I shudder all over before I manage to bring out a slow 'No-o,' while my left hand ruffles the reference pages.

She is gone; she will not come back again to-night. It is not only I who recognise that; the room changes, too. It relaxes, like an old actor. Slowly the mask is rubbed off; the look of strained attention changes to an air of heavy, sullen brooding. Every line, every fold breathes fatigue. The mirror is quenched; the ash whitens; only my shy lamp burns on ... But what a cynical indifference to me it all shows! Or should I perhaps be flattered? No, we understand each other. You know those stories of little children who are suckled by wolves and accepted by the tribe, and how for ever after they move freely among their fleet grey brothers? Something like that has happened to me. But wait – that about the wolves won't do. Curious!

Before I wrote it down, while it was still in my head, I was delighted with it. It seemed to express, and more, to suggest, just what I wanted to say. But written, I can smell the falseness immediately and the ... source of the smell is in that word fleet. Don't you agree? Fleet, grey brothers! 'Fleet.' A word I never use. When I wrote 'wolves' it skimmed across my mind like a shadow and I couldn't resist it. Tell me! Tell me! Why is it so difficult to write simply – and not only simply but *sotto voce*, if you know what I mean? That is how I long to write. No fine effects – no bravuras. But just the plain truth, as only a liar can tell it.

I light a cigarette, lean back, inhale deeply – and find myself wondering if my wife is asleep. Or is she lying in her cold bed, staring into the dark with those trustful, bewildered eyes? Her eyes are like the eyes of a cow being driven along a road. 'Why am I being driven – what harm have I done? But I really am not responsible for that look; it's her natural expression. One day, when she was turning out a cupboard, she found a little old photograph of herself, taken when she was a girl at school. In her confirmation dress, she explained. And there were the eyes, even then. I remember saying to her: 'Did you always look so sad?' Leaning over my shoulder, she laughed lightly. 'Do I look sad? I think it's just ... me.' And she waited for me to say something about it. But I was marvelling at her courage at having shown it to me at all. It was a hideous photograph! And I wondered again if she realised how plain she was, and comforted herself with the idea that people who loved each other didn't criticise but accepted everything, or if she really rather liked her appearance and expected me to say something complimentary. Oh, that was base of me! How could I have forgotten all the countless times when I have known her turn away, avoid the light, press her face into my shoulders. And above all, how could I have forgotten the afternoon of our wedding day, when we sat on the green bench in the Botanical Gardens and listened to the band, how, in an interval between two pieces, she suddenly turned to me and said in the voice in which one says: 'Do you think the grass is damp?' or 'Do you think it's time for tea?' ... 'Tell me – do you think physical beauty is so very important?' I don't like to think how often she rehearsed that question. And do you know what I answered? At that moment, as if at my command, there came a great gush of hard bright sound from the band. And I managed to shout above it – cheerfully – 'I didn't hear what you said.' Devilish! Wasn't it? Perhaps not wholly. She looked like the poor patient who hears the surgeon say, 'It will certainly be necessary to perform the operation – but not now!'

But all this conveys the impression that my wife and I were never really happy together. Not true! Not true! We were marvellously, radiantly happy. We were a model couple. If you had seen us together, any time, any place, if you had followed us, tracked us down, spied, taken us off our guard, you still would have been forced to confess, 'I have never seen a more ideally suited pair.' Until last autumn.

But really to explain what happened then I should have to go back and back, I should have to dwindle until my tiny hands clutched the bannisters, the stair-rail was higher than my head, and I peered through to watch my father padding softly up and down. There were coloured windows on the landings. As he came up, first his bald head was scarlet; then it was yellow. How frightened I was! And when they put me to bed, it was to dream that we were living inside one of my father's big coloured bottles. For he was a chemist. I was born nine years after my parents were married; I was an only child, and the effort to produce even me – small, withered bud I must have been – sapped all my mother's strength. She never left her room again. Bed, sofa, window, she moved between the three. Well I can see her, on the window days, sitting, her cheek in her hand, staring out. Her room looked over the street. Opposite there was a wall plastered with advertisement for travelling shows and circuses and so on. I stand beside her, and we gaze at the slim lady in a red dress hitting a dark gentleman over the head with her parasol, or at the tiger peering through the jungle while the clown, close by, balances a bottle on his nose, or at a little golden-haired girl sitting on the knee of an old black man in a broad cotton hat ... She says nothing. On sofa days there is a flannel dressing-gown that I loathe, and a cushion that keeps on slipping off the hard sofa. I pick it up. It has flowers and writing sewn on. I ask what the writing says, and she whispers, 'Sweet Repose!' In bed her fingers plait, in tight little plaits, the fringe of the quilt, and her lips are thin. And that is all there is of my mother, except the last queer 'episode' that comes later ...

My father – curled up in the corner on the lid of a round box that held sponges, I stared at my father so long it's as though his image, cut off at the waist by the counter, has remained solid in my memory. Perfectly bald, polished head, shaped like a thin egg, creased creamy cheeks, little bags under the eyes, large pale ears like handles. His manner was discreet, sly, faintly amused and tinged with impudence. Long before I could appreciate it I knew the mixture ... I even used to copy him in my corner, bending forward, with a small reproduction of his faint sneer. In the evening his customers were, chiefly, young women; some of them came in every day for his famous five-penny pick-me-up. Their gaudy looks, their voices, their free ways, fascinated me. I longed to be my father, handing them across the counter the little glass of bluish stuff they tossed off so greedily. God knows what it was made of. Years after I drank some, just to see what it tasted like, and I felt as though someone had given me a terrific blow on the head; I felt stunned.

One of those evenings I remember vividly. It was cold; it must have been autumn, for the flaring gas was lighted after my tea. I sat in my corner and my father was mixing something; the shop was empty. Suddenly the bell jangled and a young woman rushed in, crying so loud, sobbing so hard, that it didn't sound real. She wore a green cape trimmed with fur and a hat with cherries dangling. My father came from behind the screen. But she couldn't stop herself at first. She stood in the middle of the shop and wrung her hands, and moaned. I've never heard such crying since. Presently she managed to gasp out, 'Give me a pick-me-up.' Then she drew a long breath, trembled away from him and quavered: 'I've had *bad news*!' And in the flaring gaslight I saw the whole side of her face was puffed up and purple; her lip was cut, and her eyelid looked as though it was gummed fast over the wet eye. My father pushed the glass across the counter, and she took her purse out of her stocking and paid him. But she couldn't drink; clutching the glass, she stared in front of her as if she could not believe what she saw. Each time she put her head back the tears spurted out again. Finally she put the glass down. It was no use. Holding the cape with one hand, she ran in the same way out of the shop again. My father gave no sign. But long after she had gone I crouched in my corner, and when I think back it's as though I felt my whole body vibrating – 'So that's what it is outside,' I thought. 'That's what it's like out there.'

Do you remember your childhood? I am always coming across these marvellous accounts by writers who declare that they remember 'everything, everything'. I certainly don't. The dark stretches, the blanks, are much bigger than the bright glimpses. I seem to have spent most of my time like a plant in a cupboard. Now and again, when the sun shone, a careless hand thrust me out on to the window-sill, and a careless hand whipped me in again – and that was all. But what happened in the darkness – I wonder? Did one grow? Pale stem ... timid leaves ... white, reluctant bud. No wonder I was hated at school. Even the masters shrank from me. I somehow knew that my soft hesitating voice disgusted them. I knew, too, how they turned away from my shocked, staring eyes. I was small and thin, and I smelled of the shop; my nickname was Gregory Powder. School was a tin building stuck on the raw hillside. There were dark red streaks like blood in the oozing clay banks of the playground. I hide in the dark passage, where the coats hang, and am discovered there by one of the masters. 'What are you doing there in the dark?' His terrible voice kills me; I die before his eyes. I am standing in a ring of thrust-out heads; some are grinning, some look greedy, some are spitting. And it is always cold. Big crushed up clouds press across the sky; the rusty water in the school tank is frozen; the bell sounds numb. One day they put a dead bird in my overcoat pocket. I found it just when I reached home. Oh, what a strange flutter there was at my heart, when I drew out that terribly soft, cold little body, with the legs thin as pins and the claws wrung. I sat on the back door step in the yard and put the bird in my cap. The feathers round the neck looked wet and there was a tiny tuft just above the closed eyes that stood up too. How tightly the beak was shut; I could not see the mark where it was divided. I stretched out one wing and touched the soft, secret down underneath; I tried to make the claws curl round my little finger. But I didn't feel sorry for it – no! I wondered. The smoke from our kitchen chimney poured downwards, and flakes of soot floated – soft, light in the air. Through a big crack in the cement yard a poor-looking plant with dull reddish flowers had pushed its way. I looked at the dead bird again … And that is the first time that I remember singing, rather … listening to a silent voice inside a little cage that was me.

But what has all this to do with my married happiness? How can all this affect my wife and me? Why – to tell what happened last autumn – do I run all this way back into the Past? The Past – what is the Past? I might say the star-shaped flake of soot on a leaf of the poor-looking plant, and the bird lying on the quilted lining of my cap, and my father's pestle and my mother's cushion, belong to it. But that is not to say they are any less mine than they were when I looked upon them with my very eyes, and touched them with these fingers. No, they are more; they are a living part of me. Who am I, in fact, as I sit here at this table, but my own past? If I deny that, I am nothing. And if I were to try and divide my life into childhood, youth, early manhood and so on, it would be a kind of affectation; I should know I was doing it just because of the pleasantly important sensation it gives one to rule lines, and to use green ink for childhood, red for the next stage, and purple for the period of adolescence. For, one thing I have learnt, one thing I do believe is, Nothing Happens Suddenly. Yes, that is my religion, I suppose …

My mother's death, for instance. Is it more distant from me to-day than it was then? It is just as close, as strange, as puzzling, and in spite of all the countless times I have recalled the circumstances, I know no more now than I did then whether I dreamed them or whether they really occurred. It happened when I was thirteen and I slept in a little strip of a room on what was called the Half Landing. One night I woke up with a start to see my mother, in her nightgown, without even the hated flannel dressing-gown, sitting on my bed. But the strange thing which frightened me was, she wasn't looking at me. Her head was bent; the short thin tail of hair lay between her shoulders; her hands were pressed between her knees, and my bed shook; she was shivering. It was the first time I had ever seen her out of her own room. I said, or I think I said, 'Is that you, mother?' And as she turned round I saw in the moonlight how queer she looked. Her face looked small – quite different. She looked like one of the boys at the school baths, who sits on a step, shivering just like that, and wants to go in and yet is frightened.

'Are you awake?' she said. Her eyes opened; I think she smiled. She leaned towards me. 'I've been poisoned,' she whispered. 'Your father's poisoned me.' And she nodded. Then, before I could say a word, she was gone, and I thought I heard the door shut. I sat quite still; I couldn't move. I think I expected something else to happen. For a long time I listened for something; there wasn't a sound. The candle was by my bed, but I was too frightened to stretch out my hand for the matches. But even while I wondered what I ought to do, even while my heart thumped – everything became confused. I lay down and pulled the blankets round me. I fell asleep, and the next morning my mother was found dead of failure of the heart.

Did that visit happen? Was it a dream? Why did she come to tell me? Or why, if she came, did she go away so quickly? And her expression – so joyous under the frightened look – was that real? I believed it fully the afternoon of the funeral, when I saw my father dressed up for his part, hat and all. That tall hat so gleaming black and round was like a cork covered with black sealing-wax, and the rest of my father was awfully like a bottle, with his face for the label – *Deadly Poison*. It flashed into my mind as I stood opposite him in the hall. And Deadly Poison, or old D.P., was my private name for him from that day.

Late, it grows late. I love the night. I love to feel the tide of darkness rising slowly and slowly washing, turning over and over, lifting, floating, all that lies strewn upon the dark beach, all that lies hid in rocky hollows. I love, I love this strange feeling of drifting – whither? After my mother's death I hated to go to bed. I used to sit on the window-sill, folded up, and watch the sky. It seemed to me the moon moved much faster than the sun. And one big, bright green star I chose for my own. My star! But I never thought of it beckoning to me or twinkling merrily for my sake. Cruel, indifferent, splendid – it burned in the airy night. No matter – it was mine! But growing close up against the window there was a creeper with small, bunched up pink and purple flowers. These did know me. These, when I touched them at night, welcomed my fingers; the little tendrils, so weak, so delicate, knew I would not hurt them. When the wind moved the leaves I felt I understood their shaking. When I came to the window, it seemed to me the flowers said among themselves, 'The boy is here.'

As the months passed, there was often a light in my father's room below. And I heard voices and laughter. 'He's got some woman with him,' I thought. But it meant nothing to me. Then the gay voice, the sound of the laughter, gave me the idea it was one of the girls who used to come to the shop in the evenings – and gradually I began to imagine which girl it was. It was the dark one in the red coat and skirt, who once had given me a penny. A merry face stooped over me – warm breath tickled my neck – there were little beads of black on her long lashes, and when she opened her arms to kiss me, there came a marvellous wave of scent! Yes, that was the one. Time passed, and I forgot the moon and my green star and my shy creeper – I came to the window to wait for the light in my father's window, to listen for the laughing voice, until one night I dozed and I dreamed she came again – again she drew me to her, something soft, scented, warm and merry hung over me like a cloud. But when I tried to see, her eyes only mocked me, her red lips opened and she hissed, 'Little sneak! little sneak!' But not as if she were angry, as if she understood, and her smile somehow was like a rat ... hateful!

The night after, I lighted the candle and sat down at the table instead. By and by, as the flame steadied, there was a small lake of liquid wax, surrounded by a white, smooth wall. I took a pin and made little holes in this wall and then sealed them up faster than the wax could escape. After a time I fancied the candle flame joined in the game; it leapt up, quivered, wagged; it even seemed to laugh. But while I played with the candle and smiled and broke off the tiny white peaks of wax that rose above the wall and floated them on my lake, a feeling of awful dreariness fastened on me – yes, that is the word. It crept up from my knees to my thighs, into my arms; I ached all over with misery. And I felt so strangely that I couldn't move. Something bound me there by the table – I couldn't even let the pin drop that I held between my finger and thumb. For a moment I came to a stop, as it were.

Then the shrivelled case of the bud split and fell, the plant in the cupboard came into flower. 'Who am I?' I thought. 'What is all this?' And I looked at my room, at the broken bust of the man called Hahnemann on top of the cupboard, at my little bed with the pillow like an envelope. I saw it all, but not as I had seen before ... Everything lived, but everything. But that was not all. I was equally alive and – it's the only way I can express it – the barriers were down between us – I had come into my own world!

The barriers were down. I had been all my life a little outcast; but until that moment no one had 'accepted' me; I had lain in the cupboard – or the cave forlorn. But now – I was taken, I was accepted, claimed. I did not consciously turn away from the world of human beings; I had never known it; but I from that night did beyond words consciously turn towards my silent brothers ...

A TELEPHONE CALL

Dorothy Parker

Dorothy Parker (1893–1967) was an American critic, satirical poet, and short story writer. Best known for her wit and eye for 20th-century foibles, Parker wrote book reviews, poetry and short fiction for the fledgling magazine the *New Yorker*. She wrote the screenplay for the Hitchcock film *Saboteur*, but her involvement with Communism led to her being blacklisted in Hollywood.

Please, God, let him telephone me now. Dear God, let him call me now. I won't ask anything else of You, truly I won't. It isn't very much to ask. It would be so little to You, God, such a little, little thing. Only let him telephone now. Please, God. Please, please, please.

If I didn't think about it, maybe the telephone might ring. Sometimes it does that. If I could think of something else. If I could think of something else. Maybe if I counted five hundred by fives, it might ring by that time. I'll count slowly. I won't cheat. And if it rings when I get to three hundred, I won't stop; I won't answer it until I get to five hundred. Five, ten, fifteen, twenty, twenty-five, thirty, thirty-five, forty, forty-five, fifty ... Oh, please ring. Please.

This is the last time I'll look at the clock. I will not look at it again. It's ten minutes past seven. He said he would telephone at five o'clock. "I'll call you at five, darling." I think that's where he said "darling." I'm almost sure he said it there. I know he called me "darling" twice, and the other time was when he said good-by. "Good-by, darling." He was busy, and he can't say much in the office, but he called me "darling" twice. He couldn't have minded my calling him up. I know you shouldn't keep telephoning them – I know they don't like that. When you do that they know you are thinking about them and wanting them, and that makes them hate you. But I hadn't talked to him in three days – not in three days. And all I did was ask him how he was; it was just the way anybody might have called him up. He couldn't have minded that. He couldn't have thought I was bothering him. "No, of course you're not." he said. And he said he'd telephone me. He didn't have to say that. I didn't ask him to, truly I didn't. I'm sure I didn't. I don't think he would say he'd telephone me, and then just never do it. Please don't let him do that God. Please don't.

"I'll call you at five, darling." "Good-by, darling." He was busy, and he was in a hurry, and there were people around him, but he called me "darling" twice. That's mine, that's mine. I have that, even if I never see him again. Oh, but that's so little. That isn't enough. Nothing's enough, if I never see him again. Please let me see him again, God. Please, I want him so much. I want him so much. I'll be good, God. I will try to be better, I will, if You will let me see him again. If You let him telephone me. Oh, let him telephone me now.

Ah, don't let my prayer seem too little to You, God. You sit up there, so white and old, with all the angels about You and the stars slipping by. And I come to You with a prayer about a telephone call. Ah, don't laugh, God. You see, You don't know how it feels. You're so safe, there on Your throne, with the blue swirling under You. Nothing can touch You; no one can twist Your heart in his hands. This is suffering, God, this is bad, bad suffering. Won't You help me? For Your Son's sake, help me. You said You would do whatever was asked of You in His name. Oh, God, in the name of Thine only beloved Son, Jesus Christ, our Lord, let him telephone me now.

I must stop this. I mustn't be this way. Look. Suppose a young man says he'll call a girl up, and then something happens, and he doesn't. That isn't so terrible, is it? Why, it's going on all over the world, right this minute. Oh, what do I care what's going on all over the world? Why can't that telephone ring? Why can't it, why can't it? Couldn't you ring? Ah, please, couldn't you? You damned, ugly, shiny thing. It would hurt you to ring, wouldn't it? Oh, that would hurt you. Damn you, I'll pull your filthy roots out of the wall, I'll smash your smug black face in little bits. Damn you to hell.

No, no, no. I must stop. I must think about something else. This is what I'll do. I'll put the clock in the other room. Then I can't look at it. If I do have to look at it then I'll have to walk into the bedroom, and that will be something to do. Maybe, before I look at it again, he will call me. I'll be so sweet to him, if he calls me. If he says he can't see me tonight, I'll say, "Why, that's all right, dear. Why, of course it's all right." I'll be the way I was when I first met him. Then maybe he'll like me again. I was always sweet, at first. Oh, it's so easy to be sweet to people before you love them.

I think he must still like me a little. He couldn't have called me "darling" twice today, if he didn't still like me a little. It isn't all gone, if he still likes me a little; even if it's only a little, little bit. You see, God, if You would just let him telephone me, I wouldn't have to ask You anything more. I would be sweet to him, I would be gay, I would be just the way I used to be, and then he would love me again. And then I would never have to ask You for anything more. Don't You see, God? So won't You please let him telephone me? Won't You please, please, please?

Are You punishing me, God, because I've been bad? Are You angry with me because I did that? Oh, but God, there are so many bad people – You could not be hard only to me. And it wasn't very bad; it couldn't have been bad. We didn't hurt anybody, God. Things are only bad when they hurt people. We didn't hurt one single soul; You know that. You know it wasn't bad, don't You, God? So won't You let him telephone me now?

If he doesn't telephone me, I'll know God is angry with me. I'll count five hundred by fives, and if he hasn't called me then, I will know God isn't going to help me, ever again. That will be the sign. Five, ten, fifteen, twenty, twenty-five, thirty, thirty-five, forty, forty-five, fifty, fifty-five ... It was bad. I knew it was bad. All right, God, send me to hell. You think You're frightening me with Your hell, don't You? You think Your hell is worse than mine.

I mustn't. I mustn't do this. Suppose he's a little late calling me up – that's nothing to get hysterical about. Maybe he isn't going to call – maybe he's coming straight up here without telephoning. He'll be cross if he sees I have been crying. They don't like you to cry. He doesn't cry. I wish to God I could make him cry. I wish I could make him cry and tread the floor and feel his heart heavy and big and festering in him. I wish I could hurt him like hell.

He doesn't wish that about me. I don't think he even knows how he makes me feel. I wish he could know, without my telling him. They don't like you to tell them they've made you cry. They don't like you to tell them you're unhappy because of them. If you do, they think you're possessive and exacting. And then they hate you. They hate you whenever you say anything you really think. You always have to keep playing little games. Oh, I thought we didn't have to; I thought this was so big I could say whatever I meant. I guess you can't, ever. I guess there isn't ever anything big enough for that. Oh, if he would just telephone, I wouldn't tell him I had been sad about him. They hate sad people. I would be so sweet and so gay, he couldn't help but like me. If he would only telephone. If he would only telephpne.

Maybe that's what he is doing. Maybe he is coming on here without calling me up. Maybe he's on his way now. Something might have happened to him. No, nothing could ever happen to him. I can't picture anything happening to him. I never picture him run over. I never see him lying still and long and dead. I wish he were dead. That's a terrible wish. That's a lovely wish. If he were dead, he would be mine. If he were dead, I would never think of now and the last few weeks. I would remember only the lovely times. It would be all beautiful. I wish he were dead. I wish he were dead, dead, dead.

This is silly. It's silly to go wishing people were dead just because they don't call you up the very minute they said they would. Maybe the clock's fast; I don't know whether it's right. Maybe he's hardly late at all. Anything could have made him a little late. Maybe he had to stay at his office. Maybe he went home, to call me up from there, and somebody came in. He doesn't like to telephone me in front of people. Maybe he's worried, just a little, little bit about keeping me waiting. He might even hope that I would call him up. I could do that. I could telephone him.

I mustn't. I mustn't, I mustn't. Oh, God, please don't let me telephone him. Please keep me from doing that. I know, God, just as well as You do, that if he were worried about me, he'd telephone no matter where he was or how many people there were around him. Please make me know that God. I don't ask You to make it easy for me – You can't do that, for all that You could make a world. Only let me know it, God. Don't let me go on hoping. Don't let me say comforting things to myself. Please don't let me hope, dear God. Please don't.

I won't telephone him. I'll never telephone him again as long as I live. He'll rot in hell, before I'll call him up. You don't have to give me strength, God; I have it myself. If he wanted me, he could get me. He knows where I am. He knows I'm waiting here. He's so sure of me, so sure. I wonder why they hate you as soon as they are sure of you. I should think it would be so sweet to be sure.

It would be so easy to telephone him. Then I'd know. Maybe it wouldn't be a foolish thing to do. Maybe he wouldn't mind. Maybe he'd like it. Maybe he has been trying to get me. Sometimes people try and try to get you on the telephone, and they say the number doesn't answer. I'm not just saving that to help myself; that really happens. You know that really happens, God. Oh, God, keep me away from that telephone. Keep me away. Let me still have just a little bit of pride. I think I'm going to need it, God. I think it will be all I'll have.

Oh, what does pride matter, when I can't stand it if I don't talk to him? Pride like that is such a silly, shabby little thing. The real pride, the big pride, is in having no pride. I'm not saying that just because I want to call him. I am not. That's true, I know that's true. I will be big. I will be beyond little prides.

Please, God, keep me from telephoning him. Please, God.

I don't see what pride has to do with it. This is such a little thing, for me to be bringing in pride, for me to be making such a fuss about. I may have misunderstood him. Maybe he said for me to call him up, at five. "Call me at five, darling." He could have said that, perfectly well. It's so possible that I didn't hear him right. "Call me at five, darling." I'm almost sure that's what he said. God, don't let me talk this way to myself. Make me know, please make me know.

I'll think about something else. I'll just sit quietly. If I could sit still. If I could sit still. Maybe I could read. Oh, all the books are about people who love each other, truly and sweetly. What do they want to write about that for? Don't they know it isn't true? Don't they know it's a lie, it's a God damned lie? What do they have to tell about that for, when they know how it hurts? Damn them, damn them, damn them.

I won't. I'll be quiet. This is nothing to get excited about. Look. Suppose he were someone I didn't know very well. Suppose he were another girl. Then I'd just telephone and say, "Well, for goodness' sake, what happened to you?" That's what I'd do, and I'd never even think about it. Why can't I be casual and natural, just because I love him? I can be. Honestly. I can be. I'll call him up, and be so easy and pleasant. You see if I won't God. Oh, don't let me call him. Don't, don't, don't.

God, aren't You really going to let him call me? Are You sure, God? Couldn't You please relent? Couldn't You? I don't even ask You to let him telephone me this minute. God: only let him do it in a little while. I'll count five hundred by fives. I'll do it so slowly and so fairly. If he hasn't telephoned then, I'll call him. I will. Oh, please, dear God, dear kind God, my blessed Father in Heaven, let him call before then. Please. God. Please.

Five, ten, fifteen, twenty, twenty-five, thirty, thirty-five …

A MAN AND TWO WOMEN

Doris Lessing

> Doris Lessing (b. 1919) is a British novelist, poet, playwright, biographer and short story writer. In 2001, Lessing was awarded the David Cohen Prize for a lifetime's achievement in British Literature and she was ranked fifth on *The Times* list of the '50 Greatest British Writers Since 1945'. Lessing was awarded the 2007 Nobel Prize in Literature.

Stella's friends the Bradfords had taken a cheap cottage in Essex for the summer, and she was going down to visit them. She wanted to see them, but there was no doubt there was something of a letdown (and for them too) in the English cottage. Last summer Stella had been wandering with her husband around Italy; had seen the English couple at a cafe table, and found them sympathetic. They all liked each other, and the four went about for some weeks, sharing meals, hotels, trips. Back in London the friendship had not, as might have been expected, fallen off. Then Stella's husband departed abroad, as he often did, and Stella saw Jack and Dorothy by herself. There were a great many people she might have seen, but it was the Bradfords she saw most often, two or three times a week, at their flat or hers. They were at ease with each other. Why were they? Well, for one thing they were all artists – in different ways. Stella designed wallpapers and materials; she had a name for it.

The Bradfords were real artists. He painted, she drew. They had lived mostly out of England in cheap places around the Mediterranean. Both from the North of England, they had met at art school, married at twenty, had taken flight from England, then returned to it, needing it, then off again: and so on, for years, in the rhythm of so many of their kind, needing, hating, loving England. There had been seasons of real poverty, while they lived on pasta or bread or rice, and wine and fruit and sunshine, in Majorca, southern Spain, Italy, North Africa.

A French critic had seen Jack's work, and suddenly he was successful. His show in Paris, then one in London, made money, and now he charged in the hundreds where a year or so ago he charged ten or twenty guineas. This had deepened his contempt for the values of the markets. For a while Stella thought that this was the bond between the Bradfords and herself. They were so very much, as she was, of the new generation of artists (and poets and playwrights and novelists) who had one thing in common, a cool derision about the racket. They were so very unlike (they felt) the older generation with their Societies and their Lunches and their salons and their cliques: their atmosphere of connivance with the snobberies of success. Stella, too, had been successful by a fluke. Not that she did not consider herself talented; it was that others as talented were unfêted, and unbought. When she was with the Bradfords and other fellow spirits, they would talk about the racket, using each other as yardsticks or fellow consciences about how much to give in, what to give, how to use without being used, how to enjoy without becoming dependent on enjoyment.

Of course Dorothy Bradford was not able to talk in quite the same way, since she had not yet been "discovered"; she had not "broken through." A few people with discrimination bought her unusual delicate drawings, which had a strength that was hard to understand unless one knew Dorothy herself. But she was not at all, as Jack was, a great success. There was a strain here, in the marriage, nothing much; it was kept in check by their scorn for their arbitrary rewards of "the racket." But it was there, nevertheless.

Stella's husband had said: "Well, I can understand that, it's like me and you – you're creative, whatever that may mean, I'm just a bloody TV journalist." There was no bitterness in this. He was a good journalist, and besides he sometimes got the chance to make a good small film. All the same, there was that between him and Stella, just as there was between Jack and his wife.

After a time Stella saw something else in her kinship with the couple. It was that the Bradfords had a close bond, bred of having spent so many years together in foreign places, dependent on each other because of their poverty. It had been a real love marriage, one could see it by looking at them. It was now. And Stella's marriage was a real marriage. She understood she enjoyed being with the Bradfords because the two couples were equal in this. Both marriages were those of strong, passionate, talented individuals, they shared a battling quality that strengthened them, not weakened them.

The reason why it had taken Stella so long to understand this was that the Bradfords had made her think about her own marriage, which she was beginning to take for granted, sometimes even found exhausting. She had understood, through them, how lucky she was in her husband; how lucky they all were. No marital miseries; nothing of (what they saw so often in friends) one partner in a marriage victim to the other, resenting the other; no claiming of outsiders as sympathisers or allies in an unequal battle.

There had been a plan for these four people to go off again to Italy or Spain, but then Stella's husband departed, and Dorothy got pregnant. So there was the cottage in Essex instead, a bad second choice, but better, they all felt, to deal with a new baby on home ground, at least for the first year. Stella, telephoned by Jack (on Dorothy's particular insistence, he said), offered and received commiserations on its being only Essex and not Majorca or Italy. She also received sympathy because her husband had been expected back this weekend, but had wired to say he wouldn't be back for another month, probably – there was trouble in Venezuela. Stella wasn't really forlorn; she didn't mind living alone, since she was always supported by knowing her man would be back. Besides, if she herself were offered the chance of a month's "trouble" in Venezuela, she wouldn't hesitate, so it wasn't fair … fairness characterised their relationship. All the same, it was nice that she could drop down (or up) to the Bradfords, people with whom she could always be herself, neither more nor less.

She left London at midday by train, armed with food unobtainable in Essex: salamis, cheeses, spices, wine. The sun shone, but it wasn't particularly warm. She hoped there would be heating in the cottage, July or not.

The train was empty. The little station seemed stranded in a green nowhere. She got out, cumbered by bags full of food. A porter and a stationmaster examined, then came to succour her. She was a tallish, fair woman, rather ample; her soft hair, drawn back, escaped in tendrils, and she had great helpless-looking blue eyes.

She wore a dress made in one of the materials she had designed. Enormous green leaves laid hands all over her body, and fluttered about her knees. She stood smiling, accustomed to men running to wait on her, enjoying them enjoying her. She walked with them to the barrier where Jack waited, appreciating the scene. He was a smallish man, compact, dark. He wore a blue-green summer shirt, and smoked a pipe and smiled, watching. The two men delivered her into the hands of the third, and departed, whistling, to their duties.

Jack and Stella kissed, then pressed their cheeks together.

"Food," he said, "food," relieving her of the parcels.

"What's it like here, shopping?"

"Vegetables all right, I suppose."

Jack was still northern in this: he seemed brusque, to strangers; he wasn't shy, he simply hadn't been brought up to enjoy words. Now he put his arm briefly around Stella's waist, and said: "Marvellous, Stell, marvellous." They walked on, pleased with each other. Stella had with Jack, her husband had with Dorothy, these moments, when they said to each other wordlessly: If I were not married to my husband, if you were not married to your wife, how delightful it would be to be married to you. These moments were not the least of the pleasures of this four-sided friendship.

"Are you liking it down here?"

"It's what we bargained for."

There was more than his usual shortness in this, and she glanced at him to find him frowning. They were walking to the car, parked under a tree.

"How's the baby?"

"Little bleeder never sleeps; he's wearing us out, but he's fine."

The baby was six weeks old. Having the baby was a definite achievement: getting it safely conceived and born had taken a couple of years. Dorothy, like most independent women, had had divided thoughts about a baby. Besides, she was over thirty and complained she was set in her ways. All this – the difficulties, Dorothy's hesitations – had added up to an atmosphere which Dorothy herself described as "like wondering if some damned horse is going to take the fence." Dorothy would talk, while she was pregnant, in a soft staccato voice: "Perhaps I don't really want

a baby at all? Perhaps I'm not fitted to be a mother? Perhaps …
and if so … and how … ?"

She said: "Until recently Jack and I were always with people
who took it for granted that getting pregnant was a disaster, and
now suddenly all the people we know have young children and
baby-sitters and … perhaps … if …"

Jack said: "You'll feel better when it's born."

Once Stella had heard him say, after one of Dorothy's long
troubled dialogues with herself: "Now that's enough, that's enough,
Dorothy." He had silenced her, taking the responsibility.

They reached the car, got in. It was a secondhand job recently
bought. "They" (being the Press, the enemy generally) "wait for
us" (being artists or writers who have made money) "to buy flashy
cars." They had discussed it, decided that *not* to buy an expensive
car if they felt like it would be allowing themselves to be bullied;
but bought a secondhand one after all. Jack wasn't going to give
them so much satisfaction, apparently.

"Actually we could have walked," he said, as they shot down a
narrow lane, "but with these groceries, it's just as well."

"If the baby's giving you a tough time, there can't be much time
for cooking." Dorothy was a wonderful cook. But now again there
was something in the air as he said: "Food's definitely not too good
just now. You can cook supper, Stell, we could do with a good
feed."

Now Dorothy hated anyone in her kitchen, except, for certain
specified jobs, her husband; and this was surprising.

"The truth is, Dorothy's worn out," he went on, and now Stella
understood he was warning her.

"Well, it is tiring," said Stella soothingly.

"You were like that?"

"Like that" was saying a good deal more than just worn out, or
tired, and Stella understood that Jack was really uneasy. She said,
plaintively humorous: "You two always expect me to remember
things that happened a hundred years ago. Let me think. …"

She had been married when she was eighteen, got pregnant at
once. Her husband had left her. Soon she had married Philip, who
also had a small child from a former marriage. These two children,
her daughter, seventeen, his son, twenty, had grown up together.

She remembered herself at nineteen, alone, with a small baby. "Well, I was alone," she said. "That makes a difference. I remember I was exhausted. Yes, I was definitely irritable and unreasonable."

"Yes," said Jack, with a brief reluctant look at her.

"All right, don't worry," she said, replying aloud as she often did to things that Jack had not said aloud.

"Good," he said.

Stella thought of how she had seen Dorothy, in the hospital room, with the new baby. She had sat up in bed, in a pretty bed-jacket, the baby beside her in a basket. He was restless. Jack stood between basket and bed, one large hand on his son's stomach. "Now, you just shut up, little bleeder," he had said, as he grumbled. Then he had picked him up, as if he'd been doing it always, held him against his shoulder, and, as Dorothy held her arms out, had put the baby into them. "Want your mother, then? Don't blame you."

That scene, the ease of it, the way the two parents were together, had, for Stella, made nonsense of all the months of Dorothy's self-questioning. As for Dorothy, she had said, parodying the expected words but meaning them: "He's the most beautiful baby ever born. I can't imagine why I didn't have him before."

"There's the cottage," said Jack. Ahead of them was a small labourer's cottage, among full green trees, surrounded by green grass. It was painted white, had four sparkling windows. Next to it a long shed or structure that turned out to be a greenhouse.

"The man grew tomatoes," said Jack. "Fine studio now."

The car came to rest under another tree.

"Can I just drop in to the studio?"

"Help yourself." Stella walked into the long, glass-roofed shed. In London Jack and Dorothy shared a studio. They had shared huts, sheds, any suitable building, all around the Mediterranean. They always worked side by side. Dorothy's end was tidy, exquisite, Jack's lumbered with great canvases, and he worked in a clutter. Now Stella looked to see if this friendly arrangement continued, but as Jack came in behind her he said: "Dorothy's not set herself up yet. I miss her, I can tell you."

The greenhouse was still partly one: trestles with plants stood along the ends. It was lush and warm.

"As hot as hell when the sun's really going, it makes up. And

Dorothy brings Paul in sometimes, so he can get used to a decent climate young."

Dorothy came in, at the far end, without the baby. She had recovered her figure. She was a small dark woman, with neat, delicate limbs. Her face was white, with scarlet rather irregular lips, and black glossy brows, a little crooked. So while she was not pretty, she was lively and dramatic-looking. She and Stella had their moments together, when they got pleasure from contrasting their differences, one woman so big and soft and blond, the other so dark and vivacious,

Dorothy came forward through shafts of sunlight, stopped, and said: "Stella, I'm glad you've come." Then forward again, to a few steps off, where she stood looking at them. "You two look good together," she said, frowning. There was something heavy and over-emphasised about both statements, and Stella said: "I was wondering what Jack had been up to."

"Very good, I think," said Dorothy, coming to look at the new canvas on the easel. It was of sunlit rocks, brown and smooth, with blue sky, blue water, and people swimming in spangles of light. When Jack was in the south, he painted pictures that his wife described as "dirt and grime and misery" – which was how they both described their joint childhood background. When he was in England he painted scenes like these.

"Like it? It's good, isn't it?" said Dorothy.

"Very much," said Stella. She always took pleasure from the contrast between Jack's outward self – the small, self-contained little man who could have vanished in a moment into a crowd of factory workers in, perhaps Manchester, and the sensuous bright pictures like these.

"And you?" asked Stella.

"Having a baby's killed everything creative in me – quite different from being pregnant," said Dorothy, but not complaining of it. She had worked like a demon while she was pregnant.

"Have a heart," said Jack, "he's only just got himself born."

"Well, I don't care," said Dorothy. "That's the funny thing, I *don't* care." She said this flat, indifferent. She seemed to be looking at them both again from a small troubled distance. "You two look good together," she said, and again there was the small jar.

"Well, how about some tea?" said Jack, and Dorothy said at once: "I made it when I heard the car. I thought better inside, it's not really hot in the sun." She led the way out of the greenhouse, her white linen dress dissolving in lozenges of yellow light from the glass panes above, so that Stella was reminded of the white limbs of Jack's swimmers disintegrating under sunlight in his new picture. The work of these two people was always reminding one of each other, or each other's work, and in all kinds of ways: they were so much married, so close.

The time it took to cross the space of rough grass to the door of the little house was enough to show Dorothy was right: it was really chilly in the sun. Inside two electric heaters made up for it. There had been two little rooms downstairs, but they had been knocked into one fine lowceilinged room, stone-floored, whitewashed. A tea table, covered with a purple checked cloth, stood waiting near a window where flowering bushes and trees showed through clean panes. Charming. They adjusted the heaters and arranged themselves so they could admire the English countryside through glass. Stella looked for the baby; Dorothy said: "In the pram at the back." Then she asked: "Did yours cry a lot?"

Stella laughed and said again: "I'll try to remember."

"We expect you to guide and direct, with all your experience," said Jack.

"As far as I can remember, she was a little demon for about three months, for no reason I could see, then suddenly she became civilised."

"Roll on the three months," said Jack.

"Six weeks to go," said Dorothy, handling teacups in a languid indifferent manner Stella found new in her.

"Finding it tough going?"

"I've never felt better in my life," said Dorothy at once, as if being accused.

"You look fine."

She looked a bit tired, nothing much; Stella couldn't see what reason there was for Jack to warn her. Unless he meant the languor, a look of self-absorption? Her vivacity, a friendly, aggressiveness that was the expression of her lively intelligence, was dimmed.

She sat leaning back in a deep airchair, letting Jack manage things, smiling vaguely.

"I'll bring him in in a minute," she remarked, listening to the silence from the sunlit garden at the back.

"Leave him," said Jack. "He's quiet seldom, enough. Relax, woman, and have a cigarette."

He lit a cigarette for her, and she took it in the same vague way, and sat breathing out smoke, her eyes half-closed.

"Have you heard from Philip?" she asked, not from politeness, but with sudden insistence.

"Of course she has, she got a wire," said Jack.

"I want to know how she feels," said Dorothy. "How do you feel, Stell?" She was listening for the baby all the time.

"Feel about what?"

"About his not coming back."

"But he is coming back, it's only a month," said Stella, and heard, with surprise, that her voice sounded edgy.

"You see?" said Dorothy to Jack, meaning the words, not the edge on them.

At this evidence that she and Philip had been discussed, Stella felt, first, pleasure: because it was pleasurable to be understood by two such good friends; then she felt discomfort, remembering Jack's warning.

"See what?" she asked Dorothy, smiling.

"That's enough now," said Jack to his wife in a flash of stubborn anger, which continued the conversation that had taken place.

Dorothy took direction from her husband, and kept quiet a moment, then seemed impelled to continue: "I've been thinking it must be nice, having your husband go off, then come back. Do you realise Jack and I haven't been separated since we married? That's over ten years. Don't you think there's something awful in two grown people stuck together all the time like Siamese twins?" This ended in a wail of genuine appeal to Stella.

"No, I think it's marvellous."

"But you don't mind being alone so much?"

"It's not *so* much; it's two or three months in a year. Well of course I mind. But I enjoy being alone, really. But I'd enjoy it too if we were together all the time. I envy you two." Stella was surprised to find her eyes wet with self-pity because she had to be without her husband another month.

"And what does he think?" demanded Dorothy. "What does Philip think?"

Stella said: "Well, I think he likes getting away from time to time – yes. He likes intimacy, he enjoys it, but it doesn't come as easily to him as it does to me." She had never said this before because she had never thought about it. She was annoyed with herself that she had had to wait for Dorothy to prompt her. Yet she knew that getting annoyed was what she must not do, with the state Dorothy was in, whatever it was. She glanced at Jack for guidance, but he was determinedly busy on his pipe.

"Well, I'm like Philip," announced Dorothy. "Yes, I'd love it if Jack went off sometimes. I think I'm being stifled being shut up with Jack day and night, year in year out."

"Thanks," said Jack, short but good-humoured.

"No, but I mean it. There's something humiliating about two adult people never for one second out of each other's sight."

"Well," said Jack, "when Paul's a bit bigger, you buzz off for a month or so and you'll appreciate me when you get back."

"It's not that I don't appreciate you, it's not that at all," said Dorothy, insistent, almost strident, apparently fevered with restlessness. Her languor had quite gone, and her limbs jerked and moved. And now the baby, as if he had been prompted by his father's mentioning him, let out a cry. Jack got up, forestalling his wife, saying: "I'll get him."

Dorothy sat, listening for her husband's movements with the baby, until he came back, which he did, supporting the infant sprawled against his shoulder with a competent hand. He sat down, let his son slide on to his chest, and said: "There now, you shut up and leave us in peace a bit longer." The baby was looking up into his face with the astonished expression of the newly born, and Dorothy sat smiling at both of them. Stella understood that her restlessness, her repeated curtailed movements, meant that she longed – more, needed – to have the child in her arms, have its body against hers. And Jack seemed to feel this, because Stella could have sworn it was not a conscious decision that made him rise and slide the infant into his wife's arms. Her flesh, her needs, had spoken direct to him without words, and he had risen at once to give her what she wanted. This silent instinctive conversation between husband and wife made Stella miss her own husband violently, and with resentment against fate that kept them apart so often. She ached for Philip.

Meanwhile Dorothy, now the baby was sprawled softly against her chest, the small feet in her hand, seemed to have lapsed into good humour. And Stella, watching, remembered something she really had forgotten: the close, fierce physical tie between herself and her daughter when she had been a tiny baby. She saw this bond in the way Dorothy stroked the small head that trembled on its neck as the baby looked up into his mother's face. Why, she remembered it was like being in love, having a new baby. All kinds of forgotten or unused instincts woke in Stella. She lit a cigarette, took herself in hand; set herself to enjoy the other woman's love affair with her baby instead of envying her.

The sun, dropping into the trees, struck the windowpanes, and there was a dazzle and a flashing of yellow and white light into the room, particularly over Dorothy in her white dress and the baby. Again Stella was reminded of Jack's picture of the white-limbed swimmers in sun-dissolving water. Dorothy shielded the baby's eyes with her hand and remarked dreamily: "This is better than any man, isn't it, Stell? Isn't it better than any man?"

"Well – no," said Stella laughing. "No, not for long."

"If you say so, you should know … but I can't imagine ever … Tell me, Stell, does your Philip have affairs when he's away?"

"For God's sake!" said Jack, angry. But he checked himself.

"Yes, I am sure he does."

"Do you mind?" asked Dorothy, loving the baby's feet with her enclosing palm.

And now Stella was forced to remember, to think about having minded, minding, coming to terms, and the ways in which she now did not mind.

"I don't think about it," she said.

"Well, I don't think I'd mind," said Dorothy.

"Thanks for letting me know," said Jack, short despite himself. Then he made himself laugh.

"And you, do you have affairs while Philip's away?"

"Sometimes. Not really."

"Do you know, Jack was unfaithful to me this week," remarked Dorothy, smiling at the baby.

"That's *enough*," said Jack, really angry.

"No it isn't enough, it isn't. Because what's awful is, I don't care."

"Well why should you care, in the circumstances?" Jack turned to Stella. "There's a silly bitch Lady Edith lives across that field. She got all excited, real live artists living down her lane. Well Dorothy was lucky, she had an excuse in the baby, but I had to go to her silly party. Booze flowing in rivers, and the most incredible people – you know. If you read about them in a novel, you'd never believe ... but I can't remember much after about twelve."

"Do you know what happened?" said Dorothy. "I was feeding the baby, it was terribly early. Jack sat straight up in bed and said: 'Jesus, Dorothy, I've just remembered, I screwed, that silly bitch Lady Edith on her brocade sofa.' "

Stella laughed. Jack let out a snort of laughter. Dorothy laughed, an unscrupulous chuckle of appreciation. Then she said seriously: "But that's the point, Stella – the thing is, I don't care a tuppenny damn."

"But why should you?" asked Stella.

"But it's the first time he ever has, and surely I should have minded?"

"Don't you be too sure of that," said Jack, energetically puffing his pipe. "Don't be too sure." But it was only for form's sake, and Dorothy knew it, and said: "Surely I should have cared, Stell?"

"No. You'd have cared if you and Jack weren't so marvellous together. Just as I'd care if Philip and I weren't. ..." Tears came running down her face. She let them. These were her good friends; and besides, instinct told her tears weren't a bad thing, with Dorothy in this mood. She said, sniffing: "When Philip gets home, we always have a flaming bloody row in the first day or two, about something unimportant, but what it's really about, and we know it, is that I'm jealous of any affair he's had and vice versa. Then we go to bed and make up." She wept, bitterly, thinking of this happiness, postponed for a month, to be succeeded by the delightful battle of their day-to-day living.

"Oh Stella," said Jack. "Stell …" He got up, fished out a handkerchief, dabbed her eyes for her. "There, love, he'll be back soon."

"Yes, I know. It's just that you two are so good together and whenever I'm with you I miss Philip."

"Well, I suppose we're good together?" said Dorothy, sounding surprised. Jack, bending over Stella with his back to his wife, made a warning grimace, then stood up and turned, commanding the situation. "It's nearly six. You'd better feed Paul. Stella's going to cook supper."

"Is she? How nice," said Dorothy. "There's everything in the kitchen, Stella. How lovely to be looked after."

"I'll show you our mansion," said Jack.

Upstairs were two small white rooms. One was the bedroom, with their things and the baby's in it. The other was an overflow room, jammed with stuff. Jack picked up a large leather folder off the spare bed and said: "Look at these, Stell." He stood at the window, back to her, his thumb at work in his pipe bowl, looking into the garden. Stella sat on the bed, opened the folder and at once exclaimed: "When did she do these?"

"The last three months she was pregnant. Never seen anything like it, she just turned them out one after the other."

There were a couple of hundred pencil drawings, all of two bodies in every kind of balance, tension, relationship. The two bodies were Jack's and Dorothy's, mostly unclothed, but not all. The drawings startled, not only because they marked a real jump forward in Dorothy's achievement, but because of their bold sensuousness. They were a kind of chant, or exaltation about the marriage. The instinctive closeness, the harmony of Jack and Dorothy, visible in every movement they made towards or away from each other, visible even when they were not together, was celebrated here with a frank, calm triumph.

"Some of them are pretty strong," said Jack, the northern workingclass boy reviving in him for a moment's puritanism.

But Stella laughed, because the prudishness masked pride: some of the drawings were indecent.

In the last few of the series the woman's body was swollen in pregnancy. They showed her trust in her husband, whose body, commanding hers, stood or lay in positions of strength and confidence. In the very last Dorothy stood turned away from her husband, her two hands supporting her big belly, and Jack's hands were protective on her shoulders.

"They are marvellous," said Stella.

"They are, aren't they."

Stella looked, laughing, and with love, towards Jack; for she saw that his showing her the drawings was not only pride in his wife's talent, but that he was using this way of telling Stella not to take Dorothy's mood too seriously. And to cheer himself up. She said, impulsively: "Well that's all right then, isn't it?"

"What? Oh yes, I see what you mean, yes, I think it's all right."

"Do you know what?" said Stella, lowering her voice. "I think Dorothy's guilty because she feels unfaithful to you."

"*What?*"

"No, I mean, with the baby, and that's what it's all about."

He turned to face her, troubled, then slowly smiling. There was the same rich unscrupulous quality of appreciation in that smile as there had been in Dorothy's laugh over her husband and Lady Edith. "You think so?" They laughed together, irrepressibly and loudly.

"What's the joke?" shouted Dorothy.

"I'm laughing because your drawings are so good," shouted Stella.

"Yes, they are, aren't they?" But Dorothy's voice changed to flat incredulity: "The trouble is, I can't imagine how I ever did them, I can't imagine ever being able to do it again."

"Downstairs," said Jack to Stella, and they went down to find Dorothy nursing the baby. He nursed with his whole being, all of him in movement. He was wrestling with the breast, thumping Dorothy's plump pretty breast with his fists. Jack stood looking down at the two of them, grinning. Dorothy reminded Stella of a cat, half-closing her yellow eyes to stare over her kittens at work on her side, while she stretched out a paw where claws sheathed and unsheathed themselves, making a small rip-rip-rip on the carpet she lay on.

"You're a savage creature," said Stella, laughing.

Dorothy raised her small vivid face and smiled. "Yes, I am," she said, and looked at the two of them calm, and from a distance, over the head of her energetic baby.

Stella cooked supper in a stone kitchen, with a heater brought by Jack to make it tolerable. She used the good food she had brought with her, taking trouble. It took some time, then the three ate slowly over a big wooden table. The baby was not asleep. He grumbled for some minutes on a cushion on the floor, then his father held him briefly, before passing him over, as he had done earlier, in response to his mother's need to have him close.

"I'm supposed to let him cry," remarked Dorothy. "But why should he? If he were an Arab or an African baby he'd be plastered to my back."

"And very nice too," said Jack. "I think they come out too soon into the light of day; they should just stay inside for about eighteen months, much better all around."

"Have a heart," said Dorothy and Stella together, and they all laughed; but Dorothy added, quite serious: "Yes, I've been thinking so too."

This good nature lasted through the long meal. The light went cool and thin outside; and inside they let the summer dusk deepen, without lamps.

"I've got to go quite soon," said Stella, with regret.

"Oh, no, you've got to stay!" said Dorothy, strident. It was sudden, the return of the woman who made Jack and Dorothy tense themselves to take strain.

"We all thought Philip was coming. The children will be back tomorrow night, they've been on holiday."

"Then stay till tomorrow, I *want* you," said Dorothy, petulant.

"But I can't," said Stella.

"I never thought I'd want another woman around, cooking in my kitchen, looking after me, but I do," said Dorothy, apparently about to cry.

"Well, love, you'll have to put up with me," said Jack.

"Would you mind, Stell?"

"Mind *what*?" asked Stella, cautious.

"Do you find Jack attractive?"

"Very."

"Well I know you do. Jack, do you find Stella attractive?"

"Try me," said Jack, grinning; but at the same time signalling warnings to Stella.

"Well, then!" said Dorothy.

"A *ménage à trois*?" asked Stella, laughing. "And how about my Philip? Where does he fit in?"

"Well, if it comes to that, I wouldn't mind Philip myself," said Dorothy, knitting her sharp black brows and frowning.

"I don't blame you," said Stella, thinking of her handsome husband.

"Just for a month, till he comes back," said Dorothy. "I tell you what, we'll abandon this silly cottage, we must have been mad to stick ourselves away in England in the first place. The three of us'll just pack up and go off to Spain or Italy with the baby."

"And what else?" enquired Jack, good-natured at all costs, using his pipe as a safety valve.

"Yes, I've decided I approve of polygamy," announced Dorothy. She had opened her dress and the baby was nursing again, quietly this time, relaxed against her. She stroked his head, softly, softly, while her voice rose and insisted at the other two people: "I never understood it before, but I do now. I'll be the senior wife, and you two can look after me."

"Any other plans?" enquired Jack, angry now. "You just drop in from time to time to watch Stella and me have a go, is that it? Or are you going to tell us when we can go off and do it, give us your gracious permission?"

"Oh I don't care what you do, that's the point," said Dorothy, sighing, sounding forlorn, however.

Jack and Stella, careful not to look at each other, sat waiting.

"I read something in the newspaper yesterday, it struck me," said Dorothy, conversational. "A man and two women living together – here, in England. They are both his wives, they consider themselves his wives. The senior wife has a baby, and the younger wife sleeps with him – well, that's what it looked like, reading between the lines."

"You'd better stop reading between lines," said Jack. "It's not doing you any good."

"No, I'd like it," insisted Dorothy. "I think our marriages are silly. Africans and people like that, they know better, they've got some sense."

"I can just see you if I did make love to Stella," said Jack.

"Yes!" said Stella, with a short laugh, which, against her will, was resentful.

"But I wouldn't mind," said Dorothy, and burst into tears.

"Now, Dorothy, that's enough," said Jack. He got up, took the baby, whose sucking was mechanical now, and said: "Now listen, you're going right upstairs and you're going to sleep. This little stinker's full as a tick, he'll be asleep for hours, that's my bet."

"I don't feel sleepy," said Dorothy, sobbing.

"I'll give you a sleeping pill, then."

Then started a search for sleeping pills. None to be found.

"That's just like us," wailed Dorothy, "we don't even have a sleeping pill in the place. ... Stella, I wish you'd stay, I really do. Why can't you?"

"Stella's going in just a minute, I'm taking her to the station," said Jack. He poured some Scotch into a glass, handed it to his wife and said: "Now drink that, love, and let's have an end of it. I'm getting fed-up." He sounded fed-up.

Dorothy obediently drank the Scotch, got unsteadily from her chair and went slowly upstairs. "Don't let him cry," she demanded, as she disappeared.

"Oh you silly bitch!" he shouted after her. "When have I let him cry? Here, you hold on a minute," he said to Stella, handing her the baby. He ran upstairs.

Stella held the baby. This was almost for the first time, since she sensed how much another woman's holding her child made Dorothy's fierce new possessiveness uneasy. She looked down at the small, sleepy, red face and said softly: "Well, you're causing a lot of trouble, aren't you?"

Jack shouted from upstairs: "Come up a minute, Stell." She went up, with the baby. Dorothy was tucked up in bed, drowsy from the Scotch, the bedside light turned away from her. She looked at the baby, but Jack took it from Stella.

"Jack says I'm a silly bitch," said Dorothy, apologetic to Stella.

"Well, never mind, you'll feel different soon."

"I suppose so, if you say so. All right, I *am* going to sleep," said Dorothy, in a stubborn, sad little voice. She turned over, away from them. In the last flare of her hysteria she said: "Why don't you two walk to the station together? It's a lovely night."

"We're going to," said Jack, "don't worry."

She let out a weak giggle, but did not turn. Jack carefully deposited the now sleeping baby in the bed, about a foot from Dorothy. Who suddenly wriggled over until her small, defiant white back was in contact with the blanketed bundle that was her son.

Jack raised his eyebrows at Stella: but Stella was looking at mother and baby, the nerves of her memory filling her with sweet warmth. What right had this woman, who was in possession of such delight, to torment her husband, to torment her friend, as she had been doing – what right had she to rely on their decency as she did?

Surprised by these thoughts, she walked away downstairs, and stood at the door into the garden, her eyes shut, holding herself rigid against tears.

She felt a warmth on her bare arm – Jack's hand. She opened her eyes to see him bending towards her, concerned.

"It'd serve Dorothy right if I did drag you off into the bushes …"

"Wouldn't have to drag me," he said; and while the words had the measure of facetiousness the situation demanded, she felt his seriousness envelop them both in danger.

The warmth of his hand slid across her back, and she turned towards him under its pressure. They stood together, cheeks touching, scents of skin and hair mixing with the smells of warmed grass and leaves.

She thought: What is going to happen now will blow Dorothy and Jack and that baby sky-high; it's the end of my marriage; I'm going to blow everything to bits. There was almost uncontrollable pleasure in it.

She saw Dorothy, Jack, the baby, her husband, and two half-grown children, all dispersed, all spinning downwards through the sky like bits of debris after an explosion.

Jack's mouth was moving along her cheek towards her mouth, dissolving her whole self in delight. She saw, against closed lids, the bundled baby upstairs, and pulled back from the situation, exclaiming energetically: "Damn Dorothy, damn her, damn her, I'd like to kill her …"

And he, exploding into reaction, said in a low furious rage: "Damn you both! I'd like to wring both your bloody necks …"

Their faces were at a foot's distance from each other, their eyes staring hostility. She thought that if she had not the vision of the helpless baby they would now be in each other's arms – generating tenderness and desire like a couple of dynamos, she said to herself, trembling with dry anger.

"I'm going to miss my train if I don't go," she said.

"I'll get your coat," he said, and went in, leaving her defenceless against the emptiness of the garden.

When he came out, he slid the coat around her without touching her, and said: "Come on, I'll take you by car." He walked away in front of her to the car, and she followed meekly over rough lawn. It really was a lovely night.

HOW I FINALLY LOST MY HEART

Doris Lessing

> Doris Lessing (b. 1919) is a British novelist, poet, playwright, biographer and short story writer. In 2001, Lessing was awarded the David Cohen Prize for a lifetime's achievement in British Literature and she was ranked fifth on *The Times* list of the '50 Greatest British Writers Since 1945'. Lessing was awarded the 2007 Nobel Prize in Literature.

It would be easy to say that I picked up a knife, slit open my side, took my heart out, and threw it away; but unfortunately it wasn't as easy as that. Not that I, like everyone else, had not often wanted to do it. No, it happened differently, and not as I expected.

It was just after I had had a lunch and a tea with two different men. My lunch partner I had lived with for (more or less) four and seven-twelfths years. When he left me for new pastures, I spent two years, or was it three, half-dead, and my heart was a stone, impossible to carry about, considering all the other things weighing on one. Then I slowly, and with difficulty, got free, because my heart cherished a thousand adhesions to my first love – though from another point of view he could be legitimately described as either my second *real* love (my father being the first) or my third (my brother intervening).

As the folk song has it:

> *I have loved but three men in my life,*
> *My father, my brother, and the man that*
> *took my life.*

But if one were going to look at the thing from outside, without insight, he could be seen as (perhaps, I forget) the thirteenth, but to do that means disregarding the inner emotional truth. For we all know that those affairs or entanglements one has between *serious* loves, though they may number dozens and stretch over years, *don't really count.*

This way of looking at things creates a number of unhappy people, for it is well known that what doesn't really count for me might very well count for you. But there is no way of getting over this difficulty, for a *serious* love is the most important business in life, or nearly so. At any rate, most of us are engaged in looking for it. Even when we are in fact being very serious indeed with one person we still have an eighth of an eye cocked in case some stranger unexpectedly encountered might turn out to be even more serious. We are all entirely in agreement that we are in the right to taste, test, sip and sample a thousand people on our way to the *real* one. It is not too much to say that in our circles tasting and sampling is probably the second most important activity, the first being earning money. Or to put it another way, if you are serious about this thing, you go on laying everybody that offers until something clicks and you're all set to go.

I have digressed from an earlier point: that I regarded this man I had lunch with (we call him A) as my first love, and still do, despite the Freudians, who insist on seeing my father as A and possibly my brother as B, making my (real) first love C. And despite, also, those who might ask: What about your two husbands and all those affairs?

What about them? I did not *really* love them, the way I loved A.

I had lunch with him. Then, quite by chance, I had tea with B. When I say B, here, I mean my *second* serious love, not my brother, or the little boys I was in love with between the ages of five and fifteen, if we are going to take fifteen (arbitrarily) as the point of no return ... which last phrase is in itself a pretty brave defiance of the secular arbiters.

In between A and B (my count) there were a good many affairs, or samples, but they didn't score. B and I *clicked*, we went off like a bomb, though not quite as simply as A and I had clicked, because my heart was bruised, sullen, and suspicious because of A's throwing me over. Also there were all those ligaments and adhesions binding me to A still to be loosened, one by one. However, for a time B and

I got on like a house on fire, and then we came to grief. My heart was again a ton weight in my side.

> *If this were a stone in my side, a stone,*
> *I could pluck it out and be free ...*

Having lunch with A, then tea with B, two men who between them had consumed a decade of my precious years (I am not counting the test or trial affairs in between) and, it is fair to say, had balanced all the delight (plenty and intense) with misery (oh Lord, Lord) – moving from one to the other, in the course of an afternoon, conversing amiably about this and that, with meanwhile my heart giving no more than slight reminiscent tugs, the fish of memory at the end of a long slack line ...

To sum up, it was salutary.

Particularly as that evening I was expecting to meet C, or someone who might very well turn out to be C; though I don't want to give too much emphasis to C, the truth is I can hardly remember what he looked like, but one can't be expected to remember the unimportant ones one has sipped or tasted in between. But after all, he might have turned out to be C, we might have *clicked*, and I was in that state of mind (in which we all so often are) of thinking: He might turn out to be the one. (I use a woman's magazine phrase deliberately here, instead of saying, as I might: *Perhaps it will be serious.*)

So there I was (I want to get the details and atmosphere right) standing at a window looking into a street (Great Portland Street, as a matter of fact) and thinking that while I would not dream of regretting my affairs, or experiences, with A and B (it is better to have loved and lost than never to have loved at all), my anticipation of the heart because of spending an evening with a possible C had a certain unreality, because there was no doubt that both A and B had caused me unbelievable pain. Why, therefore, was I looking forward to C? I should rather be running away as fast as I could.

It suddenly occurred to me that I was looking at the whole phenomenon quite inaccurately. My (or perhaps I am permitted to say our?) way of looking at it is that one must search for an

A, or a B, or a C or a D with a certain combination of desirable or sympathetic qualities so that one may click, or spontaneously combust: or to put it differently, one needs a person who, like a saucer of water, allows one to float off on him/her, like a transfer. But this wasn't so at all. Actually one carries with one a sort of burning spear stuck in one's side, that one waits for someone else to pull out; it is something painful, like a sore or a wound, that one cannot wait to share with someone else.

I saw myself quite plainly in a moment of truth: I was standing at a window (on the third floor) with A and B (to mention only the mountain peaks of my emotional experience) behind me, a rather attractive woman, if I may say so, with a mellowness that I would be the first to admit is the sad harbinger of age, but is attractive by definition, because it is a testament to the amount of sampling and sipping (I nearly wrote "simpling" and "sapping") I have done in my time ... There I stood, brushed, dressed, red-lipped, kohl-eyed, all waiting for an evening with a possible C. And at another window overlooking (I think I am right in saying) Margaret Street, stood C, brushed, washed, shaved, smiling: an attractive man (I think), and *he* was thinking: Perhaps she will turn out to be D (or A or 3 or ? or %, or whatever symbol he used). We stood, separated by space, certainly, in identical conditions of pleasant uncertainty and anticipation; and we both held our hearts in our hands, all pink and palpitating and ready for pleasure and pain, and we were about to throw these hearts in each other's face like snowballs, or cricket balls (How's that?) or, more accurately, like great bleeding wounds: "Take my wound." Because the last thing one ever thinks at such moments is that he (or she) will say: Take *my* wound, please remove the spear from *my* side. No, not at all; one simply expects to get rid of one's own.

I decided I must go to the telephone and say, C! – You know that joke about the joke-makers who don't trouble to tell each other jokes, but simply say Joke 1 or Joke 2, and everyone roars with laughter, or snickers, or giggles appropriately ... Actually one could reverse the game by guessing whether it was Joke C(b) or Joke A(d) according to what sort of laughter a person made to match the silent thought ... Well, C (I imagined myself saying), the analogy is for our instruction: Let's take the whole thing as read or said. Let's not lick each other's sores; let's keep our hearts to ourselves. Because just consider it, C, how utterly absurd – here we stand at our respective windows with our palpitating hearts in our hands ...

At this moment, dear reader, I was forced simply to put down the telephone with an apology. For I felt the fingers of my left hand push outwards around something rather large, light, and slippery – hard to describe this sensation, really. My hand is not large, and my heart was in a state of inflation after having had lunch with A, tea with B, and then looking forward to C ... Anyway, my fingers were stretching out rather desperately to encompass an unknown, largish, lightish object, and I said: Excuse me a minute, to C, looked down, and there was my heart, in my hand.

I had to end the conversation there.

For one thing, to find that one has achieved something so often longed for, so easily, is upsetting. It's not as if I had been trying. To get something one wants simply by accident – no, there's no pleasure in it, no feeling of achievement. So to find myself heart-whole, or, more accurately, heart-less, or at any rate, rid of the damned thing, and at such an awkward moment, in the middle of an imaginary telephone call with a man who might possibly turn out to be C – well, it was irritating rather than not.

For another thing, a heart, raw and bleeding and fresh from one's side is not the prettiest sight. I'm not going into that at all. I was appalled, and indeed embarrassed that *that* was what had been loving and beating away all those years, because if I'd had any idea at all – well, enough of that.

My problem was how to get rid of it.

Simple, you'll say, drop it into the waste bucket.

Well, let me tell you, that's what I tried to do. I took a good look at this object, nearly died with embarrassment, and walked over to the rubbish-can, where I tried to let it roll off my fingers. It wouldn't. It was stuck. There was my heart, a large red pulsing bleeding repulsive object, stuck to my fingers. What was I going to do? I sat down, lit a cigarette (with one hand, holding the matchbox between my knees), held my hand with the heart stuck on it over the side of the chair so that it could drip into a bucket, and considered.

> *If this were a stone in my hand, a stone,*
> *I could throw it over a tree ...*

When I had finished the cigarette, I carefully unwrapped some tin foil of the kind used to wrap food in when cooking, and I fitted a sort of cover around my heart. This was absolutely and urgently necessary. First, it was smarting badly. After all, it had spent some forty years protected by flesh and ribs, and the air was too much for it. Secondly, I couldn't have any Tom, Dick and Harry walking in and looking at it. Thirdly, I could not look at it for too long myself, it filled me with shame. The tin foil was effective, and indeed rather striking. It is quite pliable and now it seemed as if there were a stylised heart balanced on my palm, like a globe, in glittering, silvery substance. I almost felt I needed a sceptre in the other hand to balance it ... But the thing was, there is no other word for it, in bad taste. I then wrapped a scarf around hand and tin-foiled heart, and felt safer. Now it was a question of pretending to have hurt my hand until I could think of a way of getting rid of my heart altogether, short of amputating my hand.

Meanwhile I telephoned (really, not in imagination) C, who now would never be C. I could feel my heart, which was stuck so close to my fingers that I could feel every beat or tremor, give a gulp of resigned grief at the idea of this beautiful experience now never to be. I told him some idiotic lie about having 'flu. Well, he was all stiff and indignant, but concealing it urbanely, as I would have done, making a joke but allowing a tiny barb of sarcasm to rankle in the last wellchosen phrase. Then I sat down again to think out my whole situation.

There I sat.

What was I going to do?

There I sat.

I am going to have to skip about four days here, vital enough in all conscience, because I simply cannot go heartbeat by heartbeat through my memories. A pity, since I suppose this is what this story is about; but in brief: I drew the curtains, I took the telephone off the hook, I turned on the lights, I took the scarf off the glittering shape, then the tin foil; then I examined the heart. There were two-fifths of a century's experience to work through, and before I had even got through the first night, I was in a state hard to describe ...

> *Or if I could pull the nerves from my skin*
> *A quick red net to drag through a sea for fish ...*

By the end of the fourth day I was worn out. By no act of will, or intention, or desire, could I move that heart by a fraction – on the contrary, it was not only stuck to my fingers, like a sucked boiled sweet, but was actually growing to the flesh of my fingers and my palm.

I wrapped it up again in tin foil and scarf, and turned out the lights and pulled up the blinds and opened the curtains. It was about ten in the morning, an ordinary London day, neither hot nor cold nor clear nor clouded nor wet nor fine. And while the street is interesting, it is not exactly beautiful, so I wasn't looking at it so much as waiting for something to catch my attention while thinking of something else.

Suddenly I heard a tap-tap-tapping that got louder, sharp and clear, and I knew before I saw her that this was the sound of high heels on a pavement though it might just as well have been a hammer against stone. She walked fast opposite my window and her heels hit the pavement so hard that all the noises of the street seemed absorbed into that single tap-tap-clang-clang. As she reached the corner at Great Portland Street two London pigeons swooped diagonally from the sky very fast, as if they were bullets aimed to kill her; and then as they saw her they swooped up and off at an angle. Meanwhile she had turned the corner. All this has taken time to write down, but the thing happening took a couple of seconds: the woman's body hitting the pavement bang-bang through her heels then sharply turning the corner in a right angle; and the pigeons making another acute angle across hers and intersecting it in a fast swoop of displaced air. Nothing to all that, of course, nothing – she had gone off down the street, her heels tip-tapping, and the pigeons landed on my windowsill and began cooing. All gone, all vanished, the marvellous exact co-ordination of sound and movement, but it had happened, it had made me happy and exhilarated, I had no problems in this world, and I realised that the heart stuck to my fingers was quite loose. I couldn't get it off altogether, though I was tugging at it under the scarf and the tin foil, but almost.

I understood that sitting and analysing each movement or pulse or beat of my heart through forty years was a mistake. I was on the wrong track altogether: this was the way to attach my red, bitter, delighted heart to my flesh for ever and ever ...

> *Ha! So you think I'm done! You think ...*
> *Watch, I'll roll my heart in a mesh of rage*
> *And bounce it like a handball off*
> *Walls, faces, railings, umbrellas and pigeons' backs ...*

No, all that was no good at all; it just made things worse. What I must do is to take myself by surprise, as it were, the way I was taken by surprise over the woman and the pigeons and the sharp sounds of heels and silk wings.

I put on my coat, held my lumpy scarfed arm across my chest, so that if anyone said: What have you done with your hand? I could say: I've banged my finger, in the door. Then I walked down into the street.

It wasn't easy to go among so many people, when I was worried that they were thinking: What has that woman done to her hand? because that made it hard to forget myself. And all the time it tingled and throbbed against my fingers, reminding me.

Now I was out, I didn't know what to do. Should I go and have lunch with someone? Or wander in the park? Or buy myself a dress? I decided to go to the Round Pond, and walk around it by myself. I was tired after four days and nights without sleep. I went down into the underground at Oxford Circus. Midday. Crowds of people. I felt self-conscious, but of course need not have worried. I swear you could walk naked down the street in London and no one would even turn round.

So I went down the escalator and looked at the faces coming up past me on the other side, as I always do; and wondered, as I always do, how strange it is that those people and I should meet by chance in such a way, and how odd that we would never see each other again, or, if we did, we wouldn't know it. And I went on to the crowded platform and looked at the faces as I always do, and got into the train, which was very full, and found a seat. It wasn't as bad as at rush hour, but all the seats were filled. I leaned back and closed my eyes, deciding to sleep a little, being so tired. I was just beginning to doze off when I heard a woman's voice muttering, or rather, declaiming:

> *"A gold cigarette case, well, that's a nice thing,*
> *isn't it, I must say, a gold case, yes ..."*

There was something about this voice which made me open my eyes: on the other side of the compartment, about eight persons away, sat a youngish woman, wearing a cheap green cloth coat, gloveless hands, flat brown shoes, and lisle stockings. She must be rather poor – a woman dressed like this is a rare sight, these days. But it was her posture that struck me. She was sitting half-twisted in her seat, so that her head was turned over her left shoulder, and she was looking straight at the stomach of an elderly man next to her. But it was clear she was not seeing it: her young staring eyes were sightless, she was looking inwards.

She was so clearly alone, in the crowded compartment, that it was not as embarrassing as it might have been. I looked around, and people were smiling, or exchanging glances, or winking, or ignoring her, according to their natures, but she was oblivious of us all.

She suddenly aroused herself, turned so that she sat straight in her seat, and directed her voice and her gaze to the opposite seat:

> *"Well so that's what you think, you think that,*
> *you think that do you, well, you think I'm just going*
> *to wait at home for you, but you gave her a gold*
> *case and ..."*

And with a clockwork movement of her whole thin person, she turned her narrow pale-haired head sideways over her left shoulder, and resumed her stiff empty stare at the man's stomach. He was grinning uncomfortably. I leaned forward to look along the line of people in the row of seats I sat in, and the man opposite her, a young man, had exactly the same look of discomfort which he was determined to keep amused. So we all looked at her, the young, thin, pale woman in her private drama of misery, who was so completely unconscious of us that she spoke and thought out loud. And again, without particular warning or reason, in between stops, so it wasn't that she was disturbed from her dream by the train stopping at Bond Street, and then jumping forward again, she twisted her body frontways, and addressed the seat opposite her (the young man had got off, and a smart grey-curled matron had got in):

> "Well I know about it now, don't I, and if you come
> in all smiling and pleased well then I know, don't
> I, you don't have to tell me, I know, and I've said
> to her, I've said, I know he gave you a gold cigarette
> case ..."

At which point, with the same clockwork impulse, she stopped, or was checked, or simply ran out, and turned herself half around to stare at the stomach – the same stomach, for the middleaged man was still there. But we stopped at Marble Arch and he got out, giving the compartment, rather than the people in it, a tolerant half-smile which said: I am sure I can trust you to realise that this unfortunate woman is stark staring mad ...

His seat remained empty. No people got in at Marble Arch, and the two people standing waiting for seats did not want to sit by her to receive her stare.

We all sat, looking gently in front of us, pretending to ourselves and to each other that we didn't know the poor woman was mad and that in fact we ought to be doing something about it. I even wondered what I should say: Madam, you're mad – shall I escort you to your home? Or: Poor thing, don't go on like that, it doesn't do any good, you know – just leave him, that'll bring him to his senses ...

And behold, after the interval that was regulated by her inner mechanism had elapsed, she turned back and said to the smart matron who received this statement of accusation with perfect self-command:

> *"Yes, I know! Oh yes! And what about my*
> *shoes, what about them, a golden cigarette*
> *case is what she got, the filthy bitch,*
> *a golden case ..."*

Stop. Twist. Stare. At the empty seat by her.

Extraordinary. Because it was a frozen misery, how shall I put it? A passionless passion – we were seeing unhappiness embodied; we were looking at the essence of some private tragedy – rather, Tragedy. There was no emotion in it. She was like an actress doing Accusation, or Betrayed Love, or Infidelity, when she has only just learned her lines and is not bothering to do more than get them right.

And whether she sat in her half-twisted position, her unblinking eyes staring at the greenish, furry, ugly covering of the train seat, or sat straight, directing her accusation to the smart woman opposite, there was a frightening immobility about her – yes, that was why she frightened us. For it was clear that she might very well (if the inner machine ran down) stay silent, forever, in either twisted or straight position, or at any point between them – yes, we could all imagine her, frozen perpetually in some arbitrary pose. It was as if we watched the shell of some woman going through certain predetermined motions.

For *she* was simply not there. *What* was there, who she was, it was impossible to tell, though it was easy to imagine her thin, gentle little face breaking into a smile in total forgetfulness of what she was enacting now. She did not know she was in a train between Marble Arch and Queensway, nor that she was publicly accusing her husband or lover, nor that we were looking at her.

And we, looking at her, felt an embarrassment and shame that was not on her account at all ...

Suddenly I felt, under the scarf and the tin foil, a lightening of my fingers, as my heart rolled loose.

I hastily took it off my palm, in case it decided to adhere there again, and I removed the scarf, leaving balanced on my knees a perfect stylised heart, like a silver heart on a Valentine card, though of course it was three-dimensional. This heart was not so much harmless, no that isn't the word, as artistic, but in very bad taste, as I said. I could see that the people in the train, now looking at me and the heart, and not at the poor madwoman, were pleased with it.

I got up, took the four or so paces to where she was, and laid the tin-foiled heart down on the seat so that it received her stare.

For a moment she did not react, then with a groan or a mutter of relieved and entirely theatrical grief, she leaned forward, picked up the glittering heart, and clutched it in her arms, hugging it and rocking it back and forth, even laying her cheek against it, while staring over its top at her husband as if to say: Look what I've got, I don't care about you and your cigarette case, I've got a silver heart.

I got up, since we were at Notting Hill Gate, and, followed by the pleased congratulatory nods and smiles of the people left behind, I went out onto the platform, up the escalators, into the street, and along to the park.

No heart. No heart at all. What bliss. What freedom ...

Hear that sound? That's laughter, yes.
That's me laughing, yes, that's me.

FAITHFUL LOVERS

Margaret Drabble

> Margaret Drabble (b. 1939) is a British novelist, biographer
> and critic. Awarded a CBE in 1980, Drabble was promoted
> to Dame Commander of the Order of the British Empire in
> the 2008 Birthday Honours. In 2011, she was awarded the
> Golden PEN Award by English PEN for a lifetime's
> distinguished service to literature.

There must have been a moment at which she decided to go down
the street and around the corner and into the café. For at one point
she was walking quite idly, quite innocently, with no recollection
or association in her head but the dimmest shadow of long-past
knowledge, and within ten yards she had made up her mind that
she would go and have her lunch in that place where they had had
lunch together once a fortnight or so over that long and lovely year.
It was the kind of place where nobody either of them knew would
ever see them. At the same time, it was not impossibly inconvenient,
not so very far from Holborn, where they both had good reason to
be from time to time. They had felt safe there – as safe as they could
ever feel – yet at the same time aware that they had not allowed
themselves to be driven into grotesque precautions.

And now, after so long, after three years, she found herself there
– and at lunchtime, too. She was hungry. There is nothing more to
it than that, she said to herself. I happened to be near, and the fact
that I wanted my lunch reminded me of this place, and moreover,
there is nowhere else possible within a five-minute walk. She had
done enough walking, she thought – from the Old Street tube
station to the place where they had made her new tooth. She ran
her tongue over the new front tooth, reassuringly, and was slightly
ashamed by the immense relief that she felt at being once more
presentable, no longer disfigured by that humiliating gap. She had
always made much of caring little for her beauty, and was always
disturbed by the accidents that brought her face to face with her

own vanity – by the inconvenient pimple, by the unperceived smudge on the cheek, by the heavy cold. And that lost tooth had been something of a test case ever since she had had it knocked out, while still a child at school. Her dentist had made her the most elaborate and delicate bridge then, but the night before last she had fallen after a party and broken it. She had rung up her dentist in the morning, and he had promised her a temporary bridge to last her until he could make her a new one. When he had told her the name of the place she should go to collect the bridge, she had noticed in herself a small flicker of recollection. He went on explaining to her, obliging yet irritable. 'You've got that then, Mrs Harvey? Eighty-two St Luke's Street? You go to Old Street Station, then turn right …' And he had explained to her that she should express her gratitude to the man at the laboratory, in view of the shortness of the notice. And she had duly expressed it to the man when, ten minutes ago, he handed her the tooth.

Then she had come out and walked along this street. And as she paused at the café door, she knew that she had been thinking of him and of that other year all this time, that she could not very well have avoided the thought of him, among so much familiar scenery. There they had sat in the car and kissed, and endlessly discussed the impossibility of their kissing; there they had stood by that lamp-post, transfixed, unable to move. The pavement seemed still to bear the marks of their feet. And yet it was all so long ago, so thoroughly slaughtered and decayed. It was two years since she had cared, more than two years since she had suffered.

She was content, she was occupied, she had got her tooth back, everything was under control. And in a way it made her almost happy to be back in this place, to find how thoroughly dead it all was. She saw no ghosts of him here; for a year after their parting she had seen him on every street corner, in every passing car, in shapes of heads and hands and forms of movement, but now he was nowhere any more, not even here. For as long as she had imagined that she saw him, she had imagined that he had remembered. Those false ghosts had been in some way the projected shadows of his love; but now she knew that surely they had both forgotten.

She pushed open the door and went in. It looked the same. She went to the side of the room that they had always favoured, away from the door and the window, and sat at the corner table, where they had always sat when they could, with her back to the door. She sat there and looked down at the red-veined Formica tabletop, with its cluster of sugar bowl, salt and pepper, mustard and ketchup, and an ashtray. Then she looked up at the dark yellow ceiling, with its curiously useless trelliswork hung with plastic lemons and bananas, and then at the wall, papered in a strange, delicate, dirty flowered print. On the wall hung the only thing that was different. It was a calendar, a gift from the garage, and the picture showed an Alpine hut in snowy mountains, for all that the month was May. In their day the calendar had been one donated by a fruit-juice firm, and they had seen it through three seasons; she recalled the anguish with which she had seen its leaves turn, more relentless even than those leaves falling so ominously from real trees, and she recalled that at the time of their parting the calendar showed an appalling photograph of an autumn evening in a country garden, with an old couple sitting by their ivy-covered doorway.

They had both been merciless deliverers of ultimatums, the one upon the other. And she had selected in her own soul the month, and the day of that month, and had said, 'Look, on the twenty-third, that's it, and I mean it this time.' She wondered if he had known that this time it was for real. Because he had taken her at her word. It was the first time that she had not relented, nor he persisted; each other time they had parted forever, a telephone call had been enough to reunite them; each time she had left him, she had sat by the telephone biting her nails and waiting for it to ring. But this time it did not ring.

The menu, when it was brought to her, had not altered much. Though she never knew why she bothered to read menus, for she always ate the same lunch – a cheese omelette and chips. So she ordered her meal, and then sat back to wait. Usually, whenever left alone in a public place, she would read, and through habit she propped a book up against the sugar bowl and opened it. But she did not look at the words. Nor was she dwelling entirely upon the past, for a certain pleasurable anxiety about that evening's show was stealing most of her attention, and she found herself wondering whether she had adequately prepared her piece about interior decoration for the discussion programme she'd been asked to appear on, and whether David Rathbone, the producer, would offer to drive her home, and whether her hair would look all right. And most of all, she wondered if she ought to wear her grey skirt. She was not at all sure that it was not just a little bit too tight. If it wasn't, then it was perfect, for it was the kind of thing that she always looked marvellous in. Then she said to herself: The very fact that I'm *worrying* about it must mean that it must be too tight after all, or the thought of its being too tight wouldn't have crossed my mind, would it? And then she saw him.

What was really most shocking about it was the way they noticed each other simultaneously, without a chance of turning away or in any way managing the shock. Their eyes met, and they both jerked, beyond hope of dissimulation.

'Oh, God,' he said, after a second, and he stood there looking at her.

And she felt at such a loss, sitting there with her book propped up against the sugar bowl, and her head full of thoughts of skirts and false teeth, that she said, hurriedly, throwing away what might after all have been really quite a moment, 'Oh, Lord, oh, well, since you're there, do sit down.' And she moved up the wooden bench, closing up her book with a snap, averting her eyes, confused, unable to look.

And he sat down by her, and then said quite suddenly and intimately, as though perfectly at home with her after so many years of silence, 'Oh, Lord, my darling Viola, what a dreadful, dreadful surprise. I don't think I shall ever recover.'

'Oh, I don't know, Kenneth,' she said, as though she too had discovered exactly where she was. 'One gets over these things quite quickly. I feel better already, don't you?'

'Why, yes, I suppose I do,' he said. 'I feel better now that I'm sitting down. I thought I was going to faint, standing there and looking at you. Didn't you feel some sort of slight tremor?'

'It's hard to tell,' she said, 'when one's sitting down. It isn't a fair test. Even of tremors.'

'No,' he said, 'no.'

Then they were silent for a moment or two, and then she said, very precisely and carefully, offering her first generous signal of intended retreat, 'I suppose that what *is* odd, really, is that we haven't come across one another before.'

'Have you ever been back here before this?' he asked.

'No, never,' she said. 'Have you?'

'Yes,' he said. 'Yes, I have. And if you had been back, you might have seen me. I looked for you.'

'You're lying,' she said quickly, elated, looking at him for the first time since he had sat down by her, and then looking away again quickly, horrified by the dangerous proximity of his head.

'No, I'm not,' he said. 'I came here, and I looked for you. I was sure that you would come.'

'It's a safe lie,' she said, 'like all your lies. A lie I could never catch you out in. Unless I really had been here, looking for you, and simply hadn't wanted to admit it.'

'But,' he said with conviction, 'you weren't here at all. I came, but you didn't. You were faithless, weren't you, my darling?'

'Faithless?'

'You forgot me quicker than I forgot you, didn't you? How long did you remember me?'

'Oh, how can one say?' she said. 'After all, there are degrees of remembrance.'

'Tell me,' he said. 'What harm can it do to tell me now?'

She moved a little on the seat, away from him, but settling at the same time into a more comfortable pose of confidence, because she had been waiting for years to tell him.

'I suffered quite horribly,' she said. 'Really quite horribly. That's what you want to hear, isn't it?'

'Of course it is,' he said.

'Oh, I really did,' she said. 'I can't tell you. I cried all the time, for weeks. For at least a month. And whenever the phone rang, I started, I jumped, like a fool, as though I'd been shot. It was pathetic, it was ludicrous. Each time I answered and it wasn't you I would stand there listening, and they would go on talking, and sometimes I would say yes or no, as I waited for them to ring off. And when they did ring off I would sit down and I would cry. Is that what you want me to say?'

'I want to hear it,' he said, 'but it can't, it can't be true.'

'It's as true as that you came to this place to look for me,' she said.

'I did come,' he said.

'And I did weep,' she said.

'Did you ever try to ring me?' he asked then, unable to resist.

'No!' she said with some pride. 'No, not once. I'd said I wouldn't, and I didn't.'

'I rang you, once,' he said.

'You didn't,' she said, and became aware at that instant that her knees under the table were trembling.

'I did,' he said. 'It was just over a year ago, and we'd just got back from a party – about three in the morning it was – and I rang you.'

'Oh, God,' she said, 'oh, God. It's true, it's not a lie, because I remember it! Oliver went to answer it, and he came back saying no one was there. But I immediately thought of you. Oh, my darling, I can't tell you how I've had to stop myself from ringing you, how I've sat there by the phone and lifted the receiver and dialled the beginning of your number, and then stopped. Wasn't that good of me?'

'Oh,' he said, 'if you knew how I'd wanted you to ring.'

'I did write to you once,' she said. 'But I couldn't bring myself to post it. But I'll tell you what I did do: I typed out an envelope to you, and I put one of those circulars from that absurd poetry club of mine into it, and I sent it off to you, because I thought that at least it might create in you a passing thought of me. And I liked the thought of something from my house reaching your house. Though perhaps she threw it away before it even got to you.'

'I remember it,' he said. 'I did think of you. But I didn't think you sent it, because the postmark was Croydon.'

'Oh,' she said, weakly. 'You got it. Oh, Lord, how alarmingly faithful we have both been.'

'Did you expect us not to be? We swore that we would be. Oh, look, my darling, here's your lunch. Are you still eating cheese omelettes every day? Now, that really *is* what I call alarming consistency. And I haven't even ordered. What about some moussaka? I always used to like that; it was always rather nice, in its own disgusting way. One moussaka, please.'

After her first mouthful, she put down her fork and said

reflectively, 'From my point of view, at least, the whole business was quite unnecessary. What I mean is, Oliver hadn't the faintest suspicion. Which, considering how ludicrously careless we were, is quite astonishing. We could have gone on forever, and he'd never have known. He was far too preoccupied with his own affairs.'

'You know,' he said, 'all those continual threats of separation, of ending it – that was really corrupt. I feel bad about it now, looking back. Don't you?'

'How do you mean, bad about it?' she said.

'I feel we ought to have been able to do better than that. Though, come to think of it, it was you that did nearly all the threatening. Every time I saw you, you said it was for the last time. Every time. And I must have seen you six days in every week for over a year. You can't have meant it each time.'

'I did mean it,' she said. 'Every time I said it. I must have meant it, because I finally did it, didn't I?'

'You mean we did it,' he said. 'You couldn't have done it without my help. If I'd rung you, if I'd written to you, it would have started all over again.'

'Do you really think so?' she said, sadly, without malice, without recrimination. 'Yes, I suppose you might be right. It takes two to part, just as it takes two to love.'

'It was corrupt,' he said, 'to make ourselves live under that perpetual threat.'

'Yes,' she said, 'but remember how lovely it was, how horribly lovely, each time that one relented. Each time one said, "I'll never see you again … all right, I'll meet you tomorrow in the usual place at half-past one." It was lovely.'

'Lovely, but wicked,' he said.

'Oh, that sensation,' she said, 'that sensation of defeat. That was so lovely, every time, every time you touched me, every time I saw you. And I felt so sure, so entirely sure that what you felt was what I felt. Lord, we were so alike. And to think that when I first knew you I couldn't think of anything to say to you at all; I thought you came from another world, that we had nothing in common at all, nothing except, well, except you know what; I feel it would be dangerous even to mention it, even now. Oh, darling, what a disaster, our being so alike.'

'I liked it, though,' he said. 'I liked breaking up together. Better than having it done to one; better than doing it.'

'Yes, but more seriously incurable,' she said. And silence threatening to fall once more, she said quickly, 'Anyway, tell me what you're doing round here. I mean to say, one has to have some reason for coming to a place like this.'

'I told you,' he said. 'I was looking for you.'

'You *are* a liar,' she said, smiling, amazed that even here she could allow herself to be amused; indeed, could not prevent herself from smiling.

'What are you doing here, then?'

'Oh, I had a perfectly good reason,' she said. 'You know that false front tooth? Well, yesterday morning I broke it, and I've got to do a programme on television tonight, so I went to my dentist and he made me a temporary new bridge, and I had to come round here to the laboratory to pick it up.'

'Have you got it in?'

'Look,' she said, and turned to face him, smiling, lifting her upper lip.

'Well, that's convincing enough, I guess,' he said.

'You still haven't told me what you're doing here,' she said. 'I bet you haven't got as good a reason as me. Mine is entirely convincing, don't you think? I mean, where else could I have had lunch? I think my reason clears me entirely of suspicion of any kind, don't you?'

'Any suspicion of sentiment?'

'That's what I meant.'

He thought for a moment, and then said, 'I had to call on a man about my income tax. Look, here's his address.' And he got an envelope out of his pocket and showed her.

'Ah,' she said.

'I came here on purpose,' he said. 'To think of you. I could have had lunch at lots of places between London Wall and here.'

'You didn't come here because of me; you came here because it's the only place you could think of,' she said.

'It comes to the same thing,' he said.

'No, it doesn't,' she said firmly. She felt creeping upon her the familiar illusion of control, created as always before by a concentration upon trivialities; she reflected that their conversations had always followed the patterns of their times in bed, and that these idle points of contention were like those frivolous, delaying gestures in which she would turn aside, in which he would lie still and stare at the ceiling, not daring to touch her, thus merely deferring the inevitable. Thinking this, and able to live only in the deferment, for now there was no inevitable outcome that she could see, she said, eating her last chip, 'And how are your children?'

'They're fine,' he said, 'fine. Saul started grammar school. We were pleased about that. What about yours?'

'Oh, they're all right, too. I've had some dreadful nights with Laura recently. I must say I thought I was through with all that – I mean, the child's five now – but she says she can't sleep and has these dreadful nightmares, so she's been in my bed every night for the last fortnight. It's wearing me out. Then in the morning she just laughs. She doesn't kick; it's just that I can't sleep with anyone else in the bed.'

'What does Oliver say?' he asked, and she said, without thinking, 'Oh, I don't sleep with Oliver any more,' and wondered as she said it how she could have made such a mistake, and wondered how to get out of it. But fortunately at that instant his moussaka arrived, making it unnecessary to pursue the subject. Though once it had become unnecessary, she regretted the subject's disappearance; she thought of saying what was the truth itself – that she had slept with nobody since she had slept with him, that for three years she had slept alone, and that she was quite prepared to sleep alone forever. But she was not entirely sure that he would want to hear it, and she knew that such a remark, once made, could never be retracted, so she said nothing.

'It looks all right,' he said, staring at the moussaka. He took a mouthful and chewed it, and then he put his fork down and said, 'Oh, Lord, oh, Lord, what a Proustian experience. I can't believe it. I can't believe that I'm sitting here with you. It tastes of you, this stuff. Oh, God, it reminds me of you. You look so beautiful, you look so lovely, my darling. Oh, God, I loved you so much. Do you believe me – that I really loved you?'

'I haven't slept with anyone,' she said, 'since I last slept with you.'

'Oh, darling,' he said. And she could feel herself fainting and sighing away, drifting downward on that fatefully descending, eddying spiral, like Paolo and Francesca in hell, helpless, the mutually entwined drifting fall of all true lovers, unresisting. It was as though three years of solitude had been nothing but a pause, nothing but a long breath before this final acknowledgement of nature, damnation and destiny. She turned towards him and said, 'Oh, my darling, I love you. What can I do? I love you.' And he, with the same breath, said, 'I love you, all the time I love you, I want you,' and they kissed there, their faces already so close that they hardly had to move.

Like many romantics, they habitually connived with fate by remembering the names of restaurants and the streets they had once walked along as lovers. Those who forget forget, he said to her later, and those who do not forget will meet again.

MASTER

Angela Carter

Angela Carter (1940–1992) was a British novelist and journalist, known for her unique blend of feminism and magical realism. In 2008, *The Times* ranked her tenth in their list of the '50 Greatest British Writers Since 1945', and in 2012 her novel, *Nights at the Circus*, was selected as the best ever winner of the James Tait Black Memorial Prize.

After he discovered that his vocation was to kill animals, the pursuit of it took him far away from temperate weather until, in time, the insatiable suns of Africa eroded the pupils of his eyes, bleached his hair and tanned his skin until he no longer looked the thing he had been but its systematic negative; he became the white hunter, victim of an exile which is the imitation of death, a willed bereavement. He would emit a ravished gasp when he saw the final spasm of his prey. He did not kill for money but for love.

He had first exercised a propensity for savagery in the acrid lavatories of a minor English public school where he used to press the heads of the new boys into the ceramic bowl and then pull the flush upon them to drown their gurgling protests. After puberty, he turned his indefinable but exacerbated rage upon the pale, flinching bodies of young women whose flesh he lacerated with teeth, fingernails and sometimes his leather belt in the beds of cheap hotels near London's great rail termini (King's Cross, Victoria, Euston …). But these pastel-coloured excesses, all the cool, rainy country of his birth could offer him, never satisfied him; his ferocity would attain the colouring of the fauves only when he took it to the torrid zones and there refined it until it could be distinguished from that of the beasts he slaughtered only by the element of self-consciousness it retained, for, if little of him now pertained to the human, the eyes of his self still watched him so that he was able to applaud his own depredations.

Although he decimated herds of giraffe and gazelle as they grazed in the savannahs until they learned to snuff their annihilation upon the wind as he approached, and dispatched heraldically plated hippopotami as they lolled up to their armpits in ooze, his rifle's particular argument lay with the silken indifference of the great cats, and, finally, he developed a speciality in the extermination of the printed beasts, leopards and lynxes, who carry ideograms of death in the clotted language pressed in brown ink upon their pelts by the fingertips of mute gods who do not acknowledge any divinity in humanity.

When he had sufficiently ravaged the cats of Africa, a country older by far than we are yet to whose innocence he had always felt superior, he decided to explore the nether regions of the New World, intending to kill the painted beast, the jaguar, and so arrived in the middle of a metaphor for desolation, the place where time runs back on itself, the moist, abandoned cleft of the world whose fructifying river is herself a savage woman, the Amazon. A green, irrevocable silence closed upon him in that serene kingdom of giant vegetables. Dismayed, he clung to the bottle as if it were a teat.

He travelled by jeep through an invariable terrain of architectonic vegetation where no wind lifted the fronds of palms as ponderous as if they had been sculpted out of viridian gravity at the beginning of time and then abandoned, whose trunks were so heavy they did not seem to rise into the air but, instead, drew the oppressive sky down upon the forest like a coverlid of burnished metal. These tree trunks bore an outcrop of plants, orchids, poisonous, iridescent blossoms and creepers the thickness of an arm with flowering mouths that stuck out viscous tongues to trap the flies that nourished them. Bright birds of unknown shapes infrequently darted past him and sometimes monkeys, chattering like the third form, leaped from branch to branch that did not move beneath them. But no motion nor sound did more than ripple the surface of the profound, inhuman introspection of the place so that, here, to kill became the only means that remained to him to confirm he himself was still alive, for he was not prone to introspection and had never found any consolation in nature. Slaughter was his only proclivity and his unique skill.

He came upon the Indians who lived among the lugubrious

trees. They represented such a diversity of ethnic types they were like a living museum of man organised on a principle of regression for, the further inland he went, the more primitive they became, as if to demonstrate that evolution could be inverted. Some of the brown men had no other habitation than the sky and, like the flowers, ate insects; they would paint their bodies with the juice of leaves and berries and ornament their heads with diadems of feathers or the claws of eagles. Placid and decorative, the men and women would come softly twittering round his jeep, a mild curiosity illuminating the inward-turning, amber suns of their eyes, and he did not recognise that they were men although they distilled demented alcohol in stills of their own devising and he drank it, in order to people the inside of his head with familiar frenzy among so much that was strange.

His half-breed guide would often take one of the brown girls who guilelessly offered him her bare, pointed breasts and her veiled, limpid smile and, then and there, infect her with the clap to which he was a chronic martyr in the bushes at the rim of the clearing. Afterwards, licking his chops with remembered appetite, he would say to the hunter: 'Brown meat, brown meat.' In drunkenness one night, troubled by the prickings of a carnality that often visited him at the end of his day's work, the hunter bartered, for the spare tyre of his jeep, a pubescent girl as virgin as the forest that had borne her.

She wore a vestigial slip of red cotton twisted between her thighs and her long, sinuous back was upholstered in cut velvet, for it was whorled and ridged with the tribal markings incised on her when her menses began – raised designs like the contour map of an unknown place. The women of her tribe dipped their hairs in liquid mud and then wound their locks into long curls around sticks and let them dry in the sun until each one possessed a hairdo of rigid ringlets the consistency of baked, unglazed pottery, so she looked as if her head was surrounded by one of those spiked haloes allotted to famous sinners in Sunday-school picture books. Her eyes held the gentleness and the despair of those about to be dispossessed; she had the immovable smile of a cat, which is forced by physiology to smile whether it wants to or not.

The beliefs of her tribe had taught her to regard herself as a sentient abstraction, an intermediary between the ghosts and the fauna, so she looked at her purchaser's fever-shaking, skeletal person with scarcely curiosity, for he was to her no more yet no less surprising than any other gaunt manifestation of the forest. If she did not perceive him as a man, either, that was because her cosmogony admitted no essential difference between herself and the beasts and the spirits, it was so sophisticated. Her tribe never killed; they only ate roots. He taught her to eat the meat he roasted over his camp fire and, at first, she did not like it much but dutifully consumed it as though he were ordering her to partake of a sacrament for, when she saw how casually he killed the jaguar, she soon realised he was death itself. Then she began to look at him with wonder for she recognised immediately how death had glorified itself to become the principle of his life. But when he looked at her, he saw only a piece of curious flesh he had not paid much for.

He thrust his virility into her surprise and, once her wound had healed, used her to share his sleeping bag and carry his pelts. He told her her name would be Friday, which was the day he bought her; he taught her to say 'master' and then let her know that was to be his name. Her eyelids fluttered for, though she could move her lips and tongue and so reproduce the sounds he made, she did not understand them. And, daily, he slaughtered the jaguar. He sent away the guide for, now he had bought the girl, he did not need him; so the ambiguous couple went on together, while the girl's father made sandals from the rubber tyre to shoe his family's feet and they walked a little way into the twentieth century in them, but not far.

Among her tribe circulated the following picturesque folk-tale. The jaguar invited the anteater to a juggling contest in which they would use their eyes to play with, so they drew their eyes out of the sockets. When they had finished, the anteater threw his eyes up into the air and back they fell – plop! in place in his head; but when the jaguar imitated him, his eyes caught in the topmost branches of a tree and he could not reach them. So he became blind. Then the anteater asked the macaw to make new eyes out of water for the jaguar and, with these eyes, the jaguar found that it could see in the dark. So all turned out well for the jaguar, and she too, the girl who did not know her own name, could see in the dark. As they moved always more deeply into the forest, away from the little settlements, nightly he extorted his pleasure from her flesh and she would gaze over her shoulder at shapes of phantoms in the thickly susurrating undergrowth, phantoms – it seemed to her – of beasts he had slaughtered that day, for she had been born into the clan of the jaguar and, when his leather belt cut her shoulder, the magic water of which her eyes were made would piteously leak.

He could not reconcile himself to the rain forest, which oppressed and devastated him. He began to shake with malaria. He killed continually, stripped the pelts and left the corpses behind him for the vultures and the flies.

Then they came to a place where there were no more roads.

His heart leaped with ecstatic fear and longing when he saw how nothing but beasts inhabited the interior. He wanted to destroy them all, so that he would feel less lonely, and, in order to penetrate this absence with his annihilating presence, he left the jeep behind at a forgotten township where a green track ended and an ancient whisky priest sat all day in the ruins of a forsaken church brewing fire-water from wild bananas and keening the stations of the cross. Master loaded his brown mistress with his guns and the sleeping bag and the gourds filled with liquid fever. They left a wake of corpses behind them for the plants and the vultures to eat.

At night, after she lit the fire, he would first abuse her with the butt of his rifle about the shoulders and, after that, with his sex; then drink from a gourd and sleep. When she had wiped the tears from her face with the back of her hand, she was herself again, and, after they had been together a few weeks she seized the opportunity of solitude to examine his guns, the instruments of his passion and, perhaps, learn a little of Master's magic.

She squinted her eye to peer down the long barrel; she caressed the metal trigger; and, pointing the barrel carefully away from her as she had seen Master do, she softly squeezed it in imitation of his gestures to see if she, too, could provoke the same shattering exhalation. But, to her disappointment, she provoked nothing. She clicked her tongue against her teeth in irritation. Exploring further, however, she discovered the secret of the safety catch.

Ghosts came out of the jungle and sat at her feet, cocking their heads on one side to watch her. She greeted them with a friendly wave of her hand. The fire began to fail but she could see clearly through the sights of the rifle since her eyes were made of water and, raising it to her shoulder as she had seen Master do, she took aim at the disc of moon stuck to the sky beyond the ceiling of boughs above her, for she wanted to shoot the moon down since it was a bird in her scheme of things and, since he had taught her to eat meat, now she thought she must be death's apprentice.

He woke from sleep in a paroxysm of fear and saw her, dimly illuminated by the dying fire, naked but for the rag that covered her sex, with the rifle in her hand; it seemed to him her clay-covered head was about to turn into a nest of birds of prey. She laughed delightedly at the corpse of the sleeping bird her bullet had knocked down from the tree and the moonlight glimmered on her curiously pointed teeth. She believed the bird she shot down had been the moon and now, in the night sky, she saw only the ghost of the moon. Though they were lost, hopelessly lost, in the trackless forest, she knew quite well where she was; she was always at home in the ghost town.

Next day, he oversaw the beginnings of her career as a markswoman and watched her tumble down from the boughs of the forest representatives of all the furred and feathered beings it contained. She always gave the same delighted laugh to see them fall for she had never thought it would be so easy to populate her fireside with fresh ghosts. But she could not bring herself to kill the jaguar, since the jaguar was the emblem of her clan; with forceful gestures of her head and hands, she refused. But, after she learned to shoot, soon she became a better hunter than he although there was no method to her killing and they went banging away together indiscriminately through the dim, green undergrowth.

The descent of the banana spirit in the gourd marked the passage of time and they left a gross trail of carnage behind them. The spectacle of her massacres moved him and he mounted her in a frenzy, forcing apart her genital lips so roughly the crimson skin on the inside bruised and festered while the bites on her throat and shoulders oozed diseased pearls of pus that brought the blowflies buzzing about her in a cloud. Her screams were a universal language; even the monkeys understood she suffered when Master took his pleasure, yet he did not. As she grew more like him, so she began to resent him.

While he slept, she flexed her fingers in the darkness that concealed nothing from her and without surprise she discovered her fingernails were growing long, curved, hard and sharp. Now she could tear his back when he inflicted himself upon her and leave red runnels in his skin; yelping with delight, he only used her the more severely and, twisting her head with its pottery appendages this way and that in pained perplexity, she gouged the empty air with her claws.

They came to a spring of water and she plunged into it in order to wash herself but she sprang out again immediately because the touch of water aroused such an unpleasant sensation on her pelt. When she impatiently tossed her head to shake away the waterdrops, her clay ringlets melted altogether and trickled down her shoulders. She could no longer tolerate cooked meat but must tear it raw between her fingers off the bone before Master saw. She could no longer twist her scarlet tongue around the two syllables of his name, 'mas-tuh'; when she tried to speak, only a diffuse and rumbling purr shivered the muscles of her throat and she dug neat holes in the earth to bury her excrement, she had become so fastidious since she grew whiskers.

Madness and fever consumed him. When he killed the jaguar, he abandoned them in the forest with the stippled pelts still on them. To possess the clawed was in itself a kind of slaughter, and, tracking behind her, his eyes dazed with strangeness and liquor, he would watch the way the intermittent dentellation of the sun through the leaves mottled the ridged tribal markings down her back until it seemed the blotched areas of pigmentation were subtly mimicking the beasts who mimicked the patterns of the sun through the leaves and, if she had not walked upright on two legs, he would have shot her. As it was, he thrust her down into the undergrowth, amongst the orchids, and drove his other weapon into her soft, moist hole whilst he tore her throat with his teeth and she wept, until, one day, she found she was not able to cry any more.

The day the liquor ended, he was alone with fever. He reeled, screaming and shaking, in the clearing where she had abandoned his sleeping bag; she crouched among the lianas and crooned in a voice like soft thunder. Though it was daylight, the ghosts of innumerable jaguar crowded round to see what she would do.

Their invisible nostrils twitched with the prescience of blood. The shoulder to which she raised the rifle now had the texture of plush.

His prey had shot the hunter, but now she could no longer hold the gun. Her brown and amber dappled sides rippled like water as she trotted across the clearing to worry the clothing of the corpse with her teeth. But soon she grew bored and bounded away.

Then only the flies crawling on his body were alive and he was far from home.

THE MAN FROM MARS

Margaret Atwood

Margaret Atwood (b. 1939) is a Canadian writer and environmental activist. She is amongst the most honoured authors of fiction in recent history. She is a winner of the Arthur C. Clarke Award and has been shortlisted for the Man Booker Prize five times, winning in 2000 for her novel *The Blind Assassin*. She is the author of more than fifty volumes of poetry, children's literature, fiction and non-fiction.

A long time ago Christine was walking through the park. She was still wearing her tennis dress; she hadn't had time to shower and change, and her hair was held back with an elastic band. Her chunky reddish face, exposed with no softening fringe, looked like a Russian peasant's, but without the elastic band the hair got in her eyes. The afternoon was too hot for April; the indoor courts had been steaming, her skin felt poached.

The sun had brought the old men out from wherever they spent the winter: she had read a story recently about one who lived for three years in a manhole. They sat weedishly on the benches or lay on the grass with their heads on squares of used newspaper. As she passed, their wrinkled toadstool faces drifted towards her, drawn by the movement of her body, then floated away again, uninterested.

The squirrels were out, too, foraging; two or three of them moved towards her in darts and pauses, eyes fixed on her expectantly, mouths with the ratlike receding chins open to show the yellowed front teeth. Christine walked faster, she had nothing to give them. People shouldn't feed them, she thought; it makes them anxious and they get mangy.

Halfway across the park she stopped to take off her cardigan. As she bent over to pick up her tennis racquet again someone touched her on her freshly bared arm. Christine seldom screamed;

she straightened up suddenly, gripping the handle of her racquet. It was not one of the old men, however it was a dark-haired boy of twelve or so.

"Excuse me," he said, "I search for Economics Building. Is it there?" He motioned towards the west.

Christine looked at him more closely. She had been mistaken: he was not young, just short. He came a little above her shoulder, but then, she was above the average height; "statuesque," her mother called it when she was straining. He was also what was referred to in their family as "a person from another culture": oriental without a doubt, though perhaps not Chinese. Christine judged he must be a foreign student and gave him her official welcoming smile. In high school she had been president of the United Nations Club; that year her school had been picked to represent the Egyptian delegation at the Mock Assembly. It had been an unpopular assignment – nobody wanted to be the Arabs – but she had seen it through. She had made rather a good speech about the Palestinian refugees.

"Yes," she said, "that's it over there. The one with the flat roof, see it?"

The man had been smiling nervously at her the whole time. He was wearing glasses with transparent plastic rims, through which his eyes bulged up at her as though through a goldfish bowl. He had not followed where she was pointing Instead he thrust towards her a small pad of green paper and a ball-point pen.

"You make map," he said.

Christine set down her tennis racquet and drew a careful map. "We are here," she said, pronouncing distinctly. "You go this way. The building is here." She indicated the route with a dotted line and an X. The man leaned close to her, watching the progress of the map attentively; he smelled of cooked cauliflower and an unfamiliar brand of hair grease. When she had finished Christine handed the paper and pen back to him with a terminal smile.

"Wait," the man said. He tore the piece of paper with the map off the pad, folded it carefully and put it in his jacket pocket; the jacket sleeves came down over his wrists and had threads at the edges. He began to write something; she noticed with a slight feeling of revulsion that his nails and the ends of his fingers were so badly bitten they seemed almost deformed. Several of his fingers were blue from the leaky ball-point.

"Here is my name," he said, holding the pad out to her.

Christine read an odd assemblage of Gs, Ys and Ns, neatly printed in block letters. "Thank you," she said.

"You now write *your* name," he said, extending the pen.

Christine hesitated. If this had been a person from her own culture she would have thought he was trying to pick her up. But then, people from her own culture never tried to pick her up; she was too big. The only one who had made the attempt was the Moroccan waiter at the beer parlour where they sometimes went after meetings, and he had been direct. He had just intercepted her on the way to the Ladies' Room and asked and she said no; that had been that. This man was not a waiter though, but a student; she didn't want to offend him. In his culture, whatever it was, this exchange of names on pieces of paper was probably a formal politeness, like saying thank you. She took the pen from him.

"That is a very pleasant name," he said. He folded the paper and placed it in his jacket with the map.

Christine felt she had done her duty. "Well goodbye," she said. "It was nice to have met you." She bent for her tennis racquet but he had already stooped and retrieved it and was holding it with both hands in front of him, like a captured banner.

"I carry this for you."

"Oh no, please. Don't bother, I am in a hurry," she said, articulating clearly. Deprived of her tennis racquet she felt weaponless. He started to saunter along the path; he was not nervous at all now, he seemed completely at ease.

"*Vous parlez français?*" he asked conversationally.

"*Oui un petit peu,*" she said. "Not very well." How am I going to get my racquet away from him without being rude? she was wondering.

"*Mais vous avez un bel accent.*" His eyes goggled at her through the glasses: was he being flirtatious? She was well aware that her accent was wretched.

"Look," she said, for the first time letting her impatience show, "I really have to go. Give me my racquet, please."

He quickened his pace but gave no sign of returning the racquet. "Where you are going?"

"Home," she said. "My house."

"I go with you now," he said hopefully.

"No," she said: she would have to be firm with him. She made a lunge and got a grip on her racquet; after a brief tug of war it came free.

"Goodbye," she said, turning away from his puzzled face and setting off at what she hoped was a discouraging jog-trot. It was like walking away from a growling dog: you shouldn't let on you were frightened. Why should she be frightened anyway? He was only half her size and she had the tennis racquet, there was nothing he could do to her.

Although she did not look back she could tell he was still following. Let there be a streetcar, she thought, and there was one, but it was far down the line, stuck behind a red light. He appeared at her side, breathing audibly, a moment after she reached the stop. She gazed ahead, rigid.

"You are my friend," he said tentatively.

Christine relented: he hadn't been trying to pick her up after all, he was a stranger, he just wanted to meet some of the local people; in his place she would have wanted the same thing.

"Yes," she said, doling him out a smile.

"That is good," he said. "My country is very far."

Christine couldn't think of an apt reply. "That's interesting," she said. "*Très interessant.*" The streetcar was coming at last; she opened her purse and got out a ticket.

"I go with you now," he said. His hand clamped on her arm above the elbow.

"*You ... stay ... here,*" Christine said, resisting the impulse to shout but pausing between each word as though for a deaf person. She detached his hand – his hold was quite feeble and could not compete with her tennis biceps – and leapt off the curb and up the streetcar steps, hearing with relief the doors grind shut behind her. Inside the car and a block away she permitted herself a glance out a side window. He was standing where she had left him; he seemed to be writing something on his little pad of paper.

When she reached home she had only time for a snack, and even then she was almost late for the Debating Society, The topic was, "Resolved: That War Is Obsolete." Her team took the affirmative and won.

Christine came out of her last examination feeling depressed. It was not the exam that depressed her but the fact that it was the last one: it meant the end of the school year. She dropped into the coffee shop as usual, then went home early because there didn't seem to be anything else to do.

"Is that you, dear?" her mother called from the living room. She must have heard the front door close. Christine went in and flopped on the sofa, disturbing the neat pattern of cushions.

"How was your exam, dear?" her mother asked.

"Fine," said Christine flatly. It had been fine; she had passed. She was not a brilliant student, she knew that, but she was conscientious. Her professors always wrote things like "A serious attempt" and "Well thought out but perhaps lacking in élan" on her term papers; they gave her Bs, the occasional B+. She was taking Political Science and Economics, and hoped for a job with the Government after she graduated; with her father's connections she had a good chance.

"That's nice."

Christine felt, resentfully, that her mother had only a hazy idea of what an exam was. She was arranging gladioli in a vase; she had rubber gloves on to protect her hands as she always did when engaged in what she called "housework." As far as Christine could tell her housework consisted of arranging flowers in vases: daffodils and tulips and hyacinths through gladioli, irises and roses, all the way to asters and mums. Sometimes she cooked, elegantly and with chafing-dishes, but she thought of it as a hobby. The girl did everything else. Christine thought it faintly sinful to have a girl. The only ones available now were either foreign or pregnant; their expressions usually suggested they were being taken advantage of somehow. But her mother asked what they would do otherwise; they'd either have to go into a Home or stay in their own countries, and Christine had to agree this was probably true. It was hard, anyway, to argue with her mother. She was so delicate, so preserved-looking, a harsh breath would scratch the finish.

"An interesting young man phoned today," her mother said. She had finished the gladioli and was taking off her rubber gloves. "He asked to speak with you and when I said you weren't in we had quite a little chat. You didn't tell me about him, dear." She put on the glasses which she wore on a decorative chain around her neck, a signal that she was in her modern, intelligent mood rather than her old-fashioned whimsical one.

"Did he leave his name?" Christine asked. She knew a lot of young men but they didn't often call her; they conducted their business with her in the coffee shop or after meetings.

"He's a person from another culture. He said he would call back later."

Christine had to think a moment. She was vaguely acquainted with several people from other cultures, Britain mostly; they belonged to the Debating Society.

"He's studying Philosophy in Montreal," her mother prompted. "He sounded French."

Christine began to remember the man in the park. "I don't think he's French, exactly," she said.

Her mother had taken off her glasses again and was poking absentmindedly at a bent gladiolus. "Well, he sounded French." She meditated, flowery sceptre in hand. "I think it would be nice if you had him to tea."

Christine's mother did her best. She had two other daughters, both of whom took after her. They were beautiful; one was well married already and the other would clearly have no trouble. Her friends consoled her about Christine by saying, "She's not fat, she's just big-bones, it's the father's side," and "Christine is so healthy." Her other daughters had never gotten involved in activities when they were at school, but since Christine could not possibly ever be beautiful even if she took off weight, it was just as well she was so athletic and political, it was a good thing she had interests. Christine's mother tried to encourage her interests whenever possible. Christine could tell when she was making an extra effort, there was a reproachful edge to her voice.

She knew her mother expected enthusiasm but she could not supply it. "I don't know, I'll have to see," she said dubiously.

"You look tired, darling," said her mother. "Perhaps you'd like a glass of milk."

Christine was in the bathtub when the phone rang. She was not prone to fantasy but when she was in the bathtub she often pretended she was a dolphin, a game left over from one of the girls who used to bathe her when she was small. Her mother was being bell-voiced and gracious in the hall; then there was a tap at the door.

"It's that nice young French student, Christine," her mother said.

"Tell him I'm in the bathtub," Christine said, louder than necessary. "He isn't French."

She could hear her mother frowning. "That wouldn't be very polite, Christine. I don't think he'd understand."

"Oh, all right," Christine said. She heaved herself out of the bathtub, swathed her pink bulk in a towel and splattered to the phone.

"Hello," she said gruffly. At a distance he was not pathetic, he was a nuisance. She could not imagine how he had tracked her down: most likely he went through the phone book, calling all the numbers with her last name until he hit on the right one.

"It is your friend."

"I know," she said. "How are you?"

"I am very fine." There was a long pause, during which Christine had a vicious urge to say, "Well goodbye then," and hang up; but she was aware of her mother poised figurine-like in her bedroom doorway. Then he said, "I hope you also are very fine."

"Yes," said Christine. She wasn't going to participate.

"I come to tea," he said.

This took Christine by surprise. "You do?"

"Your pleasant mother ask me. I come Thursday, four o'clock."

"Oh," Christine said, ungraciously.

"See you then," he said, with the conscious pride of one who has mastered a difficult idiom.

Christine set down the phone and went along the hall. Her mother was in her study, sitting innocently at her writing desk.

"Did you ask him to tea on Thursday?"

"Not exactly, dear," her mother said. "I did mention he might come round to tea sometime, though."

"Well, he's coming Thursday. Four o'clock."

"What's wrong with that?" her mother said serenely. "I think it's a very nice gesture for us to make. I do think you might try to be a little more co-operative." She was pleased with herself.

"Since you invited him," said Christine, "you can bloody well stick around and help me entertain him. I don't want to be left making nice gestures all by myself."

"Christine, *dear*," her mother said, above being shocked. "You ought to put on your dressing gown, you'll catch a chill."

After sulking for an hour Christine tried to think of the tea as a cross between an examination and an executive meeting: not enjoyable, certainly, but to be got through as tactfully as possible. And it was a nice gesture. When the cakes her mother had ordered arrived from The Patisserie on Thursday morning she began to feel slightly festive; she even resolved to put on a dress, a good one, instead of a skirt and blouse. After all, she had nothing against him, except the memory of the way he had grabbed her tennis racquet and then her arm. She suppressed a quick impossible vision of herself pursued around the living room, fending him off with thrown sofa cushions and vases of gladioli; nevertheless she told the girl they would have tea in the garden. It would be a treat for him, and there was more space outdoors.

She had suspected her mother would dodge the tea, would contrive to be going out just as he was arriving: that way she could size him up and then leave them alone together. She had done things like that to Christine before; the excuse this time was the Symphony Committee. Sure enough, her mother carefully mislaid her gloves and located them with a faked murmur of joy when the doorbell rang. Christine relished for weeks afterwards the image of her mother's dropped jaw and flawless recovery when he was introduced: he wasn't quite the foreign potentate her optimistic, veil-fragile mind had concocted.

He was prepared for celebration. He had slicked on so much hair cream that his head seemed to be covered with a tight black patent-leather cap, and he had cut the threads off his jacket sleeves. His orange tie was overpoweringly splendid. Christine noticed, however, as he shook her mother's suddenly braced white glove that the ball-point ink on his fingers was indelible. His face had broken out; possibly in anticipation of the delights in store for him he had a tiny camera slung over his shoulder and was smoking an exotic-smelling cigarette.

Christine led him through the cool flowery softly padded living room and out by the French doors into the garden. "You sit here," she said. "I will have the girl bring tea."

This girl was from the West Indies: Christine's parents had been enraptured with her when they were down at Christmas and had brought her back with them. Since that time she had become pregnant, but Christine's mother had not dismissed her. She said she was slightly disappointed but what could you expect, and she didn't see any real difference between a girl who was pregnant before you hired her and one who got that way afterwards. She prided herself on her tolerance; also there was a scarcity of girls. Strangely enough, the girl became progressively less easy to get along with. Either she did not share Christine's mother's view of her own generosity, or she felt she had gotten away with something and was therefore free to indulge in contempt. At first Christine had tried to treat her as an equal. "Don't call me 'Miss Christine,'" she had said with an imitation of light, comradely laughter. "What you want me to call you then?" the girl had said, scowling. They had begun to have brief, surly arguments in the kitchen, which Christine decided were like the arguments between one servant and another: her mother's attitude towards each of them was similar, they were not altogether satisfactory but they would have to do.

The cakes, glossy with icing, were set out on a plate and the teapot was standing ready; on the counter the electric kettle boiled. Christine headed for it, but the girl, till then sitting with her elbows on the kitchen table and watching her expressionlessly, made a dash and intercepted her. Christine waited until she had poured the water into the pot. Then, "I'll carry it out, Elvira," she said. She had just decided she didn't want the girl to see her visitor's orange tie; already, she knew, her position in the girl's eyes had suffered because no one had yet attempted to get *her* pregnant.

"What you think they pay me for, Miss Christine?" the girl said insolently. She swung towards the garden with the tray; Christine trailed her, feeling lumpish and awkward. The girl was at least as big as she was but in a different way.

"Thank you, Elvira," Christine said when the tray was in place.

The girl departed without a word, casting a disdainful backward glance at the frayed jacket sleeves, the stained fingers. Christine was now determined to be especially kind to him.

"You are very rich," he said.

"No," Christine protested, shaking her head, "we're not." She had never thought of her family as rich; it was one of her father's sayings that nobody made any money with the Government.

"Yes," he repeated, "you are very rich." He sat back in his lawn chair, gazing about him as though dazed.

Christine set his cup of tea in front of him. She wasn't in the habit of paying much attention to the house or the garden; they were nothing special, far from being the largest on the street; other people took care of them. But now she looked where he was looking, seeing it all as though from a different height: the long expanses, the border flowers blazing in the early-summer sunlight, the flagged patio and walks, the high walls and the silence.

He came back to her face, sighing a little. "My English is not good," he said, "but I improve."

"You do," Christine said, nodding encouragement.

He took sips of his tea, quickly and tenderly, as though afraid of injuring the cup. "I like to stay here."

Christine passed him the cakes. He took only one, making a slight face as he ate it; but he had several more cups of tea while she finished the cakes. She managed to find out from him that he had come over on a church fellowship – she could not decode the denomination – and was studying Philosophy or Theology, or possibly both. She was feeling well disposed towards him: he had behaved himself, he had caused her no inconvenience.

The teapot was at last empty. He sat up straight in his chair, as though alerted by a soundless gong. "You look this way, please," he said. Christine saw that he had placed his miniature camera on the stone sundial her mother had shipped back from England two years before. He wanted to take her picture. She was flattered, and settled herself to pose, smiling evenly.

He took off his glasses and laid them beside his plate. For a moment she saw his myopic, unprotected eyes turned towards her, with something tremulous and confiding in them she wanted to close herself off from knowing about. Then he went over and did something to the camera, his back to her. The next instant he was crouched beside her, his arm around her waist as far as it could reach, his other hand covering her own hands which she had folded in her lap, his cheek jammed up against hers. She was too startled to move. The camera clicked.

He stood up at once and replaced his glasses, which glittered now with a sad triumph. "Thank you, miss," he said to her. "I go now." He slung the camera back over his shoulder, keeping his hand on it as though to hold the lid on and prevent escape. "I send to my family, they will like."

He was out the gate and gone before Christine had recovered; then she laughed. She had been afraid he would attack her, she could admit it now, and he had; but not in the usual way. He had raped, *rapeo, rapere, rapui, to seize and carry off*, not herself but her celluloid image, and incidentally that of the silver tea service, which glinted mockingly at her as the girl bore it away, carrying it regally, the insignia, the official jewels.

Christine spent the summer as she had for the past three years: she was the sailing instructress at an expensive all-girls camp near Algonquin Park. She had been a camper there, everything was familiar to her; she sailed almost better than she played tennis.

The second week she got a letter from him, postmarked Montreal and forwarded from her home address. It was printed in block letters on a piece of the green paper, two or three sentences. It began, "I hope you are well," then described the weather in monosyllables and ended, "I am fine." It was signed, "Your friend." Each week she got another of these letters, more or less identical. In one of them a colour print was enclosed: himself, slightly cross-eyed and grinning hilariously, even more spindly than she remembered him against her billowing draperies, flowers exploding around them like firecrackers, one of his hands an equivocal blur in her lap, the other out of sight; on her own face, astonishment and outrage, as though he was sticking her in the behind with his hidden thumb.

She answered the first letter, but after that the seniors were in training for the races. At the end of the summer, packing to go home, she threw all the letters away.

When she had been back for several weeks she received another of the green letters. This time there was a return address printed at the top which Christine noted with foreboding was in her own city. Every day she waited for the phone to ring; she was so certain his first attempt at contact would be a disembodied voice that when he came upon her abruptly in mid-campus she was unprepared.

"How are you?"

His smile was the same, but everything else about him had deteriorated. He was, if possible; thinner; his jacket sleeves had sprouted a lush new crop of threads, as though to conceal hands now so badly bitten they appeared to have been gnawed by rodents. His hair fell over his eyes, uncut, ungreased; his eyes in the hollowed face, a delicate triangle of skin stretched on bone, jumped behind his glasses like hooded fish. He had the end of a cigarette in the corner of his mouth, and as they walked he lit a new one from it.

"I'm fine," Christine said. She was thinking, I'm not going to get involved again, enough is enough, I've done my bit for internationalism. "How are you?"

"I live here now," he said. "Maybe I study Economics."

"That's nice." He didn't sound as though he was enrolled anywhere.

"I come to see you."

Christine didn't know whether he meant he had left Montreal in order to be near her or just wanted to visit her at her house as he had done in the spring; either way she refused to be implicated. They were outside the Political Science Building. "I have a class here," she said. "Goodbye." She was being callous, she realized that, but a quick chop was more merciful in the long run, that was what her beautiful sisters used to say.

Afterwards she decided it had been stupid of her to let him find out where her class was. Though a timetable was posted in each of the colleges; all he had to do was look her up and record her every probable movement in block letters on his green notepad. After that day he never left her alone.

Initially he waited outside the lecture rooms for her to come out. She said hello to him curtly at first and kept on going, but this didn't work; he followed her at a distance, smiling his changeless smile.

Then she stopped speaking altogether and pretended to ignore him, but it made no difference, he followed her anyway. The fact that she was in some way afraid of him – or was it just embarrassment? – seemed only to encourage him. Her friends started to notice, asking her who he was and why he was tagging along behind her; she could hardly answer because she hardly knew.

As the weekdays passed and he showed no signs of letting up, she began to jog-trot between classes, finally to run. He was tireless, and had an amazing wind for one who smoked so heavily: he would speed along behind her, keeping the distance between them the same, as though he were a pull-toy attached to her by a string. She was aware of the ridiculous spectacle they must make, galloping across campus, something out of a cartoon short, a lumbering elephant stampeded by a smiling, emaciated mouse, both of them locked in the classic pattern of comic pursuit and flight; but she found that to race made her less nervous than to walk sedately, the skin on the back of her neck crawling with the feel of his eyes on it. At least she could use her muscles. She worked out routines, escapes: she would dash in the front door of the Ladies' Room in the coffee shop and out the backdoor, and he would lose the trail, until he discovered the other entrance. She would try to shake him by detours through baffling archways and corridors, but he seemed as familiar with the architectural mazes as she was herself. As a last refuge she could head for the women's dormitory and watch from safety as he was skidded to a halt by the receptionist's austere voice: men were not allowed past the entrance.

Lunch became difficult. She would be sitting, usually with other members of the Debating Society, just digging nicely into a sandwich, when he would appear suddenly as though he'd come up through an unseen manhole. She then had the choice of barging out through the crowded cafeteria, sandwich half-eaten, or finishing her lunch with him standing behind her chair, everyone at the table acutely aware of him, the conversation stilting and dwindling. Her friends learned to spot him from a distance; they posted lookouts. "Here he comes," they would whisper, helping her collect her belongings for the sprint they knew would follow.

Several times she got tired of running and turned to confront him. "What do you want?" she would ask, glowering belligerently down at him, almost clenching her fists; she felt like shaking him, hitting him.

"I wish to talk with you."

"Well, here I am," she would say. "What do you want to talk about?"

But he would say nothing; he would stand in front of her, shifting his feet, smiling perhaps apologetically (though she could never pinpoint the exact tone of that smile, chewed lips stretched apart over the nicotine-yellowed teeth, rising at the corners, flesh held stiffly in place for an invisible photographer), his eyes jerking from one part of her face to another as though he saw her in fragments.

Annoying and tedious though it was, his pursuit of her had an odd result: mysterious in itself, it rendered her equally mysterious. No one had ever found Christine mysterious before. To her parents she was a beefy heavyweight, a plodder, lacking in flair, ordinary as bread. To her sisters she was the plain one, treated with an indulgence they did not give to each other: they did not fear her as a rival. To her male friends she was the one who could be relied on. She was helpful and a hard worker, always good for a game of tennis with the athletes among them. They invited her along to drink beer with them so they could get into the cleaner, more desirable Ladies and Escorts side of the beer parlour, taking it for granted she would buy her share of the rounds. In moments of stress they confided to her their problems with women. There was nothing devious about her and nothing interesting.

Christine had always agreed with these estimates of herself. In childhood she had identified with the false bride or the ugly sister, whenever a story had begun, "Once there was a maiden as beautiful as she was good," she had known it wasn't her. That was just how it was, but it wasn't so bad. Her parents never expected her to be a brilliant social success and weren't overly disappointed when she wasn't. She was spared the manoeuvring and anxiety she witnessed among others her age, and she even had a kind of special position among men: she was an exception, she fitted none of the categories they commonly used when talking about girls; she wasn't a cock-teaser, a cold fish, an easy lay or a snarky bitch; she was an honorary person. She had grown to share their contempt for most women.

Now, however, there was something about her that could not be explained. A man was chasing her, a peculiar sort of man, granted, but still a man, and he was without doubt attracted to her, he couldn't leave her alone. Other men examined her more closely than they ever had, appraising her, trying to find out what it was those twitching bespectacled eyes saw in her. They started to ask her out, though they returned from these excursions with their curiosity unsatisfied, the secret of her charm still intact. Her opaque dumpling face, her solid bearshaped body became for them parts of a riddle no one could solve. Christine sensed this. In the bathtub she no longer imagined she was a dolphin; instead she imagined she was an elusive water-nixie; or sometimes, in moments of audacity, Marilyn Monroe. The daily chase was becoming a habit; she even looked forward to it. In addition to its other benefits she was losing weight.

All these weeks he had never phoned her or turned up at the house. He must have decided however that his tactics were not having the desired result, or perhaps he sensed she was becoming bored. The phone began to ring in the early morning or late at night when he could be sure she would be there. Sometimes he would simply breathe (she could recognize, or thought she could, the quality of his breathing), in which case she would hang up. Occasionally he would say again that he wanted to talk to her, but even when she gave him lots of time nothing else would follow. Then he extended his range: she would see him on her streetcar, smiling at her silently from a seat never closer than three away; she could feel him tracking her down her own street, though when she would break her resolve to pay no attention and would glance back he would be invisible or in the act of hiding behind a tree or hedge.

Among crowds of people and in daylight she had not really been afraid of him; she was stronger than he was and he had made no recent attempt to touch her. But the days were growing shorter and colder, it was almost November. Often she was arriving home in twilight or a darkness broken only by the feeble orange streetlamps. She brooded over the possibility of razors, knives, guns; by acquiring a weapon he could quickly turn the odds against her. She avoided wearing scarves, remembering the newspaper stories about girls who had been strangled by men. Putting on her nylons in the morning gave her a funny feeling. Her body seemed to have diminished, to have become smaller than his.

Was he deranged, was he a sex maniac? He seemed so harmless, yet it was that kind who often went berserk in the end. She pictured those ragged fingers at her throat; tearing at her clothes, though she could not think of herself as screaming. Parked cars, the shrubberies near her house, the driveways on either side of it, changed as she passed them from unnoticed background to sinister shadowed foreground, every detail distinct and harsh: they were places a man might crouch, leap out from. Yet every time she saw him in the clear light of morning or afternoon (for he still continued his old methods of pursuit), his aging jacket and jittery eyes convinced her that it was she herself who was the tormentor, the persecutor. She was in some sense responsible; from the folds and crevices of the body she had treated for so long as a reliable machine was emanating, against her will, some potent invisible odour, like a dog's in heat or a female moth's, that made him unable to stop following her.

Her mother, who had been too preoccupied with the unavoidable fall entertaining to pay much attention to the number of phone calls Christine was getting or to the hired girl's complaints of a man who hung up without speaking, announced that she was flying down to New York for the weekend; her father decided to go too; Christine panicked: she saw herself in the bathtub with her throat slit, the blood drooling out of her neck and running in a little spiral down the drain (for by this time she believed he could walk through walls, could be everywhere at once). The girl would do nothing to help; she might even stand in the bathroom door with her arms folded, watching. Christine arranged to spend the weekend at her married sister's.

When she arrived back Sunday evening she found the girl close to hysterics. She said that on Saturday she had gone to pull the curtains across the French doors at dusk and had found a strangely contorted face, a man's face, pressed against the glass, staring in at her from the garden. She claimed she had fainted and had almost had her baby a month too early right there on the living-room carpet. Then she had called the police. He was gone by the time they got there but she had recognized him from the afternoon of the tea; she had informed them he was a friend of Christine's.

They called Monday evening to investigate, two of them. They were very polite, they knew who Christine's father was. Her father greeted them heartily; her mother hovered, in the background, fidgeting with her porcelain hands, letting them see how frail and worried she was. She didn't like having them in the living room but they were necessary.

Christine had to admit he'd been following her around. She was relieved he'd been discovered, relieved also that she hadn't been the one to tell, though if he'd been a citizen of the country she would have called the police a long time ago. She insisted he was not dangerous, he had never hurt her.

"That kind don't hurt you," one of the policemen said. "They just kill you. You're lucky you aren't dead."

"Nut cases," the other one said.

Her mother volunteered that the thing about people from another culture was that you could never tell whether they were insane or not because their ways were so different. The policemen agreed with her, deferential but also condescending, as though she was a royal halfwit who had to be humoured.

"You know where he lives?" the first policeman asked. Christine had long ago torn up the letter with his address on it; she shook her head.

"We'll have to pick him up tomorrow then," he said. "Think you can keep him talking outside your class if he's waiting for you?"

After questioning her they held a murmured conversation with her father in the front hall. The girl, clearing away the coffee cups, said if they didn't lock him up she was leaving, she wasn't going to be scared half out of her skin like that again.

Next day when Christine came out of her Modem History lecture he was there, right on schedule. He seemed puzzled when she did not begin to run. She approached him, her heart thumping with treachery and the prospect of freedom. Her body was back to its usual size; she felt herself a giantess, selfcontrolled, invulnerable.

"How are you?" she asked, smiling brightly.

He looked at her with distrust.

"How have you been?" she ventured again. His own perennial smile faded; he took a step back from her.

"This the one?" said the policeman, popping out from behind a notice board like a Keystone Cop and laying a competent hand on the worn jacket shoulder. The other policeman lounged in the background; force would not be required.

"Don't *do* anything to him," she pleaded as they took him away. They nodded and grinned, respectful, scornful. He seemed to know perfectly well who they were and what they wanted.

The first policeman phoned that evening to make his report. Her father talked with him, jovial and managing. She herself was now out of the picture; she had been protected, her function was over.

"What did they *do* to him?" she asked anxiously as he came back into the living room. She was not sure what went on in police stations.

"They didn't do anything to him," he said, amused by her concern. "They could have booked him for Watching and Besetting, they wanted to know if I'd like to press charges. But it's not worth a court case: he's got a visa that says he's only allowed in the country as long as he studies in Montreal, so I told them to just ship him down there. If he turns up here again they'll deport him. They went around to his rooming house, his rent's two weeks overdue, the landlady said she was on the point of kicking him out. He seems happy enough to be getting his back rent paid and a free train ticket to Montreal." He paused. "They couldn't get anything out of him though."

"*Out* of him?" Christine asked.

"They tried to find out why he was doing it; following you, I mean." Her father's eyes swept her as though it was a riddle to him also. "They said when they asked him about that he just clammed up. Pretended he didn't understand English. He understood well enough, but he wasn't answering."

Christine thought this would be the end, but somehow between his arrest and the departure of the train he managed to elude his escort long enough for one more phone call.

"I see you again," he said. He didn't wait for her to hang up.

Now that he was no longer an embarrassing present reality, he could be talked about, he could become an amusing story. In fact, he was the only amusing story Christine had to tell, and telling it preserved both for herself and for others the aura of her strange allure. Her friends and the men who continued to ask her out speculated about his motives. One suggested he had wanted to marry her so he could remain in the country; another said that oriental men were fond of well-built women: "It's your Rubens quality."

Christine thought about him a lot. She had not been attracted to him, rather the reverse, but as an idea only he was a romantic figure, the one man who had found her irresistible; though she often wondered, inspecting her unchanged pink face and hefty body in her full-length mirror, just what it was about her that had done it. She avoided whenever it was proposed the theory of his insanity: it was only that there was more than one way of being sane.

But a new acquaintance, hearing the story for the first time, had a different explanation. "So he got you, too," he said laughing. "That has to be the same guy who was hanging around our day camp a year ago this summer. He followed all the girls like that, a short guy, Japanese or something, glasses, smiling all the time."

"Maybe it was another one," Christine said.

"There couldn't be two of them, everything fits. This was a pretty weird guy."

"What … *kind* of girls did he follow?" Christine asked.

"Oh, just anyone who happened to be around. But if they paid any attention to him at first, if they were nice to him or anything, he was unshakeable. He was a bit of a pest, but harmless."

Christine ceased to tell her amusing story. She had been one among many, then. She went back to playing tennis, she had been neglecting her game.

A few months later the policeman who had been in charge of the case telephoned her again.

"Like you to know, miss, that fellow you were having the trouble with was sent back to his own country. Deported."

"What for?" Christine asked. "Did he try to come back here?" Maybe she had been special after all, maybe he had dared everything for her.

"Nothing like it," the policeman said. "He was up to the same tricks in Montreal but he really picked the wrong woman this time – a Mother Superior of a convent. They don't stand for things like that in Quebec – had him out of here before he knew what happened. I guess he'll be better off in his own place."

"How old was she?" Christine asked, after a silence.

"Oh, around sixty, I guess."

"Thank you very much for letting me know," Christine said in her best official manner. "It's such a relief." She wondered if the policeman had called to make fun of her.

She was almost crying when she put down the phone. What *had* he wanted from her then? A Mother Superior. Did she really look sixty, did she look like a mother? What did convents mean? Comfort, charity? Refuge? Was it that something had happened to him, some intolerable strain just from being in this country; her tennis dress and exposed legs too much for him, flesh and money seemingly available everywhere but withheld from him wherever he turned, the nun the symbol of some final distortion, the robe and veil reminiscent to his nearsighted eyes of the women of his homeland, the ones he was able to understand? But he was back in his own country, remote from her as another planet; she would never know.

He hadn't forgotten her though. In the spring she got a postcard with a foreign stamp and the familiar block-letter writing. On the front was a picture of a temple. He was fine, he hoped she was fine also, he was her friend. A month later another print of the picture he had taken in the garden arrived, in a sealed manila envelope otherwise empty.

Christine's aura of mystery soon faded; anyway, she herself no longer believed in it. Life became again what she had always expected. She graduated with mediocre grades and went into the Department of Health and Welfare; she did a good job, and was seldom discriminated against for being a woman because nobody thought of her as one. She could afford a pleasant-sized apartment, though she did not put much energy into decorating it. She played less and less tennis; what had been muscle with a light coating of fat turned gradually into fat with a thin substratum of muscle. She began to get headaches.

As the years were used up and the war began to fill the

newspapers and magazines, she realized which Eastern country he had actually been from. She had known the name but it hadn't registered at the time, it was such a minor place; she could never keep them separate in her mind.

But though she tried, she couldn't remember the name of the city and the postcard was long gone – had he been from the North or the South, was he near the battle zone or safely far from it? Obsessively she bought magazines and pored over the available photographs, dead villagers, soldiers on the march, colour blowups of frightened or angry faces, spies being executed; she studied maps, she watched the late-night newscasts, the distant country and terrain becoming almost more familiar to her than her own. Once or twice she thought she could recognize him but it was no use, they all looked like him.

Finally she had to stop looking at the pictures. It bothered her too much, it was bad for her; she was beginning to have nightmares in which he was coming through the French doors of her mother's house in his shabby jacket, carrying a packsack and a rifle and a huge bouquet of richly coloured flowers. He was smiling in the same way but with blood streaked over his face, partly blotting out the features. She gave her television set away and took to reading nineteenth-century novels instead; Trollope and Galsworthy were her favourites. When, despite herself, she would think about him, she would tell herself that he had been crafty and agile-minded enough to survive, more or less, in her country, so surely he would be able to do it in his own, where he knew the language. She could not see him in the army, on either side; he wasn't the type, and to her knowledge he had not believed in any particular ideology. He would be something nondescript, something in the background, like herself perhaps he had become an interpreter.

THE BLOODY CHAMBER

Angela Carter

Angela Carter (1940–1992) was a British novelist and journalist, known for her unique blend of feminism and magical realism. In 2008, *The Times* ranked her tenth in their list of the '50 Greatest British Writers Since 1945', and in 2012 her novel, *Nights at the Circus*, was selected as the best ever winner of the James Tait Black Memorial Prize.

I remember how, that night, I lay awake in the wagon-lit in a tender, delicious ecstasy of excitement, my burning cheek pressed against the impeccable linen of the pillow and the pounding of my heart mimicking that of the great pistons ceaselessly thrusting the train that bore me through the night, away from Paris, away from girlhood, away from the white, enclosed quietude of my mother's apartment, into the unguessable country of marriage.

And I remember I tenderly imagined how, at this very moment, my mother would be moving slowly about the narrow bedroom I had left behind for ever, folding up and putting away all my little relics, the tumbled garments I would not need any more, the scores for which there had been no room in my trunks, the concert programmes I'd abandoned; she would linger over this torn ribbon and that faded photograph with all the half-joyous, half-sorrowful emotions of a woman on her daughter's wedding day. And, in the midst of my bridal triumph, I felt a pang of loss as if, when he put the gold band on my finger, I had, in some way, ceased to be her child in becoming his wife.

Are you sure, she'd said when they delivered the gigantic box that held the wedding dress he'd bought me, wrapped up in tissue paper and red ribbon like a Christmas gift of crystallized fruit. Are you sure you love him? There was a dress for her, too; black silk, with the dull, prismatic sheen of oil on water, finer than anything she'd worn since that adventurous girlhood in Indo-China, daughter of a rich tea planter. My eagle-featured, indomitable mother; what other student at the Conservatoire could boast that her mother had outfaced a junkful of Chinese pirates, nursed a village through a visitation of the plague, shot a man-eating tiger with her own hand and all before she was as old as I?

'Are you sure you love him?'

'I'm sure I want to marry him,' I said.

And would say no more. She sighed, as if it was with reluctance that she might at last banish the spectre of poverty from its habitual place at our meagre table. For my mother herself had gladly, scandalously, defiantly beggared herself for love; and, one fine day, her gallant soldier never returned from the wars, leaving his wife and child a legacy of tears that never quite dried, a cigar box full of medals and the antique service revolver that my mother, grown magnificently eccentric in hardship, kept always in her reticule, in case – how I teased her – she was surprised by footpads on her way home from the grocer's shop.

Now and then a starburst of lights spattered the drawn blinds as if the railway company had lit up all the stations through which we passed in celebration of the bride. My satin nightdress had just been shaken from its wrappings; it had slipped over my young girl's pointed breasts and shoulders, supple as a garment of heavy water, and now teasingly caressed me, egregious, insinuating, nudging between my thighs as I shifted restlessly in my narrow berth. His kiss, his kiss with tongue and teeth in it and a rasp of beard, had hinted to me, though with the same exquisite tact as this nightdress he'd given me, of the wedding night, which would be voluptuously deferred until we lay in his great ancestral bed in the sea-girt, pinnacled domain that lay, still, beyond the grasp of my imagination ... that magic place, the fairy castle whose walls were made of foam, that legendary habitation in which he had been born. To which, one day, I might bear an heir. Our destination, my destiny.

Above the syncopated roar of the train, I could hear his even, steady breathing. Only the communicating door kept me from my husband and it stood open. If I rose up on my elbow, I could see the dark, leonine shape of his head and my nostrils caught a whiff of the opulent male scent of leather and spices that always accompanied him and sometimes, during his courtship, had been the only hint he gave me that he had come into my mother's sitting room, for, though he was a big man, he moved as softly as if all his shoes had soles of velvet, as if his footfall turned the carpet into snow.

He had loved to surprise me in my abstracted solitude at the piano. He would tell them not to announce him, then soundlessly open the door and softly creep up behind me with his bouquet of hot-house flowers or his box of marrons glacés, lay his offering upon the keys and clasp his hands over my eyes as I was lost in a Debussy prelude. But that perfume of spiced leather always betrayed him; after my first shock, I was forced always to mimic surprise, so that he would not be disappointed.

He was older than I. He was much older than I; there were streaks of pure silver in his dark mane. But his strange, heavy, almost waxen face was not lined by experience. Rather, experience seemed to have washed it perfectly smooth, like a stone on a beach whose fissures have been eroded by successive tides. And sometimes that face, in stillness when he listened to me playing, with the heavy eyelids folded over eyes that always disturbed me by their absolute absence of light, seemed to me like a mask, as if his real face, the face that truly reflected all the life he had led in the world before he met me, before, even, I was born, as though that face lay underneath this mask. Or else, elsewhere. As though he had laid by the face in which he had lived for so long in order to offer my youth a face unsigned by the years.

And, elsewhere, I might see him plain. Elsewhere. But, where?

In, perhaps, that castle to which the train now took us, that marvellous castle in which he had been born.

Even when he asked me to marry him, and I said: 'Yes,' still he did not lose that heavy, fleshy composure of his. I know it must seem a curious analogy, a man with a flower, but sometimes he seemed to me like a lily. Yes. A lily. Possessed of that strange, ominous calm of a sentient vegetable, like one of those cobra-headed, funereal lilies whose white sheaths are curled out of a flesh as thick and tensely yielding to the touch as vellum. When I said that I would marry him, not one muscle in his face stirred, but he let out a long, extinguished sigh. I thought: Oh! how he must want me! And it was as though the imponderable weight of his desire was a force I might not withstand, not by virtue of its violence but because of its very gravity.

He had the ring ready in a leather box lined with crimson velvet, a fire opal the size of a pigeon's egg set in a complicated circle of dark antique gold. My old nurse, who still lived with my mother and me, squinted at the ring askance; opals are bad luck, she said. But this opal had been his own mother's ring, and his grandmother's, and her mother's before that, given to an ancestor by Catherine de Medici ... every bride that came to the castle wore it, time out of mind. And did he give it to his other wives and have it back from them? asked the old woman rudely; yet she was a snob. She hid her incredulous joy at my marital coup – her little Marquise – behind a façade of fault-finding. But, here, she touched me. I shrugged and turned my back pettishly on her. I did not want to remember how he had loved other women before me, but the knowledge often teased me in the threadbare self-confidence of the small hours.

I was seventeen and knew nothing of the world; my Marquis had been married before, more than once, and I remained a little bemused that, after those others, he should now have chosen me. Indeed, was he not still in mourning for his last wife? Tsk, tsk, went my old nurse. And even my mother had been reluctant to see her girl whisked off by a man so recently bereaved. A Romanian countess, a lady of high fashion. Dead just three short months before I met him, a boating accident, at his home, in Brittany. They never found her body but I rummaged through the back copies of the society magazines my old nanny kept in a trunk under her bed and tracked down her photograph. The sharp muzzle of a pretty, witty, naughty monkey; such potent and bizarre charm, of a dark, bright, wild yet worldly thing whose natural habitat must have been some luxurious interior decorator's jungle filled with potted palms and tame, squawking parakeets.

Before that? *Her* face is common property; everyone painted her but the Redon engraving I liked best, *The Evening Star Walking on the Rim of Night*. To see her skeletal, enigmatic grace, you would never think she had been a barmaid in a café in Montmartre until Puvis de Chavannes saw her and had her expose her flat breasts and elongated thighs to his brush. And yet it was the absinthe doomed her, or so they said.

The first of all his ladies? That sumptuous diva; I had heard her sing Isolde, precociously musical child that I was, taken to the opera for a birthday treat. My first opera; I had heard her sing Isolde. With what white-hot passion had she burned from the stage! So that you could tell she would die young. We sat high up, halfway to heaven in the gods, yet she half-blinded me. And my father, still alive (oh, so long ago), took hold of my sticky little hand, to comfort me, in the last act, yet all I heard was the glory of her voice.

Married three times within my own brief lifetime to three different graces, now, as if to demonstrate the eclecticism of his taste, he had invited me to join this gallery of beautiful women, I, the poor widow's child with my mouse-coloured hair that still bore the kinks of the plaits from which it had so recently been freed, my bony hips, my nervous, pianist's fingers.

He was rich as Croesus. The night before our wedding – a simple affair, at the Mairie, because his countess was so recently gone – he took my mother and me, curious coincidence, to see *Tristan*. And, do you know, my heart swelled and ached so during the Liebestod that I thought I must truly love him. Yes. I did. On his arm, all eyes were upon me. The whispering crowd in the foyer parted like the Red Sea to let us through. My skin crisped at his touch.

How my circumstances had changed since the first time I heard those voluptuous chords that carry such a charge of deathly passion in them! Now, we sat in a loge, in red velvet armchairs, and a braided, bewigged flunkey brought us a silver bucket of iced champagne in the interval. The froth spilled over the rim of my glass and drenched my hands, I thought: My cup runneth over. And I had on a Poiret dress. He had prevailed upon my reluctant mother to let him buy my trousseau; what would I have gone to him in, otherwise? Twice-darned underwear, faded gingham, serge skirts, hand-me-downs. So, for the opera, I wore a sinuous shift of white muslin tied with a silk string under the breasts. And everyone stared at me. And at his wedding gift.

His wedding gift, clasped round my throat. A choker of rubies, two inches wide, like an extraordinarily precious slit throat.

After the Terror, in the early days of the Directory, the aristos who'd escaped the guillotine had an ironic fad of tying a red ribbon round their necks at just the point where the blade would have sliced it through, a red ribbon like the memory of a wound. And his grandmother, taken with the notion, had her ribbon made up in rubies; such a gesture of luxurious defiance! That night at the opera comes back to me even now ... the white dress; the frail child within it; and the flashing crimson jewels round her throat, bright as arterial blood.

I saw him watching me in the gilded mirrors with the assessing eye of a connoisseur inspecting horseflesh, or even of a housewife in the market, inspecting cuts on the slab. I'd never seen, or else had never acknowledged, that regard of his before, the sheer carnal avarice of it; and it was strangely magnified by the monocle lodged in his left eye. When I saw him look at me with lust, I dropped my eyes but, in glancing away from him, I caught sight of myself in the mirror. And I saw myself, suddenly, as he saw me, my pale face, the way the muscles in my neck stuck out like thin wire. I saw how much that cruel necklace became me. And, for the first time in my innocent and confined life, I sensed in myself a potentiality for corruption that took my breath away.

The next day, we were married.

The train slowed, shuddered to a halt. Lights; clank of metal; a voice declaring the name of an unknown, never-to-be visited station; silence of the night; the rhythm of his breathing, that I should sleep with, now, for the rest of my life. And I could not sleep. I stealthily sat up, raised the blind a little and huddled against the cold window that misted over with the warmth of my breathing, gazing out at the dark platform towards those rectangles of domestic lamplight that promised warmth, company, a supper of sausages hissing in a pan on the stove for the station master, his children tucked up in bed asleep in the brick house with the painted shutters ... all the paraphernalia of the everyday world from which I, with my stunning marriage, had exiled myself.

Into marriage, into exile; I sensed it, I knew it – that, henceforth, I would always be lonely. Yet that was part of the already familiar weight of the fire opal that glimmered like a gypsy's magic ball, so that I could not take my eyes off it when I played the piano. This ring, the bloody bandage of rubies, the wardrobe of clothes from Poiret and Worth, his scent of Russian leather – all had conspired to seduce me so utterly that I could not say I felt one single twinge of regret for the world of tartines and maman that now receded from me as if drawn away on a string, like a child's toy, as the train began to throb again as if in delighted anticipation of the distance it would take me.

The first grey streamers of the dawn now flew in the sky and an eldritch half-light seeped into the railway carriage. I heard no change in his breathing but my heightened, excited senses told me he was awake and gazing at me. A huge man, an enormous man, and his eyes, dark and motionless as those eyes the ancient Egyptians painted upon their sarcophagi, fixed upon me. I felt a certain tension in the pit of my stomach, to be so watched, in such silence. A match struck. He was igniting a Romeo y Julieta fat as a baby's arm.

'Soon,' he said in his resonant voice that was like the tolling of a bell and I felt, all at once, a sharp premonition of dread that lasted only as long as the match flared and I could see his white, broad face as if it were hovering, disembodied, above the sheets, illuminated from below like a grotesque carnival head. Then the flame died, the cigar glowed and filled the compartment with a remembered fragrance that made me think of my father, how he would hug me in a warm fug of Havana, when I was a little girl, before he kissed me and left me and died.

As soon as my husband handed me down from the high step of the train, I smelled the amniotic salinity of the ocean. It was November; the trees, stunted by the Atlantic gales, were bare and the lonely halt was deserted but for his leather-gaitered chauffeur waiting meekly beside the sleek black motor car. It was cold; I drew my furs about me, a wrap of white and black, broad stripes of ermine and sable, with a collar from which my head rose like the calyx of a wildflower. (I swear to you, I had never been vain until I met him.) The bell clanged; the straining train leapt its leash and left us at that lonely wayside halt where only he and I had descended. Oh, the wonder of it; how all that might of iron and steam had paused only to suit his convenience. The richest man in France.

'Madame.'

The chauffeur eyed me; was he comparing me, invidiously, to the countess, the artist's model, the opera singer? I hid behind my furs as if they were a system of soft shields. My husband liked me to wear my opal over my kid glove, a showy, theatrical trick – but the moment the ironic chauffeur glimpsed its simmering flash he smiled, as though it was proof positive I was his master's wife. And we drove towards the widening dawn, that now streaked half the sky with a wintry bouquet of pink of roses, orange of tiger-lilies, as if my husband had ordered me a sky from a florist. The day broke around me like a cool dream.

Sea; sand; a sky that melts into the sea – a landscape of misty pastels with a look about it of being continuously on the point of melting. A landscape with all the deliquescent harmonies of Debussy, of the études I played for him, the reverie I'd been playing that afternoon in the salon of the princess where I'd first met him, among the teacups and the little cakes, I, the orphan, hired out of charity to give them their digestive of music.

And, ah! his castle. The faery solitude of the place; with its turrets of misty blue, its courtyard, its spiked gate, his castle that lay on the very bosom of the sea with seabirds mewing about its attics, the casements opening on to the green and purple, evanescent departures of the ocean, cut off by the tide from land for half a day ... that castle, at home neither on the land nor on the water, a mysterious, amphibious place, contravening the materiality of both earth and the waves, with the melancholy of a mermaiden who perches on her rock and waits, endlessly, for a lover who had drowned far away, long ago. That lovely, sad, sea-siren of a place!

The tide was low; at this hour, so early in the morning, the causeway rose up out of the sea. As the car turned on to the wet cobbles between the slow margins of water, he reached out for my hand that had his sultry, witchy ring on it, pressed my fingers, kissed my palm with extraordinary tenderness. His face was as still as ever I'd seen it, still as a pond iced thickly over, yet his lips, that always looked so strangely red and naked between the black fringes of his beard, now curved a little. He smiled; he welcomed his bride home.

No room, no corridor that did not rustle with the sound of

the sea and all the ceilings, the walls on which his ancestors in the stern regalia of rank lined up with their dark eyes and white faces, were stippled with refracted light from the waves which were always in motion; that luminous, murmurous castle of which I was the châtelaine, I, the little music student whose mother had sold all her jewellery, even her wedding ring, to pay the fees at the Conservatoire.

First of all, there was the small ordeal of my initial interview with the housekeeper, who kept this extraordinary machine, this anchored, castellated ocean liner, in smooth running order no matter who stood on the bridge; how tenuous, I thought, might be my authority here! She had a bland, pale, impassive, dislikeable face beneath the impeccably starched white linen headdress of the region. Her greeting, correct but lifeless, chilled me; daydreaming, I dared presume too much on my status ... briefly wondered how I might install my old nurse, so much loved, however cosily incompetent, in her place. Ill-considered schemings! He told me this one had been his foster mother; was bound to his family in the utmost feudal complicity, 'as much part of the house as I am, my dear'. Now her thin lips offered me a proud little smile. She would be my ally as long as I was his. And with that, I must be content.

But, here, it would be easy to be content. In the turret suite he had given me for my very own, I could gaze out over the tumultuous Atlantic and imagine myself the Queen of the Sea. There was a Bechstein for me in the music room and, on the wall, another wedding present – an early Flemish primitive of Saint Cecilia at her celestial organ. In the prim charm of this saint, with her plump, sallow cheeks and crinkled brown hair, I saw myself as I could have wished to be. I warmed to a loving sensitivity I had not hitherto suspected in him. Then he led me up a delicate spiral staircase to my bedroom; before she discreetly vanished, the housekeeper set him chuckling with some, I dare say, lewd blessing for newlyweds in her native Breton. That I did not understand. That he, smiling, refused to interpret.

And there lay the grand, hereditary matrimonial bed, itself the size, almost, of my little room at home, with the gargoyles carved on its surfaces of ebony, vermilion lacquer, gold leaf; and its white gauze curtains, billowing in the sea breeze. Our bed.

And surrounded by so many mirrors! Mirrors on all the walls, in stately frames of contorted gold, that reflected more white lilies than I'd ever seen in my life before. He'd filled the room with them, to greet the bride, the young bride. The young bride, who had become that multitude of girls I saw in the mirrors, identical in their chic navy blue tailor-mades, for travelling, madame, or walking. A maid had dealt with the furs. Henceforth, a maid would deal with everything.

'See,' he said, gesturing towards those elegant girls. 'I have acquired a whole harem for myself!'

I found that I was trembling. My breath came thickly. I could not meet his eye and turned my head away, out of pride, out of shyness, and watched a dozen husbands approach me in a dozen mirrors and slowly, methodically, teasingly, unfasten the buttons of my jacket and slip it from my shoulders. Enough! No; more! Off comes the skirt; and, next, the blouse of apricot linen that cost more than the dress I had for first communion. The play of the waves outside in the cold sun glittered on his monocle; his movements seemed to me deliberately coarse, vulgar. The blood rushed to my face again, and stayed there.

And yet, you see, I guessed it might be so – that we should have a formal disrobing of the bride, a ritual from the brothel. Sheltered as my life had been, how could I have failed, even in the world of prim bohemia in which I lived, to have heard hints of *his* world?

He stripped me, gourmand that he was, as if he were stripping the leaves off an artichoke – but do not imagine much finesse about it; this artichoke was no particular treat for the diner nor was he yet in any greedy haste. He approached his familiar treat with a weary appetite. And when nothing but my scarlet, palpitating core remained, I saw, in the mirror, the living image of an etching by Rops from the collection he had shown me when our engagement permitted us to be alone together ... the child with her sticklike limbs, naked but for her button boots, her gloves, shielding her face with her hand as though her face were the last repository of her modesty; and the old, monocled lecher who examined her, limb by limb. He in his London tailoring; she, bare as a lamb chop. Most pornographic of all confrontations. And so my purchaser unwrapped his bargain. And, as at the opera, when I had first seen my flesh in his eyes, I was aghast to feel myself stirring.

At once he closed my legs like a book and I saw again the rare movement of his lips that meant he smiled.

Not yet. Later. Anticipation is the greater part of pleasure, my little love.

And I began to shudder, like a racehorse before a race, yet also with a kind of fear, for I felt both a strange, impersonal arousal at the thought of love and at the same time a repugnance I could not stifle for his white, heavy flesh that had too much in common with the armfuls of arum lilies that filled my bedroom in great glass jars, those undertakers' lilies with the heavy pollen that powders your fingers as if you had dipped them in turmeric. The lilies I always associate with him; that are white. And stain you.

This scene from a voluptuary's life was now abruptly terminated. It turns out he has business to attend to; his estates, his companies – even on your honeymoon? Even then, said the red lips that kissed me before he left me alone with my bewildered senses – a wet, silken brush from his beard; a hint of the pointed tip of the tongue. Disgruntled, I wrapped a négligé of antique lace around me to sip the little breakfast of hot chocolate the maid brought me; after that, since it was second nature to me, there was nowhere to go but the music room and soon I settled down at my piano.

Yet only a series of subtle discords flowed from beneath my fingers: out of tune ... only a little out of tune; but I'd been blessed with perfect pitch and could not bear to play any more. Sea breezes are bad for pianos; we shall need a resident piano-tuner on the premises if I'm to continue with my studies! I flung down the lid in a little fury of disappointment; what should I do now, how shall I pass the long, sea-lit hours until my husband beds me?

I shivered to think of *that*.

His library seemed the source of his habitual odour of Russian leather. Row upon row of calf-bound volumes, brown and olive, with gilt lettering on their spines, the octavo in brilliant scarlet morocco. A deep-buttoned leather sofa to recline on. A lectern, carved like a spread eagle, that held open upon it an edition of Huysmans's *Là-bas*, from some over-exquisite private press; it had been bound like a missal, in brass, with gems of coloured glass.

The rugs on the floor, deep, pulsing blues of heaven and red of the heart's dearest blood, came from Isfahan and Bokhara; the dark panelling gleamed; there was the lulling music of the sea and a fire of apple logs. The flames flickered along the spines inside a glass-fronted case that held books still crisp and new. Eliphas Levy; the name meant nothing to me. I squinted at a title or two: *The Initiation, The Key of Mysteries, The Secret of Pandora's Box*, and yawned. Nothing, here, to detain a seventeen-year-old girl waiting for her first embrace. I should have liked, best of all, a novel in yellow paper; I wanted to curl up on the rug before the blazing fire, lose myself in a cheap novel, munch sticky liqueur chocolates. If I rang for them, a maid would bring me chocolates.

Nevertheless, I opened the doors of that bookcase idly to browse. And I think I knew, I knew by some tingling of the fingertips, even before I opened that slim volume with no title at all on the spine, what I should find inside it. When he showed me the Rops, newly bought, dearly prized, had he not hinted that he was a connoisseur of such things? Yet I had not bargained for this, the girl with tears hanging on her cheeks like stuck pearls, her cunt a split fig below the great globes of her buttocks on which the knotted tails of the cat were about to descend, while a man in a black mask fingered with his free hand his prick, that curved upwards like the scimitar he held. The picture had a caption: 'Reproof of curiosity'. My mother, with all the precision of her eccentricity, had told me what it was that lovers did; I was innocent but not naïve. *The Adventures of Eulalie at the Harem of the Grand Turk* had been printed, according to the flyleaf, in Amsterdam in 1748, a rare collector's piece. Had some ancestor brought it back himself from that northern city? Or had my husband bought it for himself, from one of those dusty little bookshops on the Left Bank where an old man peers at you through spectacles an inch thick, daring you to inspect his wares ... I turned the pages in the anticipation of fear; the print was rusty. Here was another steel engraving: 'Immolation of the wives of the Sultan'. I knew enough for what I saw in that book to make me gasp.

There was a pungent intensification of the odour of leather that suffused his library; his shadow fell across the massacre.

'My little nun has found the prayerbooks, has she?' he demanded, with a curious mixture of mockery and relish; then, seeing my painful, furious bewilderment, he laughed at me aloud, snatched the book from my hands and put it down on the sofa.

'Have the nasty pictures scared Baby? Baby mustn't play with grown-ups' toys until she's learned how to handle them, must she?'

Then he kissed me. And with, this time, no reticence. He kissed me and laid his hand imperatively upon my breast, beneath the sheath of ancient lace. I stumbled on the winding stair that led to the bedroom, to the carved, gilded bed on which he had been conceived. I stammered foolishly: We've not taken luncheon yet; and, besides, it is broad daylight ...

All the better to see you.

He made me put on my choker, the family heirloom of one woman who had escaped the blade. With trembling fingers, I fastened the thing about my neck. It was cold as ice and chilled me. He twined my hair into a rope and lifted it off my shoulders so that he could the better kiss the downy furrows below my ears; that made me shudder. And he kissed those blazing rubies, too. He kissed them before he kissed my mouth. Rapt, he intoned: 'Of her apparel she retains/Only her sonorous jewellery.'

A dozen husbands impaled a dozen brides while the mewing gulls swung on invisible trapezes in the empty air outside.

I was brought to my senses by the insistent shrilling of the telephone. He lay beside me, felled like an oak, breathing stertorously, as if he had been fighting with me. In the course of that one-sided struggle, I had seen his deathly composure shatter like a porcelain vase flung against a wall; I had heard him shriek and blaspheme at the orgasm; I had bled. And perhaps I had seen his face without its mask; and perhaps I had not. Yet I had been infinitely dishevelled by the loss of my virginity.

I gathered myself together, reached into the cloisonné cupboard beside the bed that concealed the telephone and addressed the mouthpiece. His agent in New York. Urgent.

I shook him awake and rolled over on my side, cradling my spent body in my arms. His voice buzzed like a hive of distant bees. My husband. My husband, who, with so much love, filled my bedroom with lilies until it looked like an embalming parlour.

Those somnolent lilies, that wave their heavy heads, distributing their lush, insolent incense reminiscent of pampered flesh.

When he'd finished with the agent, he turned to me and stroked the ruby necklace that bit into my neck, but with such tenderness now, that I ceased flinching and he caressed my breasts. My dear one, my little love, my child, did it hurt her? He's so sorry for it, such impetuousness, he could not help himself; you see, he loves her so … and this lover's recitative of his brought my tears in a flood. I clung to him as though only the one who had inflicted the pain could comfort me for suffering it. For a while, he murmured to me in a voice I'd never heard before, a voice like the soft consolations of the sea. But then he unwound the tendrils of my hair from the buttons of his smoking jacket, kissed my cheek briskly and told me the agent from New York had called with such urgent business that he must leave as soon as the tide was low enough. Leave the castle? Leave France! And would be away for at least six weeks.

'But it is our honeymoon!'

A deal, an enterprise of hazard and chance involving several millions, lay in the balance, he said. He drew away from me into that wax-works stillness of his; I was only a little girl, I did not understand. And, he said unspoken to my wounded vanity, I have had too many honeymoons to find them in the least pressing commitments. I know quite well that this child I've bought with a handful of coloured stones and the pelts of dead beasts won't run away. But, after he'd called his Paris agent to book a passage for the States next day – just one tiny call, my little one – we should have time for dinner together.

And I had to be content with that.

A Mexican dish of pheasant with hazelnuts and chocolate; salad; white, voluptuous cheese; a sorbet of muscat grapes and Asti spumante. A celebration of Krug exploded festively. And then acrid black coffee in precious little cups so fine it shadowed the birds with which they were painted. I had Cointreau, he had cognac in the library, with the purple velvet curtains drawn against the night, where he took me to perch on his knee in a leather armchair beside the flickering log fire. He had made me change into that chaste little Poiret shift of white muslin; he seemed especially fond of it, my breasts showed through the flimsy stuff, he said, like little soft white doves that sleep, each one, with a pink eye open. But he would not let me take off my ruby choker, although it was growing very uncomfortable, nor fasten up my descending hair, the sign of a virginity so recently ruptured that still remained a wounded presence between us. He twined his fingers in my hair until I winced; I said, I remember, very little.

'The maid will have changed our sheets already,' he said. 'We do not hang the bloody sheets out of the window to prove to the whole of Brittany you are a virgin, not in these civilized times. But I should tell you it would have been the first time in all my married lives I could have shown my interested tenants such a flag.'

Then I realized, with a shock of surprise, how it must have been my innocence that captivated him – the silent music, he said, of my unknowingness, like *La Terrasse des audiences au clair de lune* played upon a piano with keys of ether. You must remember how ill at ease I was in that luxurious place, how unease had been my constant companion during the whole length of my courtship by this grave satyr who now gently martyrized my hair. To know that my naïvety gave him some pleasure made me take heart. Courage! I shall act the fine lady to the manner born one day, if only by virtue of default.

Then, slowly yet teasingly, as if he were giving a child a great, mysterious treat, he took out a bunch of keys from some interior hidey-hole in his jacket – key after key, a key, he said, for every lock in the house. Keys of all kinds – huge, ancient things of black iron; others slender, delicate, almost baroque; wafer-thin Yale keys for safes and boxes. And, during his absence, it was I who must take care of them all.

I eyed the heavy bunch with circumspection. Until that moment, I had not given a single thought to the practical aspects of marriage with a great house, great wealth, a great man, whose key ring was as crowded as that of a prison warder. Here were the clumsy and archaic keys for the dungeons, for dungeons we had in plenty although they had been converted to cellars for his wines; the dusty bottles inhabited in racks all those deep holes of pain in the rock on which the castle was built. These are the keys to the kitchens, this is the key to the picture gallery, a treasure house filled by five centuries of avid collectors – ah! he foresaw I would spend hours there.

He had amply indulged his taste for the Symbolists, he told me with a glint of greed. There was Moreau's great portrait of his first wife, the famous *Sacrificial Victim* with the imprint of the lacelike chains on her pellucid skin. Did I know the story of the painting of that picture? How, when she took off her clothes for him for the first time, she fresh from her bar in Montmartre, she had robed herself involuntarily in a blush that reddened her breasts, her shoulders, her arms, her whole body? He had thought of that story, of that dear girl, when first he had undressed me ... Ensor, the great Ensor, his monolithic canvas: *The Foolish Virgins*. Two or three late Gauguins, his special favourite the one of the tranced brown girl in the deserted house which was called: *Out of the Night We Come, Into the Night We Go*. And, besides the additions he had made himself, his marvellous inheritance of Watteaus, Poussins and a pair of very special Fragonards, commissioned for a licentious ancestor who, it was said, had posed for the master's brush himself with his own two daughters ... He broke off his catalogue of treasures abruptly.

Your thin white face, chérie; he said, as if he saw it for the first time. Your thin white face, with its promise of debauchery only a connoisseur could detect.

A log fell in the fire, instigating a shower of sparks; the opal on my finger spurted green flame. I felt as giddy as if I were on the edge of a precipice; I was afraid, not so much of him, of his monstrous presence, heavy as if he had been gifted at birth with more specific *gravity* than the rest of us, the presence that, even when I thought myself most in love with him, always subtly oppressed me ... No. I was not afraid of him; but of myself. I seemed reborn in his unreflective eyes, reborn in unfamiliar shapes. I hardly recognized myself from his descriptions of me and yet, and yet – might there not be a grain of beastly truth in them? And, in the red firelight, I blushed again, unnoticed, to think he might have chosen me because, in my innocence, he sensed a rare talent for corruption.

Here is the key to the china cabinet – don't laugh, my darling; there's a king's ransom in Sèvres in that closet, and a queen's ransom in Limoges. And a key to the locked, barred room where five generations of plate were kept.

Keys, keys, keys. He would trust me with the keys to his office, although I was only a baby; and the keys to his safes, where he kept the jewels I should wear, he promised me, when we returned to Paris. Such jewels! Why, I would be able to change my earrings and necklaces three times a day, just as the Empress Josephine used to change her underwear. He doubted, he said, with that hollow, knocking sound that served him for a chuckle, I would be quite so interested in his share certificates although they, of course, were worth infinitely more.

Outside our firelit privacy, I could hear the sound of the tide drawing back from the pebbles of the foreshore; it was nearly time for him to leave me. One single key remained unaccounted for on the ring and he hesitated over it; for a moment, I thought he was going to unfasten it from its brothers, slip it back into his pocket and take it away with him.

'What is *that* key?' I demanded, for his chaffing had made me bold. 'The key to your heart? Give it me!'

He dangled the key tantalizingly above my head, out of reach of my straining fingers; those bare red lips of his cracked sidelong in a smile.

'Ah, no,' he said. 'Not the key to my heart. Rather, the key to my enfer.'

He left it on the ring, fastened the ring together, shook it musically, like a carillon. Then threw the keys in a jingling heap in my lap. I could feel the cold metal chilling my thighs through my thin muslin frock. He bent over me to drop a beard-masked kiss on my forehead.

'Every man must have one secret, even if only one, from his wife,' he said. 'Promise me this, my whey-faced piano-player; promise me you'll use all the keys on the ring except that last little one I showed you. Play with anything you find, jewels, silver plate; make toy boats of my share certificates, if it pleases you, and send them sailing off to America after me. All is yours, everywhere is open to you – except the lock that this single key fits. Yet all it is is the key to a little room at the foot of the west tower, behind the still-room, at the end of a dark little corridor full of horrid cobwebs that would get into your hair and frighten you if you ventured there. Oh, and you'd find it such a dull little room! But you must promise me, if you love me, to leave it well alone. It is only a private study, a hideaway, a "den", as the English say, where I can go, sometimes, on those infrequent yet inevitable occasions when the yoke of marriage seems to weigh too heavily on my shoulders. There I can go, you understand, to savour the rare pleasure of imagining myself wifeless.'

There was a little thin starlight in the courtyard as, wrapped in my furs, I saw him to his car. His last words were, that he had telephoned the mainland and taken a piano-tuner on to the staff; this man would arrive to take up his duties the next day. He pressed me to his vicuña breast, once, and then drove away.

I had drowsed away that afternoon and now I could not sleep. I lay tossing and turning in his ancestral bed until another daybreak discoloured the dozen mirrors that were iridescent with the reflections of the sea. The perfume of the lilies weighed on my senses; when I thought that, henceforth, I would always share these sheets with a man whose skin, as theirs did, contained that toad-like, clammy hint of moisture, I felt a vague desolation that within me, now my female wound had healed, there had awoken a certain queasy craving like the cravings of pregnant women for the taste of coal or chalk or tainted food, for the renewal of his caresses. Had he not hinted to me, in his flesh as in his speech and looks, of the thousand, thousand baroque intersections of flesh upon flesh? I lay in our wide bed accompanied by a sleepless companion, my dark newborn curiosity.

I lay in bed alone. And I longed for him. And he disgusted me.

Were there jewels enough in all his safes to recompense me for this predicament? Did all that castle hold enough riches to recompense me for the company of the libertine with whom I must share it? And what, precisely, was the nature of my desirous dread for this mysterious being who, to show his mastery over me, had abandoned me on my wedding night?

Then I sat straight up in bed, under the sardonic masks of the gargoyles carved above me, riven by a wild surmise. Might he have left me, not for Wall Street but for an importunate mistress tucked away God knows where who knew how to pleasure him far better than a girl whose fingers had been exercised, hitherto, only by the practice of scales and arpeggios? And, slowly, soothed, I sank back on to the heaping pillows; I acknowledged that the jealous scare I'd just given myself was not unmixed with a little tincture of relief.

At last I drifted into slumber, as daylight filled the room and chased bad dreams away. But the last thing I remembered, before I slept, was the tall jar of lilies beside the bed, how the thick glass distorted their fat stems so they looked like arms, dismembered arms, drifting drowned in greenish water.

Coffee and croissants to console this bridal, solitary waking. Delicious. Honey, too, in a section of comb on a glass saucer. The maid squeezed the aromatic juice from an orange into a chilled goblet while I watched her as I lay in the lazy, midday bed of the rich. Yet nothing, this morning, gave me more than a fleeting pleasure except to hear that the piano-tuner had been at work already. When the maid told me that, I sprang out of bed and pulled on my old serge skirt and flannel blouse, costume of a student, in which I felt far more at ease with myself than in any of my fine new clothes.

After my three hours of practice, I called the piano-tuner in, to thank him. He was blind, of course; but young, with a gentle mouth and grey eyes that fixed upon me although they could not see me. He was a blacksmith's son from the village across the causeway; a chorister in the church whom the good priest had taught a trade so that he could make a living. All most satisfactory. Yes. He thought he would be happy here. And if, he added shyly, he might sometimes be allowed to hear me play ... for, you see, he loved music. Yes. Of course, I said. Certainly. He seemed to know that I had smiled.

After I dismissed him, even though I'd woken so late, it was still barely time for my 'five o'clock'. The housekeeper, who, thoughtfully forewarned by my husband, had restrained herself from interrupting my music, now made me a solemn visitation with a lengthy menu for a late luncheon. When I told her I did not need it, she looked at me obliquely, along her nose. I understood at once that one of my principal functions as châtelaine was to provide work for the staff. But, all the same, I asserted myself and said I would wait until dinner-time, although I looked forward nervously to the solitary meal. Then I found I had to tell her what I would like to have prepared for me; my imagination, still that of a schoolgirl, ran riot. A fowl in cream – or should I anticipate

Christmas with a varnished turkey? No; I have decided. Avocado and shrimp, lots of it, followed by no entrée at all. But surprise me for dessert with every ice-cream in the ice box. She noted all down but sniffed; I'd shocked her. Such tastes! Child that I was, I giggled when she left me.

But, now ... what shall I do, now?

I could have spent a happy hour unpacking the trunks that contained my trousseau but the maid had done that already, the dresses, the tailor-mades hung in the wardrobe in my dressing room, the hats on wooden heads to keep their shape, the shoes on wooden feet as if all these inanimate objects were imitating the appearance of life, to mock me. I did not like to linger in my overcrowded dressing room, nor in my lugubriously lily-scented bedroom. How shall I pass the time?

I shall take a bath in my own bathroom! And found the taps were little dolphins made of gold, with chips of turquoise for eyes. And there was a tank of goldfish, who swam in and out of moving fronds of weeds, as bored, I thought, as I was. How I wished he had not left me. How I wished it were possible to chat with, say, a maid; or, the piano-tuner ... but I knew already my new rank forbade overtures of friendship to the staff.

I had been hoping to defer the call as long as I could, so that I should have something to look forward to in the dead waste of time I foresaw before me, after my dinner was done with, but, at a quarter before seven, when darkness already surrounded the castle, I could contain myself no longer. I telephoned my mother. And astonished myself by bursting into tears when I heard her voice.

No, nothing was the matter. Mother, I have gold bath taps.

I said, gold bath taps!

No; I suppose that's nothing to cry about, Mother.

The line was bad, I could hardly make out her congratulations, her questions, her concern, but I was a little comforted when I put the receiver down.

Yet there still remained one whole hour to dinner and the whole, unimaginable desert of the rest of the evening.

The bunch of keys lay, where he had left them, on the rug before the library fire which had warmed their metal so that they no longer felt cold to the touch but warm, almost, as my own skin. How careless I was; a maid, tending the logs, eyed me reproachfully as if I'd set a trap for her as I picked up the clinking bundle of keys, the keys to the interior doors of this lovely prison of which I was both the inmate and the mistress and had scarcely seen. When I remembered that, I felt the exhilaration of the explorer.

Lights! More lights!

At the touch of a switch, the dreaming library was brilliantly illuminated. I ran crazily about the castle, switching on every light I could find – I ordered the servants to light up all their quarters, too, so the castle would shine like a seaborne birthday cake lit with a thousand candles, one for every year of its life, and everybody on shore would wonder at it. When everything was lit as brightly as the café in the Gare du Nord, the significance of the possessions implied by that bunch of keys no longer intimidated me, for I was determined, now, to search through them all for evidence of my husband's true nature.

His office first, evidently.

A mahogany desk half a mile wide, with an impeccable blotter and a bank of telephones. I allowed myself the luxury of opening the safe that contained the jewellery and delved sufficiently among the leather boxes to find out how my marriage had given me access to a jinn's treasury – parures, bracelets, rings ... While I was thus surrounded by diamonds, a maid knocked on the door and entered before I spoke; a subtle discourtesy. I would speak to my husband about it. She eyed my serge skirt superciliously; did madame plan to dress for dinner?

She made a moue of disdain when I laughed to hear that, she was far more the lady than I. But, imagine – to dress up in one of my Poiret extravaganzas, with the jewelled turban and aigrette on my head, roped with pearl to the navel, to sit down all alone in the baronial dining hall at the head of that massive board at which King Mark was reputed to have fed his knights ... I grew calmer under the cold eye of her disapproval.

I adopted the crisp inflections of an officer's daughter. No, I would not dress for dinner. Furthermore, I was not hungry enough for dinner itself. She must tell the housekeeper to cancel the dormitory feast I'd ordered. Could they leave me sandwiches and a flask of coffee in my music room? And would they all dismiss for the night?

Mais oui, madame.

I knew by her bereft intonation I had let them down again but I did not care; I was armed against them by the brilliance of his hoard. But I would not find his heart amongst the glittering stones; as soon as she had gone, I began a systematic search of the drawers of his desk.

All was in order, so I found nothing. Not a random doodle on an old envelope, nor the faded photograph of a woman. Only the files of business correspondence, the bills from the home farms, the invoices from tailors, the billets-doux from international financiers. Nothing. And this absence of the evidence of his real life began to impress me strangely; there must, I thought, be a great deal to conceal if he takes such pains to hide it.

His office was a singularly impersonal room, facing inwards, on to the courtyard, as though he wanted to turn his back on the siren sea in order to keep a clear head while he bankrupted a small businessman in Amsterdam or – I noticed with a thrill of distaste – engaged in some business in Laos that must, from certain cryptic references to his amateur botanist's enthusiasm for rare poppies, be to do with opium. Was he not rich enough to do without crime? Or was the crime itself his profit? And yet I saw enough to appreciate his zeal for secrecy.

Now I had ransacked his desk, I must spend a cool-headed quarter of an hour putting every last letter back where I had found it, and, as I covered the traces of my visit, by some chance, as I reached inside a little drawer that had stuck fast, I must have touched a hidden spring, for a secret drawer flew open within that drawer itself; and this secret drawer contained – at last! – a file marked: *Personal*.

I was alone, but for my reflection in the uncurtained window.

I had the brief notion that his heart, pressed flat as a flower, crimson and thin as tissue paper, lay in this file. It was a very thin one.

I could have wished, perhaps, I had not found that touching, ill-spelt note, on a paper napkin marked *La Coupole*, that began: 'My darling, I cannot wait for the moment when you may make me yours completely.' The diva had sent him a page of the score of *Tristan*, the Liebestod, with the single, cryptic word: 'Until …'

scrawled across it. But the strangest of all these love letters was a postcard with a view of a village graveyard, among mountains, where some black-coated ghoul enthusiastically dug at a grave; this little scene, executed with the lurid exuberance of Grand Guignol, was captioned: 'Typical Transylvanian Scene – Midnight, All Hallows.' And, on the other side, the message: 'On the occasion of this marriage to the descendant of Dracula – always remember, "the supreme and unique pleasure of love is the certainty that one is doing evil". Toutes amitiés, C.'

A joke. A joke in the worst possible taste; for had he not been married to a Romanian countess? And then I remembered her pretty, witty face, and her name – Carmilla. My most recent predecessor in this castle had been, it would seem, the most sophisticated.

I put away the file, sobered. Nothing in my life of family love and music had prepared me for these grown-up games and yet these were clues to his self that showed me, at least, how much he had been loved, even if they did not reveal any good reason for it. But I wanted to know still more; and, as I closed the office door and locked it, the means to discover more fell in my way.

Fell, indeed; and with the clatter of a dropped canteen of cutlery, for, as I turned the slick Yale lock, I contrived, somehow, to open up the key ring itself, so that all the keys tumbled loose on the floor. And the very first key I picked out of that pile was, as luck or ill fortune had it, the key to the room he had forbidden me, the room he would keep for his own so that he could go there when he wished to feel himself once more a bachelor.

I made my decision to explore it before I felt a faint resurgence of my ill-defined fear of his waxen stillness. Perhaps I half-imagined, then, that I might find his real self in his den, waiting there to see if indeed I had obeyed him; that he had sent a moving figure of himself to New York, the enigmatic, self-sustaining carapace of his public person, while the real man, whose face I had glimpsed in the storm of orgasm, occupied himself with pressing private business in the study at the foot of the west tower, behind the still-room. Yet, if that were so, it was imperative that I should find him, should know him; and I was too deluded by his apparent taste for me to think my disobedience might truly offend him.

I took the forbidden key from the heap and left the others lying there.

It was now very late and the castle was adrift, as far as it could go from the land, in the middle of the silent ocean where, at my orders, it floated, like a garland of light. And all silent, all still, but for the murmuring of the waves.

I felt no fear, no intimation of dread. Now I walked as firmly as I had done in my mother's house.

Not a narrow, dusty little passage at all; why had he lied to me? But an ill-lit one, certainly; the electricity, for some reason, did not extend here, so I retreated to the still-room and found a bundle of waxed tapers in a cupboard, stored there with matches to light the oak board at grand dinners. I put a match to my little taper and advanced with it in my hand, like a penitent, along the corridor hung with heavy, I think Venetian, tapestries. The flame picked out, here, the head of a man, there, the rich breast of a woman spilling through a rent in her dress – the Rape of the Sabines, perhaps? The naked swords and immolated horses suggested some grisly mythological subject. The corridor wound downwards; there was an almost imperceptible ramp to the thickly carpeted floor. The heavy hangings on the wall muffled my footsteps, even my breathing. For some reason, it grew very warm; the sweat sprang out in beads on my brow. I could no longer hear the sound of the sea.

A long, a winding corridor, as if I were in the viscera of the castle; and this corridor led to a door of worm-eaten oak, low, round-topped, barred with black iron.

And still I felt no fear, no raising of the hairs on the back of the neck, no prickling of the thumbs.

The key slid into the new lock as easily as a hot knife into butter.

No fear; but a hesitation, a holding of the spiritual breath.

If I had found some traces of his heart in a file marked: *Personal*, perhaps, here, in his subterranean privacy, I might find a little of his soul. It was the consciousness of the possibility of such a discovery, of its possible strangeness, that kept me for a moment motionless, before, in the foolhardiness of my already subtly tainted innocence, I turned the key and the door creaked slowly back.

'There is a striking resemblance between the act of love and the ministrations of a torturer,' opined my husband's favourite poet; I had learned something of the nature of that similarity on my marriage bed. And now my taper showed me the outlines of a rack. There was also a great wheel, like the ones I had seen in woodcuts of the martyrdoms of the saints, in my old nurse's little store of holy books. And – just one glimpse of it before my little flame caved in and I was left in absolute darkness – a metal figure, hinged at the side, which I knew to be spiked on the inside and to have the name: the Iron Maiden.

Absolute darkness. And, about me, the instruments of mutilation.

Until that moment, this spoiled child did not know she had inherited nerves and a will from the mother who had defied the yellow outlaws of Indo-China. My mother's spirit drove me on, into that dreadful place, in a cold ecstasy to know the very worst. I fumbled for the matches in my pocket; what a dim, lugubrious light they gave! And yet, enough, oh, more than enough, to see a room designed for desecration and some dark night of unimaginable lovers whose embraces were annihilation.

The walls of this stark torture chamber were the naked rock; they gleamed as if they were sweating with fright. At the four corners of the room were funerary urns, of great antiquity, Etruscan, perhaps, and, on three-legged ebony stands, the bowls of incense he had left burning which filled the room with a sacerdotal reek. Wheel, rack and Iron Maiden were, I saw, displayed as grandly as if they were items of statuary and I was almost consoled, then, and almost persuaded myself that I might have stumbled only upon a little museum of his perversity, that he had installed these monstrous items here only for contemplation.

Yet at the centre of the room lay a catafalque, a doomed, ominous bier of Renaissance workmanship, surrounded by long white candles and, at its foot, an armful of the same lilies with which he had filled my bedroom, stowed in a four-foot-high jar glazed with a sombre Chinese red. I scarcely dared examine this catafalque and its occupant more closely; yet I knew I must.

Each time I struck a match to light those candles round her bed, it seemed a garment of that innocence of mine for which he had lusted fell away from me.

The opera singer lay, quite naked, under a thin sheet of very rare and precious linen, such as the princes of Italy used to shroud those whom they had poisoned. I touched her, very gently, on the white breast; she was cool, he had embalmed her. On her throat I could see the blue imprint of his strangler's fingers. The cool, sad flame of the candles flickered on her white, closed eyelids. The worst thing was, the dead lips smiled.

Beyond the catafalque, in the middle of the shadows, a white, nacreous glimmer; as my eyes accustomed themselves to the gathering darkness, I at last – oh, horrors! – made out a skull; yes, a skull, so utterly denuded, now, of flesh, that it scarcely seemed possible the stark bone had once been richly upholstered with life. And this skull was strung up by a system of unseen cords, so that it appeared to hang, disembodied, in the still, heavy air, and it had been crowned with a wreath of white roses, and a veil of lace, the final image of his bride.

Yet the skull was still so beautiful, had shaped with its sheer planes so imperiously the face that had once existed above it, that I recognized her the moment I saw her; face of the evening star walking on the rim of night. One false step, oh, my poor, dear girl, next in the fated sisterhood of his wives; one false step and into the abyss of the dark you stumbled.

And where was she, the latest dead, the Romanian countess who might have thought her blood would survive his depredations? I knew she must be here, in the place that had wound me through the castle towards it on a spool of inexorability. But, at first, I could see no sign of her. Then, for some reason – perhaps some change of atmosphere wrought by my presence – the metal shell of the Iron Maiden emitted a ghostly twang; my feverish imagination might have guessed its occupant was trying to clamber out, though, even in the midst of my rising hysteria, I knew she must be dead to find a home there.

With trembling fingers, I prised open the front of the upright coffin, with its sculpted face caught in a rictus of pain. Then, overcome, I dropped the key I still held in my other hand. It dropped into the forming pool of her blood.

She was pierced, not by one but by a hundred spikes, this child of the land of the vampires who seemed so newly dead, so full of blood ... oh God! how recently had he become a widower? How long had he kept her in this obscene cell? Had it been all the time he had courted me, in the clear light of Paris?

I closed the lid of her coffin very gently and burst into a tumult of sobbing that contained both pity for his other victims and also a dreadful anguish to know I, too, was one of them.

The candles flared, as if in a draught from a door to elsewhere. The light caught the fire opal on my hand so that it flashed, once, with a baleful light, as if to tell me the eye of God – his eye – was upon me. My first thought, when I saw the ring for which I had sold myself to this fate, was, how to escape it.

I retained sufficient presence of mind to snuff out the candles round the bier with my fingers, to gather up my taper, to look around, although shuddering, to ensure I had left behind me no traces of my visit.

I retrieved the key from the pool of blood, wrapped it in my handkerchief to keep my hands clean, and fled the room, slamming the door behind me.

It crashed to with a juddering reverberation, like the door of hell.

I could not take refuge in my bedroom, for that retained the memory of his presence trapped in the fathomless silvering of his mirrors. My music room seemed the safest place, although I looked at the picture of Saint Cecilia with a faint dread; what had been the nature of her martyrdom? My mind was in a tumult; schemes for flight jostled with one another ... as soon as the tide receded from the causeway, I would make for the mainland – on foot, running, stumbling; I did not trust that leather-clad chauffeur, nor the well-behaved housekeeper, and I dared not take any of the pale, ghostly maids into my confidence, either, since they were his creatures, all. Once at the village, I would fling myself directly on the mercy of the gendarmerie.

But – could I trust them, either? His forefathers had ruled this coast for eight centuries, from this castle whose moat was the Atlantic. Might not the police, the advocates, even the judge, all be in his service, turning a common blind eye to his vices since he was milord whose word must be obeyed? Who, on this distant coast, would believe the white-faced girl from Paris who came running to them with a shuddering tale of blood, of fear, of the ogre murmuring in the shadows? Or, rather, they would immediately know it to be true. But were all honour-bound to let me carry it no further.

Assistance. My mother. I ran to the telephone; and the line, of course, was dead.

Dead as his wives.

A thick darkness, unlit by any star, still glazed the windows. Every lamp in my room burned, to keep the dark outside, yet it seemed still to encroach on me, to be present beside me but as if masked by my lights, the night like a permeable substance that could seep into my skin. I looked at the precious little clock made from hypocritically innocent flowers long ago, in Dresden; the hands had scarcely moved one single hour forward from when I first descended to that private slaughterhouse of his. Time was his servant, too; it would trap me, here, in a night that would last until he came back to me, like a black sun on a hopeless morning.

And yet the time might still be my friend; at that hour, that very hour, he set sail for New York.

To know that, in a few moments, my husband would have left France calmed my agitation a little. My reason told me I had nothing to fear; the tide that would take him away to the New World would let me out of the imprisonment of the castle. Surely I could easily evade the servants. Anybody can buy a ticket at a railway station. Yet I was still filled with unease. I opened the lid of the piano; perhaps I thought my own particular magic might help me, now, that I could create a pentacle out of music that would keep me from harm for, if my music had first ensnared him, then might it not also give me the power to free myself from him?

Mechanically, I began to play but my fingers were stiff and shaking. At first, I could manage nothing better than the exercises of Czerny but simply the act of playing soothed me and, for solace, for the sake of the harmonious rationality of its sublime mathematics, I searched among his scores until I found *The Well-Tempered Clavier*. I set myself the therapeutic task of playing all Bach's equations, every one, and, I told myself, if I played them all through without a single mistake – then the morning would find me once more a virgin.

Crash of a dropped stick.

His silver-headed cane! What else? Sly, cunning, he had returned; he was waiting for me outside the door!

I rose to my feet; fear gave me strength. I flung back my head defiantly.

'Come in!' My voice astonished me by its firmness, its clarity.

The door slowly, nervously opened and I saw, not the massive, irredeemable bulk of my husband but the slight, stooping figure of the piano-tuner, and he looked far more terrified of me than my mother's daughter would have been of the Devil himself. In the torture chamber, it seemed to me that I would never laugh again; now, helplessly, laugh I did, with relief, and, after a moment's hesitation, the boy's face softened and he smiled a little, almost in shame. Though they were blind, his eyes were singularly sweet.

'Forgive me,' said Jean-Yves. 'I know I've given you grounds for dismissing me, that I should be crouching outside your door at midnight ... but I heard you walking about, up and down – I sleep in a room at the foot of the west tower – and some intuition told me you could not sleep and might, perhaps, pass the insomniac hours at your piano. And I could not resist that. Besides, I stumbled over these –'

And he displayed the ring of keys I'd dropped outside my husband's office door, the ring from which one key was missing. I took them from him, looked round for a place to stow them, fixed on the piano stool as if to hide them would protect me. Still he stood smiling at me. How hard it was to make everyday conversation.

'It's perfect,' I said. 'The piano. Perfectly in tune.'

But he was full of the loquacity of embarrassment, as though I would only forgive him for his impudence if he explained the cause of it thoroughly.

'When I heard you play this afternoon, I thought I'd never heard such a touch. Such technique. A treat for me, to hear a virtuoso! So I crept up to your door now, humbly as a little dog might, madame, and put my ear to the keyhole and listened, and listened – until my stick fell to the floor through a momentary clumsiness of mine, and I was discovered.'

He had the most touchingly ingenuous smile.

'Perfectly in tune,' I repeated. To my surprise, now I had said it, I found I could not say anything else. I could only repeat: 'In tune ... perfect ... in tune,' over and over again. I saw a dawning surprise in his face. My head throbbed. To see him, in his lovely, blind humanity, seemed to hurt me very piercingly, somewhere inside my breast; his figure blurred, the room swayed about me. After the dreadful revelation of that bloody chamber, it was his tender look that made me faint.

When I recovered consciousness, I found I was lying in the piano-tuner's arms and he was tucking the satin cushion from the piano-stool under my head.

'You are in some great distress,' he said. 'No bride should suffer so much, so early in her marriage.'

His speech had the rhythms of the countryside, the rhythms of the tides.

'Any bride brought to this castle should come ready dressed in mourning, should bring a priest and a coffin with her,' I said.

'What's this?'

It was too late to keep silent; and if he, too, were one of my husband's creatures, then at least he had been kind to me. So I told him everything, the keys, the interdiction, my disobedience, the room, the rack, the skull, the corpses, the blood.

'I can scarcely believe it,' he said, wondering. 'That man ... so rich; so well born.'

'Here's proof,' I said and tumbled the fatal key out of my handkerchief on to the silken rug.

'Oh God,' he said. 'I can smell the blood.'

He took my hand; he pressed his arms about me. Although he was scarcely more than a boy, I felt a great strength flow into me from his touch.

'We whisper all manner of strange tales up and down the coast,' he said. 'There was a Marquis, once, who used to hunt young girls on the mainland; he hunted them with dogs, as though they were foxes. My grandfather had it from his grand-father, how the Marquis pulled a head out of his saddle bag and showed it to the blacksmith while the man was shoeing his horse. "A fine specimen of the genus, brunette, eh, Guillaume?" And it was the head of the blacksmith's wife.'

But, in these more democratic times, my husband must travel

as far as Paris to do his hunting in the salons. Jean-Yves knew the moment I shuddered.

'Oh, madame! I thought all these were old wives' tales, chattering of fools, spooks to scare bad children into good behaviour! Yet how could you know, a stranger, that the old name for this place is the Castle of Murder?'

How could I know, indeed? Except that, in my heart, I'd always known its lord would be the death of me.

'Hark!' said my friend suddenly. 'The sea has changed key; it must be near morning, the tide is going down.'

He helped me up. I looked from the window, towards the mainland, along the causeway where the stones gleamed wetly in the thin light of the end of the night and, with an almost unimaginable horror, a horror the intensity of which I cannot transmit to you, I saw, in the distance, still far away yet drawing moment by moment inexorably nearer, the twin headlamps of his great black car, gouging tunnels through the shifting mist.

My husband had indeed returned; this time, it was no fancy.

'The key!' said Jean-Yves. 'It must go back on the ring, with the others. As though nothing had happened.'

But the key was still caked with wet blood and I ran to my bathroom and held it under the hot tap. Crimson water swirled down the basin but, as if the key itself were hurt, the bloody token stuck. The turquoise eyes of the dolphin taps winked at me derisively; they knew my husband had been too clever for me! I scrubbed the stain with my nail brush but still it would not budge. I thought how the car would be rolling silently towards the closed courtyard gate; the more I scrubbed the key, the more vivid grew the stain.

The bell in the gatehouse would jangle. The porter's drowsy son would push back the patchwork quilt, yawning, pull the shirt over his head, thrust his feet into his sabots ... slowly, slowly; open the door for your master as slowly as you can ...

And still the bloodstain mocked the fresh water that spilled from the mouth of the leering dolphin.

'You have no more time,' said Jean-Yves. 'He is here. I know it. I must stay with you.'

'You shall not!' I said. 'Go back to your room, now. Please.'

He hesitated. I put an edge of steel in my voice, for I knew I must meet my lord alone.

'Leave me!'

As soon as he had gone, I dealt with the keys and went to my bedroom. The causeway was empty; Jean-Yves was correct, my husband had already entered the castle. I pulled the curtains close, stripped off my clothes and pulled the bedcurtain around me as a pungent aroma of Russian leather assured me my husband was once again beside me.

'Dearest!'

With the most treacherous, lascivious tenderness, he kissed my eyes, and, mimicking the new bride newly wakened, I flung my arms around him, for on my seeming acquiescence depended my salvation.

'Da Silva of Rio outwitted me,' he said wryly. 'My New York agent telegraphed Le Havre and saved me a wasted journey. So we may resume our interrupted pleasures, my love.'

I did not believe one word of it. I knew I had behaved exactly according to his desires; had he not bought me so that I should do so? I had been tricked into my own betrayal to that illimitable darkness whose source I had been compelled to seek in his absence and, now that I had met that shadowed reality of his that came to life only in the presence of its own atrocities, I must pay the price of my new knowledge. The secret of Pandora's box; but he had given me the box, himself, knowing I must learn the secret. I had played a game in which every move was governed by a destiny as oppressive and omnipotent as himself, since that destiny was himself; and I had lost. Lost at that charade of innocence and vice in which he had engaged me. Lost, as the victim loses to the executioner.

His hand brushed my breast, beneath the sheet. I strained my nerves yet could not help but flinch from the intimate touch, for it made me think of the piercing embrace of the Iron Maiden and of his lost lovers in the vault. When he saw my reluctance, his eyes veiled over and yet his appetite did not diminish. His tongue ran over red lips already wet. Silent, mysterious, he moved away from me to draw off his jacket. He took the gold watch from his waistcoat and laid it on the dressing table, like a good bourgeois; scooped out his rattling loose change and now – oh God! – makes a great play of patting his pockets officiously, puzzled lips pursed, searching for something that has been mislaid. Then turns to me with a ghastly, a triumphant smile.

'But of course! I gave the keys to you!'

'Your keys? Why, of course. Here, they're under the pillow; wait a moment – what – Ah! No ... now, where can I have left them? I was whiling away the evening without you at the piano, I remember. Of course! The music room!'

Brusquely he flung my négligé of antique lace on the bed.

'Go and get them.'

'Now? This moment? Can't it wait until morning, my darling?'

I forced myself to be seductive. I saw myself, pale, pliant as a plant that begs to be trampled underfoot, a dozen vulnerable, appealing girls reflected in as many mirrors, and I saw how he almost failed to resist me. If he had come to me in bed, I would have strangled him, then.

But he half-snarled: 'No. It won't wait. Now.'

The unearthly light of dawn filled the room; had only one previous dawn broken upon me in that vile place? And there was nothing for it but to go and fetch the keys from the music stool and pray he would not examine them too closely, pray to God his eyes would fail him, that he might be struck blind.

When I came back into the bedroom carrying the bunch of keys that jangled at every step like a curious musical instrument, he was sitting on the bed in his immaculate shirtsleeves, his head sunk in his hands.

And it seemed to me he was in despair.

Strange. In spite of my fear of him, that made me whiter than my wrap, I felt there emanate from him, at that moment, a stench of absolute despair, rank and ghastly, as if the lilies that surrounded him had all at once begun to fester, or the Russian leather of his scent were reverting to the elements of flayed hide and excrement of which it was composed. The chthonic gravity of his presence exerted a tremendous pressure on the room, so that the blood pounded in my ears as if we had been precipitated to the bottom of the sea, beneath the waves that pounded against the shore.

I held my life in my hands amongst those keys and, in a moment, would place it between his well-manicured fingers. The evidence of that bloody chamber had showed me I could expect no mercy. Yet, when he raised his head and stared at me with his blind, shuttered eyes as though he did not recognize me, I felt a terrified pity for him, for this man who lived in such strange, secret places that, if I loved him enough to follow him, I should have to die.

The atrocious loneliness of that monster!

The monocle had fallen from his face. His curling mane was disordered, as if he had run his hands through it in his distraction. I saw how he had lost his impassivity and was now filled with suppressed excitement. The hand he stretched out for those counters in his game of love and death shook a little; the face that turned towards me contained a sombre delirium that seemed to me compounded of a ghastly, yes, shame but also of a terrible, guilty joy as he slowly ascertained how I had sinned.

That tell-tale stain had resolved itself into a mark the shape and brilliance of the heart on a playing card. He disengaged the key from the ring and looked at it for a while, solitary, brooding.

'It is the key that leads to the kingdom of the unimaginable,' he said. His voice was low and had in it the timbre of certain great cathedral organs that seem, when they are played, to be conversing with God.

I could not restrain a sob.

'Oh, my love, my little love who brought me a white gift of music,' he said, almost as if grieving. 'My little love, you'll never know how much I hate daylight!'

Then he sharply ordered: 'Kneel!'

I knelt before him and he pressed the key lightly to my forehead, held it there for a moment. I felt a faint tingling of the skin and, when I involuntarily glanced at myself in the mirror, I saw the heart-shaped stain had transferred itself to my forehead, to the space between the eyebrows, like the caste mark of a brahmin woman. Or the mark of Cain. And now the key gleamed as freshly as if it had just been cut. He clipped it back on the ring, emitting that same, heavy sigh as he had done when I said that I would marry him.

'My virgin of the arpeggios, prepare yourself for martyrdom.'

'What form shall it take?' I said.

'Decapitation,' he whispered, almost voluptuously. 'Go and

bathe yourself; put on that white dress you wore to hear *Tristan* and the necklace that prefigures your end. And I shall take myself off to the armoury, my dear, to sharpen my great-grandfather's ceremonial sword.'

'The servants?'

'We shall have absolute privacy for our last rites; I have already dismissed them. If you look out of the window you can see them going to the mainland.'

It was now the full, pale light of morning; the weather was grey, indeterminate, the sea had an oily, sinister look, a gloomy day on which to die. Along the causeway I could see trooping every maid and scullion, every pot-boy and pan-scourer, valet, laundress and vassal who worked in that great house, most on foot, a few on bicycles. The faceless housekeeper trudged along with a great basket in which, I guessed, she'd stowed as much as she could ransack from the larder. The Marquis must have given the chauffeur leave to borrow the motor for the day, for it went last of all, at a stately pace, as though the procession were a cortège and the car already bore my coffin to the mainland for burial.

But I knew no good Breton earth would cover me, like a last, faithful lover; I had another fate.

'I have given them all a day's holiday, to celebrate our wedding,' he said. And smiled.

However hard I stared at the receding company, I could see no sign of Jean-Yves, our latest servant, hired but the preceding morning.

'Go, now. Bathe yourself; dress yourself. The lustratory ritual and the ceremonial robing; after that, the sacrifice. Wait in the music room until I telephone for you. No, my dear!' And he smiled, as I started, recalling the line was dead. 'One may call inside the castle just as much as one pleases; but, outside – never.'

I scrubbed my forehead with the nail brush as I had scrubbed the key but this red mark would not go away, either, no matter what I did, and I knew I should wear it until I died, though that would not be long. Then I went to my dressing room and put on that white muslin shift, costume of a victim of an auto-da-fé, he had bought me to listen to the Liebestod in. Twelve young women combed out twelve listless sheaves of brown hair in the mirrors;

soon, there would be none. The mass of lilies that surrounded me exhaled, now, the odour of their withering. They looked like the trumpets of the angels of death.

On the dressing table, coiled like a snake about to strike, lay the ruby choker.

Already almost lifeless, cold at heart, I descended the spiral staircase to the music room but there I found I had not been abandoned.

'I can be of some comfort to you,' the boy said. 'Though not much use.'

We pushed the piano stool in front of the open window so that, for as long as I could, I would be able to smell the ancient, reconciling smell of the sea that, in time, will cleanse everything, scour the old bones white, wash away all the stains. The last little chambermaid had trotted along the causeway long ago and now the tide, fated as I, came tumbling in, the crisp wavelets splashing on the old stones.

'You do not deserve this,' he said.

'Who can say what I deserve or no?' I said. 'I've done nothing; but that may be sufficient reason for condemning me.'

'You disobeyed him,' he said. 'That is sufficient reason for him to punish you.'

'I only did what he knew I would.'

'Like Eve,' he said.

The telephone rang a shrill imperative. Let it ring. But my lover lifted me up and set me on my feet; I knew I must answer it. The receiver felt heavy as earth.

'The courtyard. Immediately.'

My lover kissed me, he took my hand. He would come with me if I would lead him. Courage. When I thought of courage, I thought of my mother. Then I saw a muscle in my lover's face quiver.

'Hoofbeats!' he said.

I cast one last, desperate glance from the window and, like a miracle, I saw a horse and rider galloping at a vertiginous speed along the causeway, though the waves crashed, now, high as the horse's fetlocks. A rider, her black skirts tucked up around her waist so she could ride hard and fast, a crazy, magnificent horsewoman in widow's weeds.

As the telephone rang again.

'Am I to wait all morning?'

Every moment, my mother drew nearer.

'She will be too late,' Jean-Yves said and yet he could not restrain a note of hope that, though it must be so, yet it might not be so.

The third, intransigent call.

'Shall I come up to heaven to fetch you down, Saint Cecilia? You wicked woman, do you wish me to compound my crimes by desecrating the marriage bed?'

So I must go to the courtyard where my husband waited in his London-tailored trousers and the shirt from Turnbull and Asser, beside the mounting block, with, in his hand, the sword which his great-grandfather had presented to the little corporal, in token of surrender to the Republic, before he shot himself. The heavy sword, unsheathed, grey as that November morning, sharp as childbirth, mortal.

When my husband saw my companion, he observed: 'Let the blind lead the blind, eh? But does even a youth as besotted as you are think she was truly blind to her own desires when she took my ring? Give it me back, whore.'

The fires in the opal had all died down. I gladly slipped it from my finger and, even in that dolorous place, my heart was lighter for the lack of it. My husband took it lovingly and lodged it on the tip of his little finger; it would go no further.

'It will serve me for a dozen more fiancées,' he said. 'To the block, woman. No – leave the boy; I shall deal with him later, utilizing a less exalted instrument than the one with which I do my wife the honour of her immolation, for do not fear that in death you will be divided.'

Slowly, slowly, one foot before the other, I crossed the cobbles. The longer I dawdled over my execution, the more time it gave the avenging angel to descend …

'Don't loiter, girl! Do you think I shall lose appetite for the meal if you are so long about serving it? No; I shall grow hungrier, more ravenous with each moment, more cruel … Run to me, run! I have a place prepared for your exquisite corpse in my display of flesh!'

He raised the sword and cut bright segments from the air with it, but still I lingered although my hopes, so recently raised, now began to flag. If she is not here by now, her horse must have stumbled on the causeway, have plunged into the sea ... One thing only made me glad; that my lover would not see me die.

My husband laid my branded forehead on the stone and, as he had done once before, twisted my hair into a rope and drew it away from my neck.

'Such a pretty neck,' he said with what seemed to be a genuine, retrospective tenderness. 'A neck like the stem of a young plant.'

I felt the silken bristle of his beard and the wet touch of his lips as he kissed my nape. And, once again, of my apparel I must retain only my gems; the sharp blade ripped my dress in two and it fell from me. A little green moss, growing in the crevices of the mounting block, would be the last thing I should see in all the world.

The whizz of that heavy sword.

And – a great battering and pounding at the gate, the jangling of the bell, the frenzied neighing of a horse! The unholy silence of the place shattered in an instant. The blade did *not* descend, the necklace did *not* sever, my head did *not* roll. For, for an instant, the beast wavered in his stroke, a sufficient split second of astonished indecision to let me spring upright and dart to the assistance of my lover as he struggled sightlessly with the great bolts that kept her out.

The Marquis stood transfixed, utterly dazed, at a loss. It must have been as if he had been watching his beloved *Tristan* for the twelfth, the thirteenth time and Tristan stirred, then leapt from his bier in the last act, announced in a jaunty aria interposed from Verdi that bygones were bygones, crying over spilt milk did nobody any good and, as for himself, he proposed to live happily ever after. The puppet master, open-mouthed, wide-eyed, impotent at the last, saw his dolls break free of their strings, abandon the rituals he had ordained for them since time began and start to live for themselves; the king, aghast, witnesses the revolt of his pawns.

You never saw such a wild thing as my mother, her hat seized by the winds and blown out to sea so that her hair was her white mane, her black lisle legs exposed to the thigh, her skirts tucked round her waist, one hand on the reins of the rearing horse while the other clasped my father's service revolver and, behind her, the breakers of the savage, indifferent sea, like the witnesses of a furious justice.

And my husband stood stock-still, as if she had been Medusa, the sword still raised over his head as in those clockwork tableaux of Bluebeard that you see in glass cases at fairs.

And then it was as though a curious child pushed his centime into the slot and set all in motion. The heavy, bearded figure roared out aloud, braying with fury, and, wielding the honourable sword as if it were a matter of death or glory, charged us, all three.

On her eighteenth birthday, my mother had disposed of a man-eating tiger that had ravaged the villages in the hills north of Hanoi. Now, without a moment's hesitation, she raised my father's gun, took aim and put a single, irreproachable bullet through my husband's head.

We lead a quiet life, the three of us. I inherited, of course, enormous wealth but we have given most of it away to various charities. The castle is now a school for the blind, though I pray that the children who live there are not haunted by any sad ghosts looking for, crying for, the husband who will never return to the bloody chamber, the contents of which are buried or burned, the door sealed.

I felt I had a right to retain sufficient funds to start a little music school here, on the outskirts of Paris, and we do well enough. Sometimes we can even afford to go to the Opéra, though never to sit in a box, of course. We know we are the source of many whisperings and much gossip but the three of us know the truth of it and mere chatter can never harm us. I can only bless the – what shall I call it? – the *maternal telepathy* that sent my mother running headlong from the telephone to the station after I had called her, that night. I never heard you cry before, she said, by way of explanation. Not when you were happy. And who ever cried because of gold bath taps?

The night train, the one I had taken; she lay in her berth, sleepless as I had been. When she could not find a taxi at that lonely halt, she borrowed old Dobbin from a bemused farmer, for some internal urgency told her that she must reach me before the incoming tide sealed me away from her for ever. My poor old nurse, left scandalized at home – what? interrupt milord on his honeymoon? – she died soon after. She had taken so much secret pleasure in the fact that her little girl had become a marquise; and now here I was, scarcely a penny the richer, widowed at seventeen in the most dubious circumstances and busily engaged in setting up house with a piano-tuner. Poor thing, she passed away in a sorry state of disillusion! But I do believe my mother loves him as much as I do.

No paint nor powder, no matter how thick or white, can mask that red mark on my forehead; I am glad he cannot see it – not for fear of his revulsion, since I know he sees me clearly with his heart – but, because it spares my shame.

1944

Ellen Gilchrist

> Ellen Gilchrist (b. 1935) is an American author and poet
> who studied creative writing under Eudora Welty. Her
> 1981 collection of stories, *In the Land of Dreamy Dreams*,
> received immense critical acclaim and, in 1984, she won
> the National Book Award for her collection of stories,
> *Victory Over Japan*.

When I was eight years old I had a piano made of nine martini glasses.

I could have had a real piano if I had been able to pay the terrible price, been able to put up with piano lessons, but the old German spy who taught piano in the small town of Seymour, Indiana, was jealous of my talent.

"Stop it! Stop it! Stop it!" she would scream in her guttural accent, hitting me on the knuckles with the stick she kept for that purpose. "Stopping this crazy business. Can't you ever listen? Can't you sit still a minute? Can't you settle down?"

God knows I tried to settle down. But the mere sight of the magnificent black upright, the feel of the piano stool against my plump bottom, the cold ivory touch of the keys would send me into paroxysms of musical bliss, and I would throw back my head and begin to pound out melodies in two octaves.

"Stop it," she would be screaming. "This is no music, this crazy banging business. Stop on my piano. Stop before I call your momma!"

I remember the day I quit for good. I got up from the piano stool, slammed the cover down on the keys, told her my father would have her arrested, and stalked out of the house without my hat and gloves. It was a cold November day, and I walked home with gray skies all around me, shivering and brokenhearted, certain the secret lives of musical instruments were closed to me forever.

So music might have disappeared from my life. With my formal training at this sorry end I might have had to content myself with tap and ballet and public speaking, but a muse looked down from heaven and took pity on me.

She arrived in the form of a glamorous war widow, was waiting for me at the bar when I walked into the officers' club with my parents that Saturday night.

There she sat, wearing black taffeta, smoking long white cigarettes, sipping her third very dry martini.

"Isn't that Doris Treadway at the bar?" my mother said. "I can't believe she's going out in public."

"What would you like her to do," my father said, "stay home and go crazy?"

"Well, after all," my mother whispered. "It's only been a month."

"Do you *know* that lady?" I asked, wondering if she was a movie star. She looked exactly like a movie star.

"She works for your daddy, Honey," my mother said. "Her husband got killed in the Philippines."

"Go talk to her," my father said. "Go cheer her up. Go tell her who you are."

As soon as we ordered dinner I did just that. I walked across the room and took up the stool beside her at the bar. I breathed deeply of her cool perfume, listening to the rustling of her sleeves as she took a long sophisticated drag on her Camel.

"So you are Dudley's daughter," she said, smiling at me. I squirmed with delight beneath her approving gaze, enchanted by the dark timbre of her voice, the marvelous fuchsia of her lips and fingertips, the brooding glamor of her widowhood.

"I'm Rhoda," I said. "The baby-sitter quit so they brought me with them."

"Would you like a drink?" she asked. "Could I persuade you to join me?"

"Sure," I said. "Sure I'll join you."

She conferred with the bartender and waved to my parents who were watching us from across the room.

"Well, Rhoda," she said. "I've been hearing about you from your father."

"What did you hear?" I asked, getting worried.

"Well," she said, "the best thing I heard was that you locked yourself in a bathroom for six hours to keep from eating fruit cocktail."

"I hate fruit cocktail," I said. "It makes me sick. I wouldn't eat fruit cocktail for all the tea in China."

"I couldn't agree with you more," she said, picking up her stirrer and tapping it on her martini glass. "I think people who hate fruit cocktail should always stick together."

The stirrer made a lovely sound against the glass. The bartender returned, bringing a wineglass foil of bright pink liquid.

"Taste it," she said, "go ahead. He made it just for you."

I picked up the glass in two fingers and brought it delicately to my lips as I had seen her do.

"It's wonderful," I said, "what's in it?"

"Something special," she said. "It's called a Shirley Temple. So little girls can pretend they're drinking." She laughed out loud and began to tap the glass stirrer against the line of empty glasses in front of her.

"Why doesn't he move the empty glasses?" I asked.

"Because I'm playing them," she said. "Listen." She tapped out a little tune. "Now, listen to this," she said, adding small amounts of water to the glasses. She tapped them again with the stirrer, calling out the notes ina very high, very clear soprano voice. "Do, Re, Mi, Fa, So, ... Bartender," she called, "bring us more glasses."

In a minute she had arranged a keyboard with nine perfect notes.

"Here," she said, moving the glasses in front of me, handing me the stirrer, "you play it."

"What should I play," I said. "I don't know any music."

"Of course you know music," she said. "Everyone knows music. Play anything you like. Play whatever comes into your head."

I began to hit the glasses with the stirrer, gingerly at first, then with more abandon. Soon I had something going that sounded marvelous.

"Is that by any chance the 'Air Corps Hymn' you're playing?" she said.

"Well ... yes it is," I said. "How could you tell?"

She began to sing along with me, singing the words in her perfect voice as I beat upon the glasses. "Off we go," she sang, "into the wild blue yonder, climbing high into the sky, dum, dum,

dum. Down we dive spouting a flame from under, off with one hell-of-a-roar, roar, roar ..."

People crowded around our end of the bar, listening to us, applauding. We finished with the air corps and started right in on the army. "Over hill, over dale, as we hit the dusty trail, and those caissons go marching along, dum, dum, dum ... In and out, hear them shout, counter march and right about, and those caissons go rolling along. For it's hie, hie, hee, in the field artilll-a-reeeee ..."

A man near me began playing the bass on a brandy glass. Another man drummed on the bar with a pair of ashtrays.

Doris broke into "Begin the Beguine." "When they begin the beguine," she sang, "it brings back a night of tropical splendor. It brings back die sound of music so te-en-de-rr. It brings back a memorreeeeee ever green."

A woman in a green dress began dancing, swaying to our rhythm. My martini glasses shone in the light from the bar. As I struck them one by one the notes floated around me like bright translucent boats.

This was music! Not the stale order of the book and the metronome, not the stick and the German. Music was this wildness rising from the dark taffeta of Doris's dress. This praise, this brilliance.

The soft delicious light, the smell of perfume and gin, the perfection of our artistry almost overwhelmed me, but I played bravely on.

Every now and then I would look up and see Doris smiling at me while she sang. Doris and I were one. And that too was the secret of music.

I do not know how long we played. Perhaps we played until my dinner was served. Perhaps we played for hours. Perhaps we are playing still.

"Oh, just let them begin the beguine, let them plaaaaay ... Let the fire that was once a flame remain an ember. Let it burn like the long lost desire I only remember. When they begin, when they begin, when they begi-i-i-i-in the begui-i-i-i-ine ..."

THE LOVER

Alice Walker

Alice Walker (b. 1944) is an American author, poet, feminist and activist. She is best known for the critically acclaimed novel *The Color Purple*, published in 1982, for which she won the National Book Award and the Pulitzer Prize. Walker's published works include seven novels, four collections of short stories, four children's books and volumes of essays and poetry.

Her husband had wanted a child and so she gave him one as a gift, because she liked her husband and admired him greatly. Still, it had taken a lot out of her, especially in the area of sexual response. She had never been particularly passionate with him, not even during the early years of their marriage; it was more a matter of being sexually comfortable. After the birth of the child she simply never thought of him sexually at all. She supposed their marriage was better than most, even so. He was a teacher at a University near their home in the Midwest and cared about his students – which endeared him to her, who had had so many uncaring teachers; and toward her own work, which was poetry (that she set very successfully to jazz), he showed the utmost understanding and respect.

She was away for two months at an artists' colony in New England and that is where she met Ellis, whom she immediately dubbed, once she had got over thinking he resembled (with his top lip slightly raised over his right eye-tooth when he smiled) a wolf, "The Lover." They met one evening before dinner as she was busy ignoring the pompous bullshit of a fellow black poet, a man many years older than she who had no concept of other people's impatience. He had been rambling on about himself for over an hour and she had at first respectfully listened because she was the kind of person whose adult behavior – in a situation like this – reflected her childhood instruction; and she was instructed as a child, to be polite.

She was always getting herself stuck in one-sided conversations of this sort because she was – the people who talked to her seemed to think – an excellent listener. She was, up to a point. She was genuinely interested in older artists in particular and would sit, entranced, as they spun out their tales of art and lust (the gossip, though old, was delicious!) of forty years ago.

But there had been only a few of these artists whose tales she had listened to until the end. For as soon as a note of bragging entered into the conversation – a famous name dropped here, an expensive Paris restaurant's menu dropped there, and especially the names of the old artist's neglected books and on what occasion the wretched creature had insulted this or that weasel of a white person – her mind began to turn about upon itself until it rolled out some of her own thoughts to take the place of the trash that was coming in.

And so it was on that evening before dinner. The old poet – whose work was exceedingly mediocre, and whose only attractions, as far as she was concerned, were his age and his rather bitter wit – fastened his black, bloodshot eyes upon her (in which she read desperation and a prayer of unstrenuous seduction) and held her to a close attention to his words. Except that she had perfected the trick – as had many of her contemporaries who hated to be rude and who, also, had a strong sense of self-preservation (because the old poet, though, she thought, approaching senility, was yet a powerful figure in black literary circles and thought nothing of using his considerable influence to thwart the careers of younger talents) – of keeping her face quite animated and turned full onto the speaker, while inside her head she could be trying out the shades of paint with which to improve the lighting of her house. In fact, so intense did her concentration appear, it seemed she read the speaker's lips.

Ellis, who would be her lover, had come into the room and sat down on a chair by the fire. For although it was the middle of summer, a fire was needed against the chilly New England evenings.

"Have you been waiting long?" he asked.

And it suddenly occurred to her that indeed she had.

"But of course," she answered absently, noting the crooked smile that reminded her of a snarling, though not disagreeable, wolf –

and turned back just as the old poet jealously reached out his hand to draw her attention to the, for him, hilarious ending of his story. She laughed and slapped her knee, a gesture of such fraudulent folksiness that she was soon laughing in earnest. Catching Ellis's eye as she thus amused herself she noticed therein a particular gleam that she instantly recognized.

"My lover," she thought, noticing for the first time his head of blue-black curls, his eyes as brown as the Mississippi, his skin that was not as successfully tanned as it might have been but which would definitely do. He was thin and tall, with practically no hips in the beige twill jeans he wore.

At dinner they sat together, looking out at the blue New England mountains in the distance, as the sun left tracings of orange and pink against the pale blue sky. He had heard she'd won some sort of prize – a prestigious one – for her "jazzed-up" poetry, and the way he said it made her glance critically at his long fingers wrapped around his wine glass. She wondered if they would be as sensitive on her skin as they looked. She had never heard of him, though she did not say so, probably because he had already said it for her. He talked a good deal – easily and early – about himself, and she was quite relaxed – even entertained – in her listener's role.

He wondered what, *if anything*, younger poets like herself had to say, since he was of the opinion that not much was learned about life until the middle years. He was in his forties. Of course he didn't look it, but he was much older than she, he said, and the reason that he was not better known was because he could not find a publisher for his two novels (still, by the way, unpublished – in case she knew publishers) or for his poetry, which an acquaintance of his had compared to something or other by Montaigne.

"You're lovely," he said into the brief silence.

"And you seem bright," she automatically replied.

She had blocked him out since his mention of the two unpublished novels. By the time he began complaining about the preferential treatment publishers now gave minorities and women she was on the point of yawning or gazing idly about the room. But she did not do either for a very simple reason: when she had first seen him she had thought – after the wolf thing – "my lover," and had liked, deep down inside, the illicit sound of it. She had never had a lover; he would be her first. Afterwards, she would be truly a woman of her time. She also responded to his curly hair and slim, almost nonexistent hips, in a surprisingly passionate way.

She was a woman who, after many tribulations in her life, few of which she ever discussed even with close friends, had reached the point of being generally pleased with herself. This self-acceptance was expressed in her eyes, which were large, dark and clear and which, more often than not, seemed predisposed to smile. Though not tall, her carriage gave the illusion of height, as did her carefully selected tall sandals and her naturally tall hair, which stood in an elegant black afro with exactly seven strands of silver hair – of which she was very proud (she was just thirty-one) – shining across the top. She wore long richly colored skirts that – when she walked – parted without warning along the side, and exposed a flash of her creamy brown thigh, and legs that were curvaceous and strong. If she came late to the dining room and stood in the doorway a moment longer than necessary – looking about for a place to sit after she had her tray – for that moment the noise from the cutlery already in use was still.

What others minded at the Colony – whether too many frogs in the frog pond (which was used for swimming) or not enough wine with the veal (there was talk of cutting out wine with meals altogether, and thereby ending a fine old Colony tradition!) – she did not seem to mind. She seemed open, bright, occasionally preoccupied, but always ready with an appreciative ear, or at times a humorous, if outdated joke of her own (which she nevertheless told with gusto and found funny herself, because she would laugh and laugh at it, regardless of what her listeners did). She seemed never to strain over her work, and literally never complained about its progress – or lack thereof. It was as if she worked only for herself, for her own enjoyment (or salvation) and was – whether working or simply thinking of working – calm about it.

Even the distraction caused by the birth of her child was a price she was ultimately prepared to pay. She did not intend to have a second one, after all – that would be too stupid – and this one would, before she knew it, be grown up enough for boarding school.

Relishing her short freedom during the summer as much as she contemplated enjoyment of her longer future one, she threw herself headlong into the interim relationship with Ellis, a professional lover of mainly older women artists who came to the Colony every year to work and play.

A New York Jew of considerable charm, intellectual pettiness, and so vast and uncritical a love of all things European it struck one as an illness (and who hated Brooklyn – where he had grown up – his parents, Jewish culture, and all he had observed of black behavior in New York City), Ellis found the listening silence of "the dark woman," as he euphemistically called her, restorative – after his endless evenings with talkative women who wrote for *Esquire* and the *New York Times*. Such women made it possible for him to be included in the proper tennis sets and swimming parties at the Colony – in which he hoped to meet contacts who would help his career along – but they were also driven to examine each and every one of their own thoughts aloud. His must be the attentive ear, since they had already "made it" and were comfortable exposing their own charming foibles to him, while he, not having made it yet, could afford to expose nothing that might discourage their assistance in his behalf.

It amused and thrilled him to almost hear the "click" when his eyes met those of the jazz poet. "Sex," he thought. And, "rest."

Of course he mistook her intensity.

After sitting before her piano for hours, setting one of her poems to music, she would fling open her cabin door and wave to him as he walked by on his way to or from the lake. He was writing a novella about his former wife and composed it in longhand down at the lake ("So if I get fed up with it I can toss myself in," he joked) and then took it back to his studio with him to type. She would call to him, her hair and clothing very loose, and entice him into her cabin with promises of sympathy and half her lunch.

When they made love she was disappointed. He did not appear to believe in unhurried pleasure, and thought the things she suggested he might do to please her very awkward at the least. But it hardly mattered, since what mattered was the fact of having a lover. She liked snuggling up to him, liked kissing him along the sides of his face – his cheeks were just beginning to be a trifle flabby but would still be good for several years – and loved to write him silly letters

– scorching with passion and promises of abandon – that made her seem head over heels in love. She enjoyed writing the letters because she enjoyed feeling to her full capacity and for as long as possible the excitement having a lover brought. It was the kind of excitement she'd felt years ago, in high school and perhaps twice in college (once when she'd fallen for a student and once when she was seduced – with her help and consent – by a teacher), and she recognized it as a feeling to be enjoyed for all it was worth. Her body felt on fire, her heart jumped in her breast, her pulse raced – she was aware, for the first time in years, of actually *needing* to make love.

He began to think he must fight her off, at least a little bit. She was too intense, he said. He did not have time for intense relationships, that's why he had finally accepted a divorce from his wife. He was also writing a great poem which he had begun in 1950 and which – now that he was at the Colony – he hoped to finish. She should concentrate on her own work if she expected to win any more prizes. She *wanted* to win more, didn't she?

She laughed at him, but would not tell him why. Instead she tried, very gently (while sitting on his lap with her bosom maternally opposite his face), to tell him he misunderstood. That she wanted nothing from him beyond the sensation of being in love itself. (His stare was at first blank, then cynical, at this.) As for her work, she did not do hers the way he apparently did his. Hers did not mean to her what he seemed to think it meant. It did not get in the way of her living, for example, and if it ever did, she felt sure she would remove it. Prizes were nice – especially if they brought one money (which one might then use to explore Barbados! China! Mozambique!) – but they were not rewards she could count on. Her life, on the other hand, *was* a reward she could count on. (He became impatient with this explanation and a little angry.)

It was their first quarrel.

When he saw her again she had spent the weekend (which had been coming up) in nearby Boston. She looked cheerful, happy and relaxed. From her letters to him – which he had thought embarrassingly self-revealing and erotic, though flattering, of course, to him – he had assumed she was on the point of declaring her undying love and of wanting to run away with him. Instead, she had gone off for two days, without mentioning it to him. And she had gone, so she said, by herself!

She soothed him as best she could. Lied, which she hated more than anything, about her work. "It was going so *poorly*," she complained (and the words rang metallic in her mouth); "I just couldn't bear staying here doing nothing where working conditions are so *idyllic*!" He appeared somewhat mollified. Actually, her work was going fine and she had sent off to her publishers a completed book of poems and jazz arrangements – which was what she had come to the Colony to do. "Your work was going swimmingly down at the lake," she giggled. "I didn't wish to disturb you."

And yet it was clear he was disturbed.

So she did not tell him she had flown all the way home.

He was always questioning her now about her town, her house, her child, her husband. She found herself describing her husband as if to a prospective bride. She lingered over the wiry bronze of his hair, the evenness of his teeth, his black, black eyes, the thrilling timbre of his deep voice. It *was* an exceptionally fine voice, it seemed to her now, listening to Ellis's rather whining one. Though, on second thought, it was perhaps nothing special.

At night, after a rousing but unsatisfactory evening with Ellis, she dreamed of her husband making love to her on the kitchen floor at home, where the sunlight collected in a pool beneath the window, and lay in bed next day dreaming of all the faraway countries, daring adventures, passionate lovers still to be found.

RUE DE LILLE

Mavis Gallant

Mavis Gallant (b. 1922) is a Canadian author. She has written two novels as well as numerous collections of stories, and is often cited as one of the best living short story writers. She was elected Companion of the Order of Canada in 1993 and, in 1989, was made a Foreign Honorary Member of the American Academy of Arts and Letters. Her work regularly appears in the *New Yorker*, often debuting there before subsequently being published in a collection.

My second wife, Juliette, died in the apartment on Rue de Lille, where she had lived – at first alone, more or less, then with me – since the end of the war. All the rooms gave onto the ivy-hung well of a court, and were for that reason dark. We often talked about looking for a brighter flat, on a top floor with southern exposure and a wide terrace, but Parisians seldom move until they're driven to. "We know the worst of what we've got," we told each other. "It's better than a bad surprise."

"And what about your books?" Juliette would add. "It would take you months to get them packed, and in the new place you'd never get them sorted." I would see myself as Juliette saw me, crouched over a slanting, shaking stack of volumes piled on a strange floor, cursing and swearing as I tried to pry out a dictionary. "Just the same, I don't intend to die here," she also said.

I once knew someone who believed drowning might be easy, even pleasant, until he almost drowned by accident. Juliette's father was a colonel who expected to die in battle or to be shot by a German firing squad, but he died of typhus in a concentration camp. I had once, long ago, imagined for myself a clandestine burial with full honors after some Resistance feat, but all I got out of the war was a few fractures and a broken nose in a motorcycle accident.

Juliette had thirty-seven years of blacked-out winter mornings in Rue de Lille. She was a few days short of her sixtieth birthday when I found her stretched out on the floor of our bedroom, a hand slackened on a flashlight. She had been trying to see under a chest of drawers, and her heart stopped. (Later, I pulled the chest away from the wall and discovered a five-franc coin.) Her gray-and-dark hair, which had grown soft and wayward with age, was tied back with a narrow satin ribbon. She looked more girlish than at any time since I'd first met her. (She fell in love with me young.) She wore a pleated flannel skirt, a tailored blouse, and one of the thick cardigans with gilt buttons she used to knit while watching television. She had been trained to believe that to look or to listen quietly is to do nothing; she would hum along with music, to show she wasn't idle. She was discreet, she was generous to a sensible degree, she was anything but contentious. I often heard her remark, a trifle worriedly, that she was never bored. She was faithful, if "faithful" means avoiding the acknowledged forms of trouble. She was patient. I know she was good. Any devoted male friend, any lover, any husband would have shown up beside her as selfish, irritable, even cruel. She displayed so little of the ordinary kinds of jealousy, the plain marital do-you-often-have-lunch-with-her? sort, that I once asked her if she had a piece missing.

"Whoever takes this place over," she said, when we spoke of moving, "will be staggered by the size of the electricity bills." (Juliette paid them; I looked after a number of other things.) We had to keep the lights turned on all day in winter. The apartment was L-shaped, bent round two sides of a court, like a train making a sharp turn. From our studies, at opposite ends of the train, we could look out and see the comforting glow of each other's working life, a lamp behind a window. Juliette would be giving some American novel a staunch, steady translation; I might be getting into shape my five-hour television series, "Stendhal and the Italian Experience," which was to win an award in Japan.

We were together for a duration of time I daren't measure against the expanse of Juliette's life; it would give me the feeling that I had decamped to a height of land, a survivor's eminence, so as to survey the point at which our lives crossed and mingled and began to move in the same direction: a long, narrow reach of time in the Rue de Lille. It must be the washy, indefinite colorations of blue that carpeted, papered, and covered floors, walls, and furniture and shaded our lamps which cast over that reach the tone of a short season. I am thinking of the patches of distant, neutral blue that appear over Paris in late spring, when it is still wet and cold in the street and tourists have come too early. The tourists shelter in doorways, trying to read their soaked maps, perennially unprepared in their jeans and thin jackets. Overhead, there are scrapings of a color that carries no threat and promises all.

That choice, Juliette's preference, I sometimes put down to her Calvinist sobriety – call it a temperament – and sometimes to a refinement of her Huguenot taste. When I was feeling tired or impatient, I complained that I had been consigned to a Protestant Heaven by an arbitrary traffic cop, and that I was better suited to a pagan Hell. Again, as I looked round our dining-room table at the calm, clever faces of old friends of Juliette's family, at their competent and unassuming wives, I saw what folly it might be to set such people against a background of buttercup yellow or apple green. The soft clicking of their upper-class Protestant consonants made conversation distant and neutral, too. It was a voice that had puzzled me the first time I'd heard it from Juliette. I had supposed, mistakenly, that she was trying it on for effect; but she was wholly natural.

The sixteenth-century map of Paris I bought for her birthday is still at the framer's; I sent a check but never picked it up. I destroyed her private correspondence without reading it, and gave armfuls of clothes away to a Protestant charity. To the personal notice of her death in *Le Monde* was attached a brief mention of her father, a hero of the Resistance for whom suburban streets are named; and of her career as a respected translator, responsible for having introduced postwar American literature to French readers; and of her husband, the well-known radio and television interviewer and writer, who survived her.

Another person to survive her was my first wife. One night when Juliette and I were drinking coffee in the little sitting room where she received her women friends, and where we watched television, Juliette said, again, "But how much of what she says does she believe? About her Catholicism, and all those fantasies running round in her head – that she is your true and only wife, that your marriage is registered in Heaven, that you and she will be together in another world?"

"Those are things people put in letters," I said. "They sit down alone and pour it out. It's sincere at that moment. I don't know why she would suddenly be insincere."

"After all the trouble she's made," said Juliette. She meant that for many years my wife would not let me divorce.

"She couldn't help that," I said.

"How do you know?"

"I don't know. It's what I think. I hardly knew her."

"You must have known *something*."

"I haven't seen her more than three or four times in the last thirty-odd years, since I started living with you."

"What do you mean?" said Juliette. "You saw her just once, with me. We had lunch. You backed off asking for the divorce."

"You can't ask for a divorce at lunch. It had to be done by mail."

"And since then she hasn't stopped writing," said Juliette. "Do you mean three or four times, or do you mean once?"

I said, "Once, probably. Probably just that once."

Viewing me at close range, as if I were a novel she had to translate, Juliette replied that one ought to be spared unexpected visions. Just now, it was as if three walls of the court outside had been bombed flat. Through a bright new gap she saw straight through to my first marriage. We – my first wife and I – postured in the distance, like characters in fiction.

I had recently taken part in a panel discussion, taped for television, on the theme "What Literature, for Which Readers, at Whose Price?" I turned away from Juliette and switched on the set, about ten minutes too early. Juliette put the empty cups and the coffeepot on a tray she had picked up in Milan, the summer I was researching the Stendhal, and carried the tray down the dim passage to the kitchen. I watched the tag end of the late news. It must have been during the spring of 1976. Because of the energy crisis, daylight saving had been established. Like any novelty, it was deeply upsetting. People said they could no longer digest their food or be nice to their children, and that they needed sedation to help them through the altered day. A doctor was interviewed; he advised a light diet and early bed until mind and body adjusted to the change.

I turned, smiling, to where Juliette should have been. My program came on then, and I watched myself making a few points before I got up and went to find her. She was in the kitchen, standing in the dark, clutching the edge of the sink. She did not move when I turned the light on. I put my arms around her, and we came back to her sitting room and watched the rest of the program together. She was knitting squares of wool to be sewn together to make a blanket; there was always, somewhere, a flood or an earthquake or a flow of refugees, and those who outlasted jeopardy had to be covered.

WORDS

Carol Shields

Carol Shields (1935–2003) was an American-born
Canadian writer. She is best known for her 1993 novel *The
Stone Diaries,* which won the Pulitzer Prize as well as the
Governor General's Award in Canada. Shields published
ten novels, three collections of poetry and five collections
of short stories.

When the world first started heating up, an international conference
was held in Rome to discuss ways of dealing with the situation.

Ian's small northern country – small in terms of population, that
is, not in size – sent him to the meetings as a junior observer, and
it was there he met Isobel, who was representing her country as
full-fledged delegate. She wore a terrible green dress the first time
he saw her, and rather clumsy shoes, but he could see that her neck
was slender, her waist narrow and her legs long and brown. For so
young a woman, she was astonishingly articulate; in fact, it was
her voice more than anything else that he fell in love with – its hills
and valleys and its pliant, easy-sided wit. It was a voice that could
be distinguished in any gathering, being both sweet and husky and
having an edging of contralto merriment that seemed to Ian as rare
and fine as a border of gold leaf.

They played truant, missing half the study sessions, the two
of them lingering instead over tall, cool drinks in the café they
found on the Via Traflori. There, under a cheerful striped canopy,
Isobel leaned across a little table and placed long, ribbony Spanish
phrases into Ian's mouth, encouraging and praising him when he
got them right. And he, in his somewhat stiff northern voice, gave
back the English equivalents. table, chair, glass, cold, hot, money,
street, people, mouth. In the evenings, walking in the gardens in
front of the institute where the conference was being held, they
turned to each other and promised with their eyes, and in two
languages as well, to love each other forever.

The second International Conference was held ten years later. The situation had become grave. One could use the word *crisis* and not be embarrassed. Ian – by then married to Isobel, who was at home with the children – attended every session and he listened attentively to the position papers of various physicists, engineers, geographers and linguists from all parts of the world. It was a solemn but distinguished assembly; many eminent men and women took their places at the lectern, including the spidery old Scottish demographer who years earlier had made the first correlation between substrata temperatures and highly verbalized societies. In every case, these speakers presented their concerns with admirable brevity, each word weighted and frugally chosen, and not one of them exceeded the two-minute time limitation. For by now no one really doubted that it was the extravagance and proliferation of language that had caused the temperature of the earth's crust to rise, and in places – California, Japan, London – to crack open and form long ragged lakes of fire. The evidence was everywhere and it was incontrovertible: thermal maps, and measurements, sonar readings, caloric separations, a network of subterranean monitoring systems – all these had reinforced the integrity of the original Scottish theories.

But the delegates, sitting in the plenary session of the second International Conference, were still reluctant to take regulatory action. It was partly a case of heads-in-the-sand; it was – human nature being what it is – partly a matter of political advantage or commercial gain. There lingered, too, a somewhat surprising nostalgia for traditional liberties and for the old verbal order of the world. Discussion at the conference had gone around and around all week, pointless and wasteful, and it looked very much as though the final meeting would end in yet another welter of indecision and deferral. It was at that point that Ian, seated in the front row, rose and requested permission to speak.

He was granted a one-minute slot on the agenda. In fact, he spoke for several minutes, but his eloquence, his sincerity (and no doubt his strong, boyish appearance, his shaggy hair and his blue eyes) seemed to merit an exception. Certainly not one person sitting in that gathering had any wish to stop him.

It was unfortunate, tragic some thought, that a freak failure in the electronic system – only a plug accidentally pulled from its socket – prevented his exact words from being recorded, but those who were present remembered afterward how passionately he pleaded his love, for the planet. (In truth – though who could know this? – he was thinking chiefly of his love for Isobel and his two children.)

We are living in a fool's dream, he told his fellow delegates, and the time has come for us to wake. Voluntary restraints were no longer adequate to preserve the little earth, which was the only home we know. Halfway measures like the old three-hour *temps tranquilles* were next to useless since they were never, or almost never, enforced. The evening curfew-lingua was ridiculously lenient. Abuses of every sort abounded, particularly the use of highly percussive words or words that were redolent with emotional potency, even though it had been established that these two classes of words were particularly damaging to bedrock and shales. Multilingualism continued to flourish. Wasteful antiphonic structures were actually on the increase in the more heavily populated regions, as was the use of elaborate ceremonial metaphor. It was as though, by refusing to make linguistic sacrifices, the human race had willed its own destruction.

When he finished speaking, the applause was prolonged and powerful. It perhaps held an element of shame, too; this young man had found the courage to say at last what should have been said long before. One after another the delegates rose to their feet, and soon their clapping fell into a steady rhythmic beat that had the effect of holding Ian hostage on the platform. The chairman whispered into his ear, begging him for a few additional words.

He assented. He could not say no. And, in a fever that was remarkably similar to the fever he had suffered as a child during a severe case of measles, or like the fever of love he had succumbed to ten years earlier in Rome, he announced to the audience, holding up a hand for attention, that he would be the first to take a vow of complete silence for the sake of the planet that had fathered him.

Almost at once he regretted his words, but hubris kept him from recanting for the first twenty-four hours and, after that, a kind of stubbornness took over. Isobel met him at the airport with the words, "You went too far." Later, after a miserable, silent attempt at lovemaking, she said, "I'll never forgive you." His children, clamoring to hear about his moment of heroism, poked at him, at his face and chest and arms, as though he were inert. He tried to tell them with his eyes that he was still their father, that he still loved them.

"Leave him alone," Isobel said sharply. "He might as well be a stranger now. He's no different than anyone else."

She became loud and shrewish. When his silent followers arrived at their door – and in time there were thousands of them, each with the same blank face and gold armband – she admitted them with bad grace. She grew garrulous. She rambled on and on, bitter and blaming, sometimes incoherent, sometimes obscene, sometimes reverting to a coarse, primitive schoolyard Spanish, sometimes shouting to herself or cursing into the mirror or chanting oaths – anything to furnish the emptiness of the house with words. She became disoriented. The solid plaster of the walls fell away from her, melting into a drift of vapor. There seemed to be no shadows, no sense of dimension, no delicate separation between one object and another. Privately, she pleaded with her husband for an act of apostasy. Later she taunted him. "Show me you're still human," she would say. "Give me just one word." The word *betrayal* came frequently out of her wide mobile mouth, and so did the scornful epithet *martyr*.

But time passes and people forget. She forgot, finally, what it was that had betrayed her. Next she forgot her husband's name. Sometimes she forgot that she had a husband at all, for how could anything be said to exist, she asked herself loudly, hoarsely – even a husband, even one's self – if it didn't also exist in the shape of a word.

He worried that she might be arrested, but for some reason – his position probably – she was always let off with a warning. In their own house she ignored him, passing him on the stairs without a look, or crossing in front of him as though he were a stuffed chair. Often she disappeared for hours, venturing out alone into the heat of the night, and he began to suspect she had taken a lover.

The thought preyed on him, though, in fact he had long since forgotten the word for *wife* and also the word for *fidelity*. One night, when she left the house, he attempted to follow her, but clearly she was suspicious because she walked very quickly, looking back over her shoulder, making a series of unnecessary turns and choosing narrow old streets whose curbs were blackened by fire. Within minutes he lost sight of her; soon after that he was driven back by the heat.

The next night he tried again, and this time he saw her disappear into an ancient dilapidated braiding, the sort of enclosure, he remembered, where children had once gone to learn to read and write. Unexpectedly, he felt a flash of pity, what a sad place for a tryst. He waited briefly, then entered the building and went up a flight of smoldering stairs that seemed on the point of collapse. There he found a dim corridor, thick with smoke, and a single room at one end.

Through the door he heard a waterfall of voices. There must have been a dozen people inside, all of them talking. The talk seemed to be about poetry. Someone – a woman – was giving a lecture. There were interruptions, a discussion, some laughter. He heard his wife's voice, her old gilt-edged contralto, asking a question, and the sound of it made him draw in his breath so sharply that something hard, like a cinder or a particle of gravel, formed in his throat.

It stayed stubbornly lodged there all night. He found it painful to breathe, and even Isobel noticed how he thrashed about in bed, gasping wildly for air. In the morning she called a doctor, who could find nothing wrong, but she remained uneasy, and that evening she stayed home and made him cups of iced honey-and-lemon tea to ease his throat. He took her hand at one point and held it to his lips as though it might be possible to find the air he needed inside the crevices of her skin. By now the scraping in his throat had become terrible, a raw agonizing rasp like a dull knife sawing through limestone. She looked at his face, from which the healthy, blood-filled elasticity had gone, and felt herself brushed by a current of air, or what might have been the memory of a name.

He began to choke violently, and she heard something grotesque come out of his mouth, a sound that was only half-human, but that rode on a curious rhythmic wave that for some reason stirred her deeply. She imagined it to be the word *Isobel*. "Isobel?" she asked, trying to remember its meaning. He said it a second time, and this time the syllables were more clearly formed.

The light of terror came into his eyes, or perhaps the beginning of a new fever; she managed to calm him by stroking his arm. Then she called the children inside the house, locked the doors and windows against the unbearable heat, and they began, slowly, patiently, hands linked, at the beginning where they had begun before – with table, chair, bed, cool, else, other, sleep, face, mouth, breath, tongue.

REVENGE

Anne Enright

Anne Enright (b. 1962) is an Irish author, born in Dublin. She has published essays, short stories, a work of non-fiction and four novels. Her novel, *The Gathering*, won the 2007 Man Booker Prize.

I work for a firm which manufactures rubber gloves. There are many kinds of protective gloves, from the surgical and veterinary (arm-length) to industrial, gardening and domestic. They have in common a niceness. They all imply revulsion. You might not handle a dead mouse without a pair of rubber gloves, someone else might not handle a baby. I need not tell you that shops in Soho sell nuns' outfits made of rubber, that some grown men long for the rubber under-blanket of their infancies, that rubber might save the human race. Rubber is a morally, as well as a sexually, exciting material. It provides us all with an elastic amnesty, to piss the bed, to pick up dead things, to engage in sexual practices, to not touch whomsoever we please.

I work with and sell an everyday material, I answer everyday questions about expansion ratios, tearing, petrifaction, I moved from market research to quality control. I have snapped more elastic in my day etcetera etcetera.

My husband and I are the kind of people who put small ads in the personal columns looking for other couples who may be interested in some discreet fun. This provokes a few everyday questions: How do people *do* that? What do they say to each other? What do they *say* to the couples who answer? To which the answers are: Easily. Very little. 'We must see each other again sometime.'

When I was a child it was carpet I loved. I should have made a career in floor-coverings. There was a brown carpet in the dining room with specks of black that was my parents' pride and joy. 'Watch the carpet!' they would say, and I did. I spent all my time sitting on it, joining up the warm, black dots. Things mean a lot to me.

The stench of molten rubber gives me palpitations. It also gives me eczema and a bad cough. My husband finds the smell anaphrodisiac in the extreme. Not even the products excite him, because after seven years you don't know who you are touching, or not touching, anymore.

My husband is called Malachy and I used to like him a lot. He was unfaithful to me in that casual, 'look, it didn't mean anything' kind of way. I was of course bewildered, because that is how I was brought up. I am supposed to be bewildered. I am supposed to say, 'What *is* love anyway? What is sex?'

Once the fiction between two people snaps then anything goes, or so they say. But it wasn't my marriage I wanted to save, it was myself. My head, you see, is a balloon on a string, my insides are elastic. I have to keep the tension between what is outside and what is in, if I am not to deflate, or explode.

So it was more than a suburban solution that made me want to be unfaithful *with* my husband, rather than *against* him. It was more than a question of the mortgage. I had my needs too: a need to be held in, to be filled, a need for sensation. I wanted revenge and balance. I wanted an awfulness of my own. Of course it was also suburban. Do you really want to know our sexual grief? How we lose our grip, how we feel obliged *to wear* things, how we are supposed to look as if we mean it.

Malachy and I laugh in bed, that is how we get over the problem of conviction. We laugh at breakfast too, on a good day, and sometimes we laugh again at dinner. Honest enough laughter, I would say, if the two words were in the same language, which I doubt. Here is one of the conversations that led to the ad in the personals:

'I think we're still good in bed.' (LAUGH)
'I think we're great in bed.' (LAUGH)
'I think we should advertise.' (LAUGH)

Here is another:

'You know John Jo at work? Well his wife was thirty-one yesterday.
I said, "What did you give her for her birthday then?" He said, "I
gave her one for every year. Beats blowing out candles." Do you
believe that?'(LAUGH)

You may ask when did the joking stop and the moment of truth
arrive? As if you didn't know how lonely living with someone can
be.

The actual piece of paper with the print on is of very little
importance. John Jo composed the ad for a joke during a coffee-
break at work. My husband tried to snatch it away from him.
There was a chase.

There was a similar chase a week later when Malachy brought the
magazine home to me. I shrieked. I rolled it up and belted him over
the head. I ran after him with a cup full of water and drenched his
shirt. There was a great feeling of relief, followed by some very
honest sex. I said, 'I wonder what the letters will say?' I said, 'What
kind of couples *do* that kind of thing? What kind of people *answer*
ads like that?' I also said, 'God, how vile!'
Some of the letters had photos attached. 'This is my wife.' Nothing
is incomprehensible, when you know that life is sad. I answered
one for a joke. I said to Malachy, 'Guess who's coming to dinner?'

I started off with mackerel pate, mackerel being a scavenger fish,
and good for the heart. I followed with veal osso buco, for reasons
I need not elaborate, and finished with a spiced fig pudding with
rum butter. Both the eggs I cracked had double yolks, which I
found poignant.

I hoovered everything in sight of course. Our bedroom is stranger-proof. It is the kind of bedroom you could die in and not worry about the undertakers. The carpet is a little more interesting than beige, the spread is an ochre brown, die pattern on the curtains is expensive and unashamed. One wall is mirrored in a sanitary kind of way; with little handles for the wardrobe doors.

'Ding Dong,' said the doorbell. Malachy let them in. I heard the sound of coats being taken and drinks offered. I took off my apron, paused at the mirror and opened the kitchen door.

Her hair was over-worked, I thought – too much perm and too much gel. Her make-up was shiny, her eyes were small. All her intelligence was in her mouth, which gave an ironic twist as she said hello. It was a large mouth, sexy and selfish. Malachy was holding out a gin and tonic for her in a useless kind of way.

Her husband was concentrating on the ice in his glass. His suit was a green so dark it looked black – very discreet, I thought, and out of our league, with Malachy in his cheap polo and jeans. I didn't want to look at his face, nor he at mine. In the slight crash of our glances I saw he was worn before his time.

I think he was an alcoholic. He drank his way through the meal and was polite. There was a feeling that he was pulling back from viciousness. Malachy, on the other hand, was over-familiar. He and the wife laughed at bad jokes and their feet were confused under the table. The husband asked me about my job and I told him about the machine I have for testing rubber squares; how it pulls the rubber four different ways at high speed. I made it sound like a joke, or something. He laughed.

I realised myself a slow, physical excitement, a kind of pornographic panic. It felt like the house was full of balloons pressing gently against the ceiling. I looked at the husband.

'Is this your first time?'

'No,' he said.

'What kind of people *do* this kind of thing?' I asked, because I honestly didn't know.

'Well they usually don't feed us so well, or even at all.' I felt guilty. 'This is much more civilised,' he said. 'A lot of them would be well on before we arrive, I'd say. As a general kind of rule.'

'I'm sorry,' I said, 'I don't really drink.'

'Listen,' he leaned forward. 'I was sitting having a G and T in someone's front room and the wife took Maria upstairs to look at the bloody grouting in the bathroom or something, when this guy comes over to me and I realise about six minutes too late that he plays for bloody Arsenal! If you see what I mean. A *very* ordinary looking guy.

'You have to be careful,' he said. 'And his wife was a cracker.'

When I was a child I used to stare at things as though they knew something I did not. I used to put them into my mouth and chew them to find out what it was. I kept three things under my bed at night; a piece of wood, a metal door-handle and a cloth. I sucked them instead of my thumb.

We climbed the stairs after Malachy and the wife, who were laughing. Malachy was away, I couldn't touch him. He had the same look in his eye as when he came home from a hurling match when the right team won.

The husband was talking in a low, constant voice that I couldn't refuse. I remember looking at the carpet, which had once meant so much to me. Everyone seemed to know what they were doing.

I thought that we were all supposed to end up together and perform and watch and all that kind of thing. I was interested in the power it would give me over breakfast, but I wasn't looking forward to the confusion. I find it difficult enough to arrange myself around one set of limbs, which are heavy things. I wouldn't know what to do with three. Maybe we would get over the awkwardness with a laugh or two, but in my heart of hearts I didn't find the idea of being with a naked woman funny. What would we joke about? Would we be expected to do things?

What I really wanted to see was Malachy's infidelity. I wanted his paunch made public, the look on his face, his bottom in the air. *That* would be funny.

I did not expect to be led down the hall and into the spare room. I did not expect to find myself sitting on my own with an alcoholic and handsome stranger who had a vicious look in his eye. I did not expect to feel anything.

I wanted him to kiss me. He leant over and tried to take off his shoes. He said, 'God, I hate that woman. Did you see her? The way she was laughing and all that bloody lip-gloss. Did you see her? She looks like she's made out of plastic. I can't get a hold of her without slipping around in some body lotion that smells like petrol and dead animals.' He had taken his shoes off and was swinging his legs onto the bed. 'She never changes, you know.' He was trying to take his trousers off. 'Oh I know she's sexy. I mean, you saw her. She is sexy. She is sexy. She is sexy. I just prefer if somebody else does it. If you don't mind.' I still wanted him to kiss me. There was the sound of laughter from the other room.

I rolled off the wet patch and lay down on the floor with my cheek on the carpet, which was warm and rough and friendly. I should go into floor-coverings. I remember when I wet the bed as a child. First it is warm then it gets cold. I would go into my parents' bedroom, with its smell, and start to cry. My mother gets up. She is half-asleep but she's not cross. She is huge. She strips the bed of the wet sheet and takes off the rubber under-blanket which falls with a thick sound to the floor. She puts a layer of newspaper on the mattress and pulls down the other sheet. She tells me to take off my wet pyjamas. I sleep in the raw between the top sheet and the rough blanket and when I turn over, all the warm newspaper under me makes a noise.

CHOIRMASTER

Elspeth Davie

Elspeth Davie (1918–1995) was a Scottish author. Although she wrote novels, she is best known for her short stories. Davie won the Katherine Mansfield Prize in 1978.

One day, out of the blue, it came to Sam, the choirmaster, that God must be very tired of people constantly flopping to the ground and begging for this and that. Rows of men, women and children on their knees – whispering, imploring, pleading, whether in song or prayer. What way was that to ask for anything? God, it was said, was all-powerful and could do anything on earth or in heaven. Heaven was an unknown quantity, of course. But, looking around the earth, people could see things had gone badly, drastically wrong. Drought and famine had ravished some lands more ferociously than others. The sickening stench of death rose from the hot earth, and from the baked mud of the riverbanks. Birth and death arrived suddenly together. Scarcely was there time to dispose of the afterbirth than the burial cloths were unwound. Gone were the days when any choir could sing cheerfully of the good seed being sown and scattered regularly by men and watered just as punctually by God. The eyes of all those in this land dried up in their sockets while staring at the terrible, brazen sky. At each dawn all the vessels in the place were brought out – the jugs, the pitchers, basins and baths in order to catch every drop of the miraculous, God-given liquid when it fell. No water fell. No water had fallen for weeks and months. Obviously, as the old choirmaster now believed, God must be weary of the bent knee and the humble, bowed head. Perhaps it was bold, abusive songs and outraged shouts He was hoping for, not the quiet, muttered prayer and the thanks which would make the lesser gods shrivel with shame. Was it not possible that God wished to be commanded for a change, not cajoled at all?

Sam had always been a lusty shouter himself. He had formed his choir as he travelled, and as he travelled continually, he gathered together a huge company of men, women and children from the remoter parts of the world. He picked his singers from the desperate and hungry, from the ill and even the dying, from people too weak to work and from some who had been almost beaten to the ground by servitude. He therefore knew that wherever they went in the world, his choir would be singing to companions in suffering; and so, whatever else it sounded like, whatever words or music were used – the song must ring true. His singers understood this, and if they were forced to compete with tornadoes, the pounding of huge waves, claps of thunder, the last rumblings of earthquake – the more they tried to rise to Sam's demands. It was true they had their own demands, but never for anything petty. Depending on what piece of land they were passing through, the men asked for what they imagined were the simple rights of every man. They demanded work, water, bread, decent huts and medicine. Occasionally they might pray to God for death. The women asked for all these as well as care and comfort for their children. Occasionally they might ask for fewer babies and sometimes even for more, as long as they still had milk to give them.

As time went on some desperate people asked if it were possible that God might be a little deaf on account of His great age. Perhaps He was no music-lover, in spite of some talk of angelic choirs. Then the choirmaster saw that he would have his work cut out, teaching, explaining, reprimanding and generally dealing with the strong emotions of his singers.

'Look,' he said one day to his hungry and unhappy crowd. 'Please, if you can possibly help it, don't cry when you're begging for anything. Begging's bad enough, but begging *and* crying must make God feel really mean. Do you want Him to feel mean?'

'Yes, I do,' said a blind old man with fly-encrusted sores around his eyes and down his legs. His feet were bound in grey bandages and he leant on a stick. It was true he was on his last legs, yet might still live for a day or so.

'No, I don't think *I* do,' said a gaunt-faced, middle-aged woman with four small children behind her, two others clutching at her cloak, and a bulge-eyed baby in her arms. 'They are all beautiful,' she said, indicating each child with a nod of her head, 'but will I have the strength to love and feed them all?'

It was true that hundreds of people in the huge choir had hardly enough strength to raise their voices. A few could do nothing but lie on the ground and wait for death for themselves and their children. This would often come quickly. But a decent burial took strength from the living and many died in the doing of it.

Not everyone in the choir agreed with Sam's method of singing loudly all the time with scarcely a break.

'Hadn't we better stop and listen once in a while?' asked one old-fashioned believer. 'Wasn't there something about a still, small voice?'

'Yes, I've heard that, but I've always been against the idea,' said the choirmaster. 'As long as we've got the strength, we're here to sing, not to listen. Sure, people want to join my choir for all kinds of reasons. They tell me they've got great voices, clear voices, that they can reach the highest notes and the lowest. And, naturally, people like that have ambitions to be the star singer. Or maybe they've no voice at all, but just want to get away from a plaguing family back home. Whatever they've come for, what help are they to a company like ours, especially if they're interested in small voices? Isn't it hard enough to get people to stand up straight and open their mouths?'

Yet for a time the old choirmaster did think of adding to his singers. And it was not only here that he looked. There were plenty of good voices back in his own country to which he returned for a short time. Many there had joined in processions and stood on platforms, for one cause or another. Groups with banners gathered outside hospitals, colleges and churches. Some he brought back to his choir, whether they had fine voices or not. He needed to make up for all he had lost through sickness or death. But he himself changed a great deal as he grew older. He had seen so much of horror, pain and misery in the land that the idea of singing songs of love or thanks for anything on earth seemed out of the question. Nowadays, outrage towards heaven was what he looked for in his singers – anything that gave force and fury to the human voice, his only rule being that they sing with chests out and heads flung back. Always they must be defiant, never suppliant.

Sam would have liked the suffering creatures of the earth to be heard in his choir – birds and animals as well as men. For he believed that many creatures might find more protection there than those outside who suffered the cruelty of human beings – the trap-setters, the cage-builders and the money-makers behind the bleeding hell of the slaughterhouses. Yet, on second thoughts, he decided to stick only to humans and allowed them to sing exactly as they pleased, whether in fear, pain, fury or sorrow. As long as they made a loud enough noise they might curse or weep as much as they liked. There was, he told them, no one God to cry to – or, if only one, he had obviously been created by all races of men, in all ages of Time, and out of every belief that had ever been attempted on earth. The choirmaster again reminded his singers that thanksgiving must sometimes be very tough on God. No doubt He might rather be bullied a bit, scolded, and even openly threatened for a change.

The choirmaster was growing old and tired. These days he was often hard put to vary the singing to every catastrophe. They came so thick and fast there was hardly time to draw breath before the next shattered the community; the flood and famine, dust and drought, disease and death, and all followed by endless questions: 'Why, why, why?' Then the hopeless non-answers. Finally silence.

But the old man kept on with his training. Above all, it was essential to teach his choir, the loud and soft notes in the human voice. They had to sing as loud as possible to be heard through the landslides and earthquakes, or simply to alert the desperate inhabitants of lonely places that help was on the way. It also took great skill to teach them to change from the loudest possible crescendo to a sound so quiet that the cry of an infant or even the whisper of a dying child might be located under some mountain of rubble.

By this time the outrage choir was pretty well established, but one day the choirmaster – ever on the look out for likely singers – picked up another possible member. His company was passing a forest one evening when a young man appeared out of the darkness between two trees. The trees were tall, their broad jungle-leaves casting great shadows around the newcomer, giving the impression that he was delicate. This was an illusion. He was thin but sturdy with strong, muscular legs and large, workman's hands. He had the unusual attraction of a darkish brown skin and clear, blue eyes.

It was hard to tell whether he came from the north, the south, the east or the west.

'I heard you coming a long way off,' he said. 'What sort of procession is it?'

'No procession at all,' Sam answered. 'This is a choir, and monstrously hard work it is too, dealing with an unruly crowd like this. But I'm not grumbling because that's exactly what I want them to be – unruly and complaining!'

'What are they complaining about?' the young man asked.

'Complaining's a poor word. I was wrong to use it,' replied the choirmaster. 'They're not girning or whingeing about some paltry thing, some petty grudge. Those who still have strength are shouting to high heaven about the hopelessness of this earth – the thirst, the hunger, the pain, the misery. Some are still singing quite sweetly, of course. Most are cursing.'

'Lord, but it must be a tough job leading a choir like that!' exclaimed the stranger.

'It certainly is. But one day I might get them to sing properly as well as shout. I confess it was I who worked them up. But still, it *is* supposed to be a choir, not only a furious rabble.'

'May I join your choir?' the young man asked.

'It all depends on the voice,' said the choirmaster.

'A tenor,' the other replied.

'Then I doubt if I can take you on,' said Sam. 'Tenors tend to sing about sweetness, peace, love, harmony and the rest of it. All the things this world is almost totally lacking in. Myself, I believed in all that once. Not now, of course.'

'And I can sing solos,' the young man went on, as if not having heard the last remark.

'Sorry, but I never allow solo singing,' said the choirmaster firmly. 'Soloists always become vain, no matter how modest they seem to be at the start. They tend to be temperamental too, and before you know where you are, they're acting like spoilt children. There is this terrific silence whenever a tenor solo gets up to sing – you must have noticed that yourself – as if he were a prince or god or some such being. People can even fall in love with tenors before the last note's out. It all plays havoc with a well-trained choir, and this *is* a well-trained choir! Once they've settled down you'll hear them sing. And I've worked so hard with them. A good choir is my one real aim in life. As in every art it's a case of balance and gravity, if you like. We can't afford too much emotion.'

'Nevertheless, you need a hell of a lot of emotion to sing well,' said the young man. 'To put anything across at all – that's a lifetime's work. Anyway, you're certainly putting it over. There's no doubt it will reach this Almighty Person you're singing to.'

'You mean He has huge, listening ears as well as everything else?'

'Possibly,' said the other. 'I've never thought about His different parts.'

'Wherever He is, I seldom think about Him nowadays,' said the old choirmaster. 'He has allowed such fearful things to happen here. I can hardly bring myself to look up at all, far less utter a respectful word. I think I'd choke if I did. Yet I can still manage to train a good choir. Imagine that!'

'You're probably best to choke and have done with it,' the newcomer replied. 'And I like people who speak their minds. Myself, I'm not so fond of the meek as I was sometimes thought to be when I was young.'

'You certainly still look young enough to me!' exclaimed the choirmaster.

'No, no, I can scarcely remember what that was like. I think I never was really young at all.'

'Well, I'll let you join us for a bit,' said the older man, 'and we can judge what kind of voice you have. Naturally, I can't promise anything right now. A great many people have wanted to join, but the moment they find it's not a church outing with picnic included, they fall away at once.'

'I've no interest in church choirs myself, nor Sunday School picnics, for that matter,' the young man assured him.

So it turned out that this newcomer was allowed to practise with the rest. But the choirmaster knew he was taking a big risk. The choir itself was never too pleased with his rare, haphazard choice of new members. Moreover, it was no longer as straightforward as in the old days when the choirmaster had been full of optimism and simple belief. Nowadays any new recruits he chose for his choir were strangely mixed. Either they would show too little anger in their voices – falling back into the old, placating tone, or else they allowed out-of-hand fury to spoil the rhythm and tempo of the song.

Yet the old choirmaster didn't hurry his new member into song. He allowed him to find his feet before he even opened his mouth. The young man was simply encouraged to walk along with the choir for a while, not singing, but just chatting with them, finding out how much strength they could still summon up for practice, hearing how they could still manage to sing in harmony even while often hating one another's guts. Some would confess how deeply they resented what they'd heard of other choirs in the cities of the world – choirs used to all the perks of wealthy companies – applause that went on for hours with endless flower-throwing, plus banquets and bouquets and beautiful women. Many, in fact, were bitter that they'd ever met up with the old choirmaster who, for reasons of his own, had, early on, gathered them into this company where they now suffered the humiliation of becoming a crowd of travelling beggars under a one-time raving idealist who could offer no food, no water, no medicine and no comfort of any kind, while gradually letting his own hopes and beliefs peter out as the arid, blazing days went on. Sometimes he appeared unsteady on his feet as the starving inhabitants of each village pressed around him, trying to claw pity from his heart. Often, at night, he would wonder what would become of him if pity ever deserted him.

As for the choir, the reasons for their present suffering gradually became clear. Long ago, when Sam took over, he had forced them to sing – no, not merely to sing but to shout – loud and triumphantly about the Love of God. Love! The scorn, the fury, the disappointment and bitterness in their singing gradually grew to a raucous crescendo as they realized what they had walked into, unawares. And now, even the old choirmaster was disintegrating before their eyes.

'So he's seen no more of this enormous love than we have!' they cried. 'This old man's taken us through deadly heat and freezing cold with nowhere to camp – through forests and deserts, all of us hungry and filthy as pariah dogs. He thinks we'll follow for the rest of our lives, like fools. Let's sing something different, so furiously blasphemous it will frighten the life out of him. Then we can run back to our homes, if there's still a home to run to. But where will our children be now? Will our husbands and wives have left long ago? They will curse us for leaving, then curse us for coming back! What a fix the old one has got us into! May he be damned!'

The new singer held up his hand. 'Wait!' he shouted. 'Don't forget your God gave you freedom – the freedom to come or to go, to turn good into bad and bad into good. But have you taken your freedom?'

Again the air was filled with furious muttering. More fierce cries and curses went up into the sky. 'There must be silence!' the young leading singer reminded them, 'or else the God will not hear that He is loved and forgiven!'

'Never! How we have suffered!' came shouts from every side. 'Where is this love? He had no love. Now we have none ourselves!'

The great trees whistled and creaked in accord. Hissing came through the dripping leaves. At least a quarter of the choir left immediately and ran back as fast as they could down the way they had come. The new singer watched them go sympathetically, while the rest hesitated, in two minds whether to follow or to stay. Many were still pondering on this unknown Love of God.

'What kind of love is this?' they demanded, this love that allows terror and torture to innocent men and beasts?' There had been loving parents in some lucky lives, of course: a few loving friends, a loving teacher or two, loving cats and dogs. A few admitted that, not clearly knowing what love meant, they had recklessly given it to all sorts of undeserving persons, and been let down, dropped, deserted, and swiftly passed over or replaced. So did this God-love have infinite meanings then – all different from anything known on earth? If so, what was the use of talking about it?

'Time to talk or sing if we ever get to heaven!' came a shout. 'Right now, let's keep our mouths shut!'

There was complete silence, so much so that the old choirmaster came back to see what had happened. 'Are you working them up about something?' he asked the new member. 'If so I'll have to ask you to leave at once. I've put a life's work into training them, and I can't afford to hear it all go for nothing. What's more, I'm afraid

I've changed my mind about the love-singing and even the love-talk. I'm into *Justice* now. *Justice* is the greatest thing on earth!'

'But will you let me stay and sing with your choir a little longer?' the young man asked.

'That's fair enough, of course. And I will stand and listen as hard as I can,' said Sam, stepping from the fringe of the forest into the sunlight.

The sound he heard was like light itself – sometimes flashing up through the trees and descending again into blackness through thick leaves, and once more climbing up a scale of brilliance till it reached a sunburst of sound. Bells, flutes and cymbals like those that herald the appearance of a new king were heard, and then a second descent into the dark evening shadow moving swiftly along the ground.

'Have they fallen on their knees to pray and praise then?' Sam asked incredulously, peering at the men and women on the ground.

'Not yet,' said the new singer. 'How on earth could they sing with tongues parched dry with thirst, with stomachs blown tight as drums with hunger?'

'But have they sung up forgiveness to God yet?' the old man asked.

'No, no,' the other answered again. 'He will not be forgiven for a long, long time. Only when the desert is green as an orchard, when the dying children get their milk and lose the look of wizened age. Only then.'

The old choirmaster stepped forward defiantly. 'Of course the *singing* sounded good,' he said. 'But I'm not sure what you're trying to do. Are you trying to be different from all other singers?'

'Yes, I suppose I am,' the other conceded.

'Then what exactly are you aiming at?' the old choirmaster went on. He had known all along that this particular singer was proud, if not actually arrogant. He had met all types in his profession – the cringing and the confident, loud-voiced braggarts and soft-voiced hypocrites, bullying voices and begging ones. Yet it was difficult to know where this particular voice fitted in. All he could vouch for was that it was a totally new and beautiful one. And so powerful it was that the man was automatically taken as leader.

The young man was silent for a while before answering Sam's

question. 'You ask what I'm aiming at. I am helping people to forgive the Almighty One for all the terrible things He has allowed on earth – the unbelievable wretchedness and frightful pain. He has forgiven them for many things. Now they can forgive Him. *He* can never be human. *They* can never be gods, but at least they can show they are human and be proud of it.'

'Don't try to change my singers,' said the old choirmaster. 'It has taken me long enough to prevent the bending knee and that horrible, begging note.'

'There'll be none of that if I have anything to do with it,' the new member assured him. 'They must go on shouting and cursing for as long as they wish. First the God must be shown fearlessly all they have endured. Then He might be forgiven. You will let me stay a short time with your singers, then?'

Again the old choirmaster could only agree. He waited, rather jealously, to hear what other sound this newcomer would bring from his choir. The old man believed that he had heard all sounds produced by animal and human throat. But this was something else. Fearful sounds and words evoking frightful images; young men, women and children of every race sliced to the bone by guns, beheaded by bombs; the frightened breath of children waiting for doors to open in the night; the roar of the wounded lion, the scream of the trapped hare, the terrified bellow of beasts with rolling eyes, slung up for slaughter; the rumbling of earthquakes spurting from unknown depths. These were not sounds only from throat or ground. These were the sounds of Hell on earth.

The young leader lifted up his arms, urging the choir to louder and louder shouts of outrage. Then he raised his hand for silence. 'That was excellent!' he called. 'You have shown a magnificent fury for the things allowed by God. Now you can show forgiveness to match!'

Again the air was filled with furious mutterings and cries of complaint.

'You see, they are not stupid,' the old choirmaster explained. 'Most of the things we heard are the fault of Man. They have nothing to do with God. Anyway, He is above thanks or blame. To think anything else would be blasphemy.'

Old Sam had once hoped to be a popular preacher in a large

city church with a decent stipend and a gathering of well-dressed ladies and gentlemen who would listen to him with unquestioning respect. How he longed, after all these years in the wilderness, to arrive at a cool, Christian building where there was no cursing, no obscenity, no endless questions and no striving on his part to offer quickfire explanations for every single horror that had ever happened upon earth!

He sidetracked a good deal of the argument nowadays. Yet he was still left with the humiliating desire to keep on with his own nagging questions, whether directed to an angel or devil in his own mind or even to some interloper who might happen, in passing, to step out of a dark wood. He turned again to the young singer for reassurance. 'It *is* the fault of human beings, isn't it?' he asked anxiously. 'The old barbaric gods would have allowed these horrors, of course, but not the great, good God of Love we have prayed and sung to day after day, year in year out.'

'I can promise great changes will come one day,' the younger man replied.

'One day, one year, one eternity,' added the old choirmaster, shaking his head dolefully.

The young man smiled. He had always foreseen more doubt than hope. One had to wait aeons and aeons of time for hope. Suddenly he left the path. He entered the forest again. Black darkness hid him.

'Is that young man gone for good?' asked one of the singers. 'I liked him. His standards were far too high, of course. He will never be popular.'

'He may well come again,' the choirmaster replied. 'He was simply here to see the damage and the pain for himself.'

'But who brought it on us?' the singer asked again.

'No doubt we brought it on ourselves,' said the old man.

'That is an easy answer,' said the other.

'Yes, I believe you're right,' the choirmaster agreed. 'It would take some superhuman power to bring all the catastrophe that has occurred on earth.'

'So that is the only answer you can find?'

'Well, I am only human,' said the old man. 'And I am tired. What more can I say? For the whole of my life I have been dumbfounded.'

Hearing this, the rest of the choir circled protectively around him. They were no longer angry. Doubt was more lovable than an iron faith, they decided. This looser circle they had formed let in both light and shadow. People felt free to break away from it and to come back again, to stand still, argue or be silent, to sing in tune or discord, to listen or to stop their ears. It was no sacred circle. Those who left were not followed or persuaded by love, the binding ties of friendship or the community spirit – to come back.

Over the centuries came changing groups of singers with their choirmasters. Rules changed. Tunes changed. Hopes rose and fell. Only music itself remained and the great forest of ancient trees. But every choirmaster taught his group not only how to sing, but to listen intently and to count the beat. Sometimes the songs were strident with bitterness, sometimes mellow with hope. Often for endless time there was no singing at all in the forest. But always an ardent listening for the return of a young leader hacking down branches to let in light – and for the terrible and confident crackle of His approaching footsteps over aeon upon aeon of fallen twigs.

ILSE'S HOUSE

Alison Lurie

> Alison Lurie (b. 1926) is an American novelist and
> academic. She won the Pulitzer Prize in 1984 for her novel
> *Foreign Affairs*. She has published ten novels, one collection
> of short stories, and a non-fiction work entitled *The
> Language of Clothes*.

Sure, I'm aware that people still theorise about why I never
married Gregor Spiegelman. I can understand that Greg was a
madly eligible man: good-looking, successful, charming, sexy. He
reminded me of those European film stars of the thirties you see
on TV reruns; he had that same suave low-key style. And then not
only was he chairman of the department, he was important in his
field. Everyone agreed that there were only two people in the world
who knew as much as he did about Balkan economic history –
some said only one.

Whereas I was just a fairly attractive young woman with a good
job as a market-research analyst. It seemed kind of a fluke that
I should have caught Greg, when so many had tried and failed.
Women had been after him for years, ever since his marriage ended
and his wife went back to Europe. I was rather pleased myself.
Though I didn't let on to anyone, privately I thought Dinah Kieran
was about the luckiest girl in upstate New York.

Of course some of my friends thought Greg was way too old
for me. But he didn't look anywhere near fifty-four. His springy
light-brown hair was scarcely grey at all, and he was really fit: he
played squash and ran two miles every day. I didn't see why his
chronological age should bother me. Back in the past it used to be
regarded as a coup to marry a man who was already established,
instead of taking a chance on some untried boy like my poor old Ma
did, to her lifelong regret.

A couple of people I knew said Greg was a male chauvinist, but
I couldn't see it. I wasn't exactly a feminist then anyhow. Sure, I

was for equal rights and equal pay; I was making as much as any man in my department, and I'd had to fight for that. But when one of my girlfriends started complaining about how having a chair pulled out for her in a restaurant was insulting, I got really bored. Holy God, why shouldn't a guy treat a woman with courtesy and consideration if he felt like it?

I rather liked being Greg's little darling, if you want to know the truth. I liked it when he helped me into my coat and gave me a secret squeeze as he settled it round me. I liked having him bring me old-fashioned presents: expensive perfume and flowers and sexy lingerie in the anemone colours that go best with my black-Irish looks: red and lavender and hot pink. I suppose he spoiled me, really, but after the kind of childhood I had there was a lot to make up for.

When we split some people blamed it on the age difference, and others said I wasn't intellectual enough for Gregor, or mature enough. Or they said our backgrounds were too different; what that meant was that I grew up in a trailer camp and didn't attend the right schools. Well, it ended so suddenly, that always makes talk. The date had been announced, the wedding invitations sent out, the caterer hired, the University chapel reserved – and then, two weeks before the ceremony, kaflooey, the whole thing was off.

In fact I was the one who broke it off. Everybody knew that, we didn't make a secret of it, and the reason we gave was the real one in a way; that I didn't want to live in Greg's house. People thought that was completely nuts, since I'd been more or less living there for months.

Greg didn't usually let on that I claimed his kitchen was haunted, because in his view that was just a crazy excuse. After all, I might not be an academic, as he said once, but I wasn't an ignorant uneducated person. I had a Master's in statistics and ought to be more rational than most women, not less. He never believed I'd really seen anything. Nobody else had had any funny experiences there, not even his hippie cleaning-lady, who believed in astrology and past lives.

You've got to understand, there was nothing intrinsically spooky about Greg's house. It was the kind of place you see in ads for paint and lawn care; a big white modern Colonial, on a broad tree-lined street in Corinth Heights. Ma would have died for it. Greg bought it when he got married, and the kitchen had been totally redone before his wife left. It was a big room with lots of cupboards and all the top-of-the-line equipment anyone could want: two ovens, microwave, disposal, dishwasher, you name it. It had avocado-green striped-and-flowered wallpaper, and the stove and fridge and cupboards and counters were that same pale sick green. Not my favourite colour, and it was kind of dark in the daytime, because of the low ceiling and the pine trees growing so close. Still, it was just about the last place you'd expect to meet a ghost.

But I did see something. At least I thought I saw something. What I thought I saw was Ilse Spiegelman, Greg's ex-wife. Of course that didn't make any sense, because how could Ilse be a ghost if she wasn't dead? And as far as I knew she was alive and well back in Czechoslovakia, or as well as you could be under the government they had then, and teaching at the university where Greg had met her.

She was probably better off there, he said. She'd liked his house, but she never cared much for the rest of America. Even after eight years she hadn't really adjusted.

'I blame myself,' he told me once. 'I didn't think enough about what I was doing, taking a woman away from her country, her family, her career. I only thought of how narrow and restricted Ilse's life was. I thought of the cold cramped two-room apartment she had to share with her sister and her parents, and how she couldn't afford a warm winter coat or the books and journals she needed for her research. I imagined how happy and grateful she would be here, but I was wrong.'

Greg said that naturally he'd expected Ilse would soon learn English. He was born in Europe himself and only came to America when he was ten, though you'd never know it. But Ilse wasn't good at languages, and she never got to the point where she was really comfortable in English, which made a problem when she started looking for work. Eventually she found a couple of temporary research jobs, and she did some part-time cataloguing for the library; but it wasn't what she wanted or was used to.

After a while Ilse didn't even try to find a job, Greg said, and she didn't make many friends. She wasn't as adaptable as he'd thought.

In fact she turned out to be a very tense, stubborn, high-strung person, and rather selfish. When things didn't go exactly as she liked she became touchy and withdrawn.

For instance, he said, Ilse got so she didn't want to go places with him. A concert was possible, or a film, especially if it was in some language she knew. But she didn't like parties. She claimed that people talked so fast she couldn't understand them, and that they didn't want to speak to her anyhow: she was only invited because she was Gregor's wife. Everyone would be happier if she didn't go, she insisted.

When Ilse stayed home she wasn't happy either, because she imagined Greg was flirting with other women at the party. I could sort of understand how she got that idea. Greg liked women and was comfortable with them. He had a way of standing close to someone attractive and lowering his voice and speaking to her with this little quiet smile. Sometimes he would raise just his left eyebrow. It wasn't deliberate; he couldn't actually move the right one, because of a bicycle accident he'd had years ago; but it was devastating.

The way he talked to women even bothered me a bit at first, though I told myself it didn't mean anything. But it made Ilse really tense and touchy. Though she must have known what a gregarious person Greg naturally was, she started trying to get him to decline invitations. And when he did persuade her to go to some party, he told me, she followed him around, holding tight to his arm. And she always wanted to leave before he did. Well, of course that wasn't much fun for either of them, so it's no wonder that after a while Greg stopped trying to persuade her to come along.

When he went out alone, he said, Ilse would always wait up for him, even though he'd asked her over and over again not to. Then while she was waiting she'd open a bottle of liqueur, Amaretto or crème de menthe or something like that, and start sipping, and by the time he came home she'd be woozy and argumentative. When Greg told her it worried him to think of her drinking alone, Ilse got hysterical. 'You have drink, at your party, why should I not have drink?' she shouted. And when Greg pointed out to her that she had finished nearly a whole bottle of Kahlúa that had been his Christmas present from his graduate students, she screamed at him and called him a tightwad, or whatever the Czech word for that is.

Finally one evening Greg came home at about one-thirty a.m. It was completely innocent, he told me: he'd been involved in a discussion about politics and forgotten the time. At first he thought Ilse had gone to sleep, but she wasn't in the bedroom and didn't answer when he called. He was worried and went all round the house looking for her. Finally he went into the kitchen and turned on the light and saw her sitting on the floor, wedged into the space between the refrigerator and the wall where the brooms and mops were kept.

Greg said he asked her what she was doing there. I could hear just how his voice would have sounded: part anxious, part irritated, part jokey. But Ilse wouldn't answer.

'So what did you do?' I said.

'Nothing.' Greg shrugged.

'Nothing?' I repeated. I didn't think he would have lost his temper, because he never did; only sometimes when he was disappointed in someone or something he'd give them this kind of cold, tight look. I expected he would have looked at Ilse like that, and then hauled her out of there and helped her upstairs.

'What could I do, darling? I knew she'd been drinking and wanted to make a scene, even though she knew how much I dislike scenes. I went upstairs and got ready for bed, and after I was almost asleep I heard her come in and fall into the other bed. Next morning she didn't apologise or say anything about what had happened, and I thought it would be kinder not to bring it up. But that was when it became clear to me that it wasn't going to work out for Ilse here.'

The next time I was alone in Greg's house I went into the kitchen and looked at the space between the fridge and the wall. It didn't seem wide enough for anyone to sit in. But when I pushed the brooms and mops and vacuum back and tried it myself I discovered that there was just barely enough room. I felt weird in there, like a kid playing hide-and-seek who's been forgotten by the other kids. All I could see was a section of avocado-green cupboard and a strip of vinyl floor in the yellowish-green swirly seasick pattern that I'd never liked too much. The cleaning-rags and the dustpan brushed against my head and neck. I wouldn't have wanted to sit there for any length of time, even if I was a kid. And I thought that anybody who did must have been in a bad way.

I think that was a mistake, trying it out, because now I had a kind of idea of how Ilse Spiegelman must have felt. But then for a while I forgot the whole thing, because Greg asked me to marry him. Up till then he had never even mentioned marriage, and neither had I. I certainly wasn't going to hint around the way he'd said his last live-in girlfriend had, or pressure him like the one before that.

That was the year there was so much excitement in the media about a survey which claimed to prove that college-educated women over thirty had just about no chance of getting married. A couple of times people said to me, Dinah, you're a statistician, aren't you worried? Well, Jesus, of course I was worried, because I was nearly twenty-nine, but I just smiled and said that everybody in my field knew that study was really badly flawed technically.

By Christmas of that year, I'd begun to sense a rising curve of possibility in the relationship; but I waited and kept my cool. Then Greg told me he'd been invited to the Rockefeller Foundation Study Center on Lake Como for a month the next summer. He said he wished I could come with him, but you weren't allowed to bring anyone but a spouse. I didn't make any suggestions. When he told me how luxurious and scenic the study centre was, I just said, 'Oh, really?' and, 'That's great.'

Three days later he brought it up again, and asked me what I'd think of our getting married before he went, because he knew I'd enjoy seeing Italy and he really didn't like the idea of leaving me behind. I didn't shriek with joy and rush into his arms, though that was what I wanted to do; I just smiled and said it sounded like a fairly good idea, as long as he didn't want us to be divorced as soon as we got back, because my poor old Ma couldn't take that.

It was the next day that I saw Ilse for the first time. I still had my apartment downtown, but I was spending a lot of time at Greg's, and sleeping over most nights. I got up early on Sunday to make sausages and waffles with maple syrup, because we'd been talking about American country breakfasts a couple of days before and he said he'd never had a good one.

It was a wet dark late-winter morning and the kitchen windows were streaked with half-frozen rain like transparent glue. When I went into the room the first thing I noticed was what looked like somebody's legs and feet in grey tights and worn black low-heel pumps sticking out between the refrigerator and the wall. I kind of screamed, but nothing came out except a sort of gurgle. Then I took a step nearer and saw a pale woman in a dark dress sitting wedged in there.

I didn't think of Ilse. If I thought anything, I thought we must have left the back door unlocked and some miserable homeless person or schizo graduate student had got in. 'Jesus Christ, what the hell!' I screeched and backed away and turned on the light.

And then I looked again and nobody was there. All I saw was Greg's black rubber galoshes, left to drip when we'd come in from a film the night before, and his long grey wool scarf hanging from a hook by the dusters. I couldn't see how my brain had assembled these variables into the figure of a woman, but the brain does funny things sometimes.

Later, after I got my breath back, I thought of Greg's story and realised that what I'd seen or imagined was Ilse Spiegelman. I didn't like that, because it meant that Greg's ex-wife was on my mind to an extent I hadn't suspected.

I didn't say anything about it. I damn sure wasn't going to tell Greg, who said sometimes that one of the things he loved most about me, besides my naturally pointed breasts, was my well-organised mind. 'You're a wonder, Dinah,' he used to tell me. 'Under those wild black curls, you're as clear-headed as any man I ever met.' Like a lot of guys his age, he believed that no matter how much education they got most women never became rational beings and their heads were essentially full of unconnected light-weight ideas, like those little white Styrofoam bubbles they pack stereo equipment in.

So I didn't say anything to anybody. What I did was, I tried to find out what Ilse had looked like. My idea was that if she was really different from the thing I thought I'd seen, it would prove I'd had a hallucination. That wouldn't be so great, but it would be better than a ghost.

Greg didn't have any photos of Ilse as far as I knew; at least I couldn't find any around the house. When I asked him what she was like he only said she was blonde and shorter than me. Then I asked if she was pretty. He looked at me and laughed out loud and said, 'Not anywhere near as pretty as you are, my lovely little cabbage.'

After that I did a sample among his friends. I didn't take it too far; I didn't want people to think I was going into some type of retrospective jealous fit. So I didn't have a significant data base, and when I averaged their statements out all I got was the profile of a medium-sized woman in her early forties with dirty-blonde hair. Some said it was wavy and others said it was straight. They all agreed that she didn't have much to say and her accent was hard to understand, but she was attractive, at least to start with. Later on, some of them said, she seemed to kind of let herself go, and towards the end she looked ill a lot of the time.

Greg's department secretary told me Ilse was slim but a little broad in the beam; but that information isn't much use if you're trying to identify somebody sitting on the floor behind a refrigerator. A couple of people said she looked 'foreign', whatever that meant; and a colleague of Greg's said she had a 'small sulky hot-looking mouth', but I had to discount that because he was always on the make.

Finally I decided that it could just possibly have been Ilse, but most likely it was my imagination. That was bad enough, because I'd never been the imaginative type, and I didn't like the idea that I was starting to see things, like one of Ma's superstitious old-lady neighbours.

The trouble was, though, I began to feel uncomfortable about Greg's kitchen. I didn't like going in there much any more; and I always made sure to switch on the overhead light first, even if it was a bright day. I had the theory that if the light was on I wouldn't think I saw Ilse Spiegelman, and in fact I didn't.

Weeks went by and my weird feeling about the kitchen should have gone away, only somehow it hung on. So one day I asked Greg casually what he thought of our moving after we married. We'd been to a cocktail party at my boss's new house on the lake. It had a big fieldstone fireplace and sliding glass doors onto a deck and a really super view. I said I'd love to live in a place like that. I think it was the first time I ever asked Greg to do anything more for me than stop at the store for a bottle of Chardonnay on his way home. Up to then he'd more or less anticipated my every wish.

Well, Greg didn't see the point of it, and from a practical view there was no point. His house was in good condition and its location was ideal: less than a mile from the University, so that on most days he could walk to his office. He said that for one thing it would be a real drag for both of us to drive to town in the kind of weather they have here from December through March. Then he reminded me how much work he'd done on his garden and grounds over the years. Next year his asparagus bed would be bearing for the first time, I wouldn't want to miss that, he said and laughed and kissed me.

So I let it pass. By that time I'd just about convinced myself that I hadn't seen anything.

Then one day in March I came in after work with two bags of groceries and set them on the counter and turned, and Holy Mother of God, there she was again, squeezed in by the refrigerator. It was nearly dark out and darker inside, but I knew it was the same woman: the hair like frayed rope, the shapeless dress and shiny grey tights and black clunky pumps, scuffed at the toes, sticking out into the room.

She didn't seem to see me. She wasn't looking in my direction anyhow, but down at the seasick-green floor, just sitting there, not moving, as if she were drunk or stunned. It was much worse than the first time. Then I was just surprised and uneasy, the way anyone would be if they found a strange woman in their kitchen, but now I was like really terrified.

I almost couldn't breathe, but somehow I stumbled back and put on the light, and when I looked round she'd disappeared again. But I was sure I'd seen someone, and I was practically sure it had been Ilse. And what was worse, I got the idea that she'd been sitting there on the floor for a long while. Or maybe she was always sitting there, only most of the time I couldn't see her.

I can tell you I was in a bad state. I figured either I'd seen a ghost, or I was losing my mind. But I didn't feel crazy, except whenever I had to go into the kitchen I panicked. The main idea I had was that I had to leave that house.

Next day at breakfast I brought up moving again, but I didn't get anywhere. Greg made all the points he'd made before, and also he mentioned the financial aspects for the first time. It turned out he had no savings to speak of and not much equity in the house. But he had an eight per cent mortgage; he couldn't possibly get that kind of rate again, he said. I was a little surprised that Greg didn't have more net worth, but it made sense when I thought about it. He liked to live well: trips to New York and to conferences all over the world, expensive food and liquor, and a new Volvo every five years.

He assumed the issue was settled, but I didn't want to let it drop. I said I was making enough money to help out and I had some savings besides; and I knew I'd be happier in a new place. Greg lowered his newspaper for a moment and glanced up at me, and for the first time I saw, just for a second, that thin cold look he gave people and things he didn't like.

But then Greg smiled slowly and folded the newspaper and put it down and came over and kissed me and said I mustn't ever worry about money. He wouldn't think of touching my little savings, he said; he had plenty for both of us.

I kissed him back, of course, and felt all warm and loved again, but at the same time just for a moment I remembered something a friend of mine at work had said when I first started going out with Greg. 'He's a really sweet guy until you cross him,' she said. 'Then, watch out.'

In a couple of days I'd more or less forgotten about that look Greg had flashed at me; but I realised I'd stuck myself with Ilse's kitchen, and my morale slid way down the chart. I didn't know what the hell to do. If I said anything to anybody they'd think I was nuts, and maybe they'd be right. Maybe I ought to just drive up to the state hospital and turn myself in. I thought of telling Ma; she believed in ghosts, and a couple of her friends had seen them; but those were always ghosts of the dead.

Then I remembered something I read in an anthropology book in college. There were sorcerers in Mexico and Central America, it said, that could project an image of themselves to anywhere they chose. The author hadn't seen it done herself, but all the locals were convinced it could happen. Well, I thought, it could be. There were some weird things in the world. Maybe Ilse Spiegelman was some kind of Czechoslovakian witch, and if she wanted to keep me from marrying Greg and moving into her house and her kitchen she might do it that way. The distance wouldn't faze her – for that kind of project two thousand miles was the same as two yards.

If I told Ma, she'd probably say I should go to a priest and ask for an exorcism. But I knew if I did that he'd give me a lot of grief for not having been to confession for three years, and living in sin with Greg. And besides, how the hell could I ask Greg to have his kitchen exorcised? I considered trying to sneak a priest into the house when Greg was at the University, but I decided it was too risky.

So I told myself okay, let's assume it was Ilse, trying to scare me off. Well, I wouldn't let her. The next time she appeared I'd make the sign of the cross and tell her to get the hell out and leave me alone. Listen, sister, I'd tell her, you had your chance with Greg, now it's my turn.

After that, instead of praying I wouldn't see Ilse, I actually tried to catch her at it. For a couple of weeks, whenever Greg went out, I set my jaw and said a Hail Mary and marched into the room. I never saw a damn thing. Then, late one evening after I'd rinsed our coffee mugs in the sink and turned out the light and was leaving the kitchen, I saw her again, sitting shadowy by the refrigerator. I wasn't expecting her, so I screamed out, 'Jesus Christ!'

Greg had gone up to bed already, and he heard me and called out, 'What's the matter, darling?' I was frightened and confused, and I called back, 'Nothing, I just cut my hand on the bread knife.' Then I switched on the light, and of course nobody was there.

I thought, oh God. That's what she wanted. She's never going to appear when I'm ready for her; she wants to surprise me, and hurt me. And now she had, because of course then I had to get out the bread knife and saw a hole in my hand to show Greg.

After that I was in a bad way. I didn't want to see Ilse when I wasn't expecting her; but I couldn't think of her the whole time. Plus I was developing a full-blown phobia about her kitchen. So

I came right out and told Greg that there were things I didn't like about his house.

He was very sweet and sympathetic. He put his arms round me and kissed one of his favourite places – the back of my neck just above the left shoulder, where I have a circle of freckles. Then he asked me to tell him what it was I didn't like and maybe it could be fixed. 'I want you to be perfectly happy here, Dinah my love,' he said.

Well, I told him there were three things. I said I'd like the downstairs bathroom repapered, because I'd never cared for goldfish, they had such stupid expressions; and I'd like a deck by the dining-room so that we could eat outdoors in the summer. 'If that's what you want, why not?' Greg said, holding me and stroking me.

Then I said I'd also like a new cabinet built in the kitchen, between the refrigerator and the wall. That was the only thing I really cared about, because I thought that if there wasn't any space there Ilse couldn't come and sit in it; and that was the only thing Greg objected to. If we put a cabinet there, he said, where would I keep my cleaning equipment? Well, I told him I'd move it out to the back entry. No, I didn't think that would be inconvenient, I said; anyhow I'd always thought a kitchen looked messy if there were old brooms and rags hanging around. I was terrified that he'd suggest building a broom cupboard, which would have been worse than nothing, but luckily it didn't occur to him.

'You want your kitchen just like your graphs, all squared away,' Greg said. 'All right, darling.' And he laughed. He liked to tease me sometimes about my passion for order.

Greg promised to have the improvements made before the wedding and he carried through. The day the new cabinet was installed I went into the kitchen the minute I got home. Just as I'd planned, it completely filled the space where Ilse had sat. There was a drawer under the counter, and a shelf under that; nobody could possibly get in there. I stooped down and looked to make sure, and then I put in a couple of baking tins and some bags of paper cups and plates.

I've done it, I thought, and I was really happy. I thought how generous and brilliant and good-looking Greg was, and how smart

I was, and how we were going to Montreal for our honeymoon and then to Europe. I'd bought a beautiful wedding dress: heavy ecru silk with a sexy low square neck and yards of lace.

Well, it got to be two weeks before the wedding. I was so high I was even starting to feel a little sorry for Ilse. I thought about how she was probably back in those two nasty little rooms again with her family. I knew what that was like, from the years I spent with my mother and sisters in the trailer camp, with cold sour air leaking through the window-frames and the kitchen faucet spitting rust and the neighbours playing the radio or screaming at each other all night. No wonder she was jealous.

Then the term was nearly over, and Greg's department was giving a reception. He called me that Friday afternoon from his office to say they were short of paper plates and could I drop some by after work? So when I got home I went into the kitchen and opened the new cabinet by the refrigerator.

It was a good thing I was alone, because I let out a real burglar-alarm screech. There was Ilse Spiegelman, just like before, only now she was shrunken down into some kind of horrible little dwarf about two and a half feet high. I didn't even try the light. I just howled and stumbled out into the hall.

It took me nearly thirty-five minutes to get up my nerve to go back into the kitchen – where of course Ilse wasn't any more, or at least I couldn't see her – and put my hand into that cabinet, maybe right through her, and take out those paper plates that Greg was waiting for.

After that I knew I was beaten. If Ilse could shrink herself like that she could appear any size, and anywhere she goddamn wanted to. Maybe she'd get into the flour bin in the pantry next, or maybe some day when I took the lid off the top of the sugar bowl she'd be in there, all scrunched up.

I was really depressed and sort of desperate. But then I thought that maybe Ilse wouldn't mind my living with Greg as long as we weren't married. After all, she hadn't even appeared until we got engaged.

So that evening I told Greg I didn't think I could go through with it. I said I was terrified of the responsibility of marriage. At first he was wonderful. He held me and kissed me and petted me and said that was perfectly natural: marriage *was* frightening. And of course, he added, I was probably apprehensive about becoming a department chairman's wife.

'Yeah, that's right,' I said, though that thought hadn't occurred to me.

He understood, Greg said. I might not think I was up to the job, but he would help me; and if anybody tried to make me feel incompetent or not worthy of him, he would give them hell.

When I kept on insisting that I didn't want to get married, Greg asked what had changed my mind. I was still afraid to tell him about Ilse; I didn't want him to think I'd gone off the deep end. So I came up with the kind of stuff you read everywhere these days about marriage being an outmoded patriarchal contract, and how the idea of owning another human being was fascist. I probably didn't make a very good presentation, because I didn't believe in what I was saying. Anyhow, Greg didn't buy it.

'You surprise me, Dinah,' he said, raising his left eyebrow. 'I've never heard you talk like this before. Who's been brainwashing you, I wonder?'

Well, I swore nobody had. I burbled on, saying I loved him so much, but I was frightened, and why couldn't we just go on the way we were? After all, I said, he'd been with other women and he hadn't wanted to marry them. That was a mistake. Greg's face changed, and he gave me that bad look again. Then he dropped his arm and sort of pushed me aside.

'What is this?' he said, laughing in an unfriendly way. 'The revenge of the bimbos?'

'Huh?' I was completely at a loss; but finally I got what he meant. There were maybe four or five women in town who had wanted to marry Greg, and some of them were still pretty hurt and angry according to rumour. He meant, was I doing it for them?

'Jesus, no,' I said. 'I don't owe those women anything. They're none of them my friends.' Then he seemed convinced and quieted down.

But I still said I didn't want to get married. Greg tried to reassure me some more, but I could see he was getting impatient. He asked if I realised that if I broke off our engagement it would embarrass him in front of everyone and make him a local joke. He'd already had to take some kidding from friends because he'd sworn so often that he was never going to marry again. And there were quite a few people on campus who weren't Greg's friends: people who envied his success and would have loved for him to mess up somehow.

I felt awful about that, and I said he could blame it all on me: he could tell everybody I was being silly and neurotic. But Greg explained that this would be almost as bad, because people would think less of him for having a relationship with someone like that.

Then he sat back and looked at me in that hard considering way, as if I was a student who'd plagiarised a paper, or some article he didn't approve of, and finally he said slowly, 'There's something else behind this, Dinah. And I can take a guess at what it is.'

What it turned out to be was, Greg thought I must have got involved with somebody else, probably some guy nearer my own age, only I was afraid to admit it. I swore there wasn't anybody. I kept saying I loved him, that he was the only person I loved, but he didn't seem to hear me any more. He pushed his face up close to mine so it filled my whole visual field and looked all distorted, like something you see in the previews of a horror film for a split second: not long enough to be sure what it is, but long enough to know it's something awful.

'All right, who is it, you bitch? Who?' he shouted, and when I kept saying 'Nobody,' he took hold of me and shook me as if I were a bottle of ketchup and he could shake out some man's name, only there wasn't any name.

When Greg let go, and I could stop trembling and crying, I told him the truth, only he didn't believe me. Instead he started going over all the other explanations he'd thought up. Gradually things got really strange and scary. Greg was cursing in this tight hard voice and saying that if I really thought I'd seen Ilse sitting in the kitchen cabinet I must be going crazy; and I was weeping. I said that if I were going crazy it would be wicked of me to marry him and ruin his life, and he said I already had.

It went on like that all weekend. We hardly slept, and finally I got so miserable and mixed-up and exhausted that I started agreeing with everything Greg said. That I had probably been brainwashed by feminists and that I was sometimes attracted to younger men;

and that I was basically irrational, deceptive, cowardly, neurotic and unconsciously envious of Greg because he was a superior person and I was nobody to speak of. The weird thing was that I didn't just agree to all this; in the state I was in by then, I'd started to believe whatever he said.

On Monday morning we were in the kitchen trying to have breakfast. I was in really bad shape; I hadn't had a bath or done anything about my hair for two days, and over my nightgown I had on an old red terry-cloth bathrobe with coffee stains. I had got to the point where I didn't care any more if I was crazy or not. I thought that if Ilse Spiegelman meant to haunt me for the rest of my life it couldn't be worse than this.

So when Greg came downstairs I told him I wanted to forget the whole thing and go ahead with the wedding. I put two pieces of Pepperidge Farm raisin toast on his plate and he looked at them. And then he looked at me and I could see that he didn't want to marry me any more, and also he didn't want to live with me.

I was right too. Later that morning Greg called my office and said that he thought it would be best if we didn't see each other or speak to each other again. So he was putting all my 'debris' out in the back entry, and would I please collect it before six p.m.?

Well, after work I went round. I could tell how upset and furious Greg still was by the way he'd pitched my belongings out the kitchen door. My lavender nightgown looked as if it had been strangled and there was raisin granola spilled everywhere; and a bottle of conditioner that he hadn't bothered to close had leaked over everything. It was a total mess. All the time I was cleaning it up I was crying and carrying on, because I still thought I was in love with Greg and that everything that had happened was my fault. And I couldn't help it, I didn't want to, but I looked through the glass of the kitchen door once more to see if Ilse was there. Maybe she would be smiling now, I thought, or even laughing. The cabinet door was hanging open, but it was empty.

I piled everything into the car and drove to my apartment; thank God the lease still had a month to run. But the place looked awful. I'd hardly been there for weeks and there was dust everywhere and the windows were grimed over with soot. I managed to unload the car and carry everything upstairs, and dumped a heap of clothes sticky with conditioner and granola into the bathtub and knelt down to turn on the water.

Then it really hit me. I felt so defeated and crazy and miserable that I slid down onto the dirty yellow vinyl and sat there in a heap between the tub and the toilet. I felt like killing myself, but I didn't have enough energy to move. I thought that maybe in a little while I would crawl across the floor and put my head in the gas oven.

Then all of a sudden I realised that I was sitting on the floor in a cramped space, just like Ilse. She'd finally reduced me to her own miserable condition.

But maybe she wasn't the only one who had done that, I thought. And for the first time I wondered if Greg had ever said the kind of things to Ilse he'd been saying to me all weekend, till she blamed herself for everything and was totally wiped out and beaten down. I remembered how his face had turned into a horror-film preview, and suddenly I felt kind of lucky to have got out of his house. I thought that even if he changed his mind now and took me back, and was as charming and affectionate as before, I would always remember this weekend and wonder if it would happen again, and I would have to sort of tiptoe round him for the rest of my life.

What if I was wrong to believe Ilse had been trying to stop me marrying Greg? I thought. What if she had been trying to warn me?

I still don't know for sure if that's right. Now that everything's changed over there, I'd really like to go to Czechoslovakia and look her up and ask her. But I don't see how I can, what with my husband and the baby.

Gregor's never married again, though he's been with a lot of different women since we separated. I wonder sometimes if any of them have seen Ilse. But maybe she hasn't had to appear, because none of his relationships seem to last very long.

IN THE SHADOW

Alison Lurie

Alison Lurie (b. 1926) is an American novelist and academic. She won the Pulitzer Prize in 1984 for her novel *Foreign Affairs*. She has published ten novels, one collection of short stories, and a non-fiction work entitled *The Language of Clothes*.

Celia Zimmern was about the last person she, or anyone else, would have expected to see a ghost. To the other women who worked at the American Embassy in London that year, she seemed almost unnaturally cool and rational. Nothing ever rattled her, or – as far as they could observe – deeply excited her.

Celia didn't even seem excited by her undoubted effect on men – which she should have been, they thought, because there was really no explanation for it. She wasn't beautiful, only rather pretty: slight, small, with a halo of crinkly dark-oak hair and oak-brown eyes with lashes so long and dense that some thought them false. Her manner wasn't flirtatious or seductive, and she always dressed quietly. Most people didn't realise that Celia's fawn wool suit was a thrift-shop Chanel, and her navy crêpe a Jean Muir; they only noticed that she wore the same clothes over and over again.

For Celia, such monotony was preferable to its alternative. If she had a failing, she knew, it was that she wanted the best or nothing. Unfortunately, the best is usually expensive, and as a result not only Celia's closet but her tiny elegant flat in Knightsbridge was almost empty. She would rather shiver all day than wear a cheap synthetic sweater, rather sit on an Afghan cushion or even her beautifully waxed parquet floor than in a plastic sling chair. Her acquisitiveness expressed itself so fastidiously that most of the time it seemed more like asceticism. But anyone who had watched Celia in a shop, stroking the surface of a beige suede skirt or lifting a perfect peach from green tissue paper, would have known otherwise.

Celia made no public show of her good taste – or of any other preference. On the job, especially, she maintained a very low profile; she took in information rather than giving it out. She'd never understood why most people strove to voluntarily repeat facts and anecdotes and opinions they already knew. Whereas by listening carefully one might hear something interesting, even something that would turn out to be useful.

Because Celia's manner was so low-key, members of the public tended to assume that she was employed at the Embassy in some low-grade clerical capacity. In fact she was a career diplomat with a responsible position in the Information Section. Her attitude at work was one of polite attention to the matter at hand; but underneath this was an almost formidable administrative intelligence and decisiveness.

Though a few of Celia's female colleagues considered her somewhat poor in spirit as well as in wardrobe, most liked and even admired her. From their point of view her only fault was that she attracted too many men, and that she continued to go out with ones in whom she had no serious interest, constantly accompanying them to restaurants, concerts, theatres, and films. She was nearly thirty, they said to each other; why couldn't she settle on one guy and give somebody else a chance? It wasn't fair. 'I don't even believe she sleeps with most of them,' one irritable young woman from the Visa Office asserted, calling Celia 'a bitch in the manger'.

Celia herself was modest and a little cynical about her social success. She knew it was mostly her gift as a listener that attracted and held men, just as it soothed irritated officials and calmed impatient journalists. Somehow, she had the ability to focus her entire attention on whomever she was with, letting them speak at length without intruding any personal opinions. 'That's very interesting,' she would say if the monologue faltered. 'Tell me more,' or 'Really! I never knew that.'

What still rather surprised her was that none of the men she knew ever caught on. They took her ready responsiveness for granted, as they would that of a superior computer system. Indeed, she sometimes privately compared herself to those computer programs that can imitate psychotherapy and even produce a transference. A similar transference usually appeared in any man Celia went out with more than once or twice: a feeling of love and trust, and the conviction that she was deeply sympathetic with all his views. So strong was this conviction that often, even when Celia declined to put out, they wanted to continue seeing her, to engross her attention for life.

Celia was aware that her acquaintances wished she would settle on one guy, and also that she was twenty-nine. Even from the point of her career, marriage would be advisable. In this connection, her mind turned most often to an economist named Dwayne Mudd. He was a large handsome young man among whose many assets were good manners, sexual energy, professional competence and a declared wish to have children. When she admitted to her friends that Dwayne was talking of marriage, they told her she could hardly do better. He was perfect, they said.

It was true, Celia admitted to herself, that Dwayne Mudd was a Rhodes Scholar, a member of a well-known midwestern political family, a former college track star, a *magna cum laude* graduate of Dartmouth, and an alumnus of Yale Law School, with what was probably a brilliant career ahead of him. Why was it, then, that when she imagined being married to him her strongest feeling was one of restless depression? Was it just his ridiculous name?

Or did it have something to do with the fact that Dwayne seemed to assume Celia was fortunate to be courted by him? When he told her that she was really very pretty, or that she would make an ideal diplomat's or politician's wife, she somehow felt he was giving himself a pep talk. He was excusing himself for not having chosen someone richer and more beautiful; above all, someone from another prominent midwestern family, because as he had once remarked, in politics it's a big advantage to have a wife with good connections.

When Celia told Dwayne that she didn't think she would ever want to marry him, he didn't seem to hear her. 'You can't mean that seriously, darling,' he said. Even though she repeated it, he insisted on treating her reluctance as feminine coquettishness. 'You'll come round,' he said, smiling. 'I can wait.'

But Celia, though she told herself that she could hardly do better, was more and more determined not to come round. Privately, she had begun to refer to Dwayne as the Wombat; not only because of his admiration for Australia, where he had spent his last posting, but because of his cropped furry hair, broad and somewhat furry hands, solid build, and stubborn tenacity.

Usually Celia kept her growing annoyance with Dwayne to herself, but occasionally it slipped out. Once, for instance, he called her office four times in a single day, mainly to say that he was thinking of her and of what he referred to as 'last night'.

'He must love you very much,' said her boss's secretary, Crystal, who was softly pretty and romantically inclined.

'Dwayne Mudd is a sentimentalist,' replied Celia. 'He probably read somewhere that women like this sort of constant nuisance and interruption.'

A few days later, a cornucopia of sugar-pink rosebuds appeared on her desk at lunchtime.

'Oh, how lovely!' Crystal exclaimed.

'Well. Maybe,' Celia said. 'What I think is, if you're going to buy flowers, you should go to a flower shop. Anything you find on those stalls outside the underground is going to be dead before you get it home.' She held the crumpled paper cone out horizontally, so that the weak stems, studded with knots of crumpled, rusting pink silk, drooped downwards.

'But it's the thought that counts, isn't it?' Crystal asked.

Celia, who disagreed, did not contradict her. 'You know what they always remind me of, flowers like these? Those shoddy cut-price umbrellas they sell in the same place, outside Bond Street station. They never open right either, and quite soon they collapse completely.'

They're kind of sweet now, though, you know.

Crystal looked at the roses in a way that caused Celia to ask, 'Would you like them?'

'Oh, yes! Thank you.' Crystal raised the paper cornucopia to her lace-trimmed blouse and buried her nose in the faint fragrance.

'I guess Dwayne still wants to marry you,' she said finally, exhaling.

'Yes.' Celia gave a little apologetic laugh. 'Of course that's impossible. I couldn't marry a man whose name was Dwayne Mudd. Imagine what it would mean – a lifetime of bad jokes.'

'You could keep your own last name. Lots of girls do that now,' Crystal suggested.

'You'd still be married to him and have to hear the jokes,' said Celia. 'Just for instance, Dwayne told me once that in elementary school he was known as "Muddy Drain".'

Crystal giggled. 'But he must believe he still has a chance,' she said. 'After all, you keep seeing him. And you still have his mother's gold watch.'

'Yes,' Celia admitted. She lifted her slim hand, admiring again an exquisite bracelet watch made in the nineteen-thirties by Cartier, with a woven gold-mesh band and a tiny oblong dial elegantly engraved with Roman numerals. 'But it's only a loan, you know. I've promised to return it the moment Dwayne finds someone else to marry.'

'He'll never find anyone as long as you go on encouraging him,' Crystal predicted.

'I don't encourage him,' Celia protested mildly.

'You must, or he wouldn't still be hanging around. He'd find another girlfriend. I think really maybe you should give back his watch and tell him you don't want to see him any more.' Crystal's voice shook slightly.

'But I do want to see Dwayne,' Celia said, smiling, not offended – indeed, Crystal had never seen her offended. 'He's quite pleasant to be with and he knows a great deal about international economics and the Common Market. I just don't want to marry him. He realises that.'

'I don't think he does,' said Crystal, who already had the difficult last name of Freeplatzer and felt she could reconcile herself to a lifetime of bad jokes quite easily if it should become Mudd. 'But I suppose he'll figure it out in time.'

Either Crystal was wrong, or Dwayne Mudd didn't have enough time. He was still stubbornly pursuing Celia when, two months later, driving home from a party in what was later determined to be a condition of .12 blood-alcohol content, he turned the wrong way up a one-way street in Belgravia and collided fatally with a heavy lorry.

Celia, in the opinion of some, didn't take this news as hard as she might have – as she should have, one of them said at lunch in the canteen.

'I don't see that,' protested Crystal loyally. 'I know Celia was really, really shocked by what happened to Dwayne.'

'Well, we all were. I'm not claiming she doesn't feel as bad as we do. But she ought to feel worse. After all, she was going out with him.'

'Yes, but she's been going out with a lot of other men too, you know. Three at least.'

Crystal's friends nodded. Oh, they knew that, they said crossly.

'I don't see how she can just go on as if nothing had happened,' one complained. 'As if she didn't really care.'

Celia *does* care, Crystal thought. She's still wearing Dwayne Mudd's mother's gold watch; doesn't that prove it?

It was true that Celia was wearing the watch. After Dwayne died she'd asked herself if perhaps she should return it – but to whom? Dwayne had no brothers or sisters; she'd have to ask someone at the Embassy who his legal heirs were, which meant appearing in the embarrassing and false public role of grieving girlfriend. Possibly Dwayne had some cousin who would want the watch, but that wasn't likely. Most people – especially people in Iowa, was the thought that crossed Celia's mind, though she quickly suppressed it as snobbish – wouldn't appreciate Dwayne's mother's watch. They'd think it old-fashioned and inconvenient; they'd much prefer the latest glittery Rolex that never had to be wound and would tell them the day of the month and the time in Hong Kong. And anyhow, wouldn't Dwayne have wanted her to have it; if he'd known – ?

A month later, as if the Fates had finally harkened to Crystal's friends, Celia abruptly removed herself from competition: not by accepting another of her current beaus, but by requesting and receiving a job transfer. What amazed everyone was her destination: a small hot West African country of no political importance.

'Of course it's a fairly responsible position: Cultural Affairs Officer,' a secretary in the department involved reported to her friends later in the canteen. 'And the salary is good, because it's a hardship post.'

'But gee, really: Goto,' Crystal exclaimed.

'I know. Nobody's ever heard of it. My boss told Celia that if she'd just hang on a while he could probably find her something much better. But Celia said she wanted to leave as soon as possible. I don't get it.'

'Maybe it's because of Dwayne Mudd,' suggested another young woman. 'Maybe she can't forget him as long as she's here in London. She might feel guilty, even.'

'I don't know,' Crystal said. 'Guilty doesn't exactly sound like her.'

All the same, she thought later, there was definitely something on Celia's mind. She had a new distracted manner, a kind of preoccupation – could she have realised that she'd been in love with Dwayne after all?

'I think I can guess why you asked for a transfer,' Crystal said when Celia took her for a farewell lunch at Wheeler's. 'It was because of Dwayne Mudd.'

Celia started as if she'd taken hold of a defective electrical appliance. 'How did you know?' she half-whispered, looking round the restaurant as if it were full of undercover agents. 'I mean, what makes you say that?' she amended, recovering her cool.

'It's – well, the way you've been sort of tense ever since he died,' Crystal said. 'I figured you might still be thinking about Dwayne and kind of, you know, imagining him everywhere in London.'

'Yes,' Celia said after a considerable pause. She lowered her fork, speared a slice of cucumber, raised it. 'Not everywhere,' she added, addressing the cucumber, 'I only see him at certain times ... Whenever I'm, you know, with somebody else.'

'You mean, in your mind's eye,' Crystal said, stirring her salad for concealed bits of shrimp.

'What?' Celia lowered the fork again.

'I mean you don't, like, really see Dwayne? Not like a spirit apparition.' Crystal leaned forward, her mouth half-open.

'Oh, no; of course not,' Celia lied. She was reminded that Crystal, though reasonably discreet, was the daughter of small-town spiritualists and had a residual fascination with their beliefs.

The truth was, though, that Celia was seeing Dwayne Mudd, or something that looked a lot like him. Mostly he appeared as a sort of wavery grey semitransparent image printed on the scene like a weak carbon copy when someone's forgotten to change the ribbon. He wasn't there all the time, only very occasionally – only, she realised after the first week, when she was alone with a man.

The first time Celia saw Dwayne she was in a taxi with a handsome, slightly stupid young merchant banker. As he bent and kissed her, she imagined or perceived something like Dwayne Mudd sitting on the jump seat. She sat up abruptly and it vanished.

It was dusk and raining, and Celia attributed the illusion to a trick of the wet half-light. But she couldn't really get into it again with the merchant banker, and when they reached her flat in Knightsbridge she checked her little gold watch, exclaimed at the lateness of the hour and didn't ask him in.

The next time Dwayne Mudd appeared was worse, because it was daylight. Celia was on a Sunday outing with an American legal expert called Mark. They were sitting in a little wood at the top of Hampstead Heath, looking out through a stand of ancient beeches at a Constable landscape of towering cumulus clouds and descending fields of grass and flowers. Celia had just had a first-rate lunch and learnt several useful things about libel law; she felt pleased, at peace.

But when Mark put his arm round her and stroked her bare shoulder the grey shadow of the Wombat wavered into view beneath the branches of a nearby tree. This time what she saw was difficult to explain as a trick of the light: it was clearly the two-dimensional image of a man; not grey now, but weakly coloured like a tinted black-and-white photograph.

'What is it?' Mark asked, following her start and fixed stare.

'I heard thunder,' Celia said, improvising. 'We'd better get back, we'll be drenched.'

When Mark, clearly much disappointed and even cross, had returned Celia to her flat and not been invited in, she poured herself a vodka and grapefruit juice and sat down to face the situation.

She refused to consider Crystal's idea that what she had seen was a 'spirit apparition' i.e. a ghost. Not only did ghosts not exist, the very idea of them was in bad taste; it went with woozy New

Age music, the fingering of greasy tarot cards and the search for people's former incarnations, who somehow always turned out to be upscale or celebrity personages.

No, there was no ghost, Celia said to herself. Rather, for some reason, she was psychologically haunted by the death of Dwayne Mudd, about which she consciously felt only a mild sadness, and also – for Dwayne had become quite a nuisance in the final month or so – a little relief.

But, Celia thought, there must be more going on subconsciously. I must believe that if I'd agreed to marry Dwayne he wouldn't be dead. Some irrational, infantile part of me must think that if I'd gone to that stuffy dinner-party with him he wouldn't have drunk too much and there wouldn't have been an accident. That's what he would probably want me to think if he were alive.

'Don't be Silly,' she told herself sharply, capitalising the adjective, which had been her nickname as a small child – perhaps on the principle of opposites, for if there was anything Celia hadn't been for a long while, it was silly. That's total nonsense about Dwayne, it's just what something neurotic in you imagines. Maybe you ought to see a shrink.

But almost as rapidly as this idea came to Celia she rejected it. She couldn't afford private therapy, she'd have to go through the Embassy medical plan. And when anyone did that it got into their medical records and stayed there. Of course no one was supposed to know what was in the records; but people often did know, because someone had to file them.

And when you came up for promotion, it usually came out. Then, even if there'd only been a minor problem, insomnia, for instance, or fear of flying, it could hurt your career. And hers wasn't a minor problem: she was having what a shrink would call delusions. Possibly she was actually coming down with a full-blown psychosis.

Celia, who up to now had always taken her mental stability for granted, began to feel depressed and even frightened. But she was a young woman of considerable courage and determination. The only thing to do, she finally decided, was to ignore her hallucinations and assume they would eventually go away.

An opportunity to test this theory appeared the following

weekend; Celia was at home, making lunch for a former lover from America, a painter named Nat. She knew, and he knew, that this lunch would probably end in bed, for old times' sake. But as she was adding fresh cream to the vichyssoise, Nat came up close behind and embraced her; and there was the greyish shape of Dwayne Mudd again, sliding about on the sunlit wall among the shadows of the hanging Swedish ivy. As Nat caressed her right breast the shape seemed to grow darker.

'No,' she said aloud.

'Sorry, love,' Nat grinned. 'Okay, I'll leave you alone while you cook.'

The shadow wavered, faded. But it reappeared after lunch as Celia stood to clear the table.

'I've missed you,' Nat said, standing also, looking directly at her.

'Yes.' They moved towards each other and then, entwined, towards the bedroom. Dwayne's image followed them from room to room, sliding over the walls and furniture.

As they sank down on the bed, Celia deliberately shut her eyes. 'You want to watch, Wombat, go ahead,' she told him silently in her mind, where of course he was located.

As if she had spoken, a voice – Dwayne Mudd's voice, though flatter now, dead-pan – in fact, dead – replied. – That's a filthy person you're with, it said. – Literally. He hasn't had a shower since Thursday.

Celia, with considerable effort, did not look round or even open her eyes. It was clear that Nat had heard nothing, for he went on kissing her enthusiastically. She cooperated, holding him close, although now his light-brown hair had an – imagined? – odour of stale turpentine.

– You like dirt and paint, look at his hands, Dwayne Mudd's voice said. – And wait till you smell how long he's been wearing those socks.

You're lying, Celia thought, but in spite of herself she glanced at Nat's hand as it lifted her grey silk Nicole Farhi jersey. There was a sour-green smudge across the knuckles and the square-cut nails were black. And when, in spite of her resolution, she raised her eyes, there was the shadow of Dwayne Mudd in the desk chair. Irrationally, because he was merely a figment of her imagination, she felt deeply embarrassed that he, fully clothed, should see her lying there naked.

The event that followed, though clearly great fun for Nat, was unsatisfactory to Celia. She concentrated on keeping her eyes shut, but she couldn't help hearing the voice.

– Well, look at that. He still doesn't wear underpants. Kind of disgusting, isn't it? Dwayne said, while Nat gasped and cried out, 'Oh, love!'

– And get a whiff of those armpits. That was why you broke up with him, wasn't it?

'Celia, my darling,' Nat murmured, subsiding, then turning to look at her. 'Are you all right?' he asked. 'I mean, is something the matter? You didn't – You usually –'

'I'm fine,' Celia assured him. 'That was lovely. But I think … Well, the thing is,' she continued, 'I'm rather involved with someone else just now.'

'Really? Oh, hell,' Nat said.

That was how it began; and it rapidly became worse. Soon, whenever Celia even shook hands with a man, the wavering image of Dwayne Mudd appeared and spoke. In life the Wombat's language had been decorous; now it was coarse.

– He's got zits on his ass.

– Notice how he stinks of stale smoke, from his lousy nicotine habit. Shit, you can smell it, you're close enough.

– How can you stand that moustache, so red and bristly, like a hog I knew in Iowa. Got a face like a goddamn hog, too, hasn't he?

– I suppose you know he's fucking the wife of the MP from that place in Surrey where he lives.

This last remark was directed at the merchant banker, whom Celia had been spending most of her time with lately – not because she liked him best but because he was the most imperceptive of her suitors and thus least apt to notice her distracted condition. But after she'd made discreet inquiries and discovered that Dwayne was right about the MP's wife, she crossed the banker off her list. Someone must have mentioned the affair and I must have remembered it subconsciously, she told herself. But she wasn't sure; she wasn't sure of anything any more.

I'm falling apart, Celia thought. I've got to get out of London before I completely crack up. No, out of England.

When she first heard of Goto, Celia had seen in her mind a comic-book panorama of jungle and swamp, crocodiles, giant snakes, political violence and malarial heat. But in fact it wasn't bad. Though she arrived in July the temperature was tolerable. The heavy rains had passed and the landscape was densely green, layered like a Henri Rousseau painting with palms and banana trees and tall grasses studded with red and magenta and white flowers. The atmosphere at the Embassy was agreeable and relaxed, and there was an Olympic-size outdoor pool embraced by blossoming shrubs.

Popti, the capital, turned out to be a seaside city of broad boulevards and red sandy alleys; of low blond and ochre and terracotta houses and shops, with here and there a shimmering high-rise hotel or bank. For years it had been a French colony; French was still the official language and there were visible survivals of French cuisine and French fashion.

There might be advantages in a place like this, Celia realised. She could practise her French and develop some regional expertise. Moreover, her professional situation was greatly improved; she had an office of her own, a secretary and the occasional use of an Embassy car and driver. She also had authority; she could cause events to happen. In just a month she'd started two film series; she was reorganising the library and negotiating with USIS in Washington for interesting speakers.

What's more, she had been assigned a four-bedroom air-conditioned villa with cook, cleaner, part-time gardener and twenty-four-hour guard service. It was not far from the Embassy and next door to the home and shop of the city's most fashionable dressmaker, Madame Miri (to some of her European clients, Madame Marie). Celia's own house was usually quiet except for the faint, almost domestic hum of the radio that would communicate instantly with the Marine guard station at the Embassy in case of emergency.

But there was always something going on in Madame's deep, leafy compound, which besides the shop contained five buildings and a large and shifting population of relatives and employees, from infants in cotton hip slings to toothless grandmothers. Celia was becoming quite friendly with Madame, who like herself was a perfectionist where dress was concerned; she had already copied a complex Issey Miyake for Celia in a remarkable black and indigo-grey local batik.

Most restful of all, Celia hadn't seen Dwayne Mudd since she arrived. That proved nothing, though, for as yet she had touched no man except to shake hands. Now that she had her life organised, she knew, it was time to test her safety – her sanity, really. Because what was the alternative? The alternative was a possibly lifelong nervous celibacy.

As a sympathetic listener, Celia had not only rapidly become popular in the European community, she had also acquired two admirers. She decided to go out with the one she liked least, an Oklahoma businessman – probably married, she guessed, though he claimed not – called Gary Mumpson. She therefore allowed Gary to take her to the most expensive French restaurant and, after dinner, to drive to the beach and park. It was pitch dark there, under a sky of intense tropical blackness speckled with stars. As Gary leant over to kiss her, rather sweatily, Celia held her breath. For a moment nothing happened; then, mixed with the sound of the heavy, treacherous surf, she seemed to discern an unmistakable voice.

– Yeah, give the creep a big hug, it said, – so you can feel that rubber tyre.

You're imagining things, Celia told herself; but her arms were already around Gary and she could not help following the Wombat's instructions.

– Anyhow, you're wasting your time, the voice seemed to say. – Not only is he married, his cock is only three inches long.

No, it was no use. 'Come on, let's drive back,' Celia said miserably, struggling upright.

'Nah, what for – oh, sure. Great idea!' Gary panted, imagining (mistakenly) that this was an invitation to Celia's apartment.

The next day was Saturday. Celia, after a sleepless night, left her house in the hope of jogging off some of her depression. The morning was cool and fresh, the street nearly empty, but as she reached the gate of the compound next door she was greeted by Madame Miri.

In the strong sunlight her landlady was an imposing figure. Her skin shone like polished mahogany and she wore a brilliant ballooning orange robe and turban printed with blue birds-of-paradise.

'What is it, *chérie*?' she inquired in her excellent French, putting a broad vermilion-nailed hand on Celia's arm.

'What?' Celia said stupidly. 'What is what?'

'You are troubled this morning.'

'No, not at all.' Celia tried to make her voice light and unconcerned.

Madame shook her head. 'I see it, in the air around you. Please, come into the shop.' She lifted a hanging curtain printed with giant golden flowers.

Blurrily, Celia followed. Madame Miri indicated that she should seat herself beside the big cutting-table heaped with fashion magazines and bolts of multicoloured cloth, and brought her a cup of scalding French coffee.

'You don't sleep well last night,' Madame Miri stated rather than inquired.

'Not very well, no,' Celia admitted.

'You have the nightmare, perhaps?'

'Well, yes, sometimes,' said Celia, thinking that the appearances of Dwayne Mudd were a kind of nightmare.

'I shall give you something.' Madame Miri rose and swept through another curtain at the dim back of the room, where she seemed to be opening drawers and unscrewing bottles, murmuring to herself in a sing-song.

I'm not going to swallow any strange medicine, Celia promised herself.

'*Voilà*.' Returning, Madame laid before Celia a small bag of reddish homespun tied with a strip of leather.

'Take this, *chérie*. You don't open it, but tonight you put it under your pillow, yes?'

'All right,' Celia promised, relieved. She knew or could guess what was in the bag: a selection of the magical and medicinal herbs and bits of bone sold at stalls in the village markets and even here in the capital. It was what people called a *gris-gris* – a protective charm.

'It's good,' Madame urged, smiling, holding out the little bag. 'Good against fear.'

Of course Madame Miri believes in spirits, she thought; almost everyone does here. The principal religion of Goto, after all, was animism: the worship of ancestors and of certain trees, rivers, and mountains. Ghosts and demons inhabited the landscape and the fields and groves often displayed, instead of a scarecrow, a bundle of leaves and powders and bones given power by spells and hung from a branch or wedged into the fork of a tree. According to local belief, it protected the crops not only against birds and animals but against thieves and evil spirits.

'Thank you,' Celia said.

When she could Celia kept her promises. She therefore put the *gris-gris* under her pillow that night and, because of it or not, slept more easily the rest of the week. Somewhat revived in spirits, she decided to risk going out with the second of her current admirers, the Marine Master Sergeant in charge of the guard at the Embassy. Jackson was an amusing young Southerner of considerable native wit who looked well in his uniform and magnificent in swim trunks. On the down side, he was four years younger than Celia, badly educated, and had terrible political convictions.

This did not surprise Celia: in her opinion, many people had peculiar views. But however much she might disagree, she made no attempt to protest or correct them. She'd always disliked argument, which in her experience never convinced anyone – only facts did that, and even then not very often. Whenever she seriously disagreed with someone she repeated a phrase her father had taught her when she was fourteen: 'You may be right.' ('It took me fifty-five years to learn to say that,' he had told her. 'Maybe it'll save you a little trouble.')

At the last moment before Jackson arrived in his red Corvette, Celia, with a superstitious impulse of which she was rather ashamed, placed Madame Miri's *gris-gris* in the bottom of her handbag. But when her date handed – or, more accurately, handled – her into the car, she thought for a moment that she saw Dwayne's image, wavering but distinct, on the whitewashed wall of the compound. It was transformed almost at once into the blowing shadows of a banyan tree, and Celia scolded herself for succumbing to nerves.

Unlike Gary, Jackson did not wait to make his move till after supper. As soon as they pulled up in front of the open-air restaurant, from which noisy, thumping local music was soaking, he turned towards Celia. 'Hey, you really look super tonight,' he said, grabbing her expertly.

Dwayne Mudd reappeared at once, sitting on the hood of the Corvette: strangely grey and semi-transparent against the sun-flooded tropical shrubbery, as if the light that shone on him was still the humid grey light of London. You better watch your step with this one, he announced.

Oh, shut up, Celia said silently. I've come all this way; I'm going to enjoy myself if I feel like it.

– He goes with whores, Dwayne continued relentlessly, pressing his grey face up against the windshield. – You should find out when he was last tested for AIDS. And check if he has a cut on his lip.

Involuntarily, Celia ran the tip of her tongue over Jackson's wide mouth. Mistaking her intention, he gasped and pulled her closer, murmuring, 'Oh, baby.'

That night, oppressed by both anxiety and frustrated desire, Celia slept worse than ever – as was immediately apparent to Madame Miri when she appeared next morning.

'But it is not yet well, *ma petite*,' she announced, after lowering herself into a chair and accepting coffee.

'No,' Celia admitted. 'I guess your charm doesn't work on Europeans.' She laughed nervously.

Madame ignored this. 'There is something heavy on your mind, is it not so?' she asked.

'No – well, yes.' Giving in, Celia told Madame Miri, gradually, everything. She'll know I'm insane now, she thought as the grotesque words fell from her mouth like the toads and snakes of the old fairy tale. She'll tell me to see a doctor.

'My poor child,' Madame said instead, when Celia fell nervously silent. 'I see how it is. This individual, he is jealous. Since he cannot have you, he wants to keep all other men away. That I have seen before, *eh oui.*' She sighed. 'And so for nothing you made this long journey.' For the first time, she used the intimate second person singular. 'Though perhaps not for nothing,' she added almost to herself.

'I thought, if I was so far from London –'

'*Chérie*, two, three thousand miles, they are like this' (she snapped her fingers) 'to a spirit. They don't figure space like we do.'

'A spirit?' Celia echoed.

'*Exactement.*' Madame Miri smiled, and Celia remembered a verse from a tribal chant that had been recited to her by the Deputy Chief of Mission.

> Those who are dead have not gone.
>
> They are in the shadow that brightens,
>
> They are in the shadow that fades,
>
> They are in the shadow that trembles.

'And how was he called in life, this *personnage*?' Madame asked.

'Dwayne Mudd,' Celia said.

Madame frowned. 'Mudd. *C'est la boue, n'est-ce pas?*'

'Yes, I suppose so,' Celia admitted.

'A bad name. Ill-omened.'

'Evidently,' Celia said. She tried an uneasy laugh, but Madame ignored the pathetic result.

'It takes a spirit to catch a spirit,' she said in a low voice, leaning across the table towards Celia as if Dwayne Mudd might be listening. 'You know perhaps some very powerful woman gone over to the other side, your mother, your grandmother *peut-être?*'

Celia shook her head. 'No, I'm sorry. They're both still alive. And my other grandmother, my father's mother – I don't know. I never liked her much and I don't think she liked me either.' She looked up at Madame Miri, who was still waiting patiently, and then down into the dark reflections of her coffee cup.

'There is someone,' she said after a pause. 'I never knew her, but I'm named after her. She was my father's stepmother.'

'*Une belle-mère, mais sympathique.*'

'Oh yes, so my father claims. He never uses the word

"wonderful" about anyone or anything, but he said once that she was a wonderful woman – I'm supposed to be like her, even though we weren't related.'

'That's well. Perhaps you have her soul.'

'Maybe,' Celia said, recalling that according to local belief ancestral spirits returned after death to inhabit their newborn descendants.

'*En tout cas*, she's without doubt watching over you, or you would not have thought of her now.' Madame Miri smiled.

'I'm not so sure about that,' Celia said. 'I mean, if she is, I guess she hasn't been watching very often, or I wouldn't be in this fix now.'

'*Pas certain, chérie*. This *belle-mère*, she was perhaps a very polite lady?'

'What?' Celia asked, feeling disorientated. Lack of sleep, she thought. 'Oh, yes. My father said she had perfect manners.'

'That explains it. She's watching over you, *oui*, but when you and some type are becoming close,' (Madame made a somewhat obscene gesture) '*elle est bien élevée*, she averts her eyes. And, *tu me l'as raconté*, that's the only time this evil spirit appears.'

'Yes,' Celia agreed. Am I really having this conversation? she thought.

'Very well, I tell you, this is what you do. Next time you see him, you call for *la belle-mère*. Not necessary to shout her name out loud, just whisper in your mind, "*Venez, venez à moi, aidez-moi*."'

'All right,' Celia promised.

For a few minutes after Madame Miri had left, she felt better. Perhaps she wasn't mad after all, only haunted. In Goto the existence of supernatural beings did not seem so impossible. Out in the country, almost every village was guarded by one or more fetish figures, which resembled large grey stone fire hydrants hung with coloured rags and garlands of flowers. They had broad faces, staring eyes and huge sexual organs, and gave off, even to a sceptic like Celia, an ominous and powerful aura.

Even here in the capital, the totemic animal of the dominant local tribe, the pigeon, was honoured by a monumental sculpture of a huge white bird, described in tourist brochures as the 'Pigeon of Peace'. Closer at hand, in a shadowy corner of Madame Miri's courtyard, squatted two household gods, smaller versions of the village fetish figures. They wore bright, constantly renewed garlands of red and orange flowers, and each day Madame's cook fed them: their open stone mouths were always smeared with dried blood and rice and fruit pulp.

But Celia's euphoria lasted only briefly. She realised that if she began to take all this seriously she would be mentally worse off than before: not only having delusions, but starting to believe in ghosts, and thinking that she could exorcise them by invoking the name of an ancestor whom she had never met and who wasn't even an ancestor. Going native, in fact, she thought. She had already heard stories about people, anthropologists mostly, who began by taking the local belief system too seriously and ended up partly or wholly off their rockers.

Some of these tales, and most of the information about Gotolese superstition, had come from a man in whom Celia was becoming seriously interested: the Deputy Chief of Mission himself, a career diplomat and former anthropologist named Charles Fenn. He was a tall, thin, very intelligent, slightly odd-looking man of about forty, with a long face, skewed eyebrows, a beaky nose, and a satirical, melancholy manner. She had liked him from the start, without ever thinking of him as a possible beau. But then, everyone at the Embassy liked Charles, from the Ambassador (a fat, elderly Texan magnate whose contributions to the Republican party had earned him this honorary post) down to the twelve-year-old Gotolese undergardener.

According to Embassy gossip, melancholy was not Charles' normal mood, but the result of events beyond his control. He was recently separated and in the process of being divorced: his ex-wife, everyone said, had been a cute and even lovable airhead, but terminally indiscreet and totally unable to adjust to West Africa. Since she left, Charles had been under the weather emotionally, while remaining unvaryingly hard-working and sympathetic to his staff. 'He really listens to you,' people often said.

'Yes, I know,' Celia always replied, feeling mildly uneasy, because this was what people often said about her.

Her unease escalated to panic at her next one-to-one meeting with Charles, after her skilled attentiveness had drawn him into describing his years as an anthropologist.

'It's a very cluttered field,' he was telling her. 'In more ways than one. You know what they say about the Navaho, that the typical family consists of a grandparent, the parents, 3.2 children, and an anthropologist. It was almost like that where I was. I realised I wasn't only going to be unnecessary and ineffectual, I was going to be superfluous.'

'Tell me more,' Celia murmured encouragingly as he paused and gazed out the window into the glossy green crown of an Embassy avocado tree.

Charles turned and looked at her. 'You always say that, don't you?' he remarked with what struck Celia as a dangerous casualness. '"Tell me more."'

'No – well, not always,' she stammered.

Charles smiled. 'Or else you say, "That's really interesting." Persuading the other person to go on talking, so you'll get to know them, and they won't know you. I recognise the technique, you see, because I do it, too.'

'I don't ...' Celia began, and swallowed the rest of the fib.

'But now I think it's your turn. *You* tell me more.' He did not take his eyes off her. They were a strange colour, she saw, between dark gold and green.

'More about what?'

'I don't care. Your childhood, your opinions, your ambitions, your dreams, whatever you like. As long as it's the truth, of course.' Charles smiled.

'I – uh.' Celia hesitated; her heart seemed to flop in her chest like a fish.

'I know. Tell me about your time in the Peace Corps, what you liked most about that.' He glanced at the wall clock. 'You have ten minutes, all right?'

'All right,' Celia said. She swallowed. 'I think it was the way the villages looked at night,' she was surprised to hear herself say. 'Especially when there was a moon ...' Why did I agree? she asked herself. Why didn't I just laugh it off and say – Not today or – I don't feel like it? I could still say that. But instead she heard her voice going on, beginning to speak of things she'd not told anyone, not because they were private or shocking, but because nobody had ever really listened, they were all just waiting their turn to talk.

It's the way he looks at me, she thought, glancing at Charles. He knows I'm here. Is that how I make people feel?

'That's very interesting,' Charles said as she paused, glancing at the clock and then back at Celia. 'Go on.'

'Well. It's because, you see, the desert isn't quiet at night. There are all the sounds in the trees and scrub outside the village, rustlings and squeaks and sighs, and you're there, you're part of it … you feel …' She looked at Charles Fenn. He was still listening; he heard her, every word. This could be important, she thought. It is important.

She thought it again after she left Charles' office, and that evening back home. She told herself that Charles was a most unusual man. That without his flighty wife he would probably go far; with Celia, even farther – if she were ever her normal self again. Otherwise she would simply screw up his career, not to mention her own, she thought wretchedly. Then she reminded herself that there was no reason to worry about this, because nothing Charles had yet done or said suggested he wanted to go anywhere with her. But for some reason that made Celia feel even more miserable.

Things were still in this condition when Charles asked Celia to accompany him and another staff member to a reception at the French Embassy. The Commercial Attaché was in the front seat with the driver; Charles and Celia in the back, and as they drove through streets illuminated by the mauve and vermilion afterglow of a tropical sunset Charles described the rank, history and personal peculiarities of the people she was about to meet.

'There's a lot of rather odd characters in the local diplomatic corps, I'm afraid,' he concluded. 'But I hope you're going to like it here all the same.' The car lurched suddenly round a corner, flinging Celia, in her gossamer-light pale mauve muslin dress, abruptly against him.

'Thanks, I think I will,' she replied distractedly, trying to catch her breath, not moving away.

'I'm very glad to hear that.' Charles also did not move; under the cover of the attaché case on his lap, he put his hand on hers.

– You're making another mistake, said the flat dead voice of

Dwayne Mudd. At first Celia could not see him; then she realised he was sitting, grey and squeezed up, between Charles and the door.

– You think he's so fucking great. He's got –'

I don't want to hear it, Celia thought desperately, feeling the steady, disturbing, desirable pressure of Charles' shoulder, arm and hand against hers.

– Athlete's foot, and –

Remembering Madame Miri, she cried out silently in her mind to the other Celia Zimmern. *Venez à moi, aidez-moi!* How stupid it sounded: like calling on herself.

Miraculously, the horrible flat voice ceased. My God, it worked, Celia thought. But the shadow of Dwayne Mudd did not vanish: it remained in the car, silently moving its greyish lips, until they reached the French Embassy.

'So, how does it go?' Madame Miri asked next morning, waylaying Celia as she went out for an early run. Narrowing her eyes in the brilliant sun, she added, 'Perhaps not completely well, yes?'

'He's still there,' Celia admitted. 'I can't hear him any more, but he's there, trying to speak, opening and shutting his mouth. Half the way to the French Embassy yesterday evening in the car, and all the way back – well, whenever I – you know. I can't bear it any more!' she cried suddenly. 'I think I'm going mad.'

'*Ah non, chérie. Come, come chez moi.* We shall consider this further.'

In a dazed condition, weakened by another night without sleep, Celia followed Madame to her shop and then, for the first time, through the curtain into the back room. It was low, dimly lit, hung with thick woven and embroidered fabrics and dominated by a kind of altar covered with an embroidered red cloth and crowded with flowers and images, including what looked like a lion with wings.

'Sit down, please.' Madame Miri indicated a low multicoloured leather pouf.

'There is something,' she said, opening her eyes after some moments of silent concentration. 'I think this spirit of mud has got some hold on you.'

'I don't know –' Celia said. 'Maybe I feel guilty –'

'Guilty, that is nothing. This is not your husband, only a stupid, jealous spirit. But I think perhaps there is some object that he has given to you, and through this he has power to come to you when he desires.'

Involuntarily, Celia glanced at her left wrist; at Dwayne's mother's gold watch. Madame Miri followed her gaze. 'So that is his?' she asked.

'Yes; well, it was his mother's.'

'So, even worse. In it, her power is joined to his. I understand well now.' She nodded several times.

'You think I shouldn't wear this watch when I go out with someone?'

'Never you should wear it,' Madame said solemnly. 'It is dangerous to you always. Give it to me; I will take care of it.'

Somewhat stunned by this development, Celia did not move.

'You must hold to persons; not to things,' said Madame Miri, putting out her hand.

Slowly, Celia unfastened the gold-mesh band and placed her Cartier watch in Madame's broad black-rimmed apricot-tinted palm, where it looked strangely small.

'But if it's so dangerous,' she said, watching what she had come to think of as her property disappear into Madame's fist. 'I mean, if you have the watch, won't he come to you?'

Madame Miri laughed. 'If he comes, let him come. He will have a large surprise, will he not?' She laughed again, more fully. 'Don't derange yourself, *ma petite*,' she said gently. 'I know how to deal with such as him, *je te le jure*.'

Five months later, Celia Zimmern and Charles Fenn were married in the garden of the American Embassy in Goto. There were well over a hundred guests; strings of coloured lanterns – ruby, sapphire, topaz, and jade-green – laced the tropical evening; fireworks were set off beside the pool. Madame Miri, who had created Celia's spectacular white tulle and lace wedding dress from a Givenchy pattern, sat at one end of the long head table, resplendent in vermilion silk brocaded in gold, with a matching fantastically folded headdress.

'A day of joy,' she said when Celia, circulating among the company, stopped beside her. 'I see that all is well with you.'

'Oh, yes.' Celia looked at Madame again. On both broad, glowing mahogany arms she wore a mass of gold bangles; among them was the gold Cartier watch. But that's mine, Celia wanted to say; then she faltered, realising that the statement was false, and that anyhow this was the wrong time and place for it; that perhaps there would never be a right time or place.

Madame Miri, unembarrassed, followed the direction of her gaze. 'That one has not appeared again to you, *n'est-ce pas?*'

'No, not since –' Celia glanced at her own slim wrist, on which there was now only a faint band of untanned skin. Out of practical necessity she had purchased a Timex from the Embassy commissary, but usually kept it in her handbag. 'Has he appeared to you?' she added, registering the emphasis in Madame's phrasing.

'*Ah oui*; I have seen him, with his little moustache,' replied Madame Miri. 'A good appearance, that fellow. But not interesting, no. *Jamais*. Not like that man of yours there, eh?' She gave an intimate laugh, bubbly with champagne, and gestured towards Charles, who was also moving among the guests.

'No,' Celia said, trying to remember if she had ever told Madame Miri that the Wombat had a small moustache. She knew she had told Charles; indeed, a month ago, without really intending to do so, she had found herself telling Charles everything about Dwayne Mudd.

His reaction, as always, was interested and sympathetic. 'I think most people see their former lovers sometimes, though not as clearly as you did. I used to see my wife; almost see her anyhow. And if you live in a place like this for a while you're not surprised by anything.'

Somehow after that Celia had at last succeeded in forgetting Dwayne Mudd. But now, dizzied by happiness and champagne, she imagined him as a fretful ghost eternally bound to Goto, a country he would probably have deplored and detested – he hated what he called 'the sticks'. She even wondered if he were present this evening, invisible and inaudible except to Madame Miri.

'Do you think Dwayne's at the party, then?' she asked, glancing round uneasily, and then back at Madame Miri. In the jewelled light of the paper lanterns Madame looked larger and more formidable than ever. What she really resembled, Celia thought, was the female of the pair of larger-than-life mahogany figures in the local museum. Heavy-limbed, heavy-lidded, they had been roughly carved a century or more ago; they were identified on their label as *Gardes des portes de l'enfer* – guardians of the gates of Hell.

'No.' Madame Miri shook her turbaned head slowly, so that her heavy earrings swayed. 'He is not here.' She was no longer laughing. 'He has gone where he should go.' She pointed down, towards the earth. But then she smiled and raised her glass. 'Do not think more of him, *chérie*,' she told Celia. 'He will not trouble you again.'

THE WATCH TRICK

Jennifer Egan

Jennifer Egan (b. 1962) is an American writer. She has published short fiction in the *New Yorker* and *Harper's*, and her journalism appears frequently in the *New York Times Magazine*. Egan's novel *A Visit from the Goon Squad* won the 2011 Pulitzer Prize and the National Book Critics Circle Award.

Sonny drove his boat straight into the middle of the lake and cut the engine. They rocked in silence, the deep, prickling hush of a Midwestern summer. The lake was flat as a rug, pushed against a wall of pale sky.

The four of them were celebrating Sonny's engagement to Billie, a girl with soft hair and a Southern accent. She kept to herself, leaning back in a chair with her legs propped on the rail. She had met Sonny the week before, at a party before her own wedding to someone else. This turn of events would have been more shocking in some lives than it was in Sonny's; he was a man who lived by his own egregiousness, who charmed, offended, and was talked about at other people's dinner parties. Stealing a bride was right up his alley.

Diana watched Sonny measure, shake, and pour martinis with the ease of a cardsharp shuffling. She was forty-two, with a worn, pretty face. Her husband, James, sat beside her, looking amused. He and Sonny had been best friends since the army. James leaned back and looked from Sonny to his bride. 'So tell us how you two happened,' he said.

Sonny just grinned, his eyes fine and vacant as crystal.

Billie swung down her legs and leaned forward, animated for the first time that day. In two sips she had finished half her martini. 'Let me tell,' she said. 'I'm dying to.'

On the night before her wedding, she explained, her father had thrown a party aboard an old steamboat. Sonny had pursued her, flirting openly whenever he found her alone, eyeing her from a distance the rest of the time. Late in the evening they were standing alone on the deck when abruptly he took off his gold Rolex, held it up in the moonlight, and threw it in the water: 'Baby, when I'm with you,' he said, 'time just stops.'

Billie narrowed her eyes as she spoke. She was very young, and strands of roller-curled hair spiraled like ribbons down her back. 'I'm like, please,' she said, 'could you possibly be more corny? But' – and here she seemed to struggle, reaching for Sonny's hand – 'it was like when you're half asleep and you hear voices, you know, from the real world, and you just think, No, I want to stay asleep and have this dream.'

She paused and tried to catch their eyes, but James and Diana were looking as far away as possible. They'd been hearing the story for years in various forms – from the Hawaiian tour guide Sonny fell in love with while gazing at the view from Kaala Peak, threatening to jump unless she agreed to come back to Chicago with him; from the astrologer who had obsessed him from the moment she divined that his mother had been killed in a small plane crash when Sonny was five. This very boat – a 34-foot Chris-Craft flybridge – he had bought twelve years before in the certainty that he would marry a professional water-skier he'd seduced the previous night. That was Sonny: music, a few drinks under his belt, the light falling a certain way, and any pretty waitress might receive a declaration of love, an impassioned lecture on their two converging fates. If she was smart, she would laugh it off and bring him his change. Not that Sonny didn't mean it – he could mean almost anything. But his attention span was short.

'So we escaped in a lifeboat,' Billie concluded. 'Daddy was mad as hell.' She grinned irrepressibly now, a young, mischievous girl whose life had taken a sudden turn for the thrilling.

'That's quite a story,' James said, with a sly look at Diana.

Sonny mixed another round of drinks. It was August, one of those hot, hot days when the sky seems to vibrate. Diana longed to strip down to her bathing suit, but her legs embarrassed her. Veins had risen to the surface in recent years. These seemed more offensive now, in the presence of Billie, who had long, gleaming legs and knees delicate as teeth.

'I hope Daddy will forgive me after Sonny and I get married,' Billie said, suddenly despondent. 'And Bobby, too, my fiancé. I've known him since the fifth grade.'

'Your ex-fiancé,' James reminded her.

'Oh yeah,' she said. 'Ex.'

James and Diana's friendship with Sonny had had its perfect moment twenty years before, in the early seventies, when Diana wore short polyester dresses and thick pale lipstick. Sonny would squire them from one Chicago nightclub to the next, and each time they went inside she felt they were expected, that the party could really begin now that they had arrived. In pictures from those days James and Sonny looked surprisingly big-eared and eager. They were typewriter salesmen for IBM, and had started a side business marketing inventions – a solar bicycle, aerosol tanning lotion – that failed one by one and left them nearly bankrupt. In the end James quit and went to law school; Sonny later cashed in on fast-food investments he'd had the prescience to make early on. But in those first days they'd been convinced success was imminent, and would wedge fat cigars between their teeth and talk about the good life. Diana pictured it coming suddenly and with violence, a shock that would leave them reeling. But like so many things, success took longer than they thought to arrive, and by the time it came, it merely seemed their due.

After a second round of drinks, Diana went down to the cabin. The sun hurt her eyes – it had been like that since she'd started researching her dissertation, 'Crisis and Catharsis in the Films of Alfred Hitchcock'. She had promised James she would cut down the hours she spent viewing, but lately she found that everything in her life – the telephone calls, the endless, hopeful pounding of their son Daniel's basketball against the garage door as he struggled to match his father, the bills and invitations – seemed like nothing but distractions from Hitchcock's tense, dreamlike world, where even the clicking of heels was significant. Diana often felt weirdly nostalgic as she watched, as if her own life had been like that once – dreamy, Technicolor – but had lost these qualities through some misstep of her own.

James came down to the cabin. He glanced up toward the deck, smiling, and shook his head. 'Nothing changes,' he said.

'Am I crazy,' Diana said, 'or is it more romantic this time?'

'You're crazy,' James said.

'I guess it's always romantic when two people fall in love,' Diana mused. 'Even if it turns out not to be real.'

'Turns out!'

'Well, never was.'

'It's been a long time since the last one,' James said, washing his hands in the sink. 'I thought maybe he was outgrowing it.'

'Oh, let's hope not!' Diana said.

James gave her an odd look, then opened the small refrigerator and peered inside it. He'd been a star basketball forward at the University of Michigan, and still had the ropey limbs and urgent, visible veins of an athlete. Lately Diana had wakened sometimes in the middle of the night to find James's eyes wide open. 'What are you thinking about?' she would ask repeatedly, nervously, though he writhed under her scrutiny. She was worried he was having an affair, or wishing he were having one.

'You know,' she said, moving near him, 'today makes me think of the old days.'

'Me, too,' James said. He was tossing things into a bowl: mayonnaise, ketchup, Tabasco, chopped celery.

Diana watched his face. 'We've changed since then,' she said. 'More than Sonny.'

'Let's hope so.' James looked up, meeting her eyes. 'How?'

'I'm not sure.'

She had noticed that she and her husband were more affectionate in public than in private nowadays, as if the presence of other people relieved some pressure between them. 'I mean, back then,' she said, 'how do you think we expected our lives to turn out?'

James picked up an egg and rolled it from one palm to the other a few times, then set it gently on the counter.

'We were kids,' he said.

Years before, while she and James were dating, Diana had once been seduced by Sonny. At the time she was twenty-three and fresh out of Smith. Sonny didn't like her. She'd been trying for weeks to win him over, but he seemed hardly to notice. She and James were staying on Lake Erie at the house Sonny had borrowed that summer, and while James made crayfish stew for dinner in the main house, Diana brought Sonny a Scotch in the cabin he used as a painting studio. He painted copies: Pollock, Motherwell, Kline, de Kooning – anything really, as long as it was abstract (he drew badly). He worked from small reproductions cut from the pages of books, and his results were uncannily good. They filled the walls of his Clark Street apartment, and first-time visitors were astonished by the daunting collection he seemed to have amassed.

Sonny surprised Diana that day by looking pleased to see her. It was raining, and while she shook the drops from her hair, Sonny shut the door behind her and lifted the drink from her hand. He sipped, then handed it back for her to share. 'I'm pretty hard on James's girlfriends,' he observed.

'I've noticed. Is that a policy?' She was nervous, and held the glass in both hands.

'I keep the boundaries clear, nobody gets the wrong idea,' he said.

It took Diana a moment to understand. 'God, it's not like anyone would,' she said. 'I mean, you're James's best friend.'

'That's why it scares me.'

He went to the window and looked outside at the rain. Diana sipped his drink, relieved it was only this he'd had against her, not something worse.

'You think I should relax about it?' he asked.

'Sonny, you have to promise.'

She crossed the room and stood beside him. She had finished the Scotch, and now she felt loopy, bold. Setting the glass at her feet, she took Sonny's hand. 'Friends?' she asked.

He nodded, then shyly put his arms around her. As they hugged, Diana teased herself, imagining what it would be like to make love to Sonny. Then he drew back, took her face in his hands, and kissed her.

Diana was as stunned as if he had slapped her. Gently she tried to pull away, but Sonny was running his palms along her back and kissing her neck as if this were all something they had agreed on. She tried to take it as a joke. 'I've heard of self-contradiction,' she said, 'but this is outrageous.' Sonny didn't pause, and as the moments passed, Diana felt drawn in by his fierce arousal, by the very fact that something so unthinkable was actually happening. The feeling was not quite desire, but something like it. It held her still while Sonny eased her onto the concrete floor, pushing a folded rag behind her head. She was crying by then, and tears ran from her eyes into both ears. She pulled Sonny to her, hooking her fingers over the thick ridges of muscle along his spine. He felt heavy and strange in her arms. His belt buckle struck the concrete – once, then again, over and over again with a thick, blunt sound. She closed her eyes at the end. When Sonny was done he stood up, slapped the dust from his hands, and picked up his paintbrush. Diana touched the floor beneath her, thinking she might have bled, though there was no reason. She ran through the rain back to the house, convinced her life would never be the same.

But nothing happened. No mention of the incident was ever made, and Sonny never again laid a hand on her except in the most benign affection. Only one thing changed: he liked her after that. It was as if she had passed some test or – and she tried not to think about this – as if she were partly his. What troubled her most was that she couldn't forget it; not Sonny himself so much as the paintbrushes soaking in their jars of cloudy water, the rolls of unstretched canvas, each detail bringing with it an ache of longing that still haunted her sometimes.

When Diana returned to the deck, Sonny and Billie were on the flybridge. 'This baby measures depth,' Sonny said, and sipped his drink. 'There's where you pump out the bilge.'

'What's a bilge?' Billie asked.

She was wearing a captain's hat, and Diana wondered if it was the same one her son, Daniel, used to wear as a little boy when they took him out on this boat. He was Danny then, and although he cringed to hear it now, Diana secretly preferred the childish name. He would sit on the tall seat, the hat nearly covering his eyes, and swing his legs while Uncle Sonny let him steer the boat. Sonny always kept one hand on the wheel; for all his recklessness, he'd been careful with Danny. 'Kid, I'm raising you for the fast lane,' he'd say.

Diana went to the stern and gazed at the lake. She was jealous of Sonny and Billie, though clearly this was absurd – they'd be lucky to last out the week. Yet in a sense it was this she envied: the fantasy, its tinge of the illicit. She stared toward shore and tried to block out Sonny's voice. A narrow strip of land was barely visible through the haze, yet it seemed, for a moment, to hold out some whispery promise – tennis courts, gin and tonics, secret, sweaty unions behind flowerbeds ... Lord, what was wrong with her?

When James came up on deck, Sonny pulled a bottle of champagne from an ice chest and popped the cork. Billie held the glasses while he poured, champagne spilling over her fingers and along the frosted stems.

'It's suicide drinking in this heat,' Sonny said with relish.

James collapsed in a chair and set the bowl of tuna salad at his feet. 'Make mine a double,' he said.

'That's a bit morbid,' Diana said, but he didn't laugh.

Sonny passed the glasses around. His white shirt was transparent with sweat, and through it Diana noticed the darkness of his chest hair, the belly rearing up under his ribcage. Today would be one more day in a long spree for Sonny, and she found this comforting. Somewhere, at least, the party never ended.

'James, baby, I toast to you,' Sonny, said, slinging an arm around James and thumping his back. He must have noticed James was down, Diana thought – Sonny was quick to notice things like that. 'You ought to be reminded every half hour you're a saint from heaven,' he declared, breathing hard.

'Should've married you, Sonny,' James said.

'Bingo,' Sonny said. 'Would've saved us both a heap of trouble.'

'Now, wait a minute,' Diana said, laughing.

Billie watched with rapt attention, her legs drawn under her chin. 'You all must've had some nice adventures, being friends so long,' she said.

'Adventures. Christ,' Sonny said, flopping onto a chair. He turned to James and Diana and all three of them laughed, helpless at how many there were.

'I wish I could've been there,' Billie said.

Sonny took her hand and swung it gently in the space between their chairs. His own hands were small and over-muscled, crowded with jeweled rings he'd smuggled in from somewhere. Billie ran her fingers over the rings.

A lazy silence fell, and they lolled back in their chairs. Diana reached for James's hand, pleased to feel his fingers relax into her own. She thought of the old days; stories they still told about parties that started calmly – like Hitchcock's movies – and then spun out of control. 'Am I imagining it,' she said, 'or was life completely different twenty years ago?'

Sonny laughed. 'Not mine.'

'Nothing changes but your body,' James said, patting Sonny's gut.

'I could have some fun in yours, that's for sure,' Sonny said.

'It's not like you're doing so badly,' Diana pointed out.

Sonny turned to her. 'I mean, what does he need it for? Parking himself in that stodgy office?'

'I work pretty hard,' James said, 'believe it or not.'

Sonny pulled another bottle from the ice chest and shot the cork into the lake. When James covered his glass, Sonny poured right over his hand until James yanked it away, shaking champagne from his fingers. Sonny filled each glass to the top, so it spilled in their laps when they tried to drink. His unflagging excess lifted Diana's spirits. She could already hear herself, weeks from now at someone's dinner party: 'We were out on Sonny's boat. His stolen bride was there, and Sonny'd been drinking for days ...'

'What will the two of you do after you're married?' she asked, unable to resist. 'What kind of lives will you have?'

James stared at her in disbelief.

'We'll give parties,' Billie said. 'Right?'

'Sure, lots of parties,' Sonny said. 'Parties every night.'

'I hope you'll invite us,' Diana said.

'Of course,' Sonny assured her. 'You'll be the guests of honor.' He waited for James to speak. 'Come on, buddy. Crash course on married life. Should we get a dog? One of those basketball hoops above the garage? Cheez Whiz and Ritz Crackers?'

Billie listened with a frown, her idea of marriage to Sonny having clearly assumed a rather different shape.

'Follow your instincts,' James said mockingly. 'You're made for marriage, Sonny. It's written all over you.'

The sarcasm caught Sonny off guard. He studied James. 'So it's that easy,' he said. 'And here I've been admiring you all these years.'

'You've kept that a secret.'

'What do you mean? I tell everyone.' Sonny refilled the glasses and shoved the bottle back inside the ice chest. 'There was a time,' he explained to Billie, 'when James and I were in business together.'

'Don't, Sonny,' James said. He hadn't touched his last drink.

'We introduced a few inventions before the world was ready for them. Then James abandoned ship.'

'The ship was sinking. I had a wife and a kid.' He, too, spoke to Billie, as if a word from her would determine, finally, who had lived the better life. She looked from one to the other, flushed from their sudden attention.

'Anyway, being a lawyer isn't so bad,' Sonny said, draining his glass and setting it on the deck. 'It's just boring as hell.'

Billie stood up and moved behind Sonny's chair. She reached her arms around his chest and rested her head on his shoulder, closing her eyes. Her long hair gathered in his lap. Sonny wound a strand around his finger. James looked away.

'What's boring as hell,' James said, 'is hearing you tell the same lies year after year.'

Sonny burst out laughing. 'Less boring than the truth,' he cried.

'What're you talking about?' Billie demanded, letting go of Sonny and turning on James.

James shook his head. Sonny continued laughing in a loud, forced way. Now Billie marched over to James and stood before him. 'How dare you insult my husband,' she declared, using a voice she must have heard somewhere and liked the sound of.

'He's not your husband yet, and I wouldn't be in such a hurry.'

Sonny let out a whoop. 'Bastard!'

'James,' Diana said.

But James was looking up at Billie, who loomed over him now, hands on her hips, her pointy elbows shaking. 'I'd marry him before you any day of the week,' she said.

'No one's asking you to marry me,' James said quietly.

They stared at each other, Billie in a stance of pure childish defiance, James with a kind of confusion, as if the anger he felt toward this young, beautiful girl were a mystery to him.

'I'd go back to my fiancé first,' Billie muttered.

'Give that some thought,' James said. 'Because if Sonny still remembers your name next month, you'll have done better than most.'

Billie hesitated, smiling uneasily. She looked unsure of what James meant at first. Then she said, 'I don't believe you. You're just jealous.'

James said nothing. He looked suddenly tired.

'And even if he used to be like that,' Billie said more loudly, 'I couldn't care less, because Sonny loves me.' She turned to Sonny. 'Right?'

But Sonny's eyes were closed, and he appeared lost in some private contemplation. Billie watched him, waiting. Finally he managed to open his eyes and look at her, squinting as if she were a piece of bright foil. 'That's right, baby,' he said. 'It's different this time.'

Billie held very still, as if waiting to experience the comfort of these words. Then she began to cry. Her shoulders curled, and she lifted her hands to her face. Diana left her chair and took the girl in her arms.

Sonny shut his eyes again. Sunlight poured over his face, and sweat glittered in the creases of his skin. He opened his eyes and looked at James. 'I slept with your wife,' he said.

Diana froze, still holding the sobbing Billie. Everything seemed to tilt, and a finger of nausea rose in her throat. 'James, it was a hundred years ago,' she said.

'I don't remember it,' Sonny said, 'but I know it happened.'

James rose slowly from his chair, and went to the edge of the boat. He gazed toward the shore. Billie had quieted down and was looking with smeary, fascinated eyes from Sonny to James.

James turned and veered toward Sonny, who rose halfway out of his chair before James hit him twice in the face, knocking him backward over the chair and into the rail. Billie screamed and clung to Diana. Sonny lay with his mouth open, blood running from his nose.

Billie and Diana went to Sonny, took his arms and tried to haul him to his feet, but he shook them off and stood up slowly. His breath stank of alcohol, not just a few drinks but a thick, rotten sweetness. Drops of red bloomed on his collar. He hovered unsteadily, pushing the hair from his eyes. 'I'm gonna kill you,' he said to James, 'I swear to God.'

'Do it,' James said.

Sonny came at James and attempted a clumsy punch, which James blocked easily. But Sonny followed almost instantly with a second, jabbing James high under his ribs, seeming to force the breath from him. Then again, in the chin, so James staggered backward.

'Stop it!' Diana screamed, and tried with Billie to come between them, but it was impossible; the men shoved them away and lunged for one another in a frenzy, pounding, grunting, as if each believed his own survival hinged purely on the other's annihilation. Blood ran from Sonny's nose over his teeth, gathering in the cracks between them. He choked and started to cough, then went at James again, slugging his ear before finally James caught him in that boxing hold Diana had seen on TV, when the fighters seem to hug each other, heads down, so neither can move.

A perfect stillness opened around them. Everyone seemed to wait. Diana noticed the whiteness of Sonny's cuffs, a scar behind James's ear from his basketball days, the slick, marmalade-colored planks at her feet. The world disappeared; the only sound was the men's breathing.

Finally James let Sonny go and waited, poised for a response. But Sonny was barely able to stand. His eyes were running – it could have been the sun or the blow to his nose. Diana had never seen him cry in all the years she had known him, and found it hard to watch. But Billie couldn't take her eyes away from Sonny. She wore a look Diana recognized, the sick, scared look of a girl whose mischief has gotten her in trouble, who suspects her life will never be the same.

Sonny went to a chair and sat down heavily. He picked up a glass and downed what was left inside it, then fumbled for the bottle. 'I can't kill you, buddy, I just realized,' he said, making an effort to smile. 'I'd be too lonely without you.'

It was not until James started the motor that the world seemed to move again. A wind blew, the boat shook, and Diana inhaled the smell of gasoline. From the deck she watched her husband swing the boat around, his knuckles on the wheel, the hollow of his spine against his shirt. She was afraid to go near him. Sonny hadn't moved from his chair. His head was thrown back, and under his nose he held a towel filled with ice Billie had brought him. One eye was already going black.

Slowly Diana inched toward James, hesitating behind him on the flybridge. He had not glanced at her once since the fight with Sonny, and she felt as if he never would again. Finally she went around in front of him and touched his cheek, which was swollen and bloody. To her surprise, James grinned. Diana studied him, not sure what this meant. 'The good old days,' he said, and shook his head. He put an arm around Diana, and they stood side by side watching Billie, who was hunched alone at the bow. As the boat thumped over the lake, she leaned forward, watching the thick folds of water peel aside. Her curls had vanished, and now her thin, straight hair whipped madly around her head. Diana had an urge to go to her, to promise Billie she would thank God one day that none of this had worked. But she doubted the girl would believe her.

More than a year passed before James and Diana saw much of Sonny again. By then Diana had earned her PhD and was teaching in the Film Studies Department at the U of I's Circle Campus. Sonny had grown even fatter, and his complexion was the color of raw oysters. The doctor issued continual warnings, but Sonny's only response had been to take up occasional smoking. Diana noticed that he flicked the cigarette constantly, so that it never had time to gather any ash.

'Remember that time I almost killed you?' he would ask James sometimes when they'd had a few drinks. 'I should've let you have it – don't know what stopped me.'

'Willpower,' James said, grinning at Diana. 'Pure self-restraint.'

'Don't kid yourself, buddy. It was pity.'

This was one story James and Diana never told at parties. Except sometimes the beginning, where Sonny made off with a bride on the eve of her own wedding. The rest they kept to themselves, hardly mentioning it, lest it take on that eerie power of old movies and faded snapshots, an allure against which the present day could only pale.

Now and then Diana still thought of Billie, who had gone back to her original fiancé and married him. Somewhere in the Deep South, Diana guessed, the girl must occasionally tell the story of her brief elopement with a madman. 'It was terrible!' she would say. 'It was something out of hell.' Yet Diana guessed that when Billie looked at the familiar trappings of her life and recalled that strange day, she was sometimes wistful.

ATLANTIC CROSSING

Jeanette Winterson

Jeanette Winterson (b. 1959) is a British writer. Her first novel, *Oranges are Not the Only Fruit,* won the 1985 Whitbread Prize for a First Novel and was adapted into a BAFTA-winning television programme. Winterson was awarded an OBE in 2006 for services to literature.

I met Gabriel Angel in 1956. The year Arthur Miller married Marilyn Monroe. I was going home. Gabriel Angel was leaving home. We were both going to the same place. We were going to London. The Millers were there too at the time.

The *Cowdenbeath* was a pre-war liner with a mahogany lining. She looked like a bath-time boat with two fat black funnels and a comfortable way of sitting in the water. She had been money and ease, the Nancy Astor generation, not the frugal fifties.

She had been requisitioned as a troop ship during the war, and now her cruising days were over, she was faded, just a ferry, when I got to her. Once a month she sailed from Southampton to St Lucia and once a month she sailed back again. One end of the bath to the other in eight days. She didn't have glamour but she had plenty of stories to tell and I've always liked that in a woman. It is what I liked about Gabriel Angel.

Journeys make me nervous, so I was up too early on the morning of my leaving, opening and shutting my trunk and bothering the porters about safe storage. The gangway up to the *Cowdenbeath* was busy with bodies run random like ants before ants. There was freight to be loaded, food to get on board, everything to be cleared before eleven o'clock embarkation.

Invisible worlds, or worlds that are supposed to be invisible interest me. I like to see the effort it takes for some people to make things go smoothly for other people. Don't misunderstand me; mostly I'm part of the invisible world myself.

*

A couple of hours after I had permanently creased my permanent press suit by sitting hunched up in a roll of rope, I saw a good-looking black woman, maybe twenty, maybe twenty-five, standing with her feet together, a little brown suitcase in her hand. She was staring at the boat as if she intended to buy it. If the sea hadn't been on one side; she would have walked right round, her head cocked like a spaniel, her eyes eager and thoughtful.

After a few moments she was joined by a much older woman with a particular dignity. The younger one said something to her, then spread out her arm towards the ship. Whatever it was, they both laughed, which did nothing for my nerves. I wanted to be reassured by the imposing vessel before me, not have it picked at like a cotton bale.

I climbed out of my rope hole, grabbed my hat, and sauntered towards them. They didn't give me a glance, but I heard the older one asking to be sent a tin of biscuits with a picture of the Queen on the lid. It is the same all over the Commonwealth; they all love the latest Queen. She's too young for me.

The steward showed me to my cabin. Mr Duncan Stewart D22. I opened my hand luggage, spread a few things on the lower bunk, and went back up on deck to watch the spectacle. I like to see the people arriving. I like to imagine their lives. It keeps me from thinking too much about my own. A man shouldn't be too introspective. It weakens him. That is the difference between Tennessee Williams and Ernest Hemingway. I'm a Hemingway man myself although I don't believe it is right to hunt lions.

Look at these two coming on deck right now; lesbians I'll bet. Both about sixty-five, shrunk into their cotton suits and wearing ancient Panamas. The stout one has a face the colour and texture of a cricket ball and the thin one looks as if she's been folded once too often.

What brogues the stout one is wearing; polished like conkers and laced too tight. Shoe lacing is a revealing and personal matter. There are criss-cross lacers; the neat brisk people who like a pattern under the surface. There are straightlacers; who pretend to be tougher than they are but when they come undone, boy, are they undone. There are the tie-tights; the ones who need to feel secure, and there are the slack-jacks, who like to leave themselves a little loose, the ones who would rather not wear shoes at all. I've met people who always use a double knot. They are liars. I'm telling you because I know.

Once the lesbians had gone by, trailing their old woman smell of heavy scent and face powder, I went back downstairs, intending to nap for an hour. I was suddenly very tired. I wanted to get my jacket off, let my feet smell, and wake up an hour later to a Scotch and Soda. In my mind I was through the sleep and tasting the drink.

I opened the door to my cabin. There was the young woman I had noticed earlier on the dock. She turned at the noise of the door and looked surprised.

'Can I help you?' she said.

'There must be some mistake' I said, 'this is my cabin.' She frowned and picked up a cabin list from the top of her little suitcase. Her voice lilted.

'D22. G Angel and D Stewart.'

'That's right. I am Duncan Stewart.'

'And I am Gabriel Angel.'

'You should be a man.'

She looked confused and examined herself in the mirror. I tried to pursue this obvious line. Obvious to me.

'Gabriel is a man's name.'

'Gabriel is an angel's name,' she said.

'Angels are men. Look at Raphael and Michael.'

'Look at Gabriel.'

I did look at her. No wings but great legs. Still I was tired and did not want to argue theology with a young woman I had never met. I thought about the bunk and the Scotch and started feeling sorry for myself. I decided to go and tackle the Purser.

'You stay here until I get back' I commanded, 'I'll straighten it out.'

I didn't straighten it out. The ship was crammed to the lifeboats. The Purser, like me, like any normal person guided by Bible basics, had assumed Gabriel was a man's name. That's why we had been yoked together. Second Class ticket holders can't be choosy. I had to explain all this to her but she didn't flinch. Either she was as innocent as she looked or she was an old hand. Some of these girls have been milking men since breast-swell. I didn't want any trouble.

'Top or bottom?' I asked, getting ready to move my stuff.

'Top' she said. 'I like heights.'

She climbed up and lay down and I eased myself below, keeping my shoes on, in case my feet smelled. I was disappointed. I had expected to share but I had hoped for some tough guy who wanted late night Scotch and a pack of cards. When you dig under the surface, past the necessities, men and women don't mix.

Her head came dipping over the side of the bunk.

'Are you asleep?'

'Yes.'

'So am I.'

There was a pause, then she asked me what I did for a living.

'I'm a business man. I do business.'

She was looking at me upside down, like a big brown bat. She was making me feel sea-sick.

'What about you?' I said, not caring.

'I'm an aviator.'

Eight days at sea. One day longer than God needed to invent the whole world, including its holiday pattern. Two days longer than he took to make her Grandmother Eve and my Grandfather Adam. This time I am not falling for the apple.

We sat up on deck today, Gabriel Angel and myself. She told me she was born in 1937, the day that Amelia Earhart had become the first woman to complete the Atlantic crossing, solo flight. Her granddaddy, as she calls him, told her it was an omen, and that's why they called her Gabriel, 'bringer of Good News', a bright flying thing.

Her granddaddy taught her to fly in the mail planes he ran between the islands. He told her she had to be smarter than life, find a way of beating gravity, and to believe in herself as angels do, their bodies bright as dragonflies, great gold wings cut across the sun.

I'm not against anyone fastening their life to an event of some significance and that way making themselves significant. God knows, we need what footholds we can find on the glass mountain of our existence. Trouble is, you climb and climb, and around middle age, you discover you have spent all the time in the same spot. You thought you were going to be somebody until you slip down into the nobody that you are. I'm telling you because I know.

She said, 'I am poor but even the poorest inherit something, their daddy's eyes, their mother's courage. I inherited the dreams.'

I leaned back. I could see in her a piece of the bright hope I once had in myself and it made me sour and angry. It made me feel sorry for her too. I wanted to take both her hands in mine, look her in the eye, and let her see that the world isn't interested in a little black girl's dreams.

She said, 'Mr Stewart, have you ever been in love?' She was leaning over the side, watching the ocean. I watched the curve of her spine, the slender tracings of her hips, beneath her dress. I wanted to touch her. I don't know why. She's too young for me.

Before I could answer, although I don't know how I would have answered, she started talking about a man with stars in his hair and arms stretched out like wings to hold her.

I moved away as soon as I could.

What is there to say about love? You could sweep up all the words and stack them in the gutter and love wouldn't be any different, wouldn't feel any different, the hurt in the heart, the headachy desire that hardly submits to language. What we can't tame we talk about. I'm talking a lot about Gabriel Angel.

If I were able to speak the truth, I'd say I had a fiancée before the War, and we're going back to 1938 now. She had a thick plait of hair that ran all the way down her back. She could wrap her hair around her as though it were a snake. I was no snake charmer.

She was a farmer's daughter, had a heart like a tractor to pull any man out of himself. Her hair was red the way the sun is red first thing in the morning. She had a look about her that took everything seriously, even the wood pile. There were plenty of men who would have traded their bodies for a split log, just to be under her hands for five minutes. I know I would. We didn't touch much. She didn't seem to want it. When we said goodnight at the bottom of her lane she let me run my index finger from her temple to her throat. Such soft hair she had on her face, invisible, but not to my hand.

If I were young again, I would have bounced up to Gabriel Angel on the dock and asked her to come with me on the later sailing. That would have been the Italian line, the real cruise ship. SS *Garibaldi* softly rocking the Mediterranean. Forget the direct Atlantic crossing, carrying workers and immigrants to a cold place they've never seen. I could have held her hand through Martinique, Las Palmas, Tenerife. I could have put my arm around her waist through the straits of Gibraltar. At Barcelona I would have bought her gem Madonnas and seed pearls. Then we would have continued by sea to Genoa and met the boat-train for England. That railway, through Italy, Switzerland and France was laid in the 1850s and was one of the first to be constructed. I'm told that Robert Browning, poet, and Mrs Elizabeth Barrett Browning, also poet, travelled along its length. I would have enjoyed that connection. I should like to run away with Gabriel Angel.

As it is, we're on this ferry boat to Southampton, the short direct brutal route, and Gabriel Angel has never been in my arms.

It turns out that the two lesbians are missionaries. Miss Bead, the one with a face like a love-note somebody crushed in his fist, tells me they have been in Trinidad for thirty years. Miss Quim, the cricket ball, has taught three generations of hockey teams. They are on their way home to buy a farmhouse together in Wales and get a dog called Rover. I realise they are happy.

I am not sleeping well. Below my cabin is dormitory accommodation, the cheapest way to travel. That's all right, what's wrong is the Barbados Banjo Band, twenty-five of them, on their way to the dancehalls of England. It isn't easy to sleep well piled on top of fifty feet, five hundred fingers and toes and forty-six eyes. Above me are the maddening curves of Gabriel Angel.

In the ship's lounge, proudly displayed, is a large map of the Atlantic threaded through with the red line of our route. Every day one of the stewards moves a gay green flag further along the red line, so that we can see where we are. Today we have reached the middle; the point of no return. Today the future is nearer than the past.

I don't have anyone to go to in England. No one will be waiting for me at Southampton or Victoria. I have a two-bedroomed terraced house in London. I have had it let for the past twelve years and I'll have to live in a boarding house until it becomes vacant again next month. I won't recognise anything familiar. I had the agents furnish it cheaply for me.

Later, my cargo will arrive and I'll start selling Caribbean crafts and trinkets and I suppose I'll go on doing that until something better comes along or until I die. Looking at my future is like looking at a rainy day through a dirty window.

'You must be excited Mr Stewart.'

'What about, Miss Angel?'

She has been reading my copy of *Wuthering Heights* by Emily Brontë and now she wishes she could live in Yorkshire. I must be careful not to lend her *Rob Roy*.

Is compassion possible between a man and a woman? When I say (as I have not said), 'I want to take care of you', do I mean 'I want you to take care of me?'

I am materially comfortable. I can provide. I could protect. I have a lot to offer a young woman in a strange place without friends or money.

'Will you marry me Miss Angel?'

It is early in the morning, not yet six o'clock. I have dressed carefully. My tie is even and my shoes are well polished and double knotted. Anyone can look at me now. Up on deck the sea chops at the boat, the waves are like grey icing, forked over. The wind is whipping my coat sleeves and making my eyes water.

Today we will dock at Southampton and I will catch the train to Victoria station and shake hands with my fellow travellers and we will wish each other well and forget each other at once. I think I'll spend tonight in a good hotel.

Last night I could not sleep, so I climbed the bunk ladder and stared at Gabriel Angel, lying peacefully under the dim yellow safety lamp. Why doesn't she want me?

The sun is rising now, but it is 93,000,000 miles away and I can't get warm. Soon Gabriel Angel will come on deck in her short sleeved blouse and carrying a pair of borrowed binoculars. She won't be cold. She has the sun inside her.

I wish the wind would drop. A man looks silly with tears in his eyes.

MY SON THE HERO

Clare Boylan

> Clare Boylan (1948–2006) was an Irish author, journalist and critic. Born in Dublin, she began her career as a journalist, winning the Journalist of the Year award in 1974 when working for the *Evening Press*. Boylan went on to concentrate on fiction, and published seven novels and three collections of short stories.

On his way home from the pub my son Ken rescued a kitten up a tree.

'Must have been a big kitten,' I said when I saw the state of his shirt. Bits of it had stuck to his chest where something had clawed through fabric and flesh.

'No,' Ken said solemnly. 'It was only small.' He made a shape with his hands about the size of a rat. His nose was cut and there were great big rusty tracks down his face.

There was something about the shirt – all bloody and chewed, like a hen left by a fox. Already I didn't like that kitten. 'If it was up a tree' – gingerly, I peeled it off and pushed it into a bucket – 'you should have left it. Cats know how to get out of trees.'

Ken scoured his head with the insides of his eyes. He had a way of considering the simplest question as if it were complex and profound, of looking back into his head for answers. 'There was a gang of kids standing round the tree. They had a dog – big, fat bastard. Cat was afraid.'

'Weren't you afraid?' I touched him and he trembled. 'They give you a hard time?'

'Yeah.' He put his hand to his bloody nose. With his fingers close to his face he gave a start and then drew back to study the purple semicircle behind the thumb, as if his hand had been caught in a gin trap. He put his two hands away carefully between his knees. 'She bit me,' he said indignantly.

'Who bit you?'

'Bloody dog.'

'Mind your language, Ken!'

To tell the truth I didn't care about the language, or the shirt. I was proud of Ken. He's not bright. People think I've wasted my life on him. Even his own father said that. Then he left us. Well, there's worse things to waste your life on. I know there's not much going on but there's courage and there's tenderness. That's worth something. You need some tenderness in the world today. Every day you read terrible things in the papers – babies murdered, old women robbed, their jaws broken and their false teeth smashed. Only the next day there was a story of some poor young girl missing. It gave me a start because it was in our own neighbourhood. I did a wash to take my mind off things, but when I went to get Ken's shirt, it was gone. 'Ken!' I said. 'Did you take that shirt from the soak?'

'N-no!' he said, and he looked as guilty as a dog.

He was watching telly, so I went upstairs and searched his room. Break your heart to go in there – trainers, size 12, and a bed full of teddies – everything in a heap on the floor. Under the mattress a stack of chocolate wrappers, and the wet shirt, seeping into a pile of magazines. It was when I looked at those magazines that my heart went through me. They were men's magazine's – not the girlie ones with women showing what they'd had for breakfast, but dirty, cruel filth. I sat there shaking as I turned the sodden pages. Then I bawled down the stain. 'Ken!'

He lumbered up and peered round the door. 'You mad at me?'

'Why would I be mad?'

'My good shirt – all torn.'

'What about these?' I held out the magazines.

He gave a sort of sneer. 'Where did you get them, Ken?' He shook his head and looked away.

'Can't say. Reg told me not to say.'

Reg Fuller? 'What have you got to do with that scum, boy?'

'I'm not a boy.' His eyes filled with tears. 'I'm a man. Reg called me a man. He said men were mad for magazines like these. He sold me them.'

I swatted him with the bundle of wet filth. 'Did you like them, son? Is that the kind of thing you like?' I was scared. To me Ken's still a child. He began to cry. I put my arms around him. 'Men don't like those magazines, pet,' I told him. 'Reg Fuller was lying. They're just dirty rubbish. Where do we put dirty rubbish?'

'In the stove,' he snivelled.

'That's right, Ken. Put them in the stove.'

Poor Ken doesn't understand much. He put the shirt in the stove along with the magazines. Wet smoke belched out and I thought I could smell blood rising over the stench of burning fabric.

He didn't go out that night, maybe because his face was scratched and bloody or it might have been that gang. We watched the news, but it was all about that poor woman appealing for information about her missing daughter. A picture of the girl was put on the screen – little blonde, face like a flower. She was last seen talking to a man with a raincoat. 'Please don't hurt Denise,' the mother kept saying, but I could tell from the way her voice squeezed on the name that she knew Denise was already dead. Ken's face mimicked the anguish of the mother. 'He knows too,' I thought. People like him often do. 'Come on, love,' I said. 'Let's go down the pub for a drink.'

Off we went, him hanging on to my arm – the odd couple. Funny to think how much we share. The instinct to protect, for one. I've passed that on to him. Then there's the other thing, never admitted, the need for sex or love, the need to connect. I've taken magazines to bed too, stupid bare-assed hunks – probably gay. We're outcasts, Ken and me. All we've got is each other. No one will have him because of the way he is and no one will have me because I've got him. Something stuck in my brain like a splinter on that walk, but it couldn't work its way out because Reg Fuller turned up with his mates and started teasing my son.

'Got a girl, have you, Ken? We saw you with a little blonde. What have you done with your girlfriend?'

'You leave him alone,' I said. Ken sank his face in his collar, puffy and bright pink. 'Have you got a girlfriend, Ken?' I said gently. He shook his head.

'Wouldn't know what to do with a girl, would you Ken?' they called after him

He shuffled on for a bit, then turned back jerkily. 'I would!'

'How would you know, Ken?'

I hurried him on. I hadn't much covered that side of life with him. Best not to stir up what's never going to crop up. 'Those magazines,' he mumbled.

'Oh, Ken, no!' I held his face. 'That's not what you do with a girl.' He didn't understand. He didn't understand anything.

Denise Carroll's body was found in a wheelie bin. Terrible things had been done to her. She was 21, an economics student, out for a drink with some friends. The thing that struck me was how she had fought to live. Bits of the man's skin and clothing were under her nails. His hair was in her fists. Extraordinary how people cling to life, even when it is most debased. Extraordinary how human evil can make an ordinary thing like a bin sinister. Ken felt it too. When I asked him to put out the bin he gave a shudder. I watched him standing in the rain, just staring at the bin. 'Where's your raincoat, Ken?' I called out. He peered down at his body as if he expected to see it there.

'Gone,' he said in surprise.

'Where?' You get exasperated, but it's no use.

'I left it somewhere.'

'Weren't you wearing it when you went to the pub the other night?' I said and suddenly I remembered what it was that had stuck in my head. He couldn't have rescued a kitten from a tree on his way home from the pub. There are no trees on that walk.

'Ken,' I said. 'Show me where the kitten was.' I grabbed his hand and dragged him back to the pub.

'It was there!' He stabbed his big blunt hand in several different directions.

'There's no tree there, Ken.' I was trying to be patient but my voice was shaking. 'You have to show me the tree.'

He looked around blankly. 'Gone,' he said with interest.

I forced him to look at me, trying to find a way past that blank expression, trying to imagine how she must have felt when she faced him. 'There was a girl, Ken, wasn't there?'

He looked vague for a minute and then he nodded.

'Why didn't you tell me about the girl?' I seized him and shook him. It was like trying to shake a bear.

'I forgot about her,' he said.

'Jesus, Ken. She must have been scared to death.'

He thought about this inside his head. He gave a sentimental smile and nodded. 'Yeah. She was really scared.'

'How could you do such a thing?'

'Because, because … ' I sometimes thought his brain must be like an old rubbish skip, where he had to throw out nearly everything before he could find anything that was useful. 'Because she wanted me to.'

That evening the police came. They said it was a routine enquiry, house to house. I had bathed Ken, scrubbed his nails, brushed his hair until it more or less sat down but I saw the way they looked at those gouge marks down his face. 'Where were you on Friday night?' they asked him. Ken peered back into his head. There was nothing I could do. There were witnesses who'd seen him – Reg Fuller, people in the pub.

'I can't remember,' he said. The thing that kept going round my head was the same phrase Denise Carroll's mother had used: 'Please don't hurt him.'

'We found a raincoat,' they said. 'We'd like you to come and take a look at it.'

Ken's face brightened. 'I lost my raincoat.'

After they'd left I gave Ken an early supper in bed – a hamburger with plenty of ketchup and four sleeping pills. I had told the police I'd bring him round the station in the morning. They were decent about that, said they'd send a car for him. Ken was quite excited about getting a ride in a cop car. When he'd eaten I sat by the side of his bed and held his hand. He's no beauty, but my heart caught on the innocent arch of his eyebrows, the mild curve of his mouth, bits of my features woven into his unfinished face. How had evil got into him? Was it evil, or just a man's desire coming through some twisted circuit, like carbon monoxide forced through a car window? Anyway, he was mine. I couldn't let them get him. I settled his pillows, slipping out the one that raised his head too high. I watched him a moment to remember how he looked asleep and then pressed the pillow over his head. I did it carefully, like pressing a cutter over pastry. It was very peaceful. Suddenly Ken's arms shot out; he reached out, wildly clawing at me. I lifted the pillow and saw the look on his face. Oh God, that face. I pressed down with all my might. Ken's strong, but the sleeping pills were against him. His arms fell. The doorbell rang. Bloody cops, back again! Of course they didn't trust me to bring him to the station. When I removed the pillow Ken looked like a squashed doll. I stood there clutching the pillow to my chest while the doorbell shrilled. As I turned to go downstairs there was a shudder from the bed and Ken regained his breathing with a mighty snore. I touched his forehead and he smiled.

At first there seemed to be no one at the door, but when I looked down there was a little girl, eight or nine. 'Is Ken there?' she said.

'Ken's in bed.' I kept my hand to my face to hide the scratches. 'So should you be.'

'I only found out tonight where he lives,' she said. 'I had to come and thank him. He got my kitten, Susie, down a tree.'

'Oh, my God,' I said.

'It was being chased by these big boys with a dog and it ran into someone's garden. They went in after it; I was terrified. Then Ken came along. He's very brave,' she, said admiringly. 'Those boys gave him a right going over. They set their dog on him.' She was about to go when she remembered the large carrier bag she was holding. 'Here's Ken's coat. He asked me to mind it when he went up the tree.'

She watched me oddly. 'Don't cry,' she said. 'Susie's all right. Oh, and she says she's very sorry. She gave Ken a terrible scraping, but we all do foolish things when we're frightened.'

THE ARTIST

Maggie Gee

Maggie Gee (b. 1948) is a British novelist who has written eleven novels and a collection of short stories. She was the first female Chair of the Royal Society of Literature, and is now one of the Vice-Presidents of the organisation. Her 2003 novel, *The White Family*, was shortlisted for the Orange Prize. She was awarded an OBE in 2012.

When Boris had only been with her a month, he came in from the garden holding a rose, a dark red complicated knot of velvet. Bowing slightly, he placed it in her fingers. 'Broke in accident,' he explained (he was repointing the brick at the back). It was her own rose he was offering her with that graceful, cavalier flourish. 'Put in water, Emma, please.'

'Beautiful, Boris,' she said, inhaling deeply, once, then again. The scent of the rose was so intense it shocked her, made her throat catch and her eyes prickle, as if life was suddenly all around her, as if she was breathing for the first time in years. Emma had hay fever, and avoided flowers. 'So beautiful, I shall write about it.' (She wrote novels, which had never been published, but she had a study, and told people she wrote.)

'I am artist,' said Boris, grinning at her with self-deprecating, dark-eyed charm. His teeth were very white, but one was chipped; he had a handsome, cherubic face. 'I am artist, you see, Emma. I am artist like you.' He jabbed his brown finger towards her, laughing. 'I make beautiful house for you.'

'Wonderful, Boris. Thank you. But really I just need the tiles laying out in squares. One black, one white, and so on.'

'Emma, I like you very much. I make you a beautiful floor, it is my present to you.' He bowed extravagantly, a knight. How old was he? Forty, fifty? 'I am artist, Emma,' he continued, showing her a piece of paper on which he had sketched an elaborate black and white design. 'You don't want one square – two square – one square – two square, black, white, same thing always. Very boring. No good!'

She took the paper from him, folded it narrowly, and slipped it back into the pocket of his jacket. 'That's just what I do want. Black, white, black, white. Like a chessboard. Simple. The tiles are in the garage. Now, I must go and work.'

Boris smiled at her forgivingly. 'Yes, you do your work, Emma, you write your books, beautiful. I like this very much, to work for an artist, like me.'

The rose was lovely, though slightly battered. She kissed it lightly before throwing it away.

'He's impossible,' she complained lazily to her husband as they lay in bed with their books, looking at Edward over her glasses, his familiar pinched profile in the cool blue room. She wanted to tell him, she wanted to tell someone, that Boris had given her a rose. 'Impossible. Edward? I'm talking to you.'

'Who is? For heaven's sake, I'm reading my book.'

'Boris,' she said.

He sat up and stared. 'Why do you keep talking about *this person*? Get a proper builder, an English one.'

'I tried, if you remember. You said the price was outrageous.'

'When you heard Boris's quote, you were very happy.'

'You found him, not me.'

'You agreed we should ask him.'

Edward couldn't deny it. He changed tack. 'You can't manage tradesmen, you never could. The cleaners never do what you tell them to.'

'The cleaners always leave. Because you won't let me pay them enough.'

'I'll talk to the fellow. I'll sort him out.'

'– No, Edward. It's fine, really.' She knew how Edward would talk to Boris, He would send him away, as he had threatened to do. Then the house would be empty every day. She liked Boris's voice, and his accent, which spoke to her of strange wide spaces somewhere far away in southeast Europe, hot stony fields, bright market-places, somewhere she would never go, she supposed, since now she so rarely went out at all. She could never tell Edward about the rose. Her memory of it wilted, faded. 'It's okay, Edward. Boris is – different.'

'What the hell does that mean?' How scornfully he spoke. Had he always spoken to her like that?

'Boris feels he's an artist. He isn't, of course. But he wants to be.' She enjoyed this thought. Poor Boris. What Emma did, he only dreamed of.

'Fraud and con man, like all the others. I want him out by the end of the week. Now could I *please* get on with my book?'

But she saw he was reading his Antiques Almanac, which surely could not have much of a plot-line. 'He lost everything, you know. In that bloody awful war. He didn't choose to come here. But now we can help him.' Saying it, Emma was suffused with love.

Edward sighed with irritation. 'He's just an illegal. That's why you're using him. Because he's cheap.' He snapped his book shut, lay down abruptly, and presented her with his navy silk back, taking off his glasses, clicking down the arms. 'A guy in the office said Afghans are cheaper. Good night, Emma.' In minutes he was snoring.

In September, when he should have been clearing out the drains, Boris had brought round his wife and daughter in a rusty, dust-covered grey saloon.

'Van break down. Very sorry.'

'Never mind, come in and get started.'

'No can do. I am in car, with wife, daughter … I can come in for cup of coffee, Emma, only.'

Boris loved her real coffee, which reminded him of home. 'Actually, I'm writing,' she protested, but he had already barrelled past her, sighing.

'What about your wife, your daughter?'

'They are well, thank you, Emma. Except only daughter –'

'I mean, you can't leave them out in the car, Boris.' It was a bore, but good manners demanded it.

'Yes, they love it.'

'Of course they don't love it. Go and ask them in.'

They trooped up the path, very straight-faced, in front of Boris, who drove them before him like sheep, looking off contemptuously to one side with a smile that seemed to say to the neighbours, 'I know, but these were all I could get.' 'Wife,' he jabbed one finger towards a thickset, grey-faced woman with hostile, uncomprehending eyes. 'Daughter,' and he put his hand on the girl's shoulder, but this time his voice was tinged with love and regret. 'Anna,' he added. 'Seventeen.' She was pretty, with her fathers white teeth and cherub nose, but her skin and lips were pale, too pale, her eyes had a slightly sunken look, and she was leaning on her mother.

'Hallo, Anna,' Emma smiled at the daughter. To the wife she tried, 'I'm sorry, I don't know your name,' but the woman's reply meant nothing to her. The words were guttural, unfamiliar.

'Will they have tea or coffee?' she asked Boris.

'No, they don't like,' said Boris, pushing them into the drawing-room, while trying to shepherd Emma back into the dining-room where the serious business of coffee would go on. 'Maybe daughter will have water.'

'Lemonade? Biscuits?'

'They don't want.'

'Water? I can hardly give them just *water*.'

Emma had broken away from Boris, doing her duty, reluctantly, and followed the two women into the drawing-room, where she found them standing together in front of the fireplace. 'Sit down,' Emma said, and they did, too promptly. 'Cake? Fruit juice? Milk? Herbal tea?'

The daughter took pity on her and explained. 'My mother speaks nothing,' she said. 'We like water, thank you, only water.'

'Water, okay then,' Emma said, reluctantly.

She got two glasses, but forgot to fill them, dreaming while Boris's coffee brewed. In the dining-room, Boris was inspecting, with what was surely self-conscious over-emphasis, the prints on the walls, frowning upwards, pursing his lips, nodding judiciously. 'Yes, very beautiful,' he said aloud, looking, not by accident, she thought, at a Lucian Freud of a naked woman. He must want her to see that he liked bare flesh. Such a terrible flirt! Though of course, she was flattered ... He made as if to notice her a few seconds later. 'Daughter is ill,' he hissed.

'Oh dear, Boris.'

'Yes, I take to the doctor. But she need clean air. Air here very dirty. She cannot breathe, Emma. London very bad. Is dust, where we live, damp also. No good.'

'Oh, has she got asthma? What a shame –'

'Asthma, yes. In my country, she hasn't got it. Now she pray every day to Virgin, but she get it very bad.'

'I am so sorry, Boris. But don't worry. I myself have atrocious hay fever. They're all allergies. Have you considered acupuncture?' She mimed little needles jabbing into her arm. 'Maybe aromatherapy?'

He shook his heavy, curly head mournfully. 'Injection? No. Too much – never mind. More coffee, please, Emma.'

Invited in, at first, on a strictly limited basis, to repoint the fireplace, then repaint the drawing-room, Boris's role slowly became a roving one, as different parts of the house demanded his attention. He would announce these impending tasks to Emma, with a mixture of sorrow and glee.

Their relationship progressed in fits and starts. Boris nearly always complimented her. She had striking blue eyes, she had always known that, but he noticed the effect of different colours that she wore, and one day told her he would like to paint her. 'First paint my house,' she said, fondly, and he looked at her with a strange regret that made her think he was a little in love. It wasn't so surprising; she was still quite pretty, and his benefactor, and a writer. But her books became a stumbling block. Boris took everything literally; she had told him she wrote books, when he first came to the house. After a few months he asked if he could see one, just to flatter her, she thought, of course, and she deflected it. But he kept on asking, becoming more pressing, and in the end she had been forced to explain: she hadn't actually published any books. He seemed unreasonably disappointed. Was there a slight dimming of his admiration?

Boris was doing the exterior paintwork when Edward put his foot down. 'When will this clown get the job finished?' he raged at his wife.

'It's been very wet.'

'It isn't now. Has he been here today?'

'His daughter's been ill this week, so he's hardly been in,' Emma said, placatingly, but Edward glared at Boris's paint-pots straggling across the patio, and his brushes in tins of cloudy white spirit, sticking up at the sky at an irritating angle.

'He's never going to darken my doors again if he doesn't get the bloody job done and this mess out of the way before Friday!' he exploded. 'I mean it, Emma. Don't think I don't. We'll get in a decent English builder at last.'

Next day Boris arrived around four, looking worried. After giving up for months, he smelled of smoke again, 'Anna is in the hospital,' he explained. 'I just come to tell you how she is, Emma.'

She didn't make him tea. 'Edward says you have to finish the job by Friday or never come back, and he means it,' she said.

'She is very bad, Emma. Tea with sugar, please.'

'No, he is *serious*,' she said. 'You have to get it done.'

But Boris suddenly clutched her fingers, with an odd little moan. 'Last night they make us stay with her in hospital. Daughter's face goes blue ...'

She pulled her hand away. 'Boris what are you going to do?' she yelled at him, feeling her power at last, losing her temper with his handsome tanned face, his white broken teeth, his thick stupid curls, his foreign problems, the swamp of his need, sucking down tea and coffee and kindness, the scruples that stopped him making love to her, his pallid, boneless daughter and grey hopeless wife, the way he'd made her husband cross with her.

He looked shocked. 'Not to shout, Emma. I am sensitive, like you. I am artist. Not to shout.' He looked as though he was going to cry.

'All right, Boris. But you must get the job done.'

He rang on the door at seven thirty next morning, half an hour earlier than ever before. Emma was bleary and vague, in a hastily donned jade silk kimono. Boris's eyes ran automatically over her body, but his mouth was a line, and his eyes were bloodshot. 'Daughter very sick last night,' he said. 'Van is no good again. And I haven't car, because wife must have it to visit hospital. Emma, you will drive me.'

'Drive you where?'

'Drive me to find men.'

'Why haven't you found them already?' she screamed at him.

Boris was frightened of this new savage woman, so different from the mild, flirtatious one he knew. 'Please, Emma. I know where we find men. But quick, drive me now, please.'

'I'm not dressed,' she said. Not that she often did get completely dressed, nowadays, for why go out? Most days Boris came in.

'Emma, put on clothes now,' he insisted. She liked him sounding masterful, and went off upstairs without protesting, returning dressed in the first thing she found in her cupboard, a smart Chanel-copy suit with gold buttons and pink braid.

He looked at her strangely as she came downstairs, but he bowed slightly, and she felt exalted. She was excited: it was an outing. She didn't listen to what he was saying.

'Slow down,' he said, in the northern suburbs. 'Here we find men, Emma.' His mobile rang and he swore and dived for it. As the traffic waited at a bottleneck, he listened intently, then shouted at the phone, finally clicking it off after an explosion of furious consonants. Emma was surprised to see tears in his eyes.

'Are you all right, Boris?' she asked him, tentative.

'Yes, Emma. Now I do work.'

'But you're crying, Boris.'

'Is only dust.'

'Oh. That's good.'

Her attention was distracted. She was driving down a long desolate road, straight, running between Victorian terraces, but there was something in front of the terraces, something that at first she mistook for trees, grey shapeless trees with aimless branches, one or two hundred metres of trees, something that struck her as strange in a city, but then she realised they were not trees. They were thickets of men, standing in clumps, mostly silent, staring at the traffic, men in rough clothes with worn brown skin, men looking furtive, men looking hungry, men with no colour beneath their tans. Dozens of them. Scores. Hundreds? Not a single woman among those thin faces. Washed out tracksuits, ill-fitting trousers. Some of their hair was white with dust. Most of them were smoking lethargically. The slogans on their chests looked tired, dated.

'What is it, Boris? What's going on?'

'Here we find men. Stop car. I do it.'

'I don't want these people!' she found herself shouting. They looked ill and strange, not exotic like Boris. Scenting interest, some had turned towards the car. They were calling out, but she couldn'tunderstand them. Then she caught some broken English: 'Only fifty!' 'Only forty!' She felt naked and stupid in her pink Chanel ribbons and terrible glittering golden buttons.

'Not to shout, Emma.' He looked very weary. 'Is okay. You leave to me.'

'They're not coming in my house. I want proper workmen.'

'Is workmen, Emma.' His phone rang again. He cursed, and threw it down on the back seat, got out of the car and left her alone.

On the pavement, Boris started talking to people. She sat inside trembling, clutching the steering-wheel. What if they suddenly rushed the car, snatched her handbag, raped her, mugged her? The phone rang again, urgent, painful. After thirteen rings she picked it up. A woman's voice shouted in an unknown language. 'I don't understand,' Emma whispered. The woman's cries became more desperate. 'I don't understand. Speak English, please,' Emma said. 'You're in England now. Please speak English.'

She felt better as she said it, briefly, in this unfamiliar place, that had no rules; she stood up for something she thought she believed in, but then the phone went silent, dead, and she laid it on the seat, and felt worse than ever. It must have been his wife. She spoke no English.

Boris came back with three hangdog giants. They got into the back without speaking a word. There was a smell of metal, and old cigarette smoke. They would make her car smell of men – for Edward was not, in that sense, a man.

'I think your wife phoned,' she said to Boris.

He shrugged. He would not look at her. 'Drive home please Emma. We finish the painting.'

The cloud had cleared by the time they got back, and the sun drilled through, fiercely hot. That long dark road with its unhealthy armies had left her with a spreading weight of terror. Boris had come to her on false pretences; he had let her imagine him framed by blue mountains, aromatic meadows, sturdy flocks, but now she saw he just came from this, a sour sad place where no one was happy.

They worked all day, the three strangers and Boris. She heard him shout at them from time to time. She went out twice, nervously, to see what they were doing, and offer tea, but Boris refused, waving one hand in dismissal, going on painting with the other one. She felt unsettled, sitting bowed in her study, trying to invent a love story, safe in her room in the cool pleasant house but uneasily aware of the four male bodies crawling all over it, obsessed, intent, locked to her hot surfaces, sweating, grunting.

The men stayed till seven, and then filed in, burnt red by the sun, hair splashed with white, lips grey-coated, refusing to look her in the eyes. They seemed barely human. She went out and inspected. The job was finished. Boris spoke to the others, who looked only at him, as if Emma herself hardly existed.

She needed Boris to smile at her, 'Would you like a drink, Boris?' she pleaded. 'You must be thirsty after all that work. While I put the money in an envelope.'

'No thank you, Emma. Men wait outside.'

'Oh, they'll be all right. They'll be perfectly happy.'

'No thank you, Emma. I go now, please.'

When Edward arrived, they had just disappeared. He was itching for a fight: the train was hellish, boiling. 'Did he bloody well turn up?' he shouted in the hallway.

'Go out and have a look,' said her voice from the study.

Five minutes later, Edward came back in and appeared at her door, actually smiling. 'At long last,' he said. 'Doesn't look too bad. And he's finally cleared all his paint pots away. The whole bloody lot. Why are you crying?'

In November, some tiles blew off the roof, and Edward instructed her to telephone Boris. She had missed him, sharply, day by day. When she tried his number, it was unobtainable. She rang it repeatedly, swearing and weeping.

Next day she got dressed as soon as Edward was gone and drove to the suburbs, remembering. Boris's sweet dark eyes, the slight roughness of his jaw. He had opened doors for her. Surely he liked her. He gave her a rose. He ... admired her.

The forest of men was there, as before. She kept nearly stopping, was afraid, drove on, and finally drew up beside a young, slight man. He had a thin clever face, and black eyes like Boris's. Perhaps he came from the same country. She thought his mouth was quite appealing.

At twelve o'clock she called him in for coffee. 'Thirsty on the roof,' she said, kindly, with elaborate mime to help things along.

'I understand you,' he said. 'It's okay. Nearly everything, I understand. In my own country, I learned good English. I am a student. I *was* a student –' (Yes, she thought, they are all students. The minicab drivers all claimed to be students.) '... sixteenth and seventeenth century history ... I am here because of the war.' He started to talk about invasions, displacements. Oh dear, she thought, he may be a bore.

'Where are you from?' she cut in. He told her.

'My last man came from there,' she said. She felt a rush of hope and pleasure. She told him the name. 'Perhaps you know him. Very hard workers, your countrymen.'

His face had changed. It was charged with interest. 'But Boris is a great man,' he said.

'Excellent worker,' she agreed.

'Is a great artist,' he said.

She laughed. It was charming, how they all praised each other. Every single one was a genius.

'No, really,' he said. 'He is an artist. We think he is a genius.'

'Yes, Boris liked to think he was an artist. That's why we got on. I am artistic, too.'

'In my country, Boris is a very great artist. Abroad you don't know him, but in my country ... But now I think he says he will do no more painting.'

She wasn't sure she had understood him. For a moment she'd thought he meant actual art. 'Yes, he's stopped working for me, since the summer,' she said. 'That's why we need a new man, really.'

She went to the kitchen to fetch some biscuits. He carried on talking in the rich, empty room. 'Boris says he will do no more painting. Is a great loss for my country. He says life is over, since his daughter died. His beautiful daughter died, in August.'

The packet wouldn't open; she was wrenching it, noisily, crashing bourbon biscuits on to bone china, but she managed to pick out the single word 'daughter', and remembered Boris's wife, her misery, the apples she ate, her grey distance. The wife and daughter had spoiled it all. 'Are you married?' she called back through from the kitchen.

He shook his head. 'Life is too hard to marry,' he said. 'Life is beautiful, but life is short.'

'I see you are sensitive,' she said, 'like me. I am an artist, you know. I write. There will be other jobs for you,' she said, smiling.

KENNY

Colette Paul

Colette Paul is a Scottish author. She has published one book of short stories, *Whoever You Choose to Love*, which was shortlisted for the Glenfiddich Spirit of Scotland Writer's Award. She won the Royal Society of Authors Tom-Gallon Trust Award in 2005.

Kenny told her last week that sometimes he forgot they weren't living together any more. Sometimes, he said, he would turn to say something to her, or switch off the telly and reach for her. It would take him a few moments to realize she wasn't there.

'Our home used to be my sanctuary,' he said. 'Not any more.'

He looked at her face for a response, and June looked away. She concentrated on a patch of wallpaper above the radiator, cream with tiny gold Chinese symbols spread along it. They were probably Chinese for Peace or Love or something. The wallpaper was torn away at one edge, and underneath someone had drawn a willy, resplendent with pubic hair.

'June,' he said, 'd'you hear me?'

'I hear you.'

He sighed and turned away. He wasn't in the habit of being serious or articulating his feelings, and it embarrassed him.

'I don't care what's wrong with you,' he said, 'you'll do for me, June.'

It seemed to June that there'd been a kind of profound silence inside her, for the past few weeks now, and she didn't know if she wanted, or even if she was able, to break it. She supposed she was depressed. She had thought, in a vague, unfocused way, that moving away might help, but nothing had changed. She was still the same.

This morning she wakes early. She lies still, looking out of the window, the sky heaped blue upon blue. A car horn beeps outside and then it's quiet except for the clock ticking. The clock ticking seems to deepen the silence. Mornings are the worst time for her. She tried to describe it to Kenny once, how what she felt, just after waking, was like grief. It was like being overcome with grief, although she didn't know what for.

'I don't understand,' he'd said. 'I don't know what you're talking about.'

'It's like being neither dead nor alive,' she said another time, and Kenny took that as an insult and reminded her of all she had to be happy about.

She gets up and walks to the kitchen, drinks a glass of water, then another one. Things used to be different; she can still remember when things were different. Remembers Kenny, up at six in the morning getting ready for work while she drifted in and out of sleep. The noise of the bathroom taps running, Kenny spitting out toothpaste and washing his face. He's very thorough when it comes to his oral hygiene, hates people with bad breath and embarrassed by the state of his own teeth. He told her once that he used to try not to smile because of them. June was surprised; she hadn't imagined he felt self-conscious about a single aspect of himself.

'They're the only charmless thing about me,' he'd said, nibbling her shoulder, 'so I can't be doing that badly.'

And then, still naked, coming into the bedroom, by the mirror, combing his hair. Him coming over to her, his face, smelling of soap, on her neck, saying, 'Aren't I a handsome devil?' and her laughing. Telling him he looked alarming, telling him to let her sleep.

'Come on, Boo, refresh me,' he'd say, and he'd make her sit up and talk to him.

He called her Boo because when they first met she was too shy to speak to him. He was staying in the hotel she was working in, doing some building work on the west wing extension. One night there'd been a party in the hotel bar and Kenny had come over and spoken to her. He asked her why she never said hello to him, and June said she did say hello to him. She'd blushed and Kenny had said he'd been watching her and he'd decided that she wouldn't say boo to a goose.

They got to know each other over that one summer. On her

nights off Kenny took her to expensive restaurants, the funfair on the other side of Ayr pier, to the ten-pin bowling and the cinema. He was earning a lot from the hotel job and was angry if she tried to pay for anything. It violated his sense of what it was to be a man. Also, he liked to spend money, and liked other people knowing he spent money. One night, walking along the beach in the rain, he asked her how much she thought his socks cost.

'Have a look,' he said and lifted up his trouser leg. 'How much?'

June said she didn't know, two pairs for a fiver? Kenny roared with laughter. He said they were Armani, fifteen pounds a pop. She'd been horrified.

'Aren't you ashamed,' she said, 'of spending that kind of money on socks?'

'Ashamed? Why should I be ashamed? I left school a dunderhead with one standard grade, and now I'm wearing Armani socks. Why should I be ashamed?' He put his arm around her and said, 'I'm still a dunderhead right enough, but we all have our crosses to bear.'

Kenny liked to turn everything into a party. He knew how to tell a story, gleefully, how to make his digressions more interesting than his original story. He dealt efficiently with interruptions, knowing when it was best to hand the floor over to someone else, and when to dismiss them. And though he never laughed at his own jokes, there was always this feeling that he was deliberately reining himself in, that he wouldn't be able to stop laughing if he started. Kenny was funny. Instinctively he understood the comic value of certain words, words that other people knew but never used. He made everyone sound ridiculous, but lovably so. Regularly, at the end of the night, June would be sitting, quiet, surrounded by a bunch of people she barely knew. Kenny would be holding court, getting higher and higher, making everyone laugh. At two or three or four in the morning, in that dismal Royale Hotel bar, Kenny'd leap up and fetch the night watchman, Mr Henry, to their table. June was frightened of Mr Henry. He seemed ancient, his face lean and ferocious, dark brown and creviced from the sun. He'd once accused June of stealing a fibreglass maid that stood at the door of the hotel.

'Right, what is it?' Mr Henry would say. Kenny would point at June and shout that they couldn't shut her up. She hadn't taken her medication, he'd shout, she was a troublemaker, and they wanted her thrown out. Everyone would scream with laughter, and Mr Henry would be furious, telling Kenny he'd no time for his tomfoolery.

'But you're laughing inside,' Kenny would say, slinging his arm over Mr Henry's shoulder.

After breakfast she cleaned the rooms on the top floor where Kenny and his workmates were staying. He would take his break at eleven and meet her up there. They would sit on the edge of the hard bed eating the complimentary shortcake and watching *Colombo*. They didn't talk much when they were alone. One morning he said he thought they should take their clothes off.

'You can keep your hat on,' he said.

'Thank goodness for that,' said June.

'If you think I'm the kind of guy who would put a girl's modesty in jeopardy,' said Kenny, 'then think again.'

Light came through the cheap blue curtains, the bed sheets hadn't been changed yet, and June could feel the grit which Kenny trailed with him from work press into her back. Afterwards he put his arm behind her neck and kissed her face.

'I didn't know you'd never, you know, done the deed,' he said.

'Well, I didn't tell you.'

'Was it okay? I didn't hurt you?'

'It was okay. I wanted to.'

They lay in silence, and after a while June said, 'You look sad.'

Sometimes she thought she could sense a sort of sadness from him. It was his eyes, she'd decided. They were pale, luminous blue, dark-lashed, and sometimes, seeing him by the door, or alone in repose, they had a dignified, sober melancholy about them.

'I am sad,' said Kenny, 'I've just missed the *Colombo* double bill.'

'Seriously,' she said, laughing. 'Aren't you ever sad?'

Kenny scrunched up his face meditatively and said, 'Do you remember when Jamie died in *EastEnders*? On Christmas fucking Eve, when Sonia was waiting for him, when he'd just bought her an engagement ring? He was all happy and excited and then that bastard Martin Fowler had to run him over. There was a definite lump in my throat that night.'

She laughed, and Kenny kissed her cheek and said, 'Why would I ever be sad? Not one bad thing's ever happened to me in my whole life.'

June said, 'It must be terrible to have a happy childhood. It doesn't prepare you for all the crap to come. I'm glad,' she said, 'that I'd such a bad one.'

'How was it so bad?'

'You tell me about yours first.'

Kenny shrugged and said there was nothing to tell. It was just happy.

'Tell me one thing you remember,' she said, 'anything at all.'

Kenny paused and then smiled. 'There was this one time in primary school,' he said. 'We had to draw pictures of Britain during the war. So I drew a wee boy with a banana skin in his hand and a big smile and one of those bubbles coming out his mouth saying YUM. And then the teacher comes round to look at all our drawings, and everyone else's drawn unhappy people and rubbly buildings and stuff. So she comes to mine and looks at it and says, "What's that?" and points to the banana skin. And I say, "A banana skin," and she goes, "But there weren't any bananas during the war," and I say, "That's why the boy's so happy. 'Cause he's found a banana." There,' Kenny said, 'will that do?'

'Yes,' she said, laughing, 'that'll do.'

June goes into the bedroom to wake Billy. He's lying with his eyes open and starts smiling when she bends down to him. He's got blue eyes and dark hair, like Kenny, and also Kenny's sunny disposition. He looks around as if he's willing the world to delight him. When he was first born, June was scared of holding him. What if she tripped, what if she dropped him? He was as breakable, as miraculous, as an eggshell, while around her the world of things had taken on a frightening solidity – the world of uncovered sockets, matches, stairs, and cookers. If you were vigilant you could guard against the danger of things, although not against cot death, measles, whooping cough. She read handbooks, memorized symptoms;

Kenny got annoyed and said she was morbid. She read a story in a magazine about a woman who'd mistakenly put her baby in the microwave when she was in a psychotic trance.

'That's enough, June,' Kenny had said when she told him about it. 'If you want to scare yourself, read a horror book.'

Sometimes, watching Kenny sling Billy over his shoulder, she was envious of how easily everything came to him. He didn't think about the precariousness of life, it didn't terrify him the way it terrified her. His love for Billy, and for her too, is unsparing, without anxiety. This is the way, she thinks, that he will love whoever he chooses to love.

She dresses Billy and feeds him porridge in the kitchen. He's getting bigger and more substantial every day – Billy Bunting, Kenny calls him – his skin soft, and fine as icing sugar, tender rolls of fat under his chin, over his knees and wrists. She lifts up his legs and kisses his feet. One day, she realizes, she won't be able to do this any more, and a terrible feeling of loss comes over her. It's not an unwelcome feeling; she's glad to feel anything. There've been days recently when she thinks that someone could drive a nail through her arm and she wouldn't even blink. She lifts Billy from his highchair and carries him round the kitchen. There's a mouldy cauliflower in the fridge, and hardly anything else. She finished the milk this morning, and there's no washing powder left. She takes out the cauliflower and puts it down on the counter, staring at it, wondering what to do next. The more she stares at the cauliflower, the more unrecognizable it becomes, the more incomprehensible. When Billy starts to wriggle, she shakes herself and throws it in the bin.

The dishes need washing, clothes need washing, she needs to buy food. If she'd bothered to get the phone connected, she could ring Kenny and ask him to bring some stuff over tonight when he picks up Billy. She could go to the shops herself, but the thought fills her with dread and she pushes it out of her mind.

She's been living here two months now. It was the first flat the council offered her, and the man who showed her round asked her if she was sure she didn't want to wait for something better to come up. No, she said, it was fine. She didn't care where she lived as long as it was away from where she'd been. She would have gone anywhere. So she found herself here. In a high-rise, nine storeys above the ground. There's a lift, but it's usually broken, and she doesn't like it anyway. It's claustrophobic and airless, full of the breath and germs of everyone who's been inside it. The stairs are just as bad, dark, smelling of urine. If you tripped and fell down the stairs you would die, and when June is on the stairs she thinks about this, and starts forgetting how to walk at all. One day last week she'd stopped on the eighth landing, Billy in her arms, too frightened to go any further.

She turns on *Sesame Street* and sits Billy on her knee. They play a game where June pretends to disappear, dropping her face behind her hand and counting one, two, three. Billy looks at her with his big serious eyes, laughing hysterically when she pops her face up over her hands. She blows raspberries onto his stomach, and then gets out his books to read. He can't talk yet, although she and Kenny used to try to decipher his gurgles, re-forming and shaping them into English. They were confident that he was going to be a genius. The book she's reading him today is about a little girl walking down a street, naming all the objects she passes. June points to the pictures and reads out the words underneath – mummy, tree, cherry, dog – until she can no longer make sense of what she's saying, pure meaningless sounds coming out of her mouth. Billy touches her lips with his fingers; he knows he's losing her. Soon he gets sleepy, and she puts him back in his cot for a nap.

She worries that she's becoming a capricious mother. Some days she'll play with Billy for hours and hours, desperately using her energy to think up new games for him. It's Billy who eventually crawls away to play by himself. Other days she can hardly be bothered to talk to him. This upsets her because, above all, she wants to be a good mum. She doesn't want Billy to go through what she went through. The days when her mother would lie in bed, tears falling silently down her face. Once June wiped her cheeks and her mother had looked up at her blankly, as if she didn't recognize her. Her Aunt Helen used to come over to clean the house and make dinner, wash her school uniform. She told June one night that her mother was ill, but that it didn't mean she didn't love her. The same night, getting out of bed for a glass of water, June overheard them talking in the kitchen.

'You have options, Elizabeth,' she heard Helen say. 'I know you don't think so, but you do.'

Her mother didn't reply.

'June could come and live with me,' said her aunt.

'I couldn't do that,' said her mum.

'You could go into hospital, get some proper medical help. See a psychiatrist.'

'I couldn't do that.'

Her aunt went on and on, until at last June heard her say, 'You don't want to die. No one wants to die.'

When her mother didn't respond, June froze. It felt as if the whole world had suddenly been stilled.

'There,' said Helen, 'that's lots of options. Let's go through them again.'

And June had stood in the hall in her nightdress, her heart thumping, listening to them haggle over her mother's life.

She goes back into the kitchen, at a loss what to do first. She starts running water for the dishes although when the basin's full she turns off the tap and looks out of the window instead. She can see the Fancy Café, where she went once for a cup of tea, the waitresses cooing over Billy; and Corinne's Hair, and Rajou's with an iron grille over the cash desk. On the other side of the road is Pollokmews train station, looking surprisingly quaint and rural amidst all the graffiti and junk and concrete ugliness of the rest of the area. At first she thought it'd be good living somewhere where everything was so close together. It'd be easier, she'd thought, to manage herself here. But it's not turned out that way: she's spent more time looking out of the window than she's spent outside. The things she sees from the window have taken on a nebulous, impalpable quality, as if they exist in a film or a dream. She finds herself concentrating on one thing at a time – a woman's hands moving, her feet, her face – unable to merge the features together to make a whole living person.

Today she looks towards the train station, watches a bald man lurch like a sleepwalker down the platform. He's got a plastic Somerfield bag round his arm; it swings as it blows in the wind. She turns to look at the clock and when she looks back, he's falling backwards over the edge of the platform. It happens in a second, the movement as neat and final as a domino toppling over. She presses her face to the window but can only see the empty platform. It takes her a few seconds to move, running to Billy's cot, pulling him up, Billy crying. Running to the door, her hands sweating, sweat all over her. Billy screaming in her arms. She's not even out of the front door when she hears the train coming. Running back to the window, she sees it gather speed and roar past the station. Then everything's exactly the same again. The sky arches on.

Inside the flat June screams, and the noise mixes with Billy wailing and a Tina Turner song someone's playing at top volume in the flat below.

When Kenny arrives she's sitting with Billy on her lap. He asks what's happened, the door was standing open. He stops and looks at her.

'What's wrong?' he says, coming close and directing her face towards him. 'What's happened?'

'I can't talk just now,' she says.

He asks if it has anything to do with Billy, and she shakes her head. He sits beside her, taking Billy from her arms.

'I think I'll stay,' he says.

When Billy goes back off to sleep, Kenny makes them a coffee. The room gets darker and darker but neither of them switches on the light.

'June,' he says.

She hears it faintly, as if it's coming over great distances to reach her.

'June.'

He kneels down in front of her, and puts his head on her lap, his arms tight around her legs.

'I'm sorry,' he says.

'Please,' she says, putting her hand on his head. 'Shh.'

REACH

Rachel Seiffert

Rachel Seiffert (b. 1971) is a British novelist and short story writer. Her first novel, *The Dark Room*, was shortlisted for the 2001 Man Booker Prize, and won the LA Times Prize for First Fiction. Her collection of short stories, *Field Study*, received an award from International PEN in 2004 and her novel, *Afterwards*, was longlisted for the 2007 Orange Prize.

Wednesday, and Kim's mother goes up to the school for parents' evening.

– She's doing badly, then.

– Well, no, not exactly. She can read and write. Quite well for a seven year old, as it happens.

Her daughter's class teacher pushes Kim's report around on the desk with her fingertips and Alice waits for her to pull the words together.

– She's just not an easy child to reach, Mrs Bell.

—

Home is the end house of the terrace above the seafront. From her bedroom window, Kim can see over the rooftops to the old pier and, beyond it, the last curve of sand before the headland. Seagulls hover on thermals, suspended, and Kim watches them at the window, swaying, waiting. From here she will see her mother when she comes home from the school.

In the door and then chopping, no sitting down between and no hello either. But this is not unusual. Kim's description of her mother in one of her schoolbooks: she always cooks with her coat on.

Kim waits after her mother has passed along the path beneath her windowsill to the back door and the kitchen. Face still pressed to the wall, and so still hidden from the street below, Kim listens a while to the pot and pan noises, then goes downstairs to find Alice. Early evening, getting dark, her mother is working by the blue light of the grill-flame, chops spitting underneath. Kim stands in the doorway a minute or so, but Alice does not turn. An evening like any other: potato peelings on the counter, mother's back at the sink. Kim wonders briefly if she got the day right, if Alice has been to the parents' evening after all, but decides against mentioning it. Joins her brother in the sitting room instead, watches TV with Joseph until dinner.

If she's staying, Alice will take her coat off and eat with her children. Tonight, she has a cup of tea and makes sure the washing-up is underway before she heads off out to work again. A reminder of bedtimes and a brisk kiss each on her way to the door. This too is normal, so Kim breathes a little easier, dries the plates slowly that Joseph washes fast. Watches the familiar sight of her mother's back receding down the garden path. She can close her eyes and see Alice making her way down the hill to the seafront. Keys gripped in her right hand, left holding her collar together against the wind.

Kim's eyes are sore tonight, scratchy, her lids heavy. She keeps them closed, keeps her mind's eye on her mother a little longer. Imagines the sea flat behind Alice as she opens the salon door, surface skimmed into ripples by the wind. She knows her mother chose the shop for its view across the beach, along the seafront. Has heard her telling the customers, watched her polish the wide glass window clean of rain and salt. Alice plays no music in her salon, she does not talk much. There is calm when she cuts and sets hair. In the summer with the door open and the sea air. In the winter with the hum of the dryers and the wide window misted against the dark afternoons.

Kim opens her eyes again at the kitchen window, her mother long gone, brother back in front of the television. She dries her hands on the damp tea towel, flicks the last crumbs of dinner off the kitchen table. Kim tries to rest her forehead on the cool surface, but can't; her neck stiff, resisting, caught somehow by her shoulders. The days before the parents' evening have been edgy, and she can't relax now, not sure what to do with all the worry.

—

When Alice is asked about her business, she says she makes a decent living for her family. Margins are tight with debts like hers, but she has no gaps in her appointment book to speak of, few concerns to raise with her accountant.

When Alice thinks about her daughter, as she does this evening, she sees her pale eyes and paler hair, the solid flesh of her face with its closed, impassive expression. Stubby thumbs sucked white and soft and drawn into tight, damp fists.

Alice has long fingers and strong nails; neat ovals without cuticles. She does them last thing before she leaves the salon, after the work is done. Alone with her thoughts and files. Rubbing the cream in, hand over hand over hand.

She didn't argue with what the teacher said this afternoon. *Not an easy child*. Alice has heard those words before now: from different sources, in different disguises, so many times she has come to expect them. Would never say so, but she agrees.

With Joseph it was simple: love arrived with him. Fury when the midwife carried him away from her across the delivery room to be washed and weighed. Kim was early. Only a few weeks after Frank had gone. Gas and air, and Alice kept telling the midwife she wasn't ready for the baby, but she came anyway. No tears and not much pain either. And then it took Alice years to get used to her: her rare smiles, her uncooperative arms and legs.

Alice hears the pigeons shuffling in the eaves above the doorway as she locks up. The soft, quivering noise they make in their throats. The water behind her is calm, just a slight breeze coming in across the sands. Breaking up the surface a little, touching her cheek as she turns the key in the lock and up the street towards home.

—

Thursday and Kim is ill.

She vomits once at school. A pile of sawdust and a smell in the corridor. Again when she gets home. Joseph heats the dinner Alice has left in the fridge for them, and when Kim throws up a third time, he phones the shop.

– Can you come home now, Mum?
– Run her a bath and put her to bed, love. Please. I'll not be late. Make sure she drinks something.

Joseph does as he is told, and his sister is silent, compliant. When Alice comes home it is dark and Kim is running a fever: dry heat and then sudden sweats which glue her pale hair to her forehead.

Friday morning, Kim can't stand up to walk to the toilet, and so when she needs to throw up again, her mother finds her crawling out into the bright hall.

– No school for you, then.

An unwieldy dead weight with limbs, Alice carries her daughter to the bathroom.

—

Cold black tea. Chalky taste of the aspirin mashed into jam and eaten with a teaspoon. Alice is home for fifteen minutes at lunchtime, keeps her coat on. Stands her daughter naked by the radiator, washes her down with a flannel and hot water in a red plastic bowl. Kneeling next to her clammy body, its awkward joints and dimples, soft belly. Kim's eyes are half-closed and she sways as Alice works. Hot cloth on face and neck, round ears, down spine, between toes and fingers. Skin turning cool where the flannel has been.

Kim lies in new pyjamas when Alice leaves for work again. Under new sheets and tucked blankets, curtains drawn against the day. The slats of the bunk above her shift and birds' eyes peep from the mattress. Beaks and wings. Kim calls for her mum, but she's gone now, back down the road. The hairspray smell of Alice left with her, and Kim is alone with the birds again. They fly out from between the slats, grey wings beating the hot air against her cheeks.

—

Alice always hoped it would come. Read about it in the leaflets she got from the midwives and the library. You will not always bond with your baby immediately, but this is normal and no cause for worry.

Kim arrived and Alice had two to care for. Frank gone and only one of her didn't seem nearly enough. Joseph was four then and she would pick him up from nursery school early. To feel his hand holding her skirt as they walked home along the seafront, to have his arms fold around her neck when she lifted him up.

Alice tried holding Kim after her evening bottle, after Joseph was asleep and they could have some quiet time together, like it said in the leaflets. But it was hard and sometimes it frightened her: sitting with her baby and still feeling so little.

—

Red-brown spots gather in the afternoon. On the soles of Kim's feet, behind her ears, inside her eyelids. Joseph sees them when the doctor shines his torch in his sister's dark bedroom. He pulls the girl's eyelids down with his thumbs.

– I'll need to use your telephone. Call an ambulance and your mother.

Joseph tells Kim later that they drove away with the siren on, but Kim remembers silence inside the ambulance. Looking at her mother and then following Alice's gaze to the trees and lamp-posts passing. The strip of world visible through the slit of clear window above the milk-glass in the doors.

—

Alice Bell's girl had meningitis and nearly died.

The customers in the salon ask concerned questions, and Alice gets a call from the health visitor, too. The woman has a good look at the clean hall, the tidy kitchen Alice leads her to. The grass in the garden is long, falls this way and that, but Alice is sure that everything else is in good order. Thinks she recognises the health visitor, too; that she has maybe cut her hair before.

Alice gets more leaflets from her. Is told about the tumbler test: roll a glass against the rash, she says. Alice thanks the woman, but thinks it's not really any good to her, this information. It's happened now, over, Kim will be home again soon.

The house is quiet after the health visitor leaves. Small. Alice sweeps her leaflets off the kitchen table, dumps them in the bin on the front on her way back to the salon.

—

Kim has scars. A tiny, round wound in the small of her back, where they tapped the fluid from her spine. And one on the back of her hand from the drip: skin and vein still slightly raised, puncture-mark already healing, fading with the black-turning-yellow bruise. She has fine, white scratch-lines on the soles of her feet, too, but these are more memory than reality. Pin-tip traces to check for sensation, pricks in the tops of her toes that drew blood-drops, which later become blood-spots on the hospital sheets.

The real scar is at her throat. Tracheotomy. Kim can't say the word, but this is where her fingers go at night in her hospital bed, and when she wakes. To feel the way the skin is pulled over, small folds overlapping and grown together. Like melted plastic, the beaker which fell in on itself when Joseph left it on the stove. At first the hairy ends of the stitches are there too. Six black bristles for Kim's fingertips to brush against under the dressing, to investigate in the bathroom mirror when no one else is there to be looking. One hand on the wheely drip, the other pushing herself up on the sink, closer to the long, clean mirror and the grey-pink pucker of skin in her reflection.

—

Kim is back at home now, back at school. Weeks have passed already, but Alice still sees the first days in the hospital with her daughter. The pictures come at her from nowhere. When she is doing the books, while she is cutting, shopping, walking, on her way home.

From her bedroom window, Kim watches her mother in the dusk light, coming up the road. She walks with her coat unbuttoned and sometimes she stops, head down, hands deep in her pockets. Stays like that for a minute or two on the pavement before walking on.

The nurses held Kim's body curled and still and Alice watched. Daughter's spine turned towards her, small feet pulled up below her bum. Brown iodine swirled on to her skin, and then her toes splayed as the needle went in: five separate soft pads on each foot, reaching.

They had a bed free for Alice in a room down the hall, but she stayed in the chair by her daughter's bed and didn't sleep much. Awake when Kim's temperature rose again and she swallowed her tongue. The doctors drew the curtain round the bed and the fitting girl while they worked. So Alice couldn't see what they were doing any longer but still she didn't move. Stayed put, listening, while they made the hole for the tube in her daughter's neck, and took her temperature down with wet sheets around her legs. No one asked Alice to leave and she sat in the chair, shoes off, coat on, pulled tight around her chest.

—

Kim has headaches, too.

Joseph watches while his sister ties the belt round her head. One of Granddad's old ones. Big buckle, cracked leather, round her forehead, over her temples. He pulls it tight for her and then she lies down, head under the blankets, nose showing. Brows pulled into a frown by the belt, jaw clenching, neck held taut against the pain.

Kim's drinks have to be warm because her teeth feel everything, and she is clumsy. Legs bruised from falls and corners, clothes stained colourful by spills. Kim has no sense of edges these days; where a glass can be placed safely, where her body can pass without damage. She creates noise and mess and the mumbling speech that the doctor said should improve quickly takes weeks to go away.

—

The school calls Alice in again. No parents' everting this time: a meeting with Kim's class teacher and headmistress, attendance register open on the desk between them.

– When does Kim leave the house, Mrs Bell?
– Quarter to nine. With her brother.
– Every morning?

Alice nods, doesn't tell them that she leaves the house at eight twenty to open the salon. Thinks they are doubtless capable of working that one out. She reminds them.

– My daughter has been very ill.
– Yes.

They are writing things down and Alice is remembering again. That Kim couldn't stop herself looking at her tracheotomy wound. That the peeled ends of the dressing curled up off her neck, giving her away, gathering dust like magnets, tacky traces on her skin turning black. Alice visited her at visiting time, whispered: it'll get infected. She smiled when she said it. Didn't want to tell her daughter off, just to tell her. Let her know that she had noticed. That she understood it, her curiosity.

Kim looked at her. Skin under her eyes flushing. Hands moving up
to cover the dressing. Alice didn't know what that meant: whether
her daughter was surprised or pleased or angry.

– Kim is what we call On Report now, Mrs Bell.
– She could have died.
– Yes.

They blink at her across the desk. Sympathetic, insistent.

– I'm afraid her attendance record has to improve.

—

Kim finds different places to spend her days. Sometimes the coast
path over the headland where the wind cuts into her legs. Sometimes
the burnt stubble of the fields inland, where she flies her kites made
out of plastic bags. Most days it is the beach, though, where she
lies down under the old pier. On her back on the cracking shingle,
waves at her feet, sea wall behind her. Sodden wood, salt, seaweed
and litter.

Above her, she can see the gulls' flapping battles through the gappy
planks of the old walkway. Lies still, watching the starlings fly their
swooping arcs around the splintered columns and rails. Cloud and
wind over the water. Storm of black beak and wing reeling above
her head.

—

Alice shuts the salon early and is home before her children. Joseph
acts as though it is normal for his mother to open the door for him;
Kim steps into the hallway, clutching her school bag as if it were
proof of something, tell-tale damp of the day in her clothes and
hair. Joseph slips upstairs to his bedroom, Kim stays silent, eyes on
the wallpaper white Alice asks her where she has been, and why.
She watches Kim's face for a reaction but cannot read anything
from her daughter's expression.

– Whatever. You'll be leaving the house with me from now on.
– No.

Later Alice goes over the scene again. In bed, light out, eyes open. Feels something closing down, tight around her ribs. Remembers the screaming battles they had when Kim was three, four, five. Doesn't want to repeat those years again. Her daughter smelled of sea and air this afternoon, it filled the corridor. Alice didn't know what to do, what to say, so she said nothing. An almost eight-year-old stranger standing in front of her. Mouth open, breath passing audibly over her small, wet teeth.

—

Kim doesn't know it, but the school keeps close tabs on her. Her teachers know she comes for registration and then dodges out of the gate behind the playing fields. They don't confront her; instead they call her mother and then Alice hangs up the phone in the back room of the salon, behind the closed curtain, under the noise of the dryers, and cries.

Alice doesn't know it, but some mornings her daughter comes down to the front. The smell leads her there: hot air, warm skin and hair, shampoo. She doesn't go in; instead she watches her mother's face at the salon window. Eyes and cheekbones amongst the reflections. Blank sky, cold sea, ragged palms. Her mother's eyes blinking, face not moving. Lamp-posts with lights strung between, rocking in the breeze.

—

Another Wednesday, another week or two later, and Kim stands in the salon doorway. Alice has had the phone call already. Knows her daughter hasn't been to school, didn't expect her to show up here. The rain slides down the windowpane and, through the open shop door, she can hear it singing in the drains.

Alice takes her daughter's coat from her, sits her down in an empty chair. The salon is quiet and Kim spends the next few minutes watching her mother working in the mirror. She sees that Alice doesn't look at her, only out of the window, or down at her fingers, turning grey hair around the pastel shades of the plastic rollers, pink and yellow and green. Her mother's cheeks are flushed, lips drawn in, and the skin around her eyes pulled taut.

When Alice steps over to her, Kim looks away. Sees the old lady's eyes on them, under the dryer. Alice knows she is watching them, too. Has felt her customers observing her ever since Kim was ill, has grown accustomed to the scrutiny. She stands behind her daughter now. A second or two passes, and she finds herself still there. Not shouting, not angry. Just looking at the slope of her daughter's shoulders, the nape of her neck, her sodden hair.

Alice gets a clean towel from the shelves at the back and then plugs in a dryer, sets to work. At first Kim watches the rain, the gulls fighting on the rail outside, but soon she closes her eyes. Feels the pressure of her mother's fingers, how strong her hands are, how warm the air is, the low noise of the dryer.

FIELD STUDY

Rachel Seiffert

Rachel Seiffert (b. 1971) is a British novelist and short story writer. Her first novel, *The Dark Room*, was shortlisted for the 2001 Man Booker Prize, and won the LA Times Prize for First Fiction. Her collection of short stories, *Field Study*, received an award from International PEN in 2004 and her novel, *Afterwards*, was longlisted for the 2007 Orange Prize.

Summer and the third day of Martin's field study. Morning, and he is parked at the side of the track, looking out over the rye he will walk through shortly to reach the river. For two days he has been alone, gathering his mud and water samples, but not today.

A boy shouts and sings in the field. His young mother carries him piggyback through the rye. Martin hears their voices, thin through the open window of his car. He keeps still. Watching, waiting for them to pass.

The woman's legs are hidden in the tall stalks of the crop and the boy's legs are skinny. He is too big to be carried comfortably, and mother and son giggle as she struggles on through the rye. The boy wears too-large trainers, huge and white, and they hang heavy at his mother's sides. Brushing the ears of rye as she walks, bumping at her thighs as she jogs an unsteady step or two. Then swinging out wide as she spins on the spot: whirling, stumbling around and around. Twice, three times, four times, laughing, lurching as the boy screams delight on her back.

They fall to the ground and Martin can't see them any more. Just the rye and the tops of the trees beyond: where the field slopes down and the river starts its wide arc around the town. Three days Martin has been here. Only another four days to cover the area, pull enough data together for his semester paper, already overdue. The young woman and her child have gone. Martin climbs out of the car, gathers his bags and locks the doors.

This river begins in the high mountains Martin cannot see but knows lie due south of where he stands. Once it passes the coal and industry of the foothills, it runs almost due west into these flat, farming lands, cutting a course through the shallow valley on which his PhD studies are centred. Past the town where he is staying and on through the provincial capital, until it finally mouths in the wide flows which mark the border between Martin's country and the one he is now in. Not a significant stretch of water historically, commercially, not even especially pretty. But a cause for concern nonetheless: here, and even more so in Martin's country, linking as it does a chemical plant on the eastern side of the border with a major population centre to the west.

Martin has a camera, notebooks and vials. Some for river water, others for river mud. Back in the town, in his room at the guesthouse, he has chemicals and a microscope. More vials and dishes. The first two days' samples, still to be analysed, a laptop on which to record his results.

The dark, uneven arc of the trees is visible for miles, marking the course of the river through the yellow-dry countryside. The harvest this year will be early and poor. Drought, and so the water level of the river is low, but the trees along its banks are still full of new growth, thick with leaves, the air beneath them moist.

Martin drinks the first coffee of the day from his flask by the water's edge. The river has steep banks, and roots grow in twisted detours down its rocky sides. He has moved steadily west along the river since the beginning of the week, covering about a kilometre each day, with a two-kilometre gap in between. Up until now, the water has been clear, but here it is thick with long fronds of weed. Martin spreads a waterproof liner on the flat rock, lays out vials and spoons in rows. He writes up the labels while he drinks his second coffee, then pulls on his long waterproof gloves. Beyond the branches, the field shimmers yellow-white and the sun is strong; under the trees, Martin is cool. Counting, measuring, writing, photographing. Long sample spoon scratching river grit against the glass of the vials.

Late morning and hot now, even under the trees. The water at this point in the river is almost deep enough to swim. Martin lays out his vials, spoons and labels for the third time that morning. Wonders a moment or two what it would be like to lie down in the lazy current, the soft weed. Touches his gloved fingertips to the surface and counts up all the toxic substances he will test his samples for later. He rolls up his trouser legs as high as they will go before he pulls on the waders, enjoys the cool pressure of the water against the rubber against his skin as he moves carefully out to about mid-stream. The weed here is at its thickest, and Martin decides to take a sample of that, too. The protective gauntlets make it difficult to get a grip, but Martin manages to pull one plant from the river bed with its root system still reasonably intact. He stands a while, feeling the current tug its way around his legs, watching the fingers of weed slowly folding over the gap he has made. Ahead is a sudden dip, a small waterfall that Martin had noted yesterday evening on the map. The noise of the cascade is loud, held in close by the dense green avenue of trees. Martin wades forward and when he stops again, he hears voices, a laugh-scream.

The bushes grow dense across the top of the drop, but Martin can just see through the leaves: young mother and son, swimming in the pool hollowed out by the waterfall. They are close. He can see the boy take a mouthful of water and spray it at his mother as she swims around the small pool. Can see the mud between her toes when she climbs out and stands on the rock at the water's edge. The long black-green weed stuck to her thigh. She is not naked, but her underwear is pale, pink-white like her skin, and Martin can also see the darker wet of nipples and pubic hair. He turns quickly and wades back to the bank, weed sample held carefully in gauntleted hands.

He stands for a moment by his bags, then pulls off the waders, pulls on his shoes again. He will walk round them, take a detour across the fields and they will have no cause to see him. He has gathered enough here already, after all. The pool and waterfall need not fall within his every 100 metres remit. No problem.

—

Martin sleeps an hour when he gets back to the guesthouse. Open window providing an occasional breeze from the small back court and a smell of bread from the kitchen. When he wakes the sun has passed over the top of the building and his room is pleasantly cool and dim.

He works for an hour or two on the first day's mud and water vials, and what he finds confirms his hypothesis. Everything within normal boundaries, except one particular metal, present in far higher concentrations than one should expect.

His fingers start to itch as he parcels up a selection of samples to send back to the university lab for confirmation. He knows this is psychosomatic, that he has always been careful to wear protection: doesn't even think that poisoning with this metal is likely to produce such a reaction. He includes the weed sample in his parcel, with instructions that a section be sent on to botany, and a photocopy of the map, with the collection sites clearly marked. In the post office, his lips and the skin around his nostrils burn, and so, despite his reasoning, he allows himself another shower before he goes down to eat an early dinner in the guesthouse café.

—

The boy from the stream is sitting on one of the high stools at the bar doing his homework, and the waitress who brings Martin his soup is his mother. She wishes him a good appetite in one of the few phrases he understands in this country, and when Martin thanks her using a couple of words picked up on his last visit, he thinks she looks pleased.

Martin watches her son while he eats. Remembers the fountain of river-water the boy aimed at his mother, wonders how much he swallowed, if they swim there regularly, how many years they might have done this for. Martin thinks he looks healthy enough, perhaps a little underweight.

His mother brings Martin a glass of wine with his main course, and when he tries to explain that he didn't order it, she just puts her finger to her lips and winks. She is thin, too, but she looks strong; broad shoulders and palms, long fingers, wide nails. She pulls her hands behind her back, and Martin is aware now that he has been staring. He lowers his eyes to his plate, watches her through his lashes as she moves on to the next table. Notes: *good posture, thick hair*. But Martin reasons while he eats that such poisons can take years to make their presence felt; nothing for a decade or two, then suddenly tumours and shortness of breath in middle age.

The woman is sitting at the bar with her son when Martin finishes his meal. She is smoking a cigarette and checking through his maths. The boy watches, kicking his trainers against the high legs of his barstool, as Martin walks towards them.

– I'm sorry. I don't really speak enough of your language. But I wanted to tell you something.

The woman looks up from her son's exercise book and blinks as Martin speaks. He stops a moment, waits to see if she understands, if she will say something, but after a small smile and a small frown, she just nods and turns away from him, back to her son. At first Martin thinks they are talking about him, and that they might still respond, but the seconds pass and the boy and his mother keep talking, and then Martin can't remember how long he has been standing there looking at the back of her head, so he looks away. Sees his tall reflection in the mirror behind the bar. One hand, *left, no right*, moving up to cover his large forehead, *sunburnt*, and red hair.

– What you want to say to my mother?

The boy speaks Martin's language. He shrugs when Martin looks at him. Martin lets his hand drop back down to his side.

– Oh, okay. Okay, good. Can you translate for me then?

The boy shrugs again, which Martin takes to be assent, and so he starts to explain. About the river, how he saw them swimming in the morning and he didn't want to disturb them, but that he has been thinking about it again this evening. And then Martin stops talking because he sees that the boy is frowning.

– Should I start again?
– You were watching my mother swimming.
– No.

The boy whispers to his mother, who flushes and then puts her hand over her mouth and laughs.

– No. No, that's not right.

Martin shakes his head again, holds both hands up, but it is loud, the woman's laughter in the quiet café, and the other two customers look up from their meals.

– I was not watching. Tell her I was not watching. I was taking samples from the river, that' s all. I'm a scientist. And I think you should know that it is polluted. The river is dirty and you really shouldn't swim there. That's all. Now please tell your mother.

The young woman keeps laughing while Martin speaks, and though he avoids looking in the mirror again, he can feel the blush making his sunburn itch, the pulse in his throat. The boy watches him a second or two, lips moving, not speaking. Martin thinks the boy doesn't believe him.

– You could get sick. The river will make you sick. I just thought you should know. Okay?

Martin is angry now. With the suspicious boy, his laughing mother. He counts out enough to pay for his meal, including the wine. Leaves it on the table without a tip and goes to his room.

—

In the morning, a man serves Martin his breakfast, but before he leaves for the river again the young mother comes into the café, pushing her son in front of her. She speaks in a low whisper to the boy, who translates for Martin in a monotone.

– My mother say she is sorry. We are both sorry. She is Ewa, I am Jacek. She say you should tell me about the river so I can tell her.

—

Martin is still annoyed when he gets back from the river in the afternoon. Doesn't expect the woman and her boy to stick to their appointment, half hopes they won't turn up, still hasn't analysed day two and three's samples. But when he comes downstairs after his shower, he finds them waiting for him in the café as arranged.

The boy helps Martin spread out his maps, asks if he can boot up the laptop. His mother murmurs something, and her son sighs.

– She says I should say please. Please.
– It's okay.

Martin shows them the path of the river from the mountains to the border and where the chemical plant lies, almost a hundred kilometres upstream from the town. Amongst his papers, he finds images of what the metal he has found in the river looks like, its chemical structure and symbol, and he tells them its common name. He says that as far as they know, the body cannot break it down, so it stores it, usually in the liver. He speaks a sentence at a time and lets the boy translate. Shows them the graphs he has plotted on his computer. Waits while the boy stumbles over his grammar, watches his mother listening, thinks: *Jacek and Ewa*.

– Where do you come from?
Ewa speaks in Martin's language, points at the map. Martin looks at her, and Jacek clears his throat.

– I am teaching her.

Martin smiles. He shows them where he is studying and then, a little further to the west, the city where he was born. And then Jacek starts to calculate how many kilometres it is from Martin's university to the border and from the border to the town. Martin asks Ewa:

– How old is he?
– Nearly eleven.

He nods. Thinks she must have been very young when she got pregnant.

– He's just about bilingual already.

An exaggeration, a silly thing to say, and Martin can see in Ewa's eyes that she knows it, but she doesn't contradict him.

– School. He is good student. Also good teacher.

She smiles and Martin is glad that they came today, Ewa and her son. Pushes last night's laughter to the back of his mind. Sees that Ewa's smile is wide and warm and that her tongue shows pink behind her teeth.

—

Day five and Martin works his way along the river again. The hot fields are empty, the road quiet. The water here is wider, deeper; flies dance above the surface.

Mid-morning and Jacek crashes through the undergrowth.

– Martin! There you are. I am here.

Martin looks up from the water, startled. He nods, then he doesn't know what to say to the boy, so he carries on working. Jacek watches him a while, and then pulls off his trainers, rolls up his trousers, picks up a vial.

– No! You shouldn't come in.
– I can help you. You work faster when I can pass them to you.
– Shouldn't you be at school?

Jacek frowns.

– Does your mother know you are here?
– She don't mind.
Martin thinks a moment.

– We don't know enough yet about this metal, you see. It's too much of a risk.

Jacek avoids eye contact, rubs his bare ankles.

– You really can't help me without boots and gloves, Jacek. I only have one pair of each. I'm sorry.

An hour later the boy is back with pink washing-up gloves and a pair of outsize rubber boots, soles caked in mud. He holds up a bag of apples.

– For you. From my mother.

—

In the evening the café is crowded and Ewa is busy; another waitress brings Martin his dinner. His table is near the bar, where Jacek is doing his homework again. New vocabulary, and he asks Martin to correct his spelling. Ewa makes a detour past his table on her way to the kitchen.

– Thank you.
– No problem.

He scratches his sunburn, stops. Feels huge at the small table after she has gone.

Jacek brings his mother with him on day six. Ewa stands at the water's edge while her son changes into his boots and washing-up gloves. Midday already, and the sky is clear, the sun high. Martin has sweat patches under his arms, on his back. He watches Ewa hold the front of her T-shirt away from her chest, and then flap it back and forth to get cool air at the hot skin beneath. He sees yellow pollen on her shoes, the hem of her skirt, damp hair at her temples.

They work for a while, and Jacek asks questions which Martin answers. Ewa says very little. She crouches on the bank and looks at the water. Lids down, lips drawn together, arms wrapped around her shins. When Martin says it's time to move downstream 100 metres, Jacek says he wants to come with him and Ewa says she will go home.

Jacek watches Martin watching his mother as she wades through the long grass back to the road.

– She used to swim here with my Tata, I think.
– Your father?

Martin tries to remember a wedding ring. Sees Ewa's strong palms, her long fingers.
– He is in your country.
– Oh?
– He is illegal. Too much problems at the border, so he don't come home.

Martin watches Jacek as they unpack the bags again. Fair with freckles. Narrow lips, pale eyes, broad nose. A good-looking boy, but not at all like his mother.

—

Day seven and Martin doesn't go to the river. After breakfast he sets up his computer, a new graph template, and plots the data from days two and three. Both agree with day one's graph, with Martin's predictions, and he starts sketching out a structure for his argument, writes a first draft conclusion. The sample results should have come back from the university yesterday, including the mud and weed from day four, which would speed up Martin's analysis. He goes downstairs to the small office mid-morning to check for faxes again, but the guesthouse is quiet, café closed, reception deserted. Sunday. So there won't be anybody at the labs, either, but Martin walks out to the phone boxes in the town square anyway.

Jacek hammers on the glass.

– Where were you?
– Wait.

Martin holds up one finger, but the phone just keeps ringing out at the other end. Jacek peels his pink gloves off while Martin leaves a message on the lab answerphone. The boy cups his hands around his eyes, presses them up to the glass, watching him. It is stifling inside the phone box and Jacek's hands leave a sweaty streak on the pane outside.

When Martin opens the door, Jacek has his fists on his hips. Rubber boots on the paving stones beside him.

– Why didn't you come?
– I've finished. I only need to do a couple more tests.
– Oh.

Jacek picks up his boots and falls into step with Martin. The sun is strong and they walk together on the shady side of the narrow street which leads back up to the guesthouse.

– I'm going home tomorrow.
– Tomorrow?

He looks up at Martin for a second or two, then turns heel and runs.

—

Martin sleeps in the afternoon and is woken by the landlady's husband with a message.

– Is it from the university?
– No. From my wife's sister.

Martin stares at the man. Eyes unfocused, face damp with heat and sleep.

– From Ewa. Jacek's mother. She works here. My wife's sister.
– Oh, yes. Yes, sorry.
– She says you should come to her house. She will cook you something to eat this evening. To say thank you.

—

Martin showers and sits down at his computer again but finds he can't work. Looks out at the birds instead, washing in a puddle on the flat roof of the building opposite. The concrete is mossy and Martin wonders where the water came from. He has been here a week and it's been 30 degrees straight through and hasn't rained once. The skin on his back is damp again, and under his arms, and he thinks he hasn't anything clean to wear this evening, so he takes a T-shirt down the hall with him and washes it in the bathroom, lays it out on his windowsill to dry.

It is still slightly damp when he goes out to find Ewa's. Bottle of wine bought from the guesthouse bar under one arm, map and address on a scrap of paper from the landlady's husband. There is a slight breeze and the T-shirt is cool against his skin. He catches sight of himself in the bakery window as he passes, pushes his hair down over his forehead a little as he turns the corner. An involuntary gesture he hopes nobody saw.

—

Jacek opens the door.

– You're early!
– Sorry.

He leads Martin up the stairs, two at a time, cartons of cigarettes and cake mix piled high along one wall. The narrow entrance hall of Ewa's flat is similarly crowded: disposable nappies, tuna fish, toothbrushes in different shades, pink and green and yellow. Jacek sees Martin looking at the boxes.

– The man we rent from. He keep things here, we pay him not so much. Every week is something new coming for him to sell.

A table stands in the middle of the room, a wardrobe in the corner. Mattress leant up against the wall and draped with a sheet. The window is open and the radio on. Martin recognises the song, a current hit, but can't understand what the announcer says afterwards. He goes into the kitchen, where Ewa is chopping and Jacek stirring.

– Can I help?
– No!

Ewa pours him a glass of wine and pushes him out into the bedroom-dining room again.

– Five minutes.

The wind is blowing into town from the river, and Martin can hear church bells ringing out the evening service.

They eat, Martin and Ewa smiling and nodding, Jacek concentrating on his food, not worried by the silence.

– Jacek, can you ask your mother to tell me a little about the town, please?

The boy looks up with his mouth full, Martin swallows.

– I know very little. I would like to know.

It is not true. He knows what she tells him already, what the boy translates for her about the nine churches, the resistance during the war and occupation, the failed collectivisation of the fruit growers during the communist era.

– There was a jam factory here when she was my age. Everybody was working there, or they were farmers. Apricots, pears, apples, and I don't know how you say those small ones. Berries?

Martin asks about the communist years.

– You want to hear about no food and unhappiness, yes?

Martin rubs his sunburn, and Ewa slaps her son's hands.

– Jacek! Sorry. I don't understand him, but I see he was bad. You translate only, yes? Yes?

Ewa points at her son and then pours them all more wine, offers to make Martin some tea.

– The way we drink it here.

Jacek's translation is sulky, sleepy. Black, in a glass so you can see the leaves floating. Boiling water, hot glass with no handles so your fingerprints get smooth and hard from the holding. Martin looks at the tips of his fingers, Ewa smiles.

– I didn't know your sister owns the guesthouse.
– Yes.

Ewa smiles, Jacek yawns.

– She gives my mother work.
– And her husband?
– Tadeusz?
– Uncle Tadeusz does no work.
– Sh! Not true.

Ewa speaks more herself now, interrupts her son's translations. She tells him her brother-in-law is a plumber. That he put his faith in the church. Her explanations are ungrammatical, sometimes nonsensical, but Martin enjoys listening to her. She says that they built new houses a year or two after the elections, a whole row, right in the centre. New times, new buildings. Flats above, shop spaces below. Brick, solid, good windows. And Tadeusz put in all the pipes, toilets, baths, taps, sinks. He got a loan to pay for all the materials. Copper piping and ceramics, imported from the west. He had the houses blessed when they were finished, but not yet painted. The priest came and threw his holy water around the empty rooms and Tadeusz was so proud. She remembers the wet, dark spots on the pink-red plasterwork, that it was a hot day, and that the dark spots left white marks behind when they dried.

– He never got paid, Tadeusz, and he cries often now.

Each time he defaults on his loan, and the houses are still empty. A while ago there was new graffiti on the wall of the last one in the row: send the nuns abroad and the priests to the moon.

Ewa looks at Jacek, who isn't listening any more, eyes half closed, head propped in his hands. She whispers to Martin:

– I think Tadeusz write that.

Martin feels her breath on his neck as she speaks, can smell wine and soap mixed.

– My sister, she wanted that Jacek and me should live with her. After Piotr left.
– Your husband?

Ewa doesn't answer, her eyes are unfocused.

– I couldn't. Not live with Tadeusz. He's not a bad man, but so much bitterness.

Martin is drunk and so is Ewa.

– I don't want my son be bitter, you see. I want that he like his life, this town, his country.

Martin nods.

– There is not so much here now, but I show him places, take him to the river.

Ewa sighs. They sit with the breeze from the open window on their bright cheeks and Jacek has his head on the tablecloth, asleep.

– I don't make him be at school this week. I think he can't swim in the river now, but it is good that he speak with you. Has some nice time, learn someone new. More than in a classroom.

Ewa smiles into the middle distance and Martin looks at her. Only half a metre between them, the corner of the table, knees almost touching underneath.

He leans towards her. But Ewa catches him.

– No.

One hand on each of his shoulders, she holds him at arms' length. Martin blinks.

An empty wine glass rolls on the table. Ewa shakes her head.

– Sorry, no.

She smiles and then Martin sits back in his chair again, sunburn itching, sweat prickling in his scalp.

He doesn't look at her and for a minute or so they sit in silence. Jacek's even breathing in the room and the church bells sounding again outside. When Martin looks up, Ewa is blinking, smiling at him.

– I am sorry.

She rights the glass on the table, then covers her mouth with her hand and laughs.

—

In the morning there is a fax from the department lab. Martin has a hangover, asks for coffee and water to be sent up to his room. His eyes skim the figures, cannot settle. He boots up the laptop, plots the lab's figures onto his graph, though he already sees the disparity between the last set of results and his predictions. Days one and two show serious levels of contamination in mud and water, and correspond with Martin's own data. Day three's samples, however, are almost low enough to be considered clear.

Martin sits on the narrow bed a while, trying to decide if he is relieved or disappointed. The weedy water, the pool under the waterfall: *Clean. As good as*. But the premise of his paper: *Void*. His headache is bad, the day hot already, the shame of yesterday evening still fresh. Martin presses the heels of his palms against his eyes.

He wants to go home, he needs to get dressed. He goes to the bathroom where the window is open, the air much cooler than in his room. He stands under the shower a long time, warm flow on face and shoulders taking the edge off his headache, filling his ears, closing his eyes, replacing Ewa and her laughter with water falling on tile.

The room he returns to is strewn with papers and clothes.

Martin works his way round it methodically, folding and sorting into piles. Before he packs, he checks through the lab technician's tidy columns once more, notes the memo at the end of the fax: the weed sample has been sent on to botany.

On the way downstairs, he reasons with himself: if the weed results are interesting, he can propose to further investigate the river fauna in the conclusion to his paper. Over breakfast, he thinks he could propose a joint venture with botany, perhaps. Something to please the department. Zoology might even be interested: the weed may be thriving, but crowding other species out. At the very least, it is good news for Ewa. She is not working this morning, but Martin thinks he will leave a note for her, tell her it's okay to take Jacek swimming again. He finishes his roll. Thinks he made a mess of the field study, the week in general, but there are still ways to make amends.

Martin stands in the narrow reception hall with his bags, sees Ewa happy by the waterfall while he waits for her sister to calculate his bill. Then he remembers how sad she looked the day she came with Jacek to the river, and he is shocked at the satisfaction the memory gives him.

There is paper on the counter in front of him. He has a pencil in his back pocket, but he doesn't get it out. He pays and picks up his bags. While he loads up the car he tells himself it is too soon to know for certain. He has yet to test all his samples, examine all the possibilities; swimming at the waterfall could still be dangerous.

On the road out of town, he sees Ewa's hand over her mouth, her eyes pressed shut, Jacek woken by her laughter and staring at him.

At the border, the road runs parallel with the river for a kilometre or so, and the traffic moves slowly. To his right, trees grow tall along the riverbanks and in his rear-view mirror Martin can see the rest of the country spread out behind him, dry and flat. His chest is tight with shame, but the border guard is waving him through now, and he is driving on again.

LOVE IN THE MARKETPLACE

Yiyun Li

> Yiyun Li (b. 1972) is a Chinese American author. Her
> debut short story collection, *A Thousand Years of Good
> Prayers*, won the 2005 Frank O'Connor International
> Short Story Award, and her second collection, *Gold Boy,
> Emerald Girl*, was shortlisted for the same award. Her
> debut novel, *The Vagrants*, was shortlisted for the 2011
> IMPAC Dublin Literary Award. She is an editor of the
> Brooklyn-based literary magazine, *A Public Space*.

Sansan is known to her students as Miss Casablanca. A beautiful
nickname if one does not pay attention to the cruel, almost
malicious smiles when the name is mentioned, and she chooses
not to see. Sansan, at thirty-two, does not have a husband, a
lover, or a close friend. Since graduation from college, she has
been teaching English at the Educators' School in the small town
where she grew up, a temporary job that has turned permanent.
For ten years she has played *Casablanca*, five or six times a
semester, for each class of students. The pattern of their response
has become familiar, and thus bearable for her. At the beginning,
they watch in awe, it being the first real American movie they
have watched, without Chinese dubbing or subtitles. Sansan
sees them struggle to understand the dialogue, but the most they
can do is catch a phrase or two now and then. Still, they seem
to have no trouble understanding the movie, and always, some
girls end the class with red teary eyes. But soon they lose their
interest. They laugh when the women in the movie cry; they
whistle when a man kisses a woman on the screen. In the end,
Sansan watches the movie alone, with the added sound track
from the chatting students.

That is what Sansan is doing with her morning class when someone taps on the door. Only when the knocking becomes urgent does she pause the tape.

"Your mother's waiting for you outside. She wants to see you," the janitor says when Sansan opens the door.

"What for?"

"She didn't say."

"Can't you see I'm busy with my students?"

"It's your mother waiting outside," the janitor says, one foot planted firmly inside the door.

Sansan stares at the janitor. After a moment, she sighs. "OK, tell her I'm coming," she says. The students all watch on amused. She tells them to keep watching the movie, and knows they will not.

Outside the school gate, Sansan finds her mother leaning onto the wooden wheelbarrow she pushes to the marketplace every day. Stacked in it are a coal stove, a big aluminum pot, packs of eggs, bottles of spices, and a small wooden stool. For forty years. Sansan's mother has been selling hard-boiled eggs in the marketplace by the train station, mostly to travelers. Sitting on the stool for all her adult life has made her a tiny stooped woman. Sansan hasn't seen her mother for a year, since her father's funeral. Her mother's hair is thinner and grayer, but so will Sansan's own be in a few years, and she feels no sentiment for either of them.

"Mama, I heard you were looking for me," Sansan says.

"How else would I know that you're alive?"

"Why? I thought people talked about me to you all the time."

"They can lie to me."

"Of course." Sansan grins.

"But whose problem is it when you make people talk about you?"

"Theirs."

"You've never known how to spell the word 'shame.'"

"Do you come just to tell me that I should be ashamed of myself? I know it by heart now."

"What god did I offend to deserve you as a daughter?" Her mother raises her voice. A few passersby slow down and look at them with amused smiles.

"Mama, do you have something to say? I'm busy."

"It won't be long before you will become an orphan, Sansan. One day I'll be drowned by all the talk about you."

"People's words don't kill a person."

"What killed your dad, then?"

"I was not the only disappointment for dad," Sansan says. Hard as she tries, she feels her throat squeezed tight by a sudden grief. Her father, before his death, worked as a meter reader, always knocking on people's doors around dinnertime, checking their gas and water meters, feeling responsible for the ever-rising rates and people's anger. One evening he disappeared after work. Later he was discovered by some kids in a pond outside the town, his body planted upside down. The pond was shallow, waist deep at most; he had plunged himself into the mud, with the force of a leap maybe, but nobody could tell for sure how he did it, or why Sansan's mother believed that it was Sansan's failure at marriage that killed him.

"Think of when you first went to college. Your dad and I thought we were the most accomplished parents in the world," her mother says, ready to reminisce and cry.

"Mama, we've been there many times. Let's not talk about it."

"Why? You think I toil all these years just to raise a daughter to shut me up?"

"I'm sorry, but I have to go," Sansan says.

"Don't go yet. Stay with me longer," her mother says, almost pleading.

Sansan tries to soften her voice. "Mama, I'm in the middle of a class."

"Come home tonight, then. I have something important to tell you."

"Why don't you tell me now? I can spare five minutes."

"Five minutes are not enough. It's about Tu." Sansan's mother steps closer and whispers, "Tu is divorced."

Sansan stares at her mother for a long moment. Her mother nods at her. "Yes, he's unoccupied now."

"I don't know what you're talking about," Sansan says.

"His parents want you to go back to him."

"Mama. I don't understand."

"That's why you have to come home and talk to me. Now go

teach," Sansan's mother says, and pushes the wheelbarrow forward
before Sansan replies.

Sansan discovered *Casablanca* the year Tu wrote a short and
apologetic letter from America, explaining his decision not to marry
her. Before the letter's arrival, she showed *The Sound of Music*
to her students, humming with every song, ready to abandon the
students for America at any minute. After the letter, she has never
sung again. *Casablanca* says all she wants to teach the students
about life.

Sansan goes back to the classroom and resumes her place on
the windowsill, letting her legs dangle the way she remembers her
American teachers did in college. At the end of the Paris scene,
when Rick gets soaked on the platform in the pouring rain, and
then boards the train, a boy says, "How funny. His coat is dry as a
camel's fur now."

Sansan is surprised that she has missed the detail all along. She
thinks of praising the boy for his keen observation, but changes her
mind. "One of life's mysteries is its inexplicability," she raises her
voice and says.

The students roar with laughter. Certainly the line will be passed
on, along with the nickname, to the next class, but Sansan does
not care. The students, recent graduates from junior high, will be
teaching elementary students after the two years of studying in the
Educators' School. Most of them are from villages, and the school
is their single chance to escape heavy farm labor. English is taught
only to comply with a regulation set by the Education Department;
they will never understand what she means, these kids living out
their petty desires.

After two classes, Sansan decides to take off, complaining to her
colleagues of a headache. Nobody believes her excuse, she knows,
but nobody would contradict her, either. They indulge her the way
people do a person with a mild and harmless craziness, whose
eccentricity adds color to their otherwise dull lives. Among the
few people in town who have college degrees, Sansan is the best-
educated one. She was one of the two children from the town who
have ever made it to the most prestigious college in Beijing, and
the only one to have returned. The other one, Tu, the childhood

companion and classmate and boyfriend and fiancé at one time or another in her life, is in America, married to a woman more beautiful than Sansan.

And divorced now, ten years too late. Back in her rented room, Sansan sits on her bed and cracks sunflower seeds. The shells rain down onto the sheet and the floor, and she lets them pile up. She craves the popping sounds in her skull, and the special flavor in her mouth. It is the sunflower seeds, sweet and salty and slightly bitter from the nameless spices Gong's Dried Goods Shop uses to process its sunflower seeds, and the English novels she bought in college – a full shelf of them, each one worthy of someone's lifetime to study – that make her life bearable. But the sunflower seeds taste different today, Tu's divorce, like a fish bone stabbed in her throat, distracts her.

Tu would never imagine her sitting among the shells of sunflower seeds and pondering his failed marriage, but she still imagines him on a daily basis. Not a surprise, as she promised Tu at their engagement ceremony. "I'll be thinking of you until the day when all the seas in the world dry up," she said. Tu must have said something similar, and Min, the only witness of the ceremony and then Tu's legal wife on paper, hugged both of them. It was odd, in retrospect, that Min did not take a vow. After all, the engagement between Sansan and Tu, just as the marriage between Min and Tu, was the contract for all three of them.

Min was the most beautiful girl Sansan had met in college, and is, ten years later, the most beautiful person in her memory. In college they lived in the same dorm with four other girls, but for a long time in their first year, they were not close. Min was a city girl, attractive, outgoing, one of the girls who would have anything they set their eyes on, and of course they only set their eyes on the best. Sansan, a girl from a small town, with a heavy accent and a plain face, was far from the best for Min, as a confidante or a friend.

Toward the end of their freshman year, the demonstrations in Tiananmen Square disrupted their study. Min became an active protester in the Square. Miss Tiananmen, the boys voted her; she dressed up as the Statue of Liberty and gestured victory to the Western reporters' cameras. After the crashing down, she had to go through a difficult time, being checked and rechecked; she ended up belonging to the category that did not need imprisonment but did not have a right to any legal job after graduation, either. When Min came back to school, still beautiful but sad and defeated, Sansan was the first and the only person in the dorm who dared to express sympathy and friendliness toward Min. Sansan was among the few who had not attended any protests. She and Tu had been the only students showing up for classes when their classmates had gone on a strike; later, when the teachers had stopped coming to classes, they had become intimate, falling in love as their parents and the whole town back home had expected them to.

Sansan never thought of her friendly gesture to Min as anything noble or brave; it was out of a simple wish to be nice to someone who deserved a better treatment from life. Sansan was overwhelmed with joy and gratitude, then, when Min decided to return the goodwill and become her best friend. Sansan felt a little uneasy, too, as if she had taken advantage of Min's bad fortune; they would have never become friends under normal circumstances, but then, what was wrong with living with the exceptional, if that's what was given by life?

At the end of their sophomore year, the Higher Education Department announced a new policy that allowed only those students who had American relatives to be granted passports for studying abroad, something that made no sense at all, but such was their life at the time, living with all the ridiculous rules that changed their lives like a willy-nilly child. Min's only hope for her future – going to America after graduation – became a burst bubble, and Sansan, when she could not stand the heartbreakingly beautiful face of Min, started to think and act with resolution.

"Are you out of your mind?" Tu said when she announced to him her plan – that he would apply to an American graduate school and help Min out through a false marriage. "I don't have any American relatives."

"Your grandfather's brother – didn't he go to Taiwan after the Liberation War? Why couldn't he have gone to America later? Listen, nobody will go to America to check your family history. As long as we get a certificate saying that he's in America ..."

"But who'll give us the certificate?"

"I'll worry about that. You think about the application," Sansan said. She saw the hesitation in Tu's eyes, but there was also a spark of hope, and she caught it before it dimmed. "Don't you want to go to America, too? We don't have to go back home after graduation, and work at some boring jobs because we don't have city residency. Nobody will care about whether you are from a small town when you get to America."

"But to marry Min?"

"Why not?" Sansan said. "We have each other, but she doesn't have anyone. The city boys – they all become turtles in their shells once she's in trouble."

Tu agreed to try. It was one of the reasons Sansan loved him – he trusted her despite his own doubt; he followed her decision. Persuading Min seemed easy, even though she too questioned the plan. Sansan alone nudged Tu and Min toward the collective American dream for all three of them; she went back to her hometown, and through bribing and pleading got a false certificate about the American grand-uncle of Tu. The plan could have gone wrong but it went right at every step. Tu was accepted by a school in Pennsylvania; Min, with the marriage certificate, got her own paperwork done to leave the country as Tu's dependent. The arrangement, a secret known only to the three of them, was too complicated to explain to outsiders, but none of the three had a doubt then. One more year and the plan would be complete, when Min would find a way to sponsor herself and Tu, with a marriage and a divorce under his belt, would come home and marry Sansan.

It did not occur to Sansan that she should have had sex with Tu before he took off. In fact, he asked for it, but she refused. She remembered reading, in her college course, *Women in Love*, and one detail had stuck with her ever since. One of the sisters, before her lover went to war, refused to have sex with him, afraid that it would make him crave women at a time when only death was available. But Tu was not going to a war but a married life with another woman. How could a man resist falling in love with a beautiful woman whose body ate, slept, peed, and menstruated in the same apartment, a thin door away from him?

Sansan started to imagine the lovemaking between Tu and Min when, after the short letter informing her of their intention to stay in the marriage, neither would write to her again. She stripped them, put them in bed, and studied their sex as if it would give her an answer. Min's silky long hair brushed against the celery stalk of Tu's body, teasing him, calling out to him; Tu pushed his large cauliflower head against Min's heavy breasts, a hungry, ugly piglet looking for his nourishment. The more she imagined, the more absurd they became. It was unfair of her, Sansan knew, to make Tu into a comic image, but Min's beauty, like a diamond, was impenetrable. Sansan had never worried about the slightest possibility of their falling in love – Min was too glamorous a girl for Tu, the boy with a big head, a thin body, and a humble smile. She had put her faith in the love between Tu and herself, and she had believed in the sacrifice they had to go through to save a friend. But inexplicable as life was, Min and Tu fell in love, and had mismatched sex in Sansan's mind. Sometimes she replaced Min with herself, and masturbated. Tu and she looked more harmonious – they had been playmates when Sansan had been a toddler sitting by her mother's stove, where Tu had been a small boy from the next stall, the fruit vendor's son; the sex, heartbreakingly beautiful, made her cry afterward.

Sansan took up the habit of eating sunflower seeds when she could no longer stand her imagination. Every night, she sits for hours cracking sunflower seeds; she reaches for the bag the first thing when she wakes up, before she gets out of bed. She calms down when the shells pop in her brain, and is able to imagine Tu and Min in their clothes. The fact that they both broke their promises to her, hurtful as it is and it will always be, no longer matters. What remains meaningful is Tu and Min's marriage vows to each other. She was the one to make them husband and wife, and even if they would be too ashamed to admit it to each other, she would always hover above their marriage bed, a guardian angel that blesses and curses them with her forgiveness.

What, then, has led them to end their marriage, ten years too late? Once they broke their promises to her; twice they did. With a divorce, what will become of her, when neither of them will be obliged to think about her nobleness?

When the bag of sunflower seeds runs out, Sansan decides to go find her mother and ask about Tu's divorce. The marketplace, the only one in town, is next to the railway station. The trains running between Beijing and the southern cities stop several times a day at the station for ten-minute breaks, and many vendors rely on these trains for their businesses.

The one-fifteen train has just pulled into the station when Sansan arrives. A few passengers show up stretching their legs and arms, and soon more flood into the marketplace. Sansan stands a few steps away and watches her mother hitting the side of the pot with a steel ladle and chanting, "Come and try – come and buy – the eight-treasure eggs – the best you'll ever taste."

A woman stops and lifts the lid, and her kid points to the biggest egg in the pot. More people slow down at the good smell of tea leaves, spices, and soy sauce. Some take out their wallets to pay; others, seeing more egg sellers, walk on without knowing they've missed the best hard-boiled eggs in the world. When Sansan was young, she was infuriated by the people who did not choose her mother's eggs – the other vendors were all stingy, never adding as many spices and tea leaves to their pots as her mother did. But when Sansan became older, she grew angry, instead, at her mother's stubbornness. All those people who buy her eggs – strangers that come and go and will not remember this place or her mother's face even if they remember the taste of the eggs – they will never know that her mother spends more money on the best spices and tea leaves.

When the train leaves, Sansan finds a brick and puts it next to her mother's stool. She sits down and watches her mother add eggs and more spices to the pot.

"Isn't it a waste of money to put in so much of the expensive spices?" Sansan says.

"Don't tell me how to boil eggs. I have done this for forty years, and have brought you up boiling eggs my way."

"But even if people can taste the difference, they will never come back to look for your eggs."

"Why not give them their one chance to eat the best eggs in the world, then?" her mother says, raising her voice. A few vendors look at them, winking at one another. The marketplace is full of eyes and ears. By dinnertime, the whole town will have known that Sansan has shown up and attacked her poor mother, and children of the town will be warned, at the dinner tables, not to follow Sansan's example, a daughter not fulfilling her filial duty, who spends money on renting when her mother has kept a room ready for her.

"Mama, why don't you think of retirement?" Sansan says in a lower voice.

"Who will feed me then, a poor old widow?"

"I will."

"You don't even know how to take care of yourself," her mother says. "What you need is a man like Tu."

Sansan looks at her own shadow on the ground, and the fragments of eggshells by her leather sandals. The eggshells were her only toys before she befriended Tu from the next stall, the fruit vendor's son. Tu's parents have retired, living in a two-bedroom flat that Tu bought for them. The next stall now sells cigarettes and lighters and palm-sized pictures of blond women whose clothes, when put close to the flame, disappear. After a moment, Sansan asks, "What happened to Tu?"

"His parents came by yesterday, and asked if you wanted to go back to him."

"Why?"

"A man needs a woman. You need a husband, too."

"Is that what I am, a substitute?"

"Don't act willful. You're not a young girl anymore."

"Why did he get a divorce?"

"People change their minds. Sansan, if you ask me, I would say just go back to Tu without questioning."

"Is that what Tu wants? Or is it his parents' idea?"

"What's the difference? He'll marry you if you want to go back to him, that's what his parents said."

"That would make it an arranged marriage."

"Nonsense. We've seen you two grow up together from the beginning," Sansan's mother says. "Even in arranged marriages, people fall in love."

Sansan feels a sting in her heart. "Sure, people fall in love in arranged marriages, but that's not the love I want."

"What do you want, then, Miss Romantic?"

Sansan does not reply. A romance is more than a love story with a man. A promise is a promise, a vow remains a vow; such is the grandeur of *Casablanca*, such is the true romance that keeps every day of her life meaningful.

Neither of them speaks. Sansan watches her mother pick up the fresh eggs with the ladle, and crack the shells carefully with a spoon so that the spices will soak the eggs well. When her mother finishes, she scoops up an egg and puts it into Sansan's hands without a word. The egg is hot but Sansan does not drop it. She looks at the cracks on the shell, darkened by the spices and soy sauce like a prophet's fractured turtle shell. When she was younger, she had to beg her mother for a long time before she was given an egg to eat, but when Tu was around, her mother always gave them each an egg without hesitation. Sansan wonders if her mother still remembers such things, the nourishing of their relationship long before she and Tu became lovers.

A few minutes pass, and then, across the street, two jeeps stop with screeching noises. Sansan looks up and sees several cops jump out and surround Gong's Dried Goods Shop. Soon the customers are driven out the door. "What's going on?" the vendors ask one another. Sansan's mother stands up and looks across the street for a minute, and hands the ladle to Sansan.

"Take care of the stove for me," her mother says, and walks across the street with a few other curious vendors.

Sansan watches her mother pushing to the front of the store, where the cops have set up red warning tapes. She wonders why, after forty years in the marketplace, her mother is still interested in other people's business.

Ten minutes later, her mother returns and says to the vendors, "You'll never imagine this – they've found opium in Gong's goods."

"What?"

"No wonder their business is always so good – they add opium when they make their nuts and seeds so people will always want to go back to them," Sansan's mother says. "What black-hearted people they are!"

"How did the police find out?" the vendor across the aisle asks.

"Someone working in the shop must have told on them."

More vendors come back. Sansan listens to them talking about

Gong's opium business, her palms wet and sticky. She was planning to go to Gong's to buy more sunflower seeds before the end of the day; even the thought of the sunflower seeds makes her eager to go home and hide herself in a pile of cracked shells, letting the taste on her tongue take her over and carry her away to a safe place, where she watches over Tu and Min serenely. Is that what she is living on, a poisoned food, a drugged dream?

Sansan's mother turns to her. "But let's not talk about other people's trouble. What do you think of the proposal, Sansan?"

"To marry Tu? No, I don't want to marry him."

"You've been waiting for him all these years. Don't be silly."

"I've never waited for him."

"But that's a lie. Everyone knows you're waiting for him."

"Everyone?"

"Why else do you never get married? Everyone knows he did this horrible thing to you, but men make mistakes. Even his parents apologized yesterday. It's time to think about forgiveness."

"What's to forgive?"

"He *had* you, and then left you for another woman. Listen, it would not be that bad a thing if you went back to him. As the old saying goes – *what belongs to someone will belong to him eventually*."

"Wait a minute, Mama. What do you mean he had me?"

Sansan's mother blushes. "Yon know what I mean."

"No, I don't know. If you mean sex, no, he's never had me."

"There's nothing to be ashamed of. It was understandable, and it was nobody's fault."

Sansan, for the first time, understands the town's tolerance of her, a pitiful woman used and then abandoned by a lover, a woman unmarriable because she will never be able to demonstrate her virginity on the snow-white sheet spread on the wedding bed. "Mama, I have nothing to do with Tu. We never had sex."

"Are you sure?" Sansan's mother asks, hopeful disbelief in her eyes.

"I'm a spinster losing my mind. If you don't believe me, why don't you ask the town to vote on my virginity?"

Sansan's mother stares at her for a long moment, and claps her hands. "That's even better. I didn't know you loved him so much.

I'll go talk to his parents tonight, and tell them you've kept your *cleanness* for him all these years."

"I did nothing for him."

"But why wouldn't you get married, if he never had you?"

Sansan does not reply. She wonders how much of the gossip about her lost virginity burdened her father before his death. She wonders why her mother has never confronted her all these years; but then, how could her mother, a proud yet humble woman of tradition, ask her daughter such a thing when they have never talked about sex in her family?

"If you can't answer the question, it's time to make up your mind," Sansan's mother says.

"My mind has been made up all along. I won't marry Tu."

"Are you going crazy?"

"Mama, why do you want to be the best egg seller in the world?"

Sansan's mother shakes her head. "I don't know what you're talking about."

"Mama, why do you put more spices in?"

"If I'm telling people I sell the best eggs in the world, I have to keep my promise."

"But nobody cares about it. You're keeping a promise that matters only to you."

"Don't talk to me like that. I'm an illiterate. Besides, what has that to do with your marriage?"

"I have my own promise to keep."

"Why are you so stubborn? Do you know we'll both end up as crazy women if you don't get married?" Sansan's mother says, and starts to cry.

Another train pulls into the station with a long whistle. Sansan listens to her mother chanting in a trembling voice, and wipes a drop of tear off. Indeed she is going crazy, hurting her mother so, the only person who loves her despite who she is. But she has no other choice. People in this world can discard their promises like used napkins, but she does not want to be one of them.

A man enters the marketplace, in a dirty shirt and jeans and carrying a shapeless bag. He hugs the bag close to his body as if it were a woman. Sansan watches the man sit down at the open space between the two stalls across the aisle from her mother's stove. He takes a flattened cardboard box and a knife out of the bag, the kind with a long and sharp blade that fruit vendors use to cut watermelons. Then he takes off his shirt, points the knife to his left arm, and with a push, carefully slices open his flesh, from the elbow to the shoulder. He seems so calm and measured in his movements that Sansan and a few other people who have noticed him all watch with quiet amazement. The man dips his index finger in the blood, checks his finger as if he is a calligrapher, and writes down the words on the cardboard box: *Give me ten yuan and I will let you slice me once wherever you like; if you finish my life with one cut, you owe me nothing.*

The man has to shout out the words twice before more people gather.

"What a crazy man," an old woman says.

"An inventive way to beg, though," another woman says.

"Why not just begging?"

"Who'd give him money? He's a strong man. He should be able to find some work."

"Young people don't like to work now. They like easy money," an old man says.

"What's easy about hurting oneself?"

"Hey, what's your story?" a young man asks. "Don't you know you have to make up some really good tragedies to beg?"

People laugh. The man sits quietly in the middle of the circle, the blood dripping from his elbow onto his jeans, but he seems not to notice it. After a while, he shouts the words again.

Sansan's mother sighs. She fumbles in her cash box and then walks to the man. "Here is ten yuan. Take it, young man, and go find a job. Don't waste your life with this nonsense."

"But there's no job to find."

"Take the money then."

The man holds the blade between his two palms, and offers the knife handle to Sansan's mother, "Here you go, Auntie."

"Why? I don't want to cut you."

"But you have to, I can't take your money without you cutting me. It's written here," the man says.

"Just take it."

"I'm not a beggar."

"What are you, then?" someone in the crowd asks.

"An idiot," someone else says, and people break out laughing. The man does not move, still holding out the knife for Sansan's mother. She shakes her head and lets the bill drop onto the cardboard. The man returns the bill to the foot of Sansan's mother, and sits back at his spot.

Sansan picks up the bill and walks to the man. The man looks up at her, and she looks into his eyes. Without a word, he puts the knife in her hand. She studies his body, the naked skin smooth and tanned, and the wound that's quietly bleeding. She touches his upper arm with one finger, testing and calculating, and then moves her fingertip to his shoulder. The man shivers slightly as her finger traces his flesh.

"Sansan, are you crazy?" her mother says.

The man's muscles loosen under her caressing finger; after all these years, she finally meets someone who understands what a promise is. Crazy as they may seem to the world, they are not alone, and they will always find each other. Such is the promise of life; such is the grandeur. "Don't worry, Mama," Sansan says, and turns to smile at her mother before she points the knife at the man's shoulder and slices, slowly opening his flesh with love and tenderness.

MOTHER TONGUE

Nadine Gordimer

Nadine Gordimer (b. 1923) is a South African writer, political activist and recipient of the 1991 Nobel Prize in Literature. She won the Man Booker Prize for her 1974 novel *The Conservationist*, and has since won numerous awards and recognition worldwide. A fierce defender of equality, Gordimer refused to accept her shortlisting for the 1998 Orange Prize because the award recognises only women writers.

But everything's by chance – how else would she ever have met him? Been here.

They fell in love in her country. Met there.

A taxi he had taken skidded into her small car. It was raining the way Europe weeps in winter, and the taxi driver slammed out of his vehicle and accosted her from the other side of her window, streaming water as if dissolving in anger. His passenger intervened, exonerating her and citing the weather as responsible. The damage to taxi and car was minimal; names, addresses and telephone numbers were exchanged for the purpose of insurance claims. – A hoo-hah about nothing. – He said that to her as if this was something he and she, in their class as taxi patron and private car owner, would rate it before the level of indignation of the Pakistani or whatever the taxi man was. The passenger spoke in English, native to him, but saw through the blur of rain the uncertain nod of one who has heard but not quite understood. He didn't know a colloquial turn of phrase to translate the passing derision into that country's language.

How he came to call her had to do with a document he was to sign, as witness; couldn't have been an opportunity to follow up any attraction to a pretty face, because the rain had made hers appear smeary as the image in a tarnished mirror. So they met again, over a piece of paper in a café near the lawyer's office where she worked. It was of course still raining, and he was able to make conversation with his cobbled-together vocabulary in the country's language, remarking that you didn't have days on end like this where he came from; that's how she learnt: from Africa. *South Africa. Mandela.* The synapses and neurons made the identifying connection in the map of every European mind. Yes, he had picked up something of her language, although the course he'd taken in preparation hadn't proved of much use when he arrived and found himself where everybody spoke it all the time and not in phrase-book style and accent. They laughed together at the way *he* spoke it, a mutual recognition closer, with the flesh-and-bone structure, shining fresh skin, deep-set but frank eyes, before him in place of the image in the tarnished mirror. Blond hair – real blond, he could tell from experience of his predilection for Nordic types, genuine or chemically concocted (once naked, anyway, they carelessly showed their natural category). She knew little of his language, the few words she remembered, learnt at school. But the other forms of recognition were making communication between them. They began to see each other every day; she would take his calls on her mobile, carried into the corridor or the women's room out of earshot of others in the lawyer's office. There among the wash-basins and toilet booths the rendezvous was decided.

He worked for one of the vast-tentacled international advertising agencies, and had got himself sent to her country by yet another kind of recognition; the director's, of his intelligence, adaptability, and sanguine acceptance of the need to learn the language of the country to which he would be sent as one of the coordinator's of the agency's conglomerate hype (global, they called it). He was not a copywriter or designer, he was a businessman who, as he told her, had many friends and contacts of his generation in different enterprises and might – as they were all on the lookout for – move on to some other participation in the opportunities of their world. By this he also meant his and hers, both of them young. He saw that world of theirs, though they were personally far apart geographically, turning round technology as the earth revolves round the sun.

She shared an apartment with a girl-friend; the first love-making was in his apartment where he lived, alone, since coming to Germany some months past. He had had his share of affairs at home – that surely must be, in view of his composed, confidently attractive face, the lean sexual exuberance of his body, and his quick mind; by lapse of e-mails and calls between them, the affair with someone back there was outworn. The girl met by chance probably had had a few experiments. She spoke of a boy-friend who had emigrated somewhere. Of course she might just be discreet and once they were in their sumptuous throes of love-making, what went before didn't matter. Her flesh was not abundant but alertly responsive – a surprising find. He'd thought of German female types as either rather hefty, athletic, or fat.

But it was her tenderness to him, the loving*ness* in the sexuality that made this foreign affair somewhat different from the others, so that – he supposed it's what's called falling in love – they married. In love. Passed that test. An odd move in his life, far from what would have been expected, among his circle at home. But powerful European countries are accustomed to all sorts of invasions, both belligerent and peaceful, and this foreign one was legal, representing big business, an individual proof of the world's acceptance of Germany's contrition over the past. He was suitably well received when she took him to her family, and as a welcome novelty among her friends. With their easy company he became more fluent in the to-and-fro of their language. And of course it was the language of the love affair and the marriage that had been celebrated in true German style, a traditional festivity which her circle of friends, who had moved on to an unceremonious life-style, nevertheless delightedly animated around the veiled bride and three-piece-suited groom. His was a personality and a growing adeptness in exchanges that, in their remaining months there, made Germany a sort of his-and-hers.

She knew when she began to love this man that the condition would be that she would live in another country. A country she had never seen, touched the earth, felt the wind or sun, rain, heard in its expression by its inhabitants, except through him, touch of his skin, sound of his voice; a country landscaped by his words. Love goes wherever the beloved must. The prospect of going home with him to Africa: her friends saw that she was – first time since they'd all grown up together – exalted. The anticipation actually showed in the burnish of the shine over her fine cheekbones and the eagerness in her readied eyes. She ceased to see the Bauhaus façade of the building where the lawyer's offices were, the familiar tower of the ancient church that had survived the bombs of the parents' war, the beer *stube* where she was among those friends. Her parents: how did that church's marriage ceremony put it? An old biblical injunction along with many of the good precepts she had learnt at the Lutheran Sunday school they had sent her to as a child. 'Leave thy father and thy mother and cleave only …' Something like that. The emotional parting with the parents, handed from the arms of one to the other, each jealous to have the last embrace of the daughter, was not a parting but an arrival in the embrace of a beloved man.

They were in Africa. His Africa, now defined out of a continent. Further defined: his city there. The property market, he was told by his friends who wanted to bring him up-to-date with what was happening while he was away 'doing the disappearing act into the married man', was 'flat on its arse' and this was the time to do what married men did, quit the bachelor pad and buy a house. So they spent only a month in his apartment that was to her a hotel room vacated by a previous occupant. She didn't know any of the objects in it which must have been personal to the man she had not known while he lived there. She looked through his books, took down one here and there as if she were in a library expecting to find some particular subject, but even when he was absent did not touch letters she saw lying in a drawer she had pulled out to find a ballpoint likely to be at hand in the unit of desk, computer, fax and photocopier. When they bought a house and he decided the only furniture worth taking along was the complex of his communications outfit, he cleared into a garbage bin the bundle of letters along with other papers, outlived.

The house new to them was in fact an old house, as age is measured in a city founded as a gold-mining camp 120 years ago. His white parents' generation were all for steel and glass or fake Californian-Spanish, didn't want to live with wooden verandah rails and coal-burning fire-places. To their offspring generation the Frank Lloyd Wright and Hispano-Californian look-alikes were symbolic of people looking to take on an identity outside the one they weren't sure of. Even if they didn't think in this way of their impulse to be worldly-fashionable, the assumed shell was also another shelter in their chosen isolation from the places, the manner in which the black people who surrounded, outnumbered them, lived: in hovels and shacks. Young whites on an economic level of choice found the old high-ceilinged, corrugated-iron-roofed houses more interestingly built, spacious for adaptation to ways of a life open to the unexpected. Everyone was doing it; fixing up old places. Blacks too, the professionals, media people and civil servants in what was called the new dispensation – civic term for what used to be called freedom. The houses were short of bathrooms, but those were easily installed, just as the kitchen, in the house he bought, was at once renovated with the equipment she knew – as the model of her mother's in Germany – was essential.

Home. A real his-and-hers. Friends came to help him thin overgrown trees, she had the beer chilled and the snacks ready for this male camaraderie. She planted flowers she had never seen before, didn't bloom where she came from. She hadn't found work yet – that wasn't urgent, anyway, her share in the creation of the house was a new and fulfilling occupation, as anything in the service of devotion is, centred by the big bed where they made love. There was the suggestion that she might find part-time employment to interest her at the local Goethe Institute. But she didn't want to be speaking German – English was her language now. She was introduced to, plunged into immersion in his circle. She talked little, although back in her own country, her circle where he'd made a place for himself so easily, she was rather animated. Here, she listened; it seemed to be her place. She was happy to feel she was understanding everything said in his language, even if she couldn't use it confidently enough to speak up.

There were many parties. Even without any special occasion, his friends black and white clustered instinctively in this or that apartment, house or bar, like agents of some cross-pollination of lives.

On a terrace the sunken sun sends pale searchlights to touch a valance of clouds here and there, the darkness seems to rise from damp grass as the drinking ignites animation in his friends. She has asked him to stop the car on the way, where there's a flower-seller on a corner. – What for? No-one's birthday, far as I know. – He forgets it's the rule, in her country, to take flowers or chocolates– – some gift – to a party. – Wine'd have been a better idea, my sweet. – And it happens that the host or one of the hosts – it's a combined get-together – dumps the bunch of lilies on a table where they are soon pushed aside by glasses and ashtrays.

When they arrived she sat beside him. At these gatherings married people don't sit together, it's not what one does, bringing a cosy domesticity into a good-time atmosphere. But she's still a newcomer, innocent of the protocol and he's too fond to tell her she should – well, circulate. She's one of the prettiest women there: looks fresh-picked; while the flowers she brought wilt. She's younger than most of the women. She sits, with the contradiction of knees and feet primly aligned and the lovely foothills of breasts showing above the neckline of her gauzy dress. Perhaps the difference between her and the others is she's prepared herself to look her best to honour him, not to attract other men.

He gets up to go over and greet someone he thinks has forgotten him – he's been away in Europe a whole year – and when the shoulder-grasping embrace, the huge laughter, is over, comes back, but by chance in the meantime someone has been waved to the seat next to his wife. So he pulls up a chair on the woman's other side. He hasn't deserted – it's a three-some. His newly imported wife happens to have already met this woman on some other occasion within the circle. The woman is very attractive, not really young any more but still wild, riling the company with barbed remarks, running hands up through her red-streaked plumage as if in a switch to despair at herself. People are distracted from their own talk by her spectacle. More wine is tilted into glasses as they come up to laugh, interject. The husband is one of her butts. He's challenging a reminiscence of an incident in the friends' circle his neighbour is recounting, flourishing loudly. All around the wife are references back and forth, a personal lingo – every clique has this, out of common experience. It was the same among her friends in that past life in Germany. Jokes you don't understand even if you know the words; understand only if you're aware what, who's being sent up. She doesn't know, either, the affectionate, patronising words, phrases, that are the means of expression of people who adapt and mix languages, exclamations, word-combinations in some sort of English that isn't the usage of educated people like themselves. There are so many languages in this country of theirs that his friends don't speak, but find it amusing to bring the flavours of into their own with the odd word or expression; so much more earthy, claiming an identity with their country as it is, now. Anecdotes are being argued – interruptions flying back and forth as voices amplify over re-filled glasses.

... so *they threw him with a stone*, right? – the director's office, *nogal* ...

... *In your face*. That's her always ... *Hai! Hamba kahle* ...

... *Awesome!* Something to do with a sports event or, once, a dessert someone made? They use the word often in talk of many different kinds; she's looked it up in a dictionary but there it means 'inspiring awe, an emotion of mingled reverence, dread and wonder'. And there are forms of address within the circle borrowed from other groups, other situations and experiences they now share. Someone calls out – *Chief*, I want to ask you something – when neither the speaker nor the pal hailed, white or black (for the party is mixed), is tribal – as she knows the title to be, whether in Indonesia, Central America, Africa, anywhere she could think of. Some address one another as *My China*. How is she to know this is some comradely endearment, cockney rhyming slang – 'my mate, my china plate' – somehow appropriated during the days of apartheid's army camps.

Smiling, silent; to be there with him is enough.

The party becomes a contest between him and the woman who sits between them. Each remembers, insists on a different version of what the incident was.

– You're confounding it with that time everyone was shagging in the bushes! –

– Well, you would be reliable about *that* –

– listen, listen, listen to me! – He slaps his arm round the back of her neck, under the hair she's flung up, laughing emphasis. She puts a hand on his thigh: – *You* never listen –

It's a wrestling match of words that come from the past, with touch that comes from the past. The hand stays on him. Then he snatches it up palm to palm, shaking it to contradict what she's jeering, laughing close to his face and drowning our the calls of others. – O-O-O you were still in *kort broek*, My China! Loverboy – you remember Isabella that time water skiing? Kama Sutra warns against games under water—

– No ways! You're the one to talk – also did some deep-diving in search of marine life, *ek sê*. No-oo, *kahle-kahle* was my line! –

– And what happened to your great fancy from where was it, Finland? That Easter. Well, why not – whatever you did's politically correct with me, they say the grave's a fine and private place but no *okes* do there embrace – Among the well-read of the friends this adaptation of Marvell was uproariously appreciated.

She was alone and laughed – she did not know what at. She sat beside the woman and her husband who were hugging, celebrating each other in the easy way of those who have old connections of intimacy encoded in exchanges of a mother tongue, released by wine and a good time had by all. She laughed when everyone else did. And then sat quiet and nobody noticed her. She understood she didn't know the language.

The only mother tongue she had was his in her mouth, at night.

THE SHARED PATIO

Miranda July

Miranda July (b. 1974) is an American filmmaker, artist and writer. Her body of work includes film, fiction, monologue and live performance art. She wrote, directed and starred in the films *Me and You and Everyone We Know* (2005) and *The Future* (2011). Her fiction has appeared in the *Paris Review*, *Harper's* and the *New Yorker*. Her collection of stories, *No One Belongs Here More Than You*, won the Frank O'Connor International Short Story Award.

It still counts, even though it happened when he was unconscious. It counts doubly because the conscious mind often makes mistakes, falls for the wrong person. But down there in the well, where there is no light and only thousand-year-old water, a man has no reason to make mistakes. God says do it and you do it. Love her and it is so. He is my neighbor. He is of Korean descent. His name is Vincent Chang. He doesn't do hapkido. When you say the word "Korean," some people automatically think of Jackie Chan's South Korean hapkido instructor, Grandmaster Kim Jin Pal; I think of Vincent.

What is the most terrifying thing that has ever happened to you? Did it involve a car? Was it on a boat? Did an animal do it? If you answered yes to any of these questions, then I am not surprised. Cars crash, boats sink, and animals are just scary. Why not do yourself a favor and stay away from these things.

Vincent has a wife named Helena. She is Greek with blond hair. It's dyed. I was going to be polite and not mention that it was dyed, but I really don't think she cares if anyone knows. In fact, I think she is going for the dyed look, with the roots showing. What if she and I were close friends. What if I borrowed her clothes and she said, That looks better on you, you should keep. it. What if she called me in tears, and I had to come over and soothe her in the kitchen, and Vincent tried to come into the kitchen and we said, Stay out, this is girl talk! I saw something like that happen on TV; these two women were talking about some stolen underwear and a man came in and they said, Stay out, this is girl talk! One reason Helena and I would never be close friends is that I am about half as tall as she. People tend to stick to their own size group because it's easier on the neck. Unless they are romantically involved, in which case the size difference is sexy. It means: I am willing to go the distance for you.

> *If you are sad, ask yourself why you are sad. Then pick up the phone and call someone and tell him or her the answer to the question. If you don't know anyone, call the operator and tell him or her. Most people don't know that the operator has to listen, it is a law. Also, the postman is not allowed to go inside your house, but you can talk to him on public property for up to four minutes or until he wants to go, whichever comes first.*

Vincent was on the shared patio. I'll tell you about this patio. It is shared. If you look at it, you will think it is only Helena and Vincent's patio, because their back door opens on to it. But when I moved in, the landlord said that it was the patio for both the upstairs and downstairs units. I'm upstairs. He said, Don't be shy about using it, because you pay just as much rent as they do. What I don't know for sure is if he told Vincent and Helena that it is a shared patio. I have tried to demonstrate ownership by occasionally leaving something down there, like my shoes, or one time I left an Easter flag. I also try to spend exactly the same amount of time on the patio as they do. That way I know we are each getting our value. Every time I see them out there, I put a little mark on my calendar. The next time the patio is empty, I go sit on it. Then I cross off the mark. Sometimes I lag behind and have to sit out there a lot toward the end of the month to catch up.

Vincent was on the shared patio. I'll tell you about Vincent. He is an example of a New Man. You might have read the article about the New Men in *True* magazine last month. New Men are more in touch with their feelings than even women, and New Men cry. New Men want to have children, they long to give birth, so sometimes when they cry, it is because they can't do this; there is just nowhere for a baby to come out. New Men just give and give and give. Vincent is like that. Once I saw him give Helena a massage on the shared patio. This is kind of ironic, because it is Vincent who needs the massage. He has a mild form of epilepsy. My landlord told me this when I moved in, as a safety precaution. New Men are often a little frail, and also Vincent's job is art director, and that is very New Man. He told me this one day when we were both leaving the building at the same time. He is the art director of a magazine called *Punt*. This is an unusual coincidence because I am the floor manager of a printer, and we sometimes print magazines. We don't print *Punt*, but we print a magazine with a similar name, *Positive*. It's actually more like a newsletter; it's for people who are HIV-positive.

Are you angry? Punch a pillow. Was it satisfying? Not hardly. These days people are too angry for punching. What you might try is stabbing. Take an old pillow and lay it on the front lawn. Stab it with a big pointy knife. Again and again and again. Stab hard enough for the point of the knife to go into the ground. Stab until the pillow is gone and you are just stabbing the earth again and again, as if you want to kill it for continuing to spin, as if you are getting revenge for having to live on this planet day after day alone.

Vincent was on the shared patio. I was already behind in my patio use, so it made me a little anxious to see him there so late in the month. Then I had an idea; I could sit there with him. I put on Bermuda shorts and sunglasses and suntan oil. Even though it was October, I still felt summery; I had a summery tableau in mind. In truth, though, it was quite windy, and I had to run back for a sweater. A few minutes later, I ran back for pants. Finally, I sat in a lawn chair beside Vincent on the shared patio and watched the suntan oil soak through the fabric of my khakis. He said he always liked the smell of suntan oil. This was a very graceful way of acknowledging my situation. A man with grace, that's the New Man. I asked him how things were going at *Punt*, and he told me a funny story about a typo. Because we are in the same business, he didn't have to explain that "typo" is short for "typographical error." If Helena had come out, we would have had to stop using our industry lingo so that she could understand us, but she didn't come out because she was still at work. She's a physician's assistant, which may or may not be the same thing as a nurse.

I asked Vincent more questions, and his answers became longer and longer until they hit a kind of cruising altitude and I didn't have to ask, he just orated. It was unexpected, like suddenly finding oneself at work on a weekend. What was I doing here? Where was my Roman Holiday? My American in Paris? This was just more of the same, an American in America. Finally he paused and squinted up at the sky, and I guessed he was constructing the perfect question for me, a fantastic question that I would have to rise up to, drawing from everything I knew about myself and mythology and this black earth. But he was pausing only to emphasize what he was saying about how the cover design was not actually his fault, and then at last he did ask me something; he asked, Did *I* think it was his fault, you know, based on everything he had just told me? I looked at the sky just to see what it felt like. I pretended I was pausing before telling him about the secret feeling of joy I hide in my chest, waiting, waiting, waiting for someone to notice that I rise each morning, seemingly with nothing to live for, but I do rise, and it is only because of this secret joy, God's love, in my chest. I looked down from the sky and into his eyes and I said, It wasn't your fault. I excused him for the cover and for everything else. For not yet being a New Man. We fell into silence then; he did not ask me any more questions. I was still happy to sit there beside him, but that is only because I have very, very low expectations of most people, and he had now become Most People.

Then he lurched forward. With a sudden motion, he leaned forward at an inhuman angle and stayed there. It was not the behavior of Most People, nor of New Men; it was perhaps something that an old man would do, an elderly man. I said, Vincent. Vincent. I yelled, Vincent Chang! But he only leaned forward silently, his chest almost to his knees. I knelt down and looked into his eyes. They were open, but closed like a store that is closed and looking ghostly with all the lights off. With the lights off, I could now see how luminous he had been the moment before, even in his selfishness. And it struck me that maybe *True* magazine had been wrong. Maybe there are no New Men. Maybe there are only the living and the dead, and all those who are living deserve each other and are equal to each other. I pushed his shoulders back so that he was upright in his chair again. I didn't know anything about epilepsy, but I had imagined more shaking. I moved his hair out of his face. I put my hand under his nose and felt gentle, even breaths. I pressed my lips against his ear and whispered again, It's not your fault. Perhaps this was really the only thing I had ever wanted to say to anyone, and be told.

I pulled up my chair and leaned my head against his shoulder. And although I was genuinely scared about this epileptic seizure I was in charge of, I slept. Why did I do this dangerous and inappropriate thing? I'd like to think I didn't do it, that it was in fact done to me. I slept and dreamed that Vincent was slowly sliding his hands up my shirt as we kissed. I could tell my breasts were small from the way his palms were curved. Larger breasts would have required a less acute angle. He held them as if he had wanted to for a long time, and suddenly, I saw things as they really were. He loved me. He was a complex person with layers of percolating emotions, some of them spiritual, some tortured in a more secular way, and he burned for me. This complicated flame of being was mine. I held his hot face and asked him the hard question.

What about Helena?

It's okay, because she's in the medical profession. They have to do whatever is the best for health.

That's right, the Hippocratic oath.

She'll be sad, but she won't interfere with us because of the oath.

Will you move your things up to my apartment?

No. I have to keep living with Helena because of our vows.

Your vows? What about the oath?

It'll be okay. All that is nothing compared to our thing.

Did you ever really love her?

Not really, no.

But me?

Yes.

Even though I have no pizzazz?

What are you talking about, you perfect thing.

You can see that I'm perfect?

It's in each thing that you do. I watch you when you hang your bottom over the side of the bathtub to wash it before bed.

You can see me do this?

Every night.

It's just in case.

I know. But no one will ever enter you in your sleep.

How can you promise that?

Because I'm watching you.

I thought I would have to wait until I died for this.

From now on I am yours.

No matter what? Even when you are with Helena and I am just the short woman upstairs, am I still yours then?

Yes, it is a fact between us, even if we never speak of it again.

I can't believe this is really happening.

And then Helena was there, shaking us both. But Vincent kept sleeping, and I wondered if he was dead and, if so, had he said the things in the dream before or after he passed away, and which was more authentic. Also, was *I* a criminal? Would I be arrested for negligence? I looked up at Helena; she was a swarm of action in her physician's-assistant clothes. All the motion made me dizzy; I shut my eyes again and was about to reenter the dream when Helena yelled, When did the seizure start? And, Why the fuck were you sleeping? But she was checking his vital signs with professional flourish, and the next time she looked at me, I knew I would not have to answer these questions because I had somehow become her assistant, the physician's assistant's assistant. She told me to run into their apartment for a plastic bag that would be on top of the refrigerator. I ran inside gratefully and shut the door.

Their apartment was very quiet. I tiptoed across the kitchen and pressed my face against the freezer, breathing in the complex smells of their life. They had pictures of children on their refrigerator. They had friends, and these friends had given birth to more friends. I had never seen anything as intimate as the pictures of these children.

I wanted to reach up and grab the plastic bag from the top of the refrigerator, but I also wanted to look at each child. One was named Trevor, and he was having a birthday party this Saturday. *Please come!* the invitation said. *We'll have a whale of a time!* and there was a picture of a whale. It was a real whale, a photograph of a real whale. I looked into its tiny wise eye and wondered where that eye was now. Was it alive and swimming, or had it died long ago, or was it dying now, right this second? When a whale dies, it falls down through the ocean slowly, over the course of a day. All the other fish see it fall, like a giant statue, like a building, but slowly, slowly. I focused my attention on the eye; I tried to reach down inside of it, toward the real whale, the dying whale, and I whispered, It's not your fault.

Helena slammed through the back door. She briefly pressed her breasts against my back as she reached over me to grab the bag, and then she ran back outside. I turned and watched her through the window. She was giving Vincent a shot. He was waking up. She was kissing Vincent, and he was rubbing his neck. I wondered what he remembered. She was sitting on his lap now, and she had her arms wrapped around his head. They did not look up when I walked past.

The interesting thing about *Positive* is that it never mentions HIV. If it weren't for the advertisements – Retrovir, Sustiva, Viramune – you would think it was a magazine about staying positive, as in upbeat. For this reason it is my favorite magazine. All the other ones build you up just to knock you down, but the editors at *Positive* understand that you have already been knocked down, again and again, and at this point you really don't need to fail a quiz called "Are You So Sexy or Just So-So?" *Positive* prints lists of ways to feel better, kind of like "Hints from Heloise." They seem easy to write, but that's the illusion of all good advice. Common sense and the truth should feel authorless, writ by time itself. It is actually hard to write something that will make a terminally ill person feel better. And *Positive* has rules, you can't just lift your guidance from the Bible or a book about Zen; they want original material. So far none of my submissions has been accepted, but I think I'm getting closer.

Do you have doubts about life? Are you unsure if it is worth the trouble? Look at the sky: that is for you. Look at each person's face as you pass on the street: those faces are for you. And the street itself, and the ground under the street, and the ball of fire underneath the ground: all these things are for you. They are as much for you as they are for other people. Remember this when you wake up in the morning and think you have nothing. Stand up and face the east. Now praise the sky and praise the light within each person under the sky. It's okay to be unsure. But praise, praise, praise.

THE THING AROUND YOUR NECK

Chimamanda Ngozi Adichie

> Chimamanda Ngozi Adichie (b. 1977) is a Nigerian author. She has published three novels, the second of which, *Half of a Yellow Sun*, won the Orange Prize, as well as an acclaimed collection of short stories, *The Thing Around Your Neck*. In 2010 she was listed in the *New Yorker's* '20 Under 40' Fiction Issue.

You thought everybody in America had a car and a gun; your uncles and aunts and cousins thought so too. Right after you won the American visa lottery, they told you: In a month, you will have a big car. Soon, a big house. But don't buy a gun like those Americans.

They trooped into the room in Lagos where you lived with your father and mother and three siblings, leaning against the unpainted walls because there weren't enough chairs to go round, to say goodbye in loud voices and tell you with lowered voices what they wanted you to send them. In comparison to the big car and house (and possibly gun), the things they wanted were minor – handbags and shoes and perfumes and clothes. You said okay, no problem.

Your uncle in America, who had put in the names of all your family members for the American visa lottery, said you could live with him until you got on your feet. He picked you up at the airport and bought you a big hot dog with yellow mustard that nauseated you. Introduction to America, he said with a laugh. He lived in a small white town in Maine, in a thirty-year-old house by a lake. He told you that the company he worked for had offered him a few thousand more than the average salary plus stock options because they were desperately trying to look diverse. They included a photo of him in every brochure, even those that had nothing to do with his unit. He laughed and said the job was good, was worth living in an all-white town even though his wife had to drive an hour to find a hair salon that did black hair. The trick was to understand America, to know that America was give-and-take. You gave up a lot but you gained a lot, too.

He showed you how to apply for a cashier job in the gas station on Main Street and he enrolled you in a community college, where the girls had thick thighs and wore bright-red nail polish, and self-tanner that made them look orange. They asked where you learned to speak English and if you had real houses back in Africa and if you'd seen a car before you came to America. They gawped at your hair. Does it stand up or fall down when you take out the braids? They wanted to know. All of it stands up? How? Why? Do you use a comb? You smiled tightly when they asked those questions. Your uncle told you to expect it; a mixture of ignorance and arrogance, he called it. Then he told you how the neighbors said, a few months after he moved into his house, that the squirrels had started to disappear. They had heard that Africans ate all kinds of wild animals.

You laughed with your uncle and you felt at home in his house; his wife called you *nwanne*, sister, and his two school-age children called you Aunty. They spoke Igbo and ate *garri* for lunch and it was like home. Until your uncle came into the cramped basement where you slept with old boxes and cartons and pulled you forcefully to him, squeezing your buttocks, moaning. He wasn't really your uncle; he was actually a brother of your father's sister's husband, not related by blood. After you pushed him away, he sat on your bed – it was his house, after all – and smiled and said you were no longer a child at twenty-two. If you let him, he would do many things for you. Smart women did it all the time. How did you think those women back home in Lagos with well-paying jobs made it? Even women in New York City?

You locked yourself in the bathroom until he went back upstairs, and the next morning, you left, walking the long windy road, smelling the baby fish in the lake. You saw him drive past – he had always dropped you off at Main Street – and he didn't honk. You wondered what he would tell his wife, why you had left. And you remembered what he said, that America was give-and-take.

You ended up in Connecticut, in another little town, because it was the last stop of the Greyhound bus you got on. You walked into the restaurant with the bright, clean awning and said you would work for two dollars less than the other waitresses. The manager, Juan, had inky-black hair and smiled to show a gold tooth. He said he had never had a Nigerian employee but all immigrants worked hard. He knew, he'd been there. He'd pay you a dollar less, but under the table; he didn't like all the taxes they were making him pay.

You could not afford to go to school, because now you paid rent for the tiny room with the stained carpet. Besides, the small Connecticut town didn't have a community college and credits at the state university cost too much. So you went to the public library, you looked up course syllabi on school Web sites and read some of the books. Sometimes you sat on the lumpy mattress of your twin bed and thought about home – your aunts who hawked dried fish and plantains, cajoling customers to buy and then shouting insults when they didn't; your uncles who drank local gin and crammed their families and lives into single rooms; your friends who had come out to say goodbye before you left, to rejoice because you won the American visa lottery, to confess their envy; your parents who often held hands as they walked to church on Sunday mornings, the neighbors from the next room laughing and teasing them; your father who brought back his boss's old newspapers from work and made your brothers read them; your mother whose salary was barely enough to pay your brothers' school fees at the secondary school where teachers gave an A when someone slipped them a brown envelope.

You had never needed to pay for an A, never slipped a brown envelope to a teacher in secondary school. Still, you chose long brown envelopes to send half your month's earnings to your parents at the address of the parastatal where your mother was a cleaner; you always used the dollar notes that Juan gave you because those were crisp, unlike the tips. Every month. You wrapped the money carefully in white paper but you didn't write a letter. There was nothing to write about.

In later weeks, though, you wanted to write because you had stories to tell. You wanted to write about the surprising openness of people in America, how eagerly they told you about their mother fighting cancer, about their sister-in-laws' preemie, the kinds of things that one should hide or should reveal only to the family members who wished them well. You wanted to write about the way people left so much food on their plates and crumpled a few dollar bills down, as though it was an offering, expiation for the wasted food. You wanted to write about the child who started to cry and pull at her blond hair and push the menus off the table and instead of the parents making her shut up, they pleaded with her, a child of perhaps five years old, and, then, they all got up and left. You wanted to write about the rich people who wore shabby clothes and tattered sneakers, who looked like the night watchmen in front of the large compounds in Lagos. You wanted to write that rich Americans were thin and poor Americans were fat and that many did not have a big house and car; you still were not sure about the guns, though, because they might have them inside their pockets.

It wasn't just to your parents you wanted to write, it was also to your friends, and cousins and aunts and uncles. But you could never afford enough perfumes and clothes and handbags and shoes to go around and still pay your rent on what you earned at the waitressing job, so you wrote nobody.

Nobody knew where you were, because you told no one. Sometimes you felt invisible and tried to walk through your room wall into the hallway, and when you bumped into the wall, it left bruises on your arms. Once, Juan asked if you had a man that hit you because he would take care of him and you laughed a mysterious laugh.

At night, something would wrap itself around your, neck, something that very nearly choked you before you fell asleep.

Many people at the restaurant asked when you had come from Jamaica, because they thought that every black person with a foreign accent was Jamaican. Or some who guessed that you were African told you that they loved elephants and wanted to go on a safari.

So when he asked you, in the dimness of the restaurant after you recited the daily specials, what African country you were from, you said Nigeria and expected him to say that he had donated money to fight AIDS in Botswana. But he asked if you were Yoruba or Igbo, because you didn't have a Fulani face. You were surprised – you thought he must be a professor of anthropology at the state university, a little young in his late twenties or so, but who was to say? Igbo, you said. He asked your name and said Akunna was pretty. He did not ask what it meant, fortunately, because you were sick of how people said, "Father's Wealth? You mean, like, your father will actually sell you to a husband?"

He told you he had been to Ghana and Uganda and Tanzania, loved the poetry of Okot p'Bitek and the novels of Amos Tutuola and had read a lot about sub-Saharan African countries, their histories, their complexities. You wanted to feel disdain, to show it as you brought his order, because white people who liked Africa too much and those who liked Africa too little were the same – condescending. But he didn't shake his head in the superior way that Professor Cobbledick back in the Maine community college did during a class discussion on decolonization in Africa. He didn't have that expression of Professor Cobbledick's, that expression of a person who thought himself better than the people he knew about. He came in the next day and sat at the same table and when you asked if the chicken was okay, he asked if you had grown up in Lagos. He came in the third day and began talking before he ordered, about how he had visited Bombay and now wanted to visit Lagos, to see how real people lived, like in the shantytowns, because he never did any of the silly tourist stuff when he was abroad. He talked and talked and you had to tell him it was against restaurant policy. He brushed your hand when you set the glass of water down. The fourth day, when you saw him arrive, you told Juan you didn't want that table anymore. After your shift that night, he was waiting outside, earphones stuck in his ears, asking you to go out with him because your name rhymed with *hakuna matata* and *The Lion King* was the only maudlin movie he'd ever liked. You didn't know what *The Lion King* was. You looked at him in the bright light and noticed that his eyes were the color of extra-virgin olive oil, a greenish gold. Extra-virgin olive oil was the only thing, you loved, truly loved, in America.

He was a senior at the state university. He told you how old he was and you asked why he had not graduated yet. This was

America, after all, it was not like back home, where universities closed so often that people added three years to their normal course of study and lecturers went on strike after strike and still were not paid. He said he had taken a couple of years off to discover himself and travel, mostly to Africa and Asia. You asked him where he ended up finding himself and he laughed. You did not laugh. You did not know that people could simply choose not to go to school, that people could dictate to life. You were used to accepting what life gave, writing down what life dictated.

You said no the following four days to going out with him, because you were uncomfortable with the way he looked at your face, that intense, consuming way he looked at your face that made you say goodbye to him but also made you reluctant to walk away. And then, the fifth night, you panicked when he was not standing at the door after your shift. You prayed for the first time in a long time and when he came up behind you and said hey, you said yes, you would go out with him, even before he asked. You were scared he would not ask again.

The next day, he took you to dinner at Chang's and your fortune cookie had two strips of paper. Both of them were blank.

You knew you had become comfortable when you told him that you watched *Jeopardy* on the restaurant TV and that you rooted for the following, in this order: women of color, black men, and white women, before, finally, white men – which meant you never rooted for white men. He laughed and told you he was used to not being rooted for, his mother taught women's studies.

And you knew you had become close when you told him that your father was really not a schoolteacher in Lagos, that he was a junior driver for a construction company. And you, told him about that day in Lagos traffic in the rickety Peugeot 504 your father drove; it was raining and your seat was wet because of the rust-eaten hole in the roof. The traffic was heavy, the traffic was always heavy in Lagos, and when it rained it was chaos. The roads became muddy ponds and cars got stuck and some of your cousins went out and made some money pushing the cars out. The rain, the swampiness, you thought, made your father step on the brakes too late that day. You heard the bump before you felt it. The car your father rammed into was wide, foreign, and dark green, with golden headlights like the eyes of a leopard. Your father started to cry and beg even before he got out of the car and laid himself flat on the road, causing much blowing of horns. Sorry, sir, sorry, sir, he chanted. If you sell me and my family, you cannot buy even one tire on your car. Sorry, sir.

The Big Man seated at the back did not come out, but his driver did, examining the damage, looking at your father's sprawled form from the corner of his eye as though the pleading was like pornography, a performance he was ashamed to admit he enjoyed. At last he let your father go. Waved him away. The other cars' horns blew and drivers cursed. When your father came back into the car, you refused to look at him because he was just like the pigs that wallowed in the marshes around the market. Your father looked like *nsi*. Shit.

After you told him this, he pursed his lips and held your hand and said he understood how you felt. You shook your hand free, suddenly annoyed, because he thought the world was, or ought to be, full of people like him. You told him there was nothing to understand, it was just the way it was.

He found the African store in the Hartford yellow pages and drove you there. Because of the way he walked around with familiarity, tilting the bottle of palm wine to see how much sediment it had, the Ghanaian store owner asked him if he was African, like the white Kenyans or South Africans, and he said yes, but he'd been in America for a long time. He looked pleased that the store owner had believed him. You cooked that evening with the things you had bought, and after he ate *garri* and *onugbu* soup, he threw up in your sink. You didn't mind, though, because now you would be able to cook *onugbu* soup with meat.

He didn't eat meat because he thought it was wrong the way they killed animals; he said they released fear toxins into the animals and the fear toxins made people paranoid. Back home, the meat pieces you ate, when there was meat, were the size of half your finger. But you did not tell him that. You did not tell him either that the *dawadawa* cubes your mother cooked everything with, because curry and thyme were too expensive, had MSG, *were* MSG. He said MSG caused cancer, it was the reason he liked Chang's; Chang didn't cook with MSG.

Once, at Chang's, he told the waiter he had recently visited Shanghai, that he spoke some Mandarin. The waiter warmed up and told him what soup was best and then asked him, "You have girlfriend in Shanghai now?" And he smiled and said nothing.

You lost your appetite, the region deep in your chest felt clogged. That night, you didn't moan when he was inside you, you bit your lips and pretended that you didn't come because you knew he would worry. Later you told him why you were upset, that even though you went to Chang's so often together, even though you had kissed just before the menus came, the Chinese man had assumed you could not possibly be his girlfriend, and he had smiled and said nothing. Before he apologized, he gazed at you blankly and you knew that he did not understand.

He bought you presents and when you objected about the cost, he said his grandfather in Boston had been wealthy but hastily added that the old man had given a lot away and so the trust fund he had wasn't huge. His presents mystified you. A fist-size glass ball that you shook to watch a tiny shapely doll in pink spin around. A shiny rock whose surface took on the color of whatever touched it. An expensive scarf hand-painted in Mexico. Finally you told him, your voice stretched in irony, that in your life presents were always useful. The rock, for instance, would work if you could grind things with it. He laughed long and hard but you did not laugh. You realized that in his life, he could buy presents that were just presents and nothing else, nothing useful. When he started to buy you shoes and clothes and books, you asked him not to, you didn't want any presents at all. He bought them anyway and you kept them for your cousins and uncles and aunts, for when you would one day be able to visit home, even though you did not know how you could ever afford a ticket *and* your rent. He said he really wanted to see Nigeria and he could pay for you both to go. You did not want him to pay for you to visit home. You did not want him to go to Nigeria, to add it to the list of countries where he went to gawk at the lives of poor people who could never gawk back at *his* life. You told him this on a sunny day, when he took you to see

Long Island Sound; and the two of you argued, your voices raised as you walked along the calm water. He said you were wrong to call him self-righteous. You said he was wrong to call only the poor Indians in Bombay the real Indians. Did it mean he wasn't a real American, since he was not like the poor fat people you and he had seen in Hartford? He hurried ahead of you, his upper body bare and pale, his flip-flops raising bits of sand, but then he came back and held out his hand for yours. You made up and made love and ran your hands through each other's, hair, his soft and yellow like the swinging tassels of growing corn, yours dark and bouncy like the filling of a pillow. He had got too much sun and his skin turned the color of a ripe watermelon and you kissed his back before you rubbed lotion on it.

The thing that wrapped itself around your neck, that nearly choked you before you fell asleep, started to loosen, to let go.

You knew by people's reactions that you two were abnormal – the way the nasty ones were too nasty and the nice ones too nice. The old white men and women who muttered and glared at him, the black men who shook their heads at you, the black women whose pitying eyes bemoaned your lack of self-esteem, your self-loathing. Or the black women who smiled swift solidarity smiles; the black men who tried too hard to forgive you, saying a too-obvious hi to him; the white men and women who said, "What a good-looking pair" too brightly, too loudly as though to prove their own open-mindedness to themselves.

But his parents were different; they almost made you think it was all normal. His mother told you that he had never brought a girl to meet them, except for his high school prom date, and he grinned stiffly and held your hand. The tablecloth shielded your clasped hands. He squeezed your hand and you squeezed back and wondered why he was so stiff, why his extra-virgin-olive-oil-colored eyes darkened as he spoke to his parents. His mother was delighted when she asked if you'd read Nawal el Saadawi and you said yes. His father asked how similar Indian food was to Nigerian food and teased you about paying when the check came. You looked at them and felt grateful that they did not examine you like an exotic trophy, an ivory tusk.

Afterwards, he told you about his issues with his parents, how they portioned out love like a birthday cake, how they would give him a bigger slice if only he'd agree to go to law school. You wanted to sympathize. But instead you were angry.

You were angrier when he told you he had refused to go up to Canada with them for a week or two, to their summer cottage in the Quebec countryside. They had even asked him to bring you. He showed you pictures of the cottage and you wondered why it was called a cottage because the buildings that big around your neighborhood back home were banks and churches. You dropped a glass and it shattered on the hardwood of his apartment floor and he asked what was wrong and you said nothing, although you thought a lot was wrong. Later, in the shower you started to cry. You watched the water dilute your tears and you didn't know why you were crying.

You wrote home finally. A short letter to your parents, slipped in between the crisp dollar bills, and you included your address. You got a reply only days later, by courier. Your mother wrote the letter herself; you knew from the spidery penmanship, from the misspelled words.

Your father was dead; he had slumped over the steering wheel of his company car. Five months now, she wrote. They had used some of the money you sent to give him a good funeral. They killed a goat for the guests and buried him in a good coffin. You curled up in bed, pressed your knees to your chest and tried to remember what you had been doing when your father died, what you had been doing for all the months when he was already dead. Perhaps your father died on the day your whole body had been covered in goosebumps, hard as uncooked rice, that you could not explain, Juan teasing you about taking over from the chef so that the heat in the kitchen would warm you up. Perhaps your father died on one of the days you took a drive to Mystic or watched a play in Manchester or had dinner at Chang's.

He held you while you cried, smoothed your hair, and offered to buy your ticket, to go with you to see your family. You said no, you needed to go alone. He asked if you would come back and you reminded him that you had a green card and you would lose it if you did not come back in one year. He said you knew what he meant, would you come back, come back?

You turned away and said nothing, and when he drove you to the airport, you hugged him tight for a long, long moment, and then you let go.

THE REDEMPTION
OF GALEN PIKE

Carys Davies

> Carys Davies is a British short story writer. She won the
> Society of Authors 2010 Olive Cook Short Story Award
> for 'The Quiet', and was then awarded the V. S. Pritchett
> Memorial Prize in 2011 for 'The Redemption of Galen
> Pike'. She curates the short fiction programme for
> Lancaster's literature festival, Litfest, where she hosts
> readings and discussions with other writers of short fiction.

They'd all seen Sheriff Nye bringing Pike into town: the two shapes
snaking down the path off the mountain through the patches of
melting snow and over the green showing beneath, each of them
growing bigger as they moved across the rocky pasture and came
down into North Street to the jailhouse – Nye on his horse, the tall
gaunt figure of Galen Pike following behind on the rope.

The current Piper City jailhouse was a low cramped brick
building containing a single square cell, Piper City being at this time,
in spite of the pretensions of its name, a small and thinly populated
town of a hundred and ninety-three souls in the foothills of the
Colorado mountains. Aside from the cell, there was a scrubby yard
behind, where the hangings took place, a front office with a table,
a chair and a broom; a hook on the wall where the cell keys hung
from a thick ring; a small stove where Knapp the jailer warmed his
coffee and cooked his pancakes in the morning.

For years, Walter's sister Patience had been visiting the felons
who found themselves incarcerated for any length of time in the
Piper City jail. Mostly they were outsiders – drifters and vagrants
drawn to the place by the occasional but persistent rumours of
gold – and whenever one came along, Patience visited him.

Galen Pike's crime revolted Patience more than she could say, and
on her way to the jailhouse to meet him for the first time, she told

herself she wouldn't think of it; walking past the closed bank, the shuttered front of the general store, the locked-up haberdasher's, the drawn blinds of the dentist, she averted her gaze.

She would do what she always did with the felons; she would bring Galen Pike something to eat and drink, she would sit with him and talk to him and keep him company in the days that he had left. She would not recite scripture, or lecture him about the Commandments or the deadly sins, and she would only read to him if he desired it – a psalm or a prayer or a few selected verses she thought might be helpful to someone in his situation but that was all.

She was a thin, plain woman, Patience Haig.

Straight brown hair scraped back from her forehead so severely that there was a small bald patch where the hair was divided in the centre. It was tied behind in a long dry braid. Her face, too, was long and narrow, her features small and unremarkable, except for her nose which was damaged and lopsided, the right nostril squashed and flattened against the bridge. She wore black flat-heeled boots and a grey dress with long sleeves and a capacious square collar. She was thirty-six years old.

If the preparation of the heart is taken seriously the right words will come. As she walked, Patience silently repeated the advice Abigail Warner had given her when she'd passed on to Patience the responsibility of visiting the jail. Patience was always a little nervous before meeting a new prisoner for the first time, and as she came to the end of Franklin Street and turned the corner into North, she reminded herself that the old woman's advice had always stood her in good stead: if she thought about how lonely it would be – how bleak and frightening and uncomfortable – to be shut up in a twelve foot box far from home without company or kindness, then whatever the awfulness of the crime that had been committed, she always found that she was able, with the help of her basket of biscuits and strawberry cordial, to establish a calm and companionable atmosphere in the grim little room. Almost always, she had found the men happy to see her.

"Good morning, Mr Pike," she said, stepping through the barred door and hearing it clang behind her.

Galen Pike loosened the phlegm in his scrawny throat, blew out his hollow cheeks and hawked on the ground.

"I have warm biscuits," continued Patience, setting her basket on the narrow table between them, "and strawberry cordial."

Pike looked her slowly up and down. He looked at her flat-heeled tightly laced boots, her grey long-sleeved dress and scraped-back hair and asked her, in a nasty smoke-cracked drawl, if she was a preacher.

"No," said Patience, "I am your friend."

Pike burst out laughing.

He bared his yellow teeth and threw back his mane of filthy black hair and observed that if she was his friend she'd have brought him something a little stronger than strawberry cordial to drink.

If she was his friend, he said, lowering his voice and pushing his vicious ravenous-looking face close to hers and rocking forward on the straight-backed chair to which he was trussed with rope and a heavy chain, she'd have used her little white hand to slip the key to his cell off its hook on her way in and popped it in her pretty Red Riding Hood basket instead of leaving it out there on the goddamn wall with that fat pancake-scoffing fucker of a jailer.

Patience blinked and took a breath and replied crisply that he should know very well she couldn't do the second thing, and she certainly wouldn't do the first because she didn't believe anyone needed anything stronger than strawberry cordial to refresh themselves on a warm day.

She removed the clean white cloth that covered the biscuits. The cloth was damp from the steam and she used it to wipe the surface of the greasy little table which was spotted and streaked with thick unidentifiable stains, and poured out three inches of cordial into the pewter mug she'd brought from home that belonged to her brother Walter.

She told Galen Pike that she would sit with him; that she would come every morning between now and Wednesday unless he told her not to, and on Wednesday she would come too, to be with him then also, if he desired it. In the meantime, if he wanted to, he could unburden himself about what he had done, she would not judge him. Or they could talk about other things, or if he liked she would read to him, or they might sit in silence if he preferred. She didn't mind in the least, she said, if they sat in silence, she was used to silence, she liked it almost more than speaking.

Pike looked at her, frowning and wrinkling his big hooked nose, as if he was trying to figure out whether he'd been sent a mad person. When he didn't make any reply to what she'd said, Patience settled herself in the chair opposite him and took out her knitting and for half an hour neither she nor Galen Pike spoke a word, until Pike, irritated perhaps by the prolonged quiet or the rapid clickety-clack of her wooden needles, leaned across the table with the top half of his scrawny body and twisted his face up close to hers like before and asked, what was a dried-up old lady like her doing knitting a baby's bootie?

Patience coloured at the insult but ignored it and told Pike that she and the other women from the Franklin Street Friends' Meeting House were preparing a supply of clothing for Piper City's new hostel for unwed mothers. A lot of girls, she said, ended up coming this way, dragging themselves along the Boulder Road, looking for somewhere to lay their heads.

Pike slouched against the back of his chair. He twisted his grimy-fingered hands which were fastened together in a complicated knot and roped tightly, one on top of the other, across his lap.

"Unwed mothers?" he said in a leering unpleasant way. "Where all is that then?"

"Nowhere at present," Patience replied, looking up from her work, "but when it opens it will be here on North Street. The application is with the mayor."

When Patience Haig wasn't visiting the occasional residents of the Piper City jail, she was fighting the town's Republican mayor, Byron Lym.

Over the years, she and her brother Walter and the other Friends from the Franklin Street Meeting House had joined forces with the pastor and congregation of the Episcopalian church and a number of other Piper City residents to press for certain improvements in the town: a new roof for the dilapidated schoolhouse; a road out to Piet Larson's so they could get a cart out there from time to time and bring the old man into town so he could feel a bit of life about him; a library; a small fever hospital; a hostel on North Street for unwed mothers.

So far, Lym had blocked or sabotaged each and every one of the projects. He'd said no to the new roof for the school, no to Piet Larson's road, no to the library, no to the hospital and a few days from now, they would find out if he was going to say no to the hostel too.

"He is a difficult man, the mayor," said Patience, but Pike wasn't listening, he was looking out through the cell's tiny window at the maroon peaks of the mountains and when, at the end of an hour, he had asked no more questions about the hostel or anything else, or shown any desire at all to enter into any kind of conversation, Patience put her needles together and placed the finished bootie in her basket and told him that she would come again in the morning if he'd like her to.

Pike yawned and without turning his eyes from the window told her to suit herself, it was all the same to him whether she came or not. In another week he would be dead and that would be that.

Over the next three days, Patience visited Galen Pike every morning.

She brought fresh biscuits and cordial and asked Pike if he wished to talk, or have her read to him. When he didn't reply she took out her knitting and they sat together in silence.

On the fifth morning, a Sunday, Patience arrived a little later than usual, apologising as she stepped in past Knapp when he unlocked, and then locked, the barred door behind her; she'd been at Meeting for Worship, she said, and there'd been a great quantity of notices afterwards, mostly on the subject of the hostel, as the mayor had indicated he'd be making his decision shortly, possibly as early as tomorrow.

Pike yawned and spat on the floor and said he didn't give a shit where she'd been or what she'd been doing and the only thing he wanted to know was how she'd got that pretty nose.

Knapp, in his office, peeped out from behind his newspaper. He'd never known any of the men to be so unmannerly to Miss Haig. He craned his neck a little farther to see if anything interesting would happen now, if Patience Haig would put Pike in his place, or maybe get up and walk out and leave him to rot in there by hisself for the last three days of his life like he deserved.

"I fell off a gate, Mr Pike," said Patience. "When I was nine."

"Ain't that a shame," said Pike in his nasty drawl, and Knapp kept his eye on Patience, but all she said was that it was quite all right, she'd got used to it a long time ago and didn't notice it unless people remarked on it, which in her experience they never did unless they meant to be rude or unkind, and after that the two of them settled into their customary silence.

Patience took out her knitting.

In his office Knapp folded up the newspaper and began heating his coffee and cooking his pancakes. The fat in his skillet began to pop and smoke and then he poured in the batter and when the first pancake was cooked he slid it onto a plate and then he cooked another and another and when he had a pile of half a dozen he drew his chair up to his table and began to eat. Every so often he looked up and over into the cell where Patience Haig and Galen Pike sat together, as if he was still hoping for some significant event or exchange of words, something he might tell his wife about on Wednesday when he was done keeping an eye on Pike and could go home. It was creepy, he thought, as he munched on his pancakes and gulped his coffee, the way the fellow was so scrawny and thin.

"QUIT SNOOPING!" yelled Pike all of a sudden into the silence, opening his mouth wide in a big yellow-toothed snarl that made Knapp jump like a frightened squirrel and drop his fork.

"Jesus Christ," growled Pike. "Nosy fat curly-tailed fuckin' hog."

He turned to Patience. "What all d'y'all do then? At the worship meeting?"

Patience laid down her knitting and explained that there were nineteen members of the Piper City Friends' Meeting, including herself and her brother Walter, and on Sunday mornings they gathered together at the Franklin Street Meeting House where they sat on two rows of benches arranged around a small central table.

"What about the preacher?"

"No preacher," said Patience. Instead, they abided in silence and sought the light of God within themselves and no one spoke out loud unless the spirit moved them.

"What light of God?" said Galen Pike.

"The light of God that shines in every man," said Patience.

On the following day Byron Lym summoned Patience Haig and the pastor of the Episcopalian church and a handful of the other Piper City residents who supported the creation of the hostel for unwed mothers and told them they couldn't have it.

Afterwards, walking home, Patience passed Mayor Lym's big yellow house with its screened-in porch and its magical square of mown green lawn and its herbaceous borders and its sweeping driveway of twinkling smooth-rolled macadam out in front. She passed the schoolhouse with its perished square of flapping tarpaulin tethered to the beams of the broken roof; she passed the plot of unused ground next to the lumber yard where they'd hoped to build the library; the empty warehouse that could so easily be converted into a fever hospital; and by the time she reached Franklin Street she felt so low, so crushed and despondent and depressed, that she didn't go to the jail at all that day to visit Galen Pike.

She ate lunch with her brother Walter and let loose a tirade against the mayor. "Byron Lym has no interest in the unfortunate people of this world," she said, speaking quickly and breathlessly. Boiling fury and exasperated irritation bordering on despair made her burst out: "He is selfish and corrupt and bad for the town."

Walter served the macaroni cheese and Patience sat without eating, fuming.

Byron Lym had won every election in Piper City for fifteen years. The margin was narrow, but on election day, the Republican vote always seemed to win out: there were enough people in Piper City who didn't seem to mind Byron Lym stealing their taxes and spending them on himself, as long as he kept them low.

"It's wrong, Walter," she declared, "the way that man manages to hold onto those votes. It's like a greedy child with a handful of sticky candies and it shouldn't be allowed when there's not one ounce of goodness in him, not one single solitary drop."

Walter raised his eyebrows and looked at his sister with his mild smile. "No light of God, sister?"

Patience threw her napkin at him across the table. "Don't tease me, Walter. Doubtless it is there in some dark silk-lined pocket of his embroidered waistcoat but if it is he keeps it well hidden."

When they'd finished eating she asked her brother to please excuse her, she was going out for some air and for an hour Walter could hear her out on the porch glider, rocking furiously back and forth, the rusty rings creaking and tugging in the porch roof as if they might pull the whole thing down at any moment.

In his cell, Pike sat with the rope cutting into his wrists, the chain grinding against his hips every time he shifted himself in the chair. He looked around at the bare brick walls and the thick bars, at Knapp reading his newspaper or hunched over his skillet or dragging the twigs of his old broom across the office floor.

He closed his eyes and sat listening to the rustle of the aspen trees outside, and from time to time he turned his head and looked out through the tiny window at the maroon peaks of the mountains.

Eleven o'clock had come and gone, then twelve and the woman in the grey dress with the lopsided nose had not appeared. Three o'clock, four, still no sign, and Galen Pike discovered that he missed her.

He missed the gentle tapping of her knitting needles, the soft reedy tooting of the stale air of his cell as it went in and out of her squashed nostril. He realised that from the moment he woke up in the mornings, he was listening for her quick light step in the street outside. From the moment Knapp pushed his oatmeal through the bars and reached in for his potty, he was looking over at the office door and waiting for it to open. She was the only person in the world who did not recoil from him in disgust. In the courthouse people had held themselves against the wall, gawping at his wild black hair and straggly vagabond's beard, shaking their heads as if they had seen the devil. This one, with her neat hair and her long plain face and her flat polished shoes, sat there straight and stiff and looked him in the eye. He felt bad about calling her an old lady and being rude about her nose. He missed the way she gathered the silence of his cell about her like something warm that did not exclude him from it. He'd even come to enjoy the strawberry cordial.

Slowly, inch by careful inch, and with the greatest difficulty, he began working his hands loose from the tight coils of the rope.

*

"Forgive me, Mr Pike," said Patience when she came in the morning.

She would have come yesterday, she said, but the mayor had turned down their application for the hostel. He said it would be "a blister in the eye of any visitor to Piper City and an affront to the respectability of its inhabitants." Afterwards her spirits had been so low she'd gone straight home. "My company would have been very poor I'm afraid, Mr Pike, even for someone who makes as few demands on it as you."

Pike wished Knapp wasn't there. He hated the way the fat jailer spied on them.

"Ain't that a shame," he said, his voice low, hoarse.

"Yes."

Suddenly there were tears in Patience Haig's eyes. Her plain narrow face looked even longer than ever, pulled down by the twitching corners of her thin mouth.

Pike studied her. He didn't know what to say.

Knapp had edged closer, attracted no doubt by the soft sound of Patience Haig crying. When Pike saw him he jumped up with his chair on his back and shook his chains and roared and rushed towards the bars like a gorilla, sending the terrified Knapp scurrying back to his stove on the far side of his little office. When Pike returned to the table he found Patience laughing quietly.

"He's like the winged lion in the Book of Revelation," she said, blowing her nose. "Full of eyes before, behind and within."

"Ain't that the truth."

Patience sniffed and dried her cheeks with a half-made bootie. She straightened her long dry braid and squared her bony shoulders.

"Well," she said. "Enough of my disappointments, Mr Pike. How are you today?"

Pike wanted to tell her he'd missed her yesterday when she hadn't come.

"I'm okay," he said.

"That's good," said Patience.

"I have something for you," said Galen Pike, laying his hand upon the table.

He had made it, he said, to brighten her frock.

It was a kind of rosette, or flower, woven from what appeared to be loose threads from the rope that had been twined about his hands, which Patience saw now was no longer there. Four rough stringy petals; at the centre a button from his putrid blood-soaked shirt. Patience held it for a moment in the palm of her hand. The rough petals scraped her skin. She wondered if Pike meant it as a romantic gesture of some sort.

If the preparation of the heart is taken seriously the right words will come.

"Thank you, Mr Pike," she said gently. Thank you but she couldn't accept it, she was against adornment, material decoration.

She placed the flower back in the hollow of his cupped hand. His dirty fingers closed around it.

"You hate me."

"No."

Knapp held his breath. He watched Pike turn the rope flower over in his hand and shake his head, the foul matted tangle of snakes and rat-tails, and heard him tell Patience Haig she was wrong about the light of God being in every man. He didn't have it. It had passed him by. Where he was, was dark and swampy and bad.

"Nonsense," said Patience.

It was true, said Pike, looking out through the tiny window at the maroon-coloured peaks beyond. Since his mother died he'd done all manner of wicked things. Since she passed away, years and years and years ago, there'd been no one to tell him how to behave; no one in the world he'd wanted to please, whose good opinion mattered at all. If he'd wanted to do something, he'd gone ahead and done it. He looked at Patience. What was her name? he asked.

"Patience," she said. "Patience Haig."

"You remind me, a little, Miss Haig, of my mother."

Knapp's beady eyes moved from Galen Pike to the thin Quaker lady in her drab frock. It was hard to tell from her expression if she enjoyed this comparison with Pike's mother. Her face showed no emotion, her long braid lay neatly down her back, her hands folded in her lap.

"I am afraid of the hangman, Miss Haig," said Galen Pike.

He touched his hand to his throat. Would she shave him, in the morning? And cut his hair? Would she bring him a clean shirt so he wouldn't look so dirty and overgrown when they came for him in the morning? That is, he added with an awkward kind of grimace, if she didn't disapprove too much of him being anxious about his appearance.

Patience looked at her hands. Of course she would shave him, she said softly. If he thought it would help.

And then, because she wanted very much to lighten the heaviness of the moment, she smiled, and said she hoped she wouldn't make too much of a mess of it; she'd watched her brother Walter shaving a few times but had no experience herself. Pike said he was sure it would be all right. He trusted her not to hurt him.

When she'd finished shaving him the next morning, and given him Walter's clean shirt to put on instead of his stinking one, Patience asked him if he wanted her to read something. The twenty-third Psalm was beautiful, she said. It would give him strength, she was sure. Pike said all he wanted was for her to go with him. For ten minutes more they sat quietly. There was the sound of Knapp's broom moving across the floor of his little office, outside in the yard the rustle of the aspen trees, and then Knapp came with the key, and Sheriff Nye and two of his men, and Dr Harriman and the hangman from Boulder.

Nye unlocked the chain around Pike's waist and untied the remaining rope that fastened his legs to the chair, and took him by the arm.

In the yard he asked him if he had any last words and in a strong voice Pike said he wanted to thank Miss Patience Haig for the tasty biscuits and the cordial and the clean shirt and the shave but most of all he wanted to thank her for her sweet quiet company. She was the best and kindest person he had ever known. He had not deserved her but he was grateful and he wished he had something to give her, some small remembrance or lasting token of appreciation to show his gratitude, but he had nothing and all he could hope was that if she ever thought of him after he was dead, it would not be badly.

It was hard to tell, Knapp said later to his wife, what effect this short speech of Pike's had on Patience Haig, but when the burlap bag came smartly down over Pike's black eyes and repulsive ravenous features and the floor opened beneath his feet, he was certain Miss Haig struggled with her famous composure; that behind the rough snap of the cloth and the clatter of the scaffold's wooden machinery, he heard a small high cry escape from her plain upright figure.

When it was over Patience asked Knapp if she might sit for while in the empty cell. She looked for the rope flower but it wasn't there. Knapp must have spirited it away, or perhaps Pike had taken it with him.

It seemed an eternity since he'd first wandered into town. There'd still been snow on the ground, though the worst of the winter had been over. For months before there'd been talk of a little gold to the south, and she remembered seeing the four Piper City men heading off on their expedition to look for it, Pike making the fifth as bag-carrier and general dogsbody, loaded up with cooking pots and shovels, dynamite, fuel, picks.

She walked slowly away from the jailhouse, trying to empty her mind of everything that had happened since the four Piper City men had failed to return and their horrible fate had been discovered. She tried to empty her mind of the quiet hours she'd spent with Galen Pike at the jail, of Byron Lym's crushing rejection of her latest project, of the terrible hanging. She had never felt so miserable in her entire life. She turned out of North Street into Franklin and passed in front of the shuttered front of the general store, the closed bank, the locked-up haberdasher's, the drawn blinds of the dentist. She paused before the heavy pine doors of the bank. On the brass knocker someone had tied an evergreen wreath with a thick black ribbon. Poor Mr Shrigley, she thought. Poor Mr Palgrave. Poor Damon Archer and Dawson Mew.

She walked on a little way and then she stopped and turned and looked back at the silent premises of the four dead men.

It had not occurred to her before.

"Oh dear Lord," she whispered, thinking of Byron Lym's stubborn but wafer-thin majority at the polls.

In Piper City everyone knew how everyone else voted and if Patience's memory served her and she was not mistaken, there'd been forty-eight Republican voters at the last election, and since then Galen Pike had eaten four of them. It was doubtful Lym could succeed next time without them.

Patience turned on her heel.

She squared her bony shoulders and tucked her basket into the crook of her arm.

Quickened her step along Franklin Street towards home.

Ran up the steps onto the porch and in through the screen door, to tell Walter the news.

THE HEART OF DENIS NOBLE

Alison MacLeod

> Alison MacLeod is a British novelist, short story writer
> and essayist. She was awarded the Society of Authors Tom-
> Gallon Trust Award in 2008 and was shortlisted for the
> BBC National Short Story Award in 2011 for 'The Heart
> of Denis Noble'.

As Denis Noble, Professor of Cardiovascular Physiology, succumbs
to the opioids – a meandering river of fentanyl from the IV drip
– he is informed his heart is on its way. In twenty, perhaps thirty
minutes' time, the Cessna air ambulance will land in the bright,
crystalline light of December, on the small landing strip behind the
Radcliffe Hospital.

A bearded jaw appears over him. From this angle, the mouth is
oddly labial. Does he understand? Professor Noble nods from the
other side of the ventilation mask. He would join in the team chat
but the mask prevents it, and in any case, he must lie still so the
nurse can shave the few hairs that remain on his chest.

No cool-box then. No heart on ice. This is what they are telling
him. Instead, the latest technology. He remembers the prototype
he was once shown. His new heart will arrive in its own state-
of-the-art reliquary. It will be lifted, beating, from a nutrient-rich
bath of blood and oxygen. So he can rest easy, someone adds. It's
beating well at 40,000 feet, out of range of all turbulence. 'We
need your research, Professor,' another voice jokes from behind the
ECG. 'We're taking no chances!'

Which isn't to say that the whole thing isn't a terrible gamble.

The nurse has traded the shaver for a pair of nail-clippers. She
sets to work on the nails on his right hand, his plucking hand. Is
that necessary? he wants to ask. It will take him some time to grow
them back, assuming of course he still has 'time'. As she slips the

pulse-oximeter over his index finger, he wonders if Joshua will show any interest at all in the classical guitar he is destined to inherit, possibly any day now. According to his mother, Josh is into electronica and urban soul.

A second nurse bends and whispers in his ear like a lover. 'Now all you have to do is relax, Denis. We've got everything covered.' Her breath is warm. Her breast is near. He can imagine the gloss of her lips. He wishes she would stay by his ear forever. 'We'll have you feeling like yourself again before you know it.'

He feels he might be sick.

Then his choice of pre-op music – the second movement of Schubert's Piano Trio in E-Flat Major – seems to flow, sweet and grave, from her mouth into his ear, and once more he can see past the red and golden treetops of Gordon Square to his attic room of half a century ago. A recording of the Schubert is rising through the floorboards, and the girl beside him in his narrow student bed is warm; her lips brush the lobe of his ear; her voice alone, the whispered current of it, is enough to arouse him. But when her fingers find him beneath the sheet, they surprise him with a catheter, and he has to shut his eyes against the tears, against the absurdity of age.

The heart of Denis Noble beat for the first time on the fifth of March, 1936 in the body of Ethel Noble as she stitched a breast pocket to a drape-cut suit in an upstairs room at Wilson & Jeffries, the tailoring house where she first met her husband George, a trainee cutter, across a flashing length of gold silk lining.

As she pierced the tweed with her basting needle, she remembered George's tender, awkward kiss to her collarbone that morning, and, as if in reply, Denis's heart, a mere tube at this point, beat its first of more than two billion utterances – da dum. Unknown to Ethel, she was twenty-one days pregnant. Her thread dangled briefly in mid-air.

Soon, the tube that was Denis Noble's heart, a delicate scrap of mesoderm, would push towards life. In the dark of Ethel, it would twist and grope, looping blindly back towards itself in the primitive knowledge that circulation, the vital whoosh of life, deplores a straight line. With a tube, true, we can see from end to end, we can blow clear through or whistle a tune – a tube is nothing if not straightforward – but a loop, a *loop*, is a circuit of energy understood only by itself.

In this unfolding, intra-uterine drama, Denis Noble – a dangling button on the thread of life – would begin to take shape, to hold fast. He would inherit George's high forehead and Ethel's bright almond-shaped, almost Oriental, eyes. His hands would be small but unusually dexterous. A birthmark would stamp itself on his left hip. But inasmuch as he was flesh, blood and bone, he was also, deep within Ethel, a living stream of sound and sensation, a delicate flux of stimuli, the influence of which eluded all known measure, then as now.

He was the cloth smoothed beneath Ethel's cool palm, and the pumping of her foot on the pedal of the Singer machine. He was the hiss of her iron over the sleeve press and the clink of brass pattern-weights in her apron pocket. He was the soft spring light through the open window, the warmth of it bathing her face, and the serotonin surging in her synapses at the sight of a magnolia tree in flower. He was the manifold sound waves of passers-by: of motor cars hooting, of old men hawking and spitting, and delivery boys teetering down Savile Row under bolts of cloth bigger than they were. Indeed it is impossible to say where Denis stopped and the world began.

Only on a clear, cloudless night in November 1940 did the world seem to unstitch itself from the small boy he was and separate into something strange, something other. Denis opened his eyes to the darkness. His mother was scooping him from his bed and running down the stairs so fast, his head bumped up and down against her shoulder.

Downstairs, his father wasn't in his armchair with the newspaper on his lap, but on the sitting room floor cutting cloth by the light of a torch. Why was Father camping indoors? 'Let's sing a song,' his mother whispered, but she forgot to tell him which song to sing.

The kitchen was a dark place and no, it wasn't time for eggs and soldiers, not yet, she shooshed, and even as she spoke, she was depositing him beneath the table next to the fat yellow bundle that was his sister, and stretching out beside him, even though her feet in their court shoes stuck out the end. 'There, there,' she said as she pulled them both to her. Then they turned their ears towards a sky they couldn't see and listened to the planes that droned like wasps in the jar of the South London night.

When the bang came, the floor shuddered beneath them and plaster fell in lumps from the ceiling. His father rushed in from the sitting room, pins still gripped between his lips. Before his mother had finished thanking God, Denis felt his legs propel him, without permission, not even his own, to the window to look. Beneath a corner of the black-out curtain, at the bottom of the garden, flames were leaping. 'Fire!' he shouted, but his father shouted louder, nearly swallowing his pins – 'GET AWAY from the window!' – and plucked him into the air.

They owed their lives, his mother would later tell Mrs West next door, to a cabinet minister's suit. Their Anderson shelter, where they would have been huddled were it not for the demands of bespoke design, had taken a direct hit.

That night, George and a dicky stirrup pump waged a losing battle against the flames until neighbours joined in with rugs, hoses and buckets of sand. Denis stood behind his mother's hip at the open door. His baby sister howled from her Moses basket. Smoke gusted as he watched his new red wagon melt in the heat. Ethel smiled down at him, squeezing his hand, and it seemed very odd because his mother shook as much as she smiled and she smiled as much as she shook. It should have been very difficult, like rubbing your tummy and patting your head at the same time, and as Denis beheld his mother – her eyes wet with tears, her hair unpinned, her arms goose-pimpled – he felt something radiate through his chest. The feeling was delicious. It warmed him through. He felt light on his toes. If his mother hadn't been wearing her heavy navy blue court shoes, the two of them, he thought, might have floated off the doorstep and into the night.

At the same time, the feeling was an ache, a hole, a sore inside him. It made him feel heavy. His heart was like something he'd swallowed that had gone down the wrong way. It made it hard to breathe. Denis Noble, age four, didn't understand. As the tremor in his mother's arm travelled into his hand, up his arm, through his armpit and into his chest, he felt for the first time the mysterious life of the heart.

*

He had of course been briefed in the weeks prior to surgery. His consultant, Mr Bonham, had sat at his desk – chins doubling with the gravity of the situation – reviewing Denis's notes. The tests had been inconclusive but the 'rather urgent' need for transplantation remained clear.

Naturally he would, Mr Bonham said, be familiar with the procedure. An incision in the ribcage. The removal of the pericardium – 'a slippery business, but routine'. Denis's heart would be emptied, and the aorta clamped prior to excision. 'Textbook.' The chest cavity would be cleared, though the biatrial cuff would be left in place. Then the new heart would be 'unveiled – voilà!', and the aorta engrafted, followed by the pulmonary artery.

Most grafts, Mr Bonham assured him, recovered normal ventricular function without intervention. There were risks, of course: bleeding, RV failure, bradyarrhythmias, conduction abnormalities, sudden death …

Mr Bonham surveyed his patient through his half-moon specs. 'Atheist, I presume?'

'I'm afraid not.' Denis regarded his surgeon with polite patience. Mr Bonham was widely reputed to be one of the last eccentrics still standing in the NHS.

'A believer then. Splendid. More expedient at times like this. And fear not. The Royal Society won't hear it from me!'

'Which is perhaps just as well,' said Denis, 'as I'm afraid I make as poor a "believer" as I do an atheist.'

Mr Bonham removed his glasses. 'Might be time to sort the muddle out.' He huffed on his specs, gave them a wipe with a crumpled handkerchief, and returned them to the end of his nose. 'I have a private hunch, you see, that agnostics don't fare quite as well in major surgery. No data for *The Lancet* as yet but' – he ventured a wink – 'even so. See if you can't muster a little … certainty.'

A smile crept across Denis's face. 'The Buddhists advise against too much metaphysical certainty.'

'You're a Buddhist?' A Buddhist at Oxford? At Balliol?

Denis's smile strained. 'I try to keep my options open.'

'I see.' Mr Bonham didn't. There was an embarrassment of

categories. A blush spread up his neck, and as Denis watched his surgeon shuffle his notes, he felt his chances waver.

The *allegro* now. The third movement of the Piano Trio – *faster, faster* – but the Schubert is receding, and as Denis surfaces from sleep, he realises he's being whisked down the wide, blanched corridors of the Heart Unit. His trolley is a precision vehicle. It glides. It shunts around corners. There's no time to waste – the heart must be fresh – and he wonders if he has missed his stop. Kentish Town. Archway. Highgate. East Finchley. The names of the stations flicker past like clues in a dream to a year he cannot quite summon. Tunnel after tunnel. He mustn't nod off again, mustn't miss the stop, but the carriage is swaying and rocking, it's only quarter past five in the morning, and it's hard to resist the ramshackle lullaby of the Northern Line.

West Finchley. Woodside Park.

1960.

That's the one.

It's 1960, but no one, it seems, has told the good people of Totteridge. Each time he steps onto the platform at the quaint, well-swept station, he feels as if he has been catapulted back in time.

The slaughterhouse is a fifteen-minute walk along a B-road, and Denis is typically the first customer of the day. He feels underdressed next to the workers in their whites, their hard hats, their metal aprons and steel-toed Wellies. They stare, collectively, at his loafers.

Slaughter-men aren't talkers by nature, but nevertheless, over the months, Denis has come to know each by name. Front of house, there's Alf the Shackler, Frank the Knocker, Jimmy the Sticker, Marty the Plucker, and Mike the Splitter. Frank tells him how, years ago, a sledgehammer saw him through the day's routine, but now it's a pneumatic gun and a bolt straight to the brain; a few hundred shots a day, which means he has to wear goggles, 'cos of all the grey matter flying'. He's worried he's developing 'trigger-finger', and he removes his plastic glove so Denis can see for himself 'the finger what won't uncurl.'

Alf is brawny but soft-spoken with kind, almost womanly eyes. Every morning on the quiet, he tosses Denis a pair of Wellies to spare his shoes. No one mentions the stink of the place, a sharp kick to the lungs of old blood, manure and offal. The breeze block walls exhale it and the floor reeks of it, even though the place is mopped down like a temple every night.

Jimmy is too handsome for a slaughterhouse, all dirty blond curls and American teeth, but he doesn't know it because he's a farmboy who's never been further than East Finchley. Marty, on the other hand, was at Dunkirk. He has a neck like a battering ram and a lump of shrapnel in his head. Every day, at the close of business, he brings his knife home with him on the passenger seat of his Morris Mini-Minor. He explains to Denis that he spends a solid hour each night sharpening and sanding the blade to make sure it's smooth with no pits. 'An' 'e wonders,' bellows Mike, 'why 'e can't get a bird!'

Denis pays £4 for two hearts a day, a sum that left him stammering with polite confusion on his first visit. At Wilson and Jeffries, his father earns £20 per week.

Admittedly, they bend the rules for him. Frank 'knocks' the first sheep as usual. Alf shackles and hoists. But Jimmy, who grasps his sticking knife – Jimmy, the youngest, who's always keen, literally, to 'get stuck in' – doesn't get to slit the throat and drain the animal. When Denis visits, there's a different protocol. Jimmy steps aside, and Marty cuts straight into the chest and scoops out 'the pluck'. The blood gushes. The heart and lungs steam in Marty's hands. The others tssktssk like old women at the sight of the spoiled hide, but Marty is butchery in motion. He casts the lungs down a chute, passes the warm heart to Denis, rolls the stabbed sheep down the line to Mike the Splitter, shouts 'Chop, chop, ha ha' at Mike, and waits like a veteran for Alf to roll the second sheep his way.

Often Denis doesn't wait to get back to the lab. He pulls a large pair of scissors from his hold-all, grips the heart at arm's length, cuts open the meaty ventricles, checks to ensure the Purkinje fibres are still intact, then pours a steady stream of Tyrode solution over and into the heart. When the blood is washed clear, he plops the heart into his Thermos and waits for the next heart as the gutter in the floor fills with blood. The Tyrode solution, which mimics the sugar and salts of blood, is a simple but strange elixir. Denis still can't help but take a schoolboy sort of pleasure in its magic. There in his Thermos, at the core of today's open heart, the Purkinje fibres have started to beat again in their Tyrode bath. Very occasionally, a whole ventricle comes to life as he washes it down. On those occasions, he lets Jimmy hold the disembodied heart as if it is a wounded bird fluttering between his palms.

Then the Northern Line flickers past in reverse until Euston Station re-appears, where Denis hops out and jogs – Thermos and scissors clanging in the hold-all – down Gower Street, past the main quad, through the Anatomy entrance, up the grand, century-old staircase to the second floor, and into the empty lab before the clock on the wall strikes seven.

In the hush of the Radcliffe's principal operating theatre, beside the anaesthetised, intubated body of Denis Noble, Mr Bonham assesses the donor heart for a final time.

The epicardial surface is smooth and glistening. The quantity of fat is negligible. The aorta above the valve reveals a smooth intima with no atherosclerosis. The heart is still young, after all; sadly, just seventeen years old, though – in keeping with protocol – he has revealed nothing of the donor identity to the patient, and Professor Noble knows better than to ask. The lumen of the coronary artery is large, without any visible narrowing. The muscular arterial wall is of sound proportion.

Pre-operative monitoring has confirmed strong wall motion, excellent valve function, good conduction and regular heart rhythm.

It's a ticklish business at the best of times, he reminds his team, but yes, he is ready to proceed.

In the lab of the Anatomy Building, Denis pins out the heart like a valentine in a Petri dish. The buried trove, the day's booty, is nestled at the core; next to the red flesh of the ventricle, the Purkinje network is a skein of delicate yellow fibres. They gleam like the bundles of pearl cotton his mother used to keep in her embroidery basket.

Locating them is one thing. Getting them is another. It is tricky work to lift them free; trickier still to cut away sections without destroying them. He needs a good eye, a small pair of surgical scissors, and the steady cutting hand he inherited, he likes to think, from his father. If impatience gets the better of him, if he sneezes, if his scissors slip, it will be a waste of a fresh and costly heart. Beyond the lab door, an undergrad class thunders down the staircase. Outside, through the thin Victorian glass panes, Roy Orbison croons 'Only the Lonely' on a transistor radio.

Denis drops his scissors and reaches for a pair of forceps. He works like a watchmaker, lifting another snipped segment free. A second Petri dish awaits. A fresh bath of Tyrode solution, an oxygenated variety this time, will boost their recovery. If all goes well, he can usually harvest a dozen segments from each heart. But the ends will need to close before the real work can begin. Sometimes they need an hour, sometimes longer.

Coffee. He needs a coffee. He boils water on the Bunsen burner someone pinched from the chemistry lab. The instant coffee is on the shelf with the belljars. He pours, using his sleeve as a mitt, and, in the absence of a spoon, uses the pencil that's always tucked behind his ear.

At the vast chapel-arch of a window, he can just see the treetops of Gordon Square, burnished with autumn, and far below, the gardeners raking leaves and lifting bulbs. Beyond it, from this height, he can see as far as Tavistock Square, though the old copper beech stands between him and a view of his own attic window at the top of Connaught Hall.

He tries not to think about Ella, whom he hopes to find, several hours from now, on the other side of that window, in his room – i.e., his bed – where they have agreed to meet to 'compare the findings' of their respective days. Ella, a literature student, has been coolly bluffing her way into the Press Box at the Old Bailey for the last week or so. For his part, he'd never heard of the infamous novel until the headlines got hold of it, but Ella is gripped and garrulous, and even the sound of her voice in his ear fills him with a desire worthy of the finest dirty book.

He paces, mug in hand. He can't bring himself to leave his fibres unattended while they heal.

He watches the clock.

He checks the fibres. Too soon.

He deposits his mug on the windowsill and busies himself

with his prep. He fills the first glass micro-pipette with potassium chloride, inserts the silver thread-wire and connects it to the valve on his home-made amp. The glass pipette in his hand always brings to mind the old wooden dibber, smooth with use, that his father used during spring planting. Denis can see him still, in his weekend pullover and tie, on his knees in the garden, as he dibbed and dug for a victory that was in no hurry to come. Only his root vegetables ever rewarded his efforts.

Soon, Antony and Günter, his undergrad assistants, will shuffle in for duty. He'll post Antony, with the camera and a stockpile of film, at the oscilloscope's screen. Günter will take to the darkroom next to the lab, and emerge pale and blinking at the end of the day.

Outside, the transistor radio and its owner take their leave. He drains his coffee, glances at the clock, and checks his nails for sheep's blood. How much longer? He allows himself to wander as far as the stairwell and back again. He doodles on the blackboard – a sickle moon, a tree, a stick man clinging to a branch – and erases all three.

At last, at last. He prepares a slide, sets up the Zeiss, switches on its light and swivels the lens into place. At this magnification, the fibre cells are pulsing minnows of life. His 'dibbers' are ready; Günter passes him the first and checks its connection to the amp. Denis squints over the Zeiss and inserts the micro-pipette into a cell membrane. The view is good. He can even spot the two boss-eyed nuclei. If the second pipette penetrates the cell successfully, he'll make contact with the innermost life of the cell.

His wrist is steady, which means every impulse, every rapid-fire excitation, should travel up the pipette through the thread-wire and into the valve of the amplifier. The oscilloscope will 'listen' to the amp. Fleeting waves of voltage will rise and fall across its screen, and Antony will snap away on the Nikon, capturing every fluctuation, every trace. Günter, for his part, has already removed himself like a penitent to the darkroom. There, if all goes well, he'll capture the divine spark of life on Kodak paper, over and over again.

Later still, they'll convert the electrical ephemera of the day into scrolling graphs; they'll chart the unfolding peaks and troughs; they'll watch on paper the ineffable currents that compel the heart to life.

Cell after cell. Impulse upon impulse. An ebb and flow of voltage. The unfolding story of a single heartbeat in thousandths of a second.

'Tell me,' says Ella, 'about your excitable cells. I like those.' Their heads share the one pillow. Schubert's piano trio is rising through the floorboards of the student hall. A cellist he has yet to meet lives below.

'I'll give you excitable.' He pinches her bottom. She bites the end of his nose. Through the crack of open window, they can smell trampled leaves, wet pavement and frostbitten earth. In the night above the attic window, the stars throb.

She sighs luxuriously and shifts, so that Denis has to grip the mattress of the narrow single bed to steady himself. 'Excuse me, Miss, but I'm about to go over the edge.'

'Of the bed or your mental health? Have you found those canals yet?'

'Channels.'

'Precisely. Plutonium channels. See? I listen. You might not think I do, but I do.'

'Potassium. Potassium channels.'

'That's what I said.'

'I'm afraid you didn't. Which means ...'

'Which means ...?'

He rumples his brow in a display of forethought. 'Which means – and I say this with regret – I might just have to spank you.' He marvels at his own audacity. He is someone new with her and, at the same time, he has never felt more himself.

'Cheek!' she declares, and covers her own with the eiderdown. 'But I'm listening now. Tell me again. What do you do with these potassium channels?'

'I map their electrical activity. I demonstrate the movement of ions – electrically charged particles – through the cell membranes.' From the mattress edge, he gets a purchase by grabbing hold of her hip.

'Why aren't you more pleased?'

'Tell me about the trial today.'

'I thought you said those channels of yours were *the* challenge. The new discovery. The biologist's New World.'

'I'm pleased. Yes. Thanks. It's going well.' He throws back the eiderdown, springs to his feet and rifles through her shoulder bag for her notebook. 'Is it in here?'

'Is what?'

'Your notebook.'

'A man's testicles are never at their best as he bends,' she observes.

'So did The Wigs put on a good show today?'

She folds her arms across the eiderdown. 'I'm not talking dirty until you tell me about your potassium what-nots.'

'Channels.' From across the room, his back addresses her. 'They're simply passages or pores in the cell membrane that allow a mass of charged ions to be shunted into the cell – or out of it again if there's an excess.'

She sighs. 'If it's all so matter of fact, why are you bothering?'

He returns to her side, kisses the top of her head and negotiates his way back into the bed. 'My supervisor put me on the case, and, like I say, all's well. I'm getting the results, rather more quickly than I expected, so I'm pleased. Relieved even. Because in truth, I would have looked a little silly if I hadn't found them. They're already known to exist in muscle cells, and the heart is only another muscle after all.'

'Only another muscle?'

'Yes.' He nips through her notebook.

'But this is something that has you running through Bloomsbury in the middle of the night and leaving me for a date with a computer.'

He kisses her shoulder. 'The computer isn't nearly so amiable.'

'Denis Noble, are you doing interesting work or aren't you?'

'I have a dissertation to produce.'

'Please. Never be, you know ... take it or leave it. Never be bored. Men who are bored bore me.'

'Then I shall stifle every yawn.'

'You'll have to do better than that. Tell me what you aim to discover next.' She divests him of his half of the eiderdown, and he grins, in spite of the cold.

'Whatever it is, you'll be the first to know.'

'Perhaps it isn't an "it",' she muses. 'Have you thought of that?'

'How can "it" not be an "it"?'

'I'm not sure,' she says, and she wraps herself up like the Queen of Sheba. The eiderdown crackles with static, and her fine, shiny hair flies away in the light of the desk-lamp. 'But a book, for example, is not an "it".'

'Of course it's an "it". It's an object, a thing. Ask any girl in her deportment class, as she walks about with one on her head.'

'Then I'll re-phrase, shall I? A story is not an "it". If it's any good, it's more alive than an "it". Every part of a great story "contains" every other part. Every small part anticipates the whole. Nothing can be passive or static. Nothing is just a part. Not really. Because the whole, if it's powerful enough that is, cannot be divided. That's what a great creation is. It has its own marvellous unity.' She pauses to examine the birthmark on his hip, a new discovery. 'Of course, I'm fully aware I sound like a) a girl and b) a dreamy arts student, but I suspect the heart *is* a great creation and that the same rule applies.'

'And which *rule* might that be?' He loves listening to her, even if he has no choice but to mock her, gently.

'The same principle then.'

He raises an eyebrow.

She adjusts her generous breasts. 'The principle of Eros. Eros is an attractive force. It binds the world; it makes connections. At best, it gives way to a sense of wholeness, a sense of the sacred even; at worst, it leads to fuzzy vision. Logos, your contender, particularises. It makes the elements of the world distinct. At best, it is illuminating; at worst, it is reductive. It cheapens. Both are vital. The balance is the thing. You need Eros, Denis. You're missing Eros.'

He passes her her notebook and taps it. 'On that point, we agree entirely. I wait with the utmost patience.'

She studies him with suspicion, then opens the spiral-bound stenographer's notebook. In the days before the trial, she taught herself shorthand in record time simply to capture, like any other putative member of the press, the banned passages of prose. She was determined to help carry their erotic charge into the world. 'T. S. Eliot was supposed to give evidence for the defense today, but apparently he sat in his taxi and couldn't bring himself to "do the deed".'

'Old men – impotent. Young men' – he smiles shyly and nods to his exposed self – 'ready.' He opens her notebook to a random page of shorthand. The ink is purple.

'My little joke,' she says. 'A sense of humour is *de rigueur* in the Press Box.' She nestles into the pillow and relinquishes his half of the eiderdown. He pats down her fly-away hair. 'From Chapter Ten,' she begins. '"Then with a quiver of exquisite pleasure he touched the warm soft body, and touched her navel for a moment in a kiss. And he had to come into her at once, to enter the peace on earth of her soft quiescent body. It was the moment of pure peace for him, the entry into the body of a woman." '

'That gamekeeper chap doesn't hang about,' he says, his smile twitching.

'Quiet,' she chides. 'He is actually a very noble sort. Not sordid like you.'

'My birth certificate would assure you that I'm a Noble sort.'

'Ha ha.'

Denis lays his head against her breast and listens to the beat of her heart as she reads. Her voice enters him like a current and radiates through him until he feels himself almost hum with it, as if he is the body of a violin or cello that exists only to amplify her voice. He suspects he is not in love with her – and that is really just as well – but it occurs to him that he has never known such sweetness, such delight. He tries to stay in the moment, to loiter in the beats between the words she reads, between the breaths she takes. He runs his hand over the bell of her hip and tries not to think that in just four hours he will set off into the darkened streets of Bloomsbury, descend a set of basement steps and begin his night shift in the company of the only computer at the University of London powerful enough to crunch his milliseconds of data into readable equations.

As a lowly biologist, an ostensible lightweight among the physicists and computer guys, he has been allocated the least enviable slot on the computer, from two till four a.m. By five, he'll be on the Northern Line again, heading for the slaughterhouse.

Ella half wakes as he leaves.

'Go back to sleep,' he whispers. He grabs his jacket and the hold-all.

She sits up in bed, blinking in the light of the lamp which he has turned to the wall. 'Are you going now?'

'Yes.' He smiles, glancing at her, finds his wallet and checks he has enough for the hearts of the day.

'Goodbye, Denis,' she says softly.

'Sweet dreams,' he says.

But she doesn't stretch and settle back under the eiderdown. She remains upright and naked even though the room is so cold, their breath has turned to frost on the inside of the window. He wonders if there isn't something odd in her expression. He hovers for a moment before deciding it is either a shadow from the lamp or the residue of a dream. Whatever the case, he can't be late for his shift. If he is, the porter in the unit won't be there to let him in – which means he has no more time to think on it.

He switches off the lamp.

*

In his later years, Denis Noble has allowed himself to wonder, privately, about the physiology of love. He has loved – with gratitude and frustration – parents, siblings, a spouse and two children. What, he asks himself, is love if not a force within? And what is a force within if not something *lived through* the body? Nevertheless, as Emeritus Professor of Cardiovascular Physiology, he has to admit he knows little more about love than he did on the night he fell in love with his mother; the night their shelter was bombed; the night he felt with utter certainty the strange and secret life of the heart within his chest.

Before 1960 drew to a close, he would – like hundreds of thousands of other liberated readers – buy the banned book and try to understand it as Ella had understood it. Later still in life, he would dedicate himself to the music and poetry of the Occitan troubadours. ('*I only know the grief that comes to me, to my love-ridden heart, out of over-loving ...*') He would read and re-read the ancient sacred-sexual texts of the Far East. He would learn, almost by heart, St Theresa's account of her vision of the seraph: '*I saw in his hands a long spear of gold, and at the iron's point there seemed to be a little fire. He appeared to me to be thrusting it at times into my heart, and to pierce my very entrails; when he drew it out, he seemed to draw them out also, and to leave me all on fire with a great love of God. The pain was so great that it made me moan;*

*and yet so surpassing was the sweetness of this excessive pain that
I could not wish to be rid of it.'*

But *what*, he wanted to ask St Theresa, could the heart, that feat
of flesh, blood and voltage, have to do with love? *Where*, he'd like
to know, is love? *How* is love?

On the train to Totteridge, he can still smell the citrus of Ella's
perfume on his hands, in spite of all the punched paper-tape
offerings he's been feeding to the computer through the night. He
only left its subterranean den an hour ago. These days, the slots of
his schedule are his daily commandments.

He is allowed 'to live' and to sleep from seven each evening to
half past one the next morning, when his alarm wakes him for his
shift in the computer unit. He closes the door on the darkness of
Connaught Hall and sprints across Bloomsbury. After his shift, he
travels from the Comp. Science basement to the Northern Line, from
the Northern Line to the slaughterhouse, from the slaughterhouse
to Euston, and from Euston to the lab for his twelve-hour day.
'Seven to seven,' he declares to his supervisor. He arrives home to
Connaught Hall for supper at seven-thirty, Ella at eight, sleep at
ten and three hours' oblivion until the alarm rings and the cycle
starts all over again.

He revels briefly in the thought of a pretty girl still asleep in his
bed, a luxury he'd never dared hope to win as a science student.
Through the smeared carriage windows, the darkness is thinning
into a murky dawn. The Thermos jiggles in the hold-all at his feet,
the carriage door rattles and clangs, and his head falls back.

Up ahead, Ella is standing naked and grand on a bright woodland
path in Tavistock Square. She doesn't seem to care that she can be
seen by all the morning commuters and the students rushing past
on their way to classes. She slips through the gate at the western
end of the square and turns, closing it quickly. As he reaches it, he
realises it is a kissing-gate. She stands on the other side but refuses
him her lips. 'Gates open,' she says tenderly, 'and they close.' He
tries to go through but she shakes her head. When he pulls on the
gate, he gets an electric shock. 'Why are you surprised?' she says.
Then she's disappearing through another gate into Gordon Square,

and her hair is flying away in the morning light, as if she herself is electric. He pulls again on the gate, but it's rigid.

The dream returns to him only later as Marty is scooping the pluck from the first sheep on the line.

He feels again the force of that electric shock.

The gate was conductive ...

It opened ... It closed.

It *closed.*

He receives from Marty the first heart of the day. It's hot between his palms but he doesn't reach for his scissors. He doesn't open the Thermos. He hardly moves. Deep within him, it's as if his own heart has been jump-started to life.

In the operating theatre, Mr Bonham and his team have been at work for three-and-a-half hours, when at last he gives the word. Professor Noble can be disconnected from the bypass machine. His pulse is strong. The new heart, declares Mr Bonham, 'is going great guns'.

His dream of Ella at the gate means he can't finish at the slaughterhouse quickly enough. On the train back into town, he swears under his breath at the eternity of every stop. In the lab, he wonders if the ends of the Purkinje fibres will ever close and heal. He has twelve hours of lab time. Seven to seven. Will it be enough?

Twelve hours pass like two. The fibres are tricky today. He botched more than a few in the dissection, and the insertion of the micro-pipette has been hit and miss. Antony and Günter exchange looks. They discover he has amassed untold quantities of film, and he tells Antony he wants a faster shutter speed. When they request a lunch break, he simply stares into the middle distance. When Günter complains that his hands are starting to burn from the fixatives, Denis looks up from his micro-pipette, as if at a tourist who requires something of him in another language.

Finally, when the great window is a chapel arch of darkness and rain, he closes and locks the lab door behind him. There is nothing in his appearance to suggest anything other than a long day's work. No one he passes on the grand staircase of the Anatomy Building pauses to look. No one glances back, pricked by an intuition or an afterthought. He has remembered his hold-all and the Thermos for tomorrow's hearts. He has forgotten his jacket, but the sight of a poorly dressed student is nothing to make anyone look twice.

Yet as he steps into the downpour of the night, every light is blazing in his head. His brain is Piccadilly Circus, and in the dazzle, he hardly sees where he's going but he's running, across Gordon Square and on towards Tavistock ... He wants to shout the news to the winos who shelter from the rain under dripping trees. He wants to holler it to every lit window, to every student in his or her numinous haze of thought. He wants to dash up the stairs of Connaught Hall, knock on the door of the mystery cellist, and blurt out the words. Tomorrow at the slaughterhouse, he tells himself, he might even have to hug Marty and Alf. 'They *close*!'

He saw it with his own eyes: potassium channels that *closed*.

They did just the opposite of what everyone expected.

He assumed some sort of experimental error. He went back through Günter's contact sheets. He checked the amp and the connections. He wondered if he wasn't merely observing his own wishful thinking. He started again. He shook things up. He subjected the cells to change – changes of voltage, of ions, of temperature. Antony asked, morosely, for permission to leave early. He had an exam – Gross Anatomy – the next day. Didn't Antony understand? 'They're not simply open,' he announced over a new ten-pound cylinder of graph paper. 'They *opened*.'

Antony's face was blank as an egg.

Günter suggested they call it a day.

But the channels opened. They were active. They opened *and*, more remarkably still, they *closed*.

Ella was right. He'll tell her she was. He'll be the first to admit it. The channels aren't merely passive conduits. They're not just machinery or component parts. They're alive and responsive.

Too many ions inside the cell – too much stress, exercise, anger, love, lust or despair – and they close. They stop all incoming electrical traffic. They preserve calm in the midst of too much life. They allow the ion gradient to stabilise.

He can hardly believe it himself. The heart 'listens' to itself. Causation isn't just upward; it's unequivocally downward too. It's a beautiful loop of feedback. The parts of the heart listen to each other as surely as musicians in an ensemble listen to each other. That's what he's longing to tell Ella. *That's* what he's discovered. Forget the ensemble. The heart is an *orchestra*. It's the BBC Proms. It's the Boston Pops. Even if he only understands its rhythm section today he knows this now. The heart is infinitely more than the sum of its parts.

And he can prove it mathematically. The super computer will vouch for him, he feels sure of it. He'll design the equations. He'll come up with a computer model that will make even the physicists and computer scientists stand and gawp.

Which is when it occurs to him: what if the heart doesn't stop at the heart? What if the connections don't end?

Even he doesn't quite know what he means by this.

He will ask Ella. He will tell her of their meeting at the kissing-gate. He will ask for the kiss her dream-self refused him this morning. He'll enjoy the sweet confusion on her face.

Ella at eight.

Ella always at eight.

He waits by the window until the lights go out over Tavistock Square and the trees melt into darkness.

He waits for three days. He retreats under the eiderdown. He is absent from the slaughterhouse, the lab and the basement.

A fortnight passes. A month. The new year.

When the second movement of the Piano Trio rises through the floorboards, he feels nothing. It has taken him months, but finally, he feels nothing.

*

As he comes round, the insult of the tube down his throat assures him he hasn't died.

The first thing he sees is his grandson by the foot of his bed tapping away on his new mobile phone. 'Hi, Granddad,' Josh says, as if Denis has only been napping. He bounces to the side of the ICU bed, unfazed by the bleeping monitors and the tubes. 'Put your index finger here, Denis. I'll help you ... No, like right *over* the camera lens. That's it. This phone has an Instant Heart Rate App. We'll see if you're working yet.'

'Cool,' Denis starts to say, but the irony is lost to the tube in his throat.

Josh's brow furrows. He studies his phone screen like a doctor on a medical soap. 'Sixty-two beats per minute at rest. Congratulations, Granddad. You're like … alive.' Josh squeezes his hand and grins.

Denis has never been so glad to see him.

On the other side of the bed, his wife touches his shoulder. Her face is tired. The fluorescence of the lights age her. She has lipstick on her front tooth and tears in her eyes as she bends to whisper, hoarsely, in his ear, 'You came back to me.'

The old words.

After a week, he'd given up hope. He realised he didn't even know where she lived, which student residence, which flat, which telephone exchange. He'd never thought to ask. Once he even tried waiting for her outside The Old Bailey, but the trial was over, someone told him. Days before. Didn't he read the papers?

When she opened his door in January of '61, she stood on the threshold, like an apparition who might at any moment disappear again. She simply waited, her shiny hair still flying away from her in the light of the bare bulb on the landing. He was standing at the window through which he'd given up looking. On the other side, the copper beech was bare with winter. In the room below, the Schubert recording was stuck on a scratch.

Her words, when they finally came, were hushed and angry. They rose and fell in a rhythm he'd almost forgotten. 'Why don't you *know* that you're in love with me? What's wrong with you, Denis Noble?'

Cooking smells – boiled vegetables and mince – wafted into his room from the communal kitchen on the floor below. It seemed impossible that she should be here. Ella. Not Ella at eight. *Ella*.

Downstairs, the cellist moved the needle on the record.

'You came back to me,' he said.

His eyes filled.

As his recuperation begins, he will realise, with not a little impatience, that he knows nothing at all about the whereabouts of love. He knows only where it isn't. It is not in the heart, or if it is, it is not only in the heart. The organ that first beat in the depths of Ethel in the upstairs room of Wilson & Jeffries is now consigned to the scrap heap of cardiovascular history. Yet in this moment, with a heart that is not strictly his, he loves Ella as powerfully as he did the night she re-appeared in his room on Tavistock Square.

But if love is not confined to the heart, nor would it seem is memory confined to the brain. The notion tantalises him. Those aspects or qualities which make the human condition human – love, consciousness, memory, affinity – are, Denis feels more sure than ever, *distributed* throughout the body. The single part, as Ella once claimed so long ago, must contain the whole.

He hopes his new heart will let him live long enough to see the proof. He'll have to chivvy the good folk at the Physiome Project along.

He wishes he had a pencil.

In the meantime, as Denis adjusts to his new heart hour by hour, day by day, he will demonstrate, in Josh's steadfast company, an imperfect but unprecedented knowledge of the lyrics of Jay-Z and OutKast. He will announce to Ella that he is keen to buy a BMX bike. He won't be sure himself whether he is joking or not. He will develop an embarrassing appetite for doner kebabs, and he will not be deterred by the argument, put to him by Ella, his daughter and Josh, that he has never eaten a doner kebab in his entire life.

He will surprise even himself when he hears himself tell Mr Bonham, during his evening rounds, that he favours Alton Towers over the Dordogne this year.

THE LOST SEED

Emma Donoghue

Emma Donoghue (b. 1969) is an Irish-born playwright, literary historian and novelist. She has published seven novels, eleven plays and four collections of short stories. Her 2010 novel, *Room*, was a finalist for the Man Booker Prize.

In this world we are as seed scattered from God's hand. Some fall on the fat soil and thrive. Some fall among thorns and are choked as they grow. Some fall on hard ground, and their roots get no purchase, for the bitter rocks lie all around.

I, Richard Berry, make this record in the margins of the Good Book for those who come after, lest our plantation fail and all trace of our endeavors be wiped from the earth. Shielded by the Lord's arm, our ship has traveled safe across the ocean through all travails, to make landfall at the colony of Plymouth. Today we stretched our legs on land again. The snow reaches our knees. We never saw stuff like this before. It is bright as children's teeth and squeaks underfoot.

On the first day of June came the quake. So powerful is the mighty hand of the Lord, it makes both the earth and the sea to shake. Many of our thatched huts fell down.

But we and the settlers who came before us keep faith with our Maker and our mission. We go on hacking ourselves a space in the wilderness of Cape Cod: our settlement is to be called Yarmouth. The mosquitoes bite us till we are striped with blood. May we cast off the old sins of England like dust from our boots.

I have written nothing in this book for a time, being much occupied with laboring for the good of the Lord and this plantation. We have made new laws, and set down on paper the liberties of all freemen. The Indians have shown us how to bury dead fish with our seeds to sweeten the soil. We have sold them guns.

I am still unmarried. I thought on Sarah White but she laughs overmuch.

Of late I have been troubled by a weakness of spirit. I dwell on my mother and father and come near to weeping, for I will never see them again in this life. But I must remember that those who till the soil beside me are my brethren.

There are few enough of our congregation aboveground. Edward Preston lost his wife this past month, and so did Teague Joanes, a godly man whose field lies next to mine. For ye know not the hour. There are others in Yarmouth who seek to stir up division like mud in a creek. At Meeting they grasp at privilege and make much of themselves. But our dissensions must be thrust aside. If we do not help each other, who will help us? We are all sojourners in a strange land: we must lend aid, and stand guard against attack, and carry our faith like a precious stone. We hear of other plantations where there is not a Christian left alive.

Our court sentenced Seb Mitchel to be fined three pounds for his unseemly and blasphemous speeches. He spoke against his Maker for taking all three of Seb's children. He will have to give his hog to pay the fine.

Our numbers in Yarmouth are increased with the coming of ships, yet I dislike these incomers, who are all puffed up and never think of our sweat that built this town. I pray they be not like the seed that springs up quick and eager but is soon parched and blasted by the noonday sun.

Sarah White is married to Hugh Norman these two months past. She is lightsome of countenance and speech. She forgets the saying of the Apostle, that wives should submit. If she does not take care, her behavior will be spoken of at Meeting. I went by her house the other day, and she was singing a song. I could not make out the words, but it was no hymn.

These days some play while others work. Things that are lawful in moderation, whether archery or foot-racing, tobacco or ale, are become traps for the weak. Each man goes his own way, it seems; there is little concord or meekness of spirit. I remind my brethren that we are not separate, one from the other. Another bad winter could extinguish us. In this rough country we stand together or we fall.

God has not yet granted me a helpmeet. I look about me diligently at the sisters in our plantation, but some are shrewish, and others have a barren look about them, or a limp, or a cast in the eye.

In the first days, I remember, we were all one family in the Lord. But now each household shuts its doors at night. Every man looks to his own wife and his own children. I think on the first days, when there was great fellowship, through all trials.

Last night there was a snow so heavy that the whole plantation was made one white. I stood in my door and saw some flakes as wide as my hand, that came down faster than the others. Every flake falls alone, and yet on the ground they are all one.

Twice in these last months a woman has come big-bellied to be married, and she and the man put a shame-face on and paid their fine to the court, but it is clear think little of their sin.

Our court sentenced Joan Younge's master to pay her fine of two pounds, for she was rude to her mistress on the Lord's day and blocked her ears when the Bible was read, and the master should have kept her under firm governance. I would have had the girl whipped down to the bone.

Teague Joanes is the only man now who says more to me than yea or nay.

At sunset most evenings I meet him where our cornfields join. He tells me that though marriage be our duty, it brings much grief, and from the hour a child is born his father is never without fear.

Hugh Norman's daughter was found in the well, five years old. I went by their house and offered a word of succor to the mother, Sarah, but she would not leave off howling like a beast. One of John Vincent's daughters was there.

Good news on the last ship. King Charles has been cast down for his Popish wickedness. Men of conscience govern England. Heathenish festivities no longer defile the name of the Lord, and there is no more Christmas.

Here we work till the light fails. We have indentured men, some blacks among them, to hoe the land, but still too much of the crop is lost in the weeds, and strangled in rankness.

Mary Vincent is fifteen, and comely, but not overmuch.

Our court found Nathaniel Hatch and his sister Lydia Hatch guilty of unclean practices. They have strayed so far from the path, they are sheep who cannot be brought home. He is to be banished to the south and she to the north. We are not to break bread with them, or so much as throw them a crust. If we happen to pass either of them in the road, we are to turn our faces away. If either tries to speak to any of our community, we are to stop up our ears. No other town in Plymouth, or any other Christian plantation, will take in a cast-out.

I gave my view in Meeting that the pair should have been put to death for their incest, as a sign to waverers. (And after all, to be cast out is itself a sort of death, for who would wish to roam this wilderness alone?) It has seemed to me for some time that our laws are too soft. If any man go after strange flesh, or children, or fowl or other beasts, even if the deed be not accomplished, it should be death. If any man act upon himself so as to spill his seed on the ground, it should be exile, at least. For the seed is most precious in these times and must not be lost.

I spoke to Mary Vincent's father, and he was not opposed, but the girl would not have me.

I am a fruitless man. My grievous sins of pride and hard-heartedness have made me to bury my coin in the ground, like the bad servant in the parable. I have begot no children to increase our plantation. All I can do is work.

There is talk of making a law against the single life, so that every unmarried man or woman would have to go and live in some godly family. But what house would take me in?

Nathaniel Hatch is rumored to be living still in the woods to the south of Yarmouth. I wonder if he has repented of his filth. Even if the wolves have spared him, he has no people now. As for his sister, no one has set eyes on her.

Mary Vincent is to marry Benjamin Hammon.

My face is furrowed like a cornfield. The ice leaves its mark, and the burning summer turns all things brown. But I will cast off vanity. The body is but the husk that is tossed aside in the end.

Benjamin Hammon said to Teague Joanes that Sarah Norman told his wife I was an old killjoy.

It matters not.

Sin creeps around like a fog in the night. Too many of us forget to be watchful. Too many have left their doors open for the Tempter to slip in. I puzzle over it as I lie on my bed in the darkness, but

I cannot tell why stinking lusts and things fearful to name should arise so commonly among us. It may be that our strict laws stop up the channel of wickedness, but it searches everywhere and at last breaks out worse than before.

I consider it my pressing business to stand sentry. Where vice crawls out of the shadows, I shine a light on it. Death still seizes so many of our flock each winter, we cannot spare a single soul among the survivors. Better I should anger my neighbor than stand by and watch the Tempter pluck up his soul as the eagle fastens on the lamb. Better I should be spurned and despised, and feel myself to be entirely alone on this earth, than that I should relinquish my holy labor. They call me killjoy, but let them tell me this, what business have we with joy? What time have we to spare for joy, and what have we done to deserve it?

The Lord has entered into the Temple and the cleansing has begun. Let the godless tremble, but the clean of heart rejoice.

This day by my information charges were laid against Sarah Norman, together with Mary Hammon, fifteen years old and newly a wife, the more her shame. I testified to what I witnessed. With my own eyes I saw them, as I stood by Hugh Norman's window in the heat of the day. His wife and Benjamin Hammon's were lying on the one bed together. They were naked as demons, and there was not a hand-span between their bodies.

It is time now to put our feet to the spades to dig up evil and all its roots.

But already there is weakening. Our court was prevailed upon to let the girl go, with only an admonition, on account of her youth. The woman's case has been held over until the weight of business allows it to be heard. But I have faith she will be brought to judgment at last after all these years of giddiness. In the meantime, Hugh Norman has sworn he will put her and her children out of his house. I gave my belief that she should be cast out of Yarmouth.

Teague Joanes came to my house last night after dark, a thing he has never done before. He said, was it not likely the woman and the girl were only comforting each other when I saw them through the window, and what soul did not need some consolation in these hard times? I reminded him that consolation was not to be sought nor found in this life, but the next. He would have prevailed upon me to show mercy, as the Father did to his Prodigal. But I gave my belief that by their transgression Sarah Norman and Mary Hammon have strayed far beyond the reach of mercy.

Then he asked me a curious thing, did I never feel lonely? In the depth of winter, say, when the snow fills up all the pathways.

I told him I never did. But this was akin to a lie.

Teague said he could not believe I was such a hard man. I gave him no answer, for my thoughts were all confounded. Then he said at any rate he would not part with me on bad terms, and came up to me and held on to me, and his leg lay against my leg.

All that was last night. And today charges were laid by my information against Teague Joanes for an attempt at sodomy.

These are bitter times. The wind of opposition blows full in my face, but I must not turn aside, for fear of my soul.

At last our court found Sarah Norman guilty of lewd behavior with Mary Hammon, but sentenced her merely to make a public acknowledgment on the Lord's day following. She lives now in a mud hut on the edge of our plantation, and her children with her, as Hugh Norman has taken ship back to England. With my own eyes I have seen some of the brethren stop to speak with her on the road. I ask why she has not been exiled, and there is none will answer me.

The case against Teague Joanes has not yet been heard. He is well liked among those who are deceived by a show of friendliness and the Tempter's own sweet smile. Many whisper that the charges should be struck out as unfounded. No one says a word to me these days. But I know what I know.

Our paths crossed on the Lord's day, and he spat on my back.

I am not a dreaming man, but last night the most dreadful sight was shown to me. I saw Teague Joanes and Sarah Norman consorting uncleanly on a bed, the man behind the woman, turning the natural use to that which is against nature, and laughing all the while.

And when I woke I knew this was no fancy but a true vision, granted me by the Lord, so that with the eyes of sleep I could witness what is hidden in the light of day. So I walked to the court and laid charges against them both for sodomy.

The clerk did not want to write down my dream. So I took him by the collar and I asked, would he wrestle with God's own angel?

In the whole town there is none who will greet me. I hear the slurs they cast upon me as I go down the street.

I work in my own field, though these days my bones creak like dead trees. I keep my head down if ever someone passes by. I wait for the court to hear my evidence. I must stand fast.

Today I was called to the court. I stepped out my door, and over my head were hanging icicles as thick as my fist and sharp like swords of glass.

There in the court were Teague Jones and Sarah Norman and Benjamin Hammon and his wife Mary together with many others, the whole people of Plymouth. And I read on their faces that they were my enemies and God's.

At first I spoke up stoutly and told of the wickedness that is spreading through this plantation, and of the secrets that hide in the folds of men's hearts. And then Teague Joanes stood up and shouted out that I was a madman and that I had no heart.

It was quiet for a moment, a quietness I have never heard before.

Then I was asked over and over again about what I had seen, and what I had imagined, and what I knew for sure. But I could not answer. I felt a terrible spinning. All I could think on was the evening Teague Joanes walked in my door. Not of the words he spoke, but the way he stood there, looking in my eyes as few know how to in these times. The way he laid his arms around me, fearless, and pressed me to him, as one brother to another. And all of a sudden I remembered the treacherous stirring between us, the swelling of evil, and I knew whose body began it.

So I said out very loud in front of the whole court that I had perjured myself and that I withdrew the charges and that I was damned for all time. And when I walked to the door, the people moved out of my way so as not to touch me.

I went across the fields for fear of meeting any human creature on the road. And it seemed to me the snow was like a face, for its crust is an image of perfection, but underneath is all darkness and slime. And I wept, a thing I have not done since I was a child, and the water turned to ice on my cheeks.

THE TURTLE

Roshi Fernando

Roshi Fernando was born in London. She was awarded the Impress Prize for New Writers in 2009 for her composite novel *Homesick*, which portrays a community of Sri Lankan immigrants in London through a series of inter-linked short stories. In 2011, her story, 'The Fluorescent Jacket', was shortlisted for the Sunday Times EFG Private Bank Short Story Award.

In the dark they are back to the people they always were, Jenny and Mike with their son Lucas. They are three stumbling human beings, walking in black air, with multitudinous stars above them, and Jenny and Mike, with Lucas in between, can just be people on holiday.

With her pashmina wrapped about her, and Mike holding Lucas's other hand, she feels safer in their family, stronger in her belief in it. The guide with the torch is far ahead, and a group of worthy Germans and Italians walk his invisible footsteps in the sand one step behind. Mike and Jenny and Lucas take their time because Lucas is only four and Lucas does not like the feel of the sand as it enters the holes of his Crocs. 'I like wet sand,' he says to Jenny, 'but not *this* sand.'

'That's funny, because I would have thought it would be the other way round,' Mike says.

'No, no, Daddy. It is *this* way round,' Lucas says. 'I think this sand is yucky,' he says to Jenny, conspiratorially. She nods in the dark. 'I SAID ...' Lucas shouts –

'Yes, sorry, I heard you,' Jenny whispers. 'Remember the deal, Lucas? We whisper, and then the turtles will come out. Do you remember?' she asks urgently. Up ahead, she has seen a few of the Germans' heads turning towards them.

'Would you like a carry, littley?' Mike says.

'No, Daddy,' Lucas says. He has developed a habit of calling

Mike 'Daddy' in a formal manner, as if addressing a newly bought dog that needs to learn his name. It is done kindly, but Jenny hears it every time as an admonishment to them both.

'Let me carry you,' Mike continues. 'We could catch up, and see the turtles sooner.' Jenny feels the change in the air as he stoops to pick his son up. She stiffens as she feels the child's hand become rigid in her own.

'No, Mike, don't ...' she says sharply, and it is nearly too late, but he has learnt, from her emails and her sobbing phone calls in the middle of the night, to stop as soon as she says no, to do as she says, at least where Lucas is concerned. They walk on, but she feels she is dragging Lucas, and she realises he has let go of Mike's hand.

There are dips in the sand, great hollows where her foot thinks there will be ground and instead there is air and she unbalances two or three times, giggling embarrassedly, without humour. She pulls Lucas down with her once, and he shouts again. Mike lags behind, then comes up unexpectedly at her shoulder, holding her arm with his hand. She wants to shake him off, but she contains the anger.

They reach the group, and the group acknowledge them, Jenny is sure, with stares and disapprobation, but she can't see; it is so dark she cannot see her own hand. She looks down at Lucas; his face reflects the guide's red light and is an ecstasy of expectation. She only notices now that the guide is still waiting for a group of Japanese who straggle up behind them.

'Where is the turtle?' Lucas asks, quite reasonably, she thinks. It is a rational request in this circumstance. It is fine for him to ask that, at that pitch of voice. The guide does not reply, simply looks ahead towards the older Japanese couple still struggling towards them. Lucas steps forward and tugs at the guide's *dish dasha*. 'I said,' he says louder, 'where is the turtle?' The guide flicks Lucas's hand away. Jenny hushes him, takes Lucas's hand, leads him off into the dark. Mike follows.

'Can I have attention, *please*?' the guide says. 'My assistant is now looking for turtle. There is turtle nearby, but we have to wait, so please to sit. Sit ...' He gestures expansively. He has wide eyes, a broad smile, satanic in the red-bulbed torch he uses to search out the laying turtles. Mike and Jenny take Lucas up a dune, behind the rest of the group, and kneel gingerly. Lucas does not want to sit.

'The sand is yucky,' he repeats.

'Look,' Mike says, 'look at the stars,' and slowly he coaxes Lucas into sitting between his knees, with stories about Hercules and Orion. Stars shoot across the wide sky, as Mike's story takes hold. Jenny imagines this as ordinary, imagines they could live here, as Mike wants them to, and she could take for granted stars that transverse the sky.

Twenty minutes later, when they are starting to cramp and Lucas is beginning to shiver, there is sudden movement, an exchange of texts and the guide says, 'Please! Please! Quiet! There is a turtle very near here! She is in process of laying eggs, please!'

'Did you hear that, Lucas? We're going to see a turtle now,' Mike says. Lucas is still with the stars.

'Lukey, did you hear?' Jenny whispers. 'A real turtle!'

He is dreamy, tired perhaps. They get up, Mike lifting Lucas to his feet, and Jenny notices he is careful not to do more. She is grateful. The group all stand and murmur. Suddenly Lucas shouts, 'We're going to see a turtle!' and Mike and Jenny gasp, shush him, tell him no. Some of the group laugh.

The guide says 'Quiet! Quiet …' He tells them facts and figures about the turtle, how she will not lay until she is between thirty-six and forty-two years old. She is two metres long. She swims back to the same beach every year, and the turtles that are born on this beach will return to lay their eggs. He says the turtle lays, then she covers them in a large mound and goes back to the water. Jenny takes the information and speaks it into Lucas's ear. Lucas interrupts her sometimes, to ask her to repeat the words; she knows he is encapsulating the knowledge. She knows these words will stay now, that each kick of a turtle's flipper is a neural pathway opened and connected to another in her son's brain. She is an enabler, that is all, helpless in this assimilation of facts, lacking courage to deny it and make him play as any other child. She fills him up, day after day, and it seems to make him stronger, seems to make him more.

'Come now,' the guide says. 'Let us go. But when we approach, be calm and quiet please. The mother lays eggs *now*! Now!' They follow his torchlight down on to the main beach, falling in and out of holes which Jenny now realises must be old nests. The assistant is squatting next to a hole containing a dark green, hexagonally patterned rock. The rock has a head, which moves from side to side like a toy. Lucas has started to tremble.

'See, it's a turtle, Lukey, can you see it?' Mike and Jenny and Lucas stand back, away from the rest of the group, letting Lucas understand.

'I need to see,' he whispers. He allows Mike to pick him up. Jenny watches him crane forward, his arm carelessly about Mike's neck. She does not look at the turtle, only at that arm, the skin in full contact with Mike's skin. It is simply there, and she is nearly faint with not breathing.

'Come!' the guide whispers to them. 'Come and see the eggs!' As they approach, the guide asks others to stand and move away. He kneels again, shows them where they should sit. He takes Lucas's chin in his hand and points it, just so, like a midwife. 'Look!' he says, and Lucas does not object to his touch, simply looks and there are large pearls dropping from the turtle's tail, precise and round, a pile of luminescent blobs of matter, perfect in their potential.

'Oohhhh!' Lucas says wildly. The guide nods, pats Lucas's head. He does not move them away:

It was the hottest night of the year, the night Lucas was born. He was stuck in her birth canal, his English head too wide for her. 'You are made for roundheaded Sri Lankan babies,' the Chinese midwife said. 'We need to unhook him. Episiotomy … forceps.' Words mentioned, not understood: she was feral with fear and pain and anxiety for the child. Mike stood between her and the doctor, stood with his eyes to hers, cradling her head as cuts were made, holding her hands as tight as she clung to his, while cold metal plunged high into her abdomen to retrieve the tiny man stuck inside.

'It hurts, Mike!' she screamed, and he held her, telling her she was the bravest, telling her the baby was nearly there. 'Ohhhh!' she screamed.

And it was this noise she heard, when Lucas cried out. It was this red-hot anguish she thought of, the white light, the blackness inside her skull.

Jenny looks down at the turtle: there are tears rolling from the creature's eyes. 'She's crying,' she says to the guide.

'Yes, tears. But she is secreting excess salt, nothing more. It is not pain. It is not sadness!' He laughs, as if it were a joke. His phone beeps, and he reads the message. 'Oh! My goodness! You are lucky group! There is baby here! Baby!' He turns to Lucas. 'Come! You see baby?' Mike and Lucas stand and follow the others. But Jenny stays there, in the dark with the turtle, in fellowship.

Much later, in bed finally, Lucas's limbs are still, and he settles into her. She holds him close, as if he were a normal child. 'My egg,' he says. His T-shirt is damp with sweat in the closeness of the night room.

'You're a little egg, all tucked up and safe in our bed,' she coos.

'No. *My* egg.' He struggles awake. 'Be careful with it. It's in my pocket.'

When he's asleep, she looks in his trouser pockets. There is an egg there, dented, worn by the world it seems, still pale but its skin dull, dead. Mike is making tea in the kitchen of their suite. She shows him, and he reverently washes out a yoghurt pot, places tissues inside, and puts the egg in, tucking more tissues around it. Its value to Lucas somehow brings them together. Yet, when they go to bed, they say goodnight, nothing more, and stares at the ceiling, listening to the waves outside their window, knowing the sky above them is still full of stars.

The egg focuses Lucas, Mike thinks. There are fewer scenes than in England. Perhaps Lucas is growing out of it, he thinks, but he knows it is a foolish thought. He has always chosen to ignore the worst of Lucas's foibles: the way he crawled back and forth on top of the patch that was burnt by a falling iron in the carpet in their sitting room, running his hand along its texture, then crawling, then backing up and doing the whole procedure over and over, as they both watched helplessly. His mouth dribbling from a sticking-out tongue. Jenny's anxiety made Mike ashamed – of himself, of his family.

'You were the same,' his mother said, when he broached the subject. Had he been? He asked his eldest sister, who was ten when he was born. Had he been madly obsessive, too bright, easily upset? She was part of the problem – she had the same symptoms, so could not provide the solution. 'But we did OK, didn't we?' she emailed back. Did we, he wonders? Did we? Jenny and he on this cusp – and his brothers and sisters all divorced or near enough. Lucas is going to be happy, he decides. This holiday, this childhood, this life.

They wake up early every morning, and Lucas is awake before them, singing in his bed, as if in answer to the call to prayer at five.

His egg sits by his bed: it is the first thing he sees when he wakes. He has replaced the tissue with sand from the beach at Ras Al Jinz: he brought it back in his jacket pocket. Lucas had taken in everything. The guide said, 'The sand of this beach is the mother of these turtles, and it is to their mother they return when they too become mothers!' Lucas's egg is at the bottom of the yoghurt cup, weighed down by sand. Sometimes he tops the sand up from other beaches, but he is careful not to allow the cup to tip so that the 'Mummy sand', as he calls it, stays integral to the egg.

'How can you tell the difference?' Mike asks.

'Oh, I can,' Lucas says, showing the fineness of the Ras Al Jinz sand compared to the rice-like desiccated shells of the Ras Al Haad sand. He is now an expert on turtles and an expert on sand.

As they have travelled about, Lucas has held the egg in its carton, with its clingfilm (with holes) lid, on his lap in the back of the car. He has refused air conditioning, preferring the temperature of the car to be the temperature of the warm dry air of Oman. As they drive past mountain after mountain of pinky orange rock and plains of sandy earth, Lucas looks steadily and calmly about him, understanding little, 'not engaging' as Jenny puts it, but holding his yoghurt pot. Mike is fine with this. It *is* fine, he thinks. It is perfectly ordinary for a four-year-old child to behave in this way.

The driving makes Jenny talk to him, and Mike is grateful and quick to reply, so that the friendship that began their relationship is rekindled soon enough. They do not laugh yet, as they used to, but the interest shown and given is enough for Mike to be encouraged.

'I used to love stick insects when I was his age, you know.'

'Really?' she smiles. She is the most beautiful of women, pale brown, with her long black hair making her seem paler in this deeply coloured, heavily sunned country. He cannot see her eyes under her over-large sunglasses, but he has noticed that she has steadily lost weight since Lucas was born, and her wrists are tiny, her cheekbones too prominent. He dares not look at her breasts, her waist. He looks at the empty road as he drives and they speak. He does not dare imagine making love to her.

When he was offered the job in Oman, he expected her to be negative. The vehemence, though, her downright refusal to contemplate a move, disquieted them both. But the break away from the family, from the pity, from the routine visits to various caring professions: all would be banished, he argued, and we could do it ourselves. It would be just *us*, he said, bringing up *our* child. She had not considered it. Had not thought it through, he realised. He took the job. He knew it was the right moment, the right opportunity, and she would follow or she would not. And with the extra money Oman offered, he would be able to pay for Lucas and Jenny to have the life they needed, in Oman or England. There were no other choices. He came to Oman.

'I had a snail farm,' she says. 'I collected snails for a whole week or so – you know, those ugly grey-brown things that eat everything, and I let them crawl up my arm, and Mum took pictures and thought I was some sort of science genius, but I wasn't.' He notices a line of sweat-dots glistening on her upper lip. He would like to lick them off. She looks out of the open window.

'Camel!' she cries. 'Did you see, Lucas? Oh, slow down, Mike!' and she puts her hand out and touches his forearm. It tingles; the warmth of her fingers he feels down in the base of his penis. He cannot help his erection, and he slows the car down, stops on the hard shoulder of the highway, so she can hang out of the window with a camera, and he adjusts himself, and shifts in his seat. Lucas is asleep behind him, and the pot is sideways in his lap. Mike leans over and takes the yoghurt pot, puts it into the drinks holder at the front. He starts the car again.

'You don't have to be a tourist, Jen,' he says.

'Let's not talk about it,' she says.

'Why? Why not?'

She does not say anything. He drives up the last hill, in a culvert cut through orange cliffs. He knows at the top there will be the first sight of the ocean, navy and straight, the dash of a child's loaded brush across this white day. They are on their way back to Sur. They will soon be passing the Sur lagoon where young men play football at dusk. Sometimes, he plays football with the office crowd in a park in Muttrah, a rowdy, good-humoured game where often he finds himself floored by a handsome Omani who picks him up and slaps his back. Football is the language here – even in the desert, a Bedouin served them coffee in a Beckham shirt. He could teach Lucas, he thinks, and then smiles at his optimism.

'Shall we stop for a drink?' he asks, pointing to the hotel on the lagoon. Its door stands open invitingly. The tide is receding, and here the water is yellow with silt and glinting around the already stranded dhows lying on their sides.

'Lucas is still asleep,' she says.

'We can leave him in the car. It's safe here. We can sit over there, look,' he says, pulling in through the gates. In England he is never so decisive. In England Jenny tells him where to park.

'OK,' she says.

They sit at the table, and he drinks a mango lassi, and she drinks lime juice through a delicate, opaque straw. Everything about her looks taut, as if about to break. They are Mike and Jenny, Jenny and Mike, who hold hands and drink in pubs by the river.

'Please, Jenny?' he says. And just this question brings it all pouring out, the misgivings, the resentment, the torture of being left by herself in England, the 'I will *never* …' that she has stored up for this occasion, the quiet reflection after the tears, the talk of divorce. And he hears it all, but it is as if it is something that can be dealt with in the morning, on a fresh day, like a bad Excel spreadsheet that has come in at 5.30. Tomorrow it will seem easier, and when she has finished her drink, and takes off her sunglasses to really look at him (a technique he is wise to), he only says, 'Oh, my, you are lovely,' and she smiles, she – smiles. At least, she smiles.

Just down the road, he can see the men pulling up in their cars, in shorts and vests and mirrored shades. They don't wear shoes, but slip swiftly over the rocks on to the lagoon bed. Lucas's scream, 'My egg!' he greets calmly, and Mike walks steadily to the car, takes his son from his seat and the yoghurt pot from the front, and they stay for another drink and watch the sunset game.

Jenny wakes up abruptly on the beach. She watches a bird fly out across the waves. It has come to her, the sudden idea. It does not make her lift her head from the towel. She lies there, still, and thinks – if he is to drown Lucas, he must do it soon. Now. I will give him *this moment*.

Just as suddenly as the idea has come, it becomes anathema, and she sits up, curling her legs beneath her. She feels the breath judder into her, her head twitching to the side. In the distance, Mike and Lucas walk along the sea edge, hand in hand, looking down at the water. They stop to silently watch an Omani family in the sea. A father struggles with a ball against the tide and two boys run in and out of the water. She hears the boys' laughter, and she turns away.

On their last day, they stop in Muttrah. He has taken them to the Grand Mosque, and round the Sultan Qaboos University Campus, should she be tempted to take up the provisional teaching post he has begged for. He drove past the International School. He did not need to point it out. She saw it: he saw her head turn.

They sit at a juice bar, opposite the bay, fanning themselves with menus, the heat swabbing them, getting between them. Will she launch into another tirade? Not yet. She sips. He hears the sigh.

'You see, what I'm afraid of ...' she says. Here it comes. 'You see me as some kind of catalogue bride. Bring me out here and I'll facilitate for you. I'll look after your fucked-up son ...' His fucked-up son is playing with an ugly black street cat under the next table.

'... and be waiting at home with my sexed-up clothes under my hijab ...' And so she goes on. He waits silently for her to finish. She can see his jaw twitch in patient frustration. 'I don't want to talk about it any more,' she finishes.

'Have you thought,' he says suddenly, 'that Lucas may benefit –' But she does not let him carry on. Off again, the het-up, angry words, female and hot. He talks over them: 'Maybe a new country ... maybe it is not stepping backwards. Maybe a new culture ... Maybe you'll be free to be *you* ...' But Jenny does not see the new culture, the new life. She sees a turtle, in a hole, flapping its back flippers to bury its eggs, its head nodding this way and that in exhaustion. She sees the lady on the next table, her hijab-ed head nodding this way and that.

'No, Mike. I *can't*. I can't be *trapped* ... ' but as she says it, she thinks of the turtle climbing out of her hole, walking down to the foam, swimming out to sea.

'Oh, Jen. I hate to say it, but you have got to – *shut up*!' He sees she is shocked. He has spoilt her, being so polite, so gentle. 'I'm sorry, but you have to *listen*.'

She will not, and she stumbles up, he knows in tears, and takes Lucas's hand roughly, so that as he stands, he glances his head against the corner of the table. He shouts, and begins to cry, but a painful, ordinary child's cry.

'Be quiet, Lucas,' she says, in anger, and Lucas is quiet. She starts to march away, pulling at his wrist. Lucas drags back, and they tug at each other. Lucas says: 'I want Daddy. I want to stay with Daddy.' Mike takes three Omani Real from his wallet and tucks them under the ashtray. He picks up Lucas's rucksack and takes Lucas's hand. Lucas shakes Jenny away.

They walk back into the soukh, Jenny ahead of them. Around them, men offer pashminas, perfume. The smoke of frankincense carries them through.

'You know you're going on the aeroplane tonight, don't you?' Mike says.

'Yes. Can you check my egg?' It is a ritual now. Where is the egg? It is in the main pocket on the right side. It is in the dark, under your muslin. Mike opens the bag, makes a pantomime one-eyed probe, and Lucas giggles. Jenny has disappeared around a corner into the gold soukh. He saw which way she went, but he is in no hurry to find her.

'Lucas. So you know you're going home, don't you?' He wants to appeal to the logic in the child, make it easier, the way things were made easier when he was a child, by teachers at boarding school.

'Yes,' Lucas says. But unexpectedly, he says, 'And when will you come for us?'

'Come for you?'

'Yes,' Lucas says. 'When?' And he has learnt that use of a deep, direct look into Mike's eyes.

'I don't want you to go,' Mike says, and he looks away, towards Jenny.

At the airport, they are dreadfully alone. Mike has kissed Lucas again and again, and Lucas has kissed Mike tenderly and carefully. Jenny allows him to kiss her cheek. It is night, almost ten. Lucas is tired as Mike picks him up, holds his full length against him as if to memorise it. Lucas walks backwards through the security doors. Jenny looks back once, sees Mike brush a tear away. She and Lucas have to become a team again. She pushes the trolley, and he carries his rucksack. She tries to check in, but they have not opened the desk yet, so she sits Lucas on the trolley and they wait, watching the men and women in their flowing robes. She is grateful for the air conditioning, the vacuum of the airport. An Omani manager is kind and beckons them to a different desk. The bags are on the conveyor belt when Lucas says, 'My turtle.' It is a low-pitched gurgle of a noise.

'Did you pack these bags yourself?'

'Yes.'

'Mummy,' he whispers. 'My turtle.'

'Lucas,' she says sharply. '*Wait!*' She has learnt that his feelings are not always precious, and that he will not break.

'Did anyone ask you to carry any packages for them?'

'No,' she says, talking to both of them. Lucas looks as if he needs the toilet. 'Do you need to go?'

'Yes,' he says urgently. 'Mummy, my turtle. It's hatching. It is.'

The man at the desk smiles at Lucas.

'It isn't, Lucas,' she says, chattily. She wants to get through this, get back to England, and the cold and dark, which make her safe. The taxi is booked to meet their flight. The old shuffling George who takes them to Lucas's appointments will be there, white bristles on his cheeks; hair unkempt and the black anorak pervading smoke and Fisherman's Friends. Lucas jumps from one foot to the other. He is going red.

'He needs toilet?' the man says.

'I think so.' She is embarrassed, the way she always is, in a matter-of-fact, my-child-is-special-needs way.

'Go – go,' he says with a smile, and points towards the lavatories across the hall. She takes Lucas's hand roughly and they go through the double doors.

'See?' Lucas says, unzipping his rucksack. Inside, clambering over his muslin, his colouring pencils and his shells is a small black creature. It is comical, its head bobbing about, and it tries to climb up the black nylon interior. Its eyes look up at her, and Jenny yelps. Someone is coming in. Jenny pulls Lucas into the toilet and locks it.

'Oh, God, what are we going to do?'

'I want to take him home,' Lucas says stoutly. He slides to the floor with the bag on his lap. Jenny looks at him and sees Mike. She thinks of Mike carrying the yoghurt pot through Oman, and it makes her cry, the suddenness of the turtle's appearance. Oh, Mike, she thinks.

'We have to take him home,' Lucas whines. He is looking at Jenny, the way he looks at her when she is to say no, no, Lucas, we can't.

'Take him home? Where to?' she asks him. She will not say no.

'To the beach, of course,' he says. She was sure he meant his little room, with its dinosaur mural and plastic animals on the floor.

'Lucas! We're just about to get on a plane! We're going home!'

'No! Jenny.' He calls her Jenny in moments of crisis, like an old man, like a friend. 'We need to take him to his beach.'

'Lucas …' As Lucas begins to shout, she realises she had never imagined a time when Mike was not part of her, when she was simply Jenny again.

She calls Mike from the desk, but he is not home. She cannot remember his mobile number in her fluster. She takes the bags off the conveyor belt, tells the man they are not going. They fight their way out of security, and all the while Lucas laughs, and is manic, allowing his rucksack to be held safely by his mother, while running up and down the concourse, skidding on his knees, getting in the way of busy men and tourists. It is nearly midnight. She should take a cab, but instead she goes to a desk and hires a car.

She asks the man for a map, pays by credit card, loads the bags in with no help from anyone, straps the rucksack into the seat next to Lucas. 'You do *not* touch him, understand? You allow him air to breathe, but you do *not* touch him, OK?'

'I won't hurt him … '

'Lucas. I'm warning you … what did the man do when you saw the baby turtle?'

'He guided him down the beach with his torch.'

'Exactly. We will do the same.'

'At Ras Al Jinz?' Lucas's eyes are wide, excited.

'No. I don't know,' she says. 'We'll ask Daddy.'

They stand at Ras Al Haad, watching the sea. Lucas's shoulders still heave from the crying, and the singing of the muezzin is unexpected and disturbs them. The sun will come up soon. Lucas holds Mike's hand, and Jenny stands apart from them. It will take time, she thinks. And later, months and years later, when Lucas and her daughters are willowy and stand tall next to her, she thinks of this moment, on this beach, as the moment of knowledge. The moment she covered what was exposed. The moment she opened what was shut away.

EVEN PRETTY EYES COMMIT CRIMES

M. J. Hyland

M. J. Hyland (b. 1968) is a British-born author who grew up in Australia. Her first short story was published when she was seventeen. She has written three novels, the second of which, *Carry Me Down,* was shortlisted for the 2006 Man Booker Prize.

My father was sitting on my doorstep. He was wearing khaki shorts, his bare head was exposed to the full bore of the sun, and he was holding a pineapple. I hadn't a clue what he was doing there. He hadn't given me any warning.

As I crossed the street, I raised my hand, but his eyes were closed, and he didn't see me until I was standing right in front of him.

'Dad. What are you doing here so early?'

'Relax,' he said. 'There's nothing to worry about.'

I looked at my watch. It wasn't yet eight-thirty and I wasn't in the mood for him. I'd walked home to save on bus fares after working a ten-hour night shift and I needed a shower and sleep.

'Did you knock?'

'No,' he said. 'I didn't knock. I didn't want to wake anybody. I was just going to leave the pineapple on your doorstep, but then I sat down to rest for a minute and you turned up.'

The neighbour's dogs were barking. My father frowned at the pampas grass that grew wild along the length of the broken fence.

'Your neighbours need to train those bloody kelpies to stop barking.'

I held out my hand.

'Here, Dad. Grab hold.'

'I'm alright,' he said. 'No need.'

I'd had twenty-nine years to get used to Australia; its boiling summers, long days with no distinct parts – hot in the morning, noon and night – but I still couldn't stomach the heat or the glare that came off every footpath and every parked car. My father was the opposite. He was made better by the sun; it made him buoyant and though he was sixty-five, on that morning, I was much more beaten and tired than he'd ever been.

'Do you want to come into the flat for a minute,' I said.

'If that's alright.'

'We'd best be quiet, though. Janice won't be out of bed yet.'

But Janice wasn't home. As soon as we were inside the hall I saw she'd left the bedroom door open and it was clear the bed hadn't been slept in. I'd made the bed and it was just as I'd left it. We'd had an argument about money before I left for work and when I was walking out the door she said, 'You're boring now, Paul.'

She said this in the cool and expert way my mother used to say things about couples who sit in cafés reading the newspaper and not talking to each other. 'They're boring each other,' she used to say. 'They're probably only days away from divorce.'

My father looked into the bedroom, just as I had done. He suspected Janice of straying, just as he'd suspected my mother.

'Janice must be out,' I said.

I straightened my shoulders and tried to hide my worry and fatigue. I was at the end of a long run of night shifts, and I wasn't in the mood for the grilling he'd give me if he knew about my marriage troubles.

'Where's your uniform?' he asked.

'In my locker. I don't like walking home wearing it. I get changed first.'

'So, you have a clean one for tomorrow's shift?'

'Yes, Dad. I have a few.'

He looked into the bedroom again. 'Where do you think she is?'

'Keep your hat on, Dad. She's probably just popped out to do some shopping.'

I owed my father some money, and mentioning shops was a mistake. He was well-off and enjoyed his riches, but he didn't like giving money away, not without arrangements for its 'fair return'.

When I was eighteen my father asked me to have a drink with him. It was the first time he'd asked to meet me in a pub and he picked the day and time of the meeting months in advance.

'It's time we had a proper man-to-man chat,' he said.

It was a perfect spring day, a gentle day, and we sat in the corner of the dark pub under a TV screen, in a suburb miles from his surgery, and even further away from my university digs.

'It's time I told you a few home-truths,' he said.

'OK,' I said. 'Go ahead.'

'Well, for starters, I knew your mother was up to no good years before she left us.'

As far as I was concerned, she hadn't left *us* when I was ten years old, she'd left *him*. She'd got sick of him and found somebody else. I was only ten, but I wasn't stupid. I'd heard her say, 'Men shouldn't talk as much as you do, Richard.'

My father sipped his beer slowly and looked at the TV screen above my head.

'She was a very good liar, your mother,' he said.

I was too angry to speak. What he'd said got me in the gut, a weird kind of wetness low in my stomach. I'd have got blind drunk that day if I'd had some spare money of my own but I had to listen to him curse my mother with nothing but a warm glass of beer froth in front of me.

When he came back to the table after ordering another round, he put the drinks down on our corner table and sat close and, after a moment, as though he was a different person, he put his hand on my knee.

'I'll tell you something now,' he said. 'Even pretty eyes commit crimes. You should bear that in mind when you start making lady friends.'

'Right,' I said.

'You prefer ladies, don't you?'

'Of course I do,' I said. 'Jesus Christ!'

My father didn't like sitting close to people, and he didn't like touching, and said he loathed displays of affection of any kind, but he was sitting very close, and his hand stayed on my knee a bit too long, and he softly squeezed, and my knee got hotter and hotter, and he kept looking at me, as though waiting for me to do something, and I had an idea that he was going to ask if we could have sex, father and son. It was a crazy idea, but I was certain of it. I moved my leg.

'Well then,' he said, 'you've been warned. You thought your mother was an angel because she looked like one, but you were completely wrong about that.'

I didn't want to hear any more. I told him I needed to use the toilet and I went to the bar and used the last of my money to pay for our drinks. I wasn't going to say goodbye, I couldn't stand him anymore, but he came round the corner, and saw me.

'What are you doing?' he said.

'I need to go back to Uni. I just remembered I have to meet my tutor.'

My father and I had lived alone together for seven years and, for seven years, when he got home from work, I'd be stuck with him, trapped with his talking in the kitchen or lounge, and if he wanted me when I went into my bedroom, he'd barge in, and I'd have to yawn my head right off its hinges to get rid of him. Nearly every weekend I'd pretend to be going into the city to see a film with friends and instead, catch the bus to an internet café three suburbs away, and drink coffee and play games online.

He followed me to the front door of the pub. 'Did you hear what I said? Were you listening?'

'Yes, but I have to go to a lecture.'

'You're a stinking liar,' he said. 'I'm staying on and I'll finish these beers. I don't like people who waste time and money. Do you follow me?'

'Yes,' I said.

He opened the door for me, and saw me out to the street.

We saw very little of each other after that spring afternoon; once or twice a year, my birthday and Christmas, but that changed when I married Janice. On our wedding day, at a small outdoor ceremony by the lake, he gave me our wedding gift; a Tartan picnic flask, six blue plastic cups, and a matching rug.

'You'll have a family of your own, soon,' he said. 'And I want to help you along. I can help you get on with things. I can help you sort things out.'

After the wedding, he formed a habit of stopping by the flat, donating furniture, giving me loans, calling me late in the night and saying things like, 'I'm just around the corner. Have you got a minute?'

And here he was again, only two months since his last visit, standing beside my kitchen table and holding a pineapple in the crook of his arm.

I turned my back to him and checked the whiteboard on the fridge to see if Janice had left me a message. She hadn't. I pretended to check the clock over the sink and looked into the backyard. Her bike was leaning against the shed, but her helmet wasn't in the basket. She might be gone for good and my father would be here to see it happen.

As I turned round to face him, he gave me the pineapple, offered it to me as though it were something of great value.

'It fell off the tree when I was heading home last night,' he said. 'What a glorious country, eh?'

'I don't really like pineapples, Dad. Why don't you give it to somebody at work?'

'Give it back to me, then. It's not going to waste.'

I gave it back to him.

'You should eat more fruit,' he said.

'You're right,' I said. 'I should.'

I thought he was going to leave but he sat at the table and put the pineapple in his lap. He was going to stay, and there was nothing I could do about it.

'What do you want to drink?' I said. 'Will a cup of tea do?'

'That'd be nice.'

I opened the fridge and looked out to the backyard again. The neighbour's ginger cat was curled up, asleep, on the Greek family's trampoline.

'Sorry, Dad. There's no milk.'

There was always milk in the fridge. Janice bought two litres every night when she went to the 7-Eleven on the corner for her cigarettes.

'Then I'll have water,' he said. 'Do you have ice?'

'You don't want a beer?'

'Christ, no,' he said. 'It's too early. I'm working today.'

'What time do you start?'

'I'm supposed to be there by nine. But there's no mad rush. I've arranged for the locum to do the mornings.'

There was no ice in the ice-tray, but I rummaged in the freezer as though there was hope it might be found. The breeze from the frost took some of the heat off my hands.

'There's no ice,' I said.

'Forget the water, then. I'll suck on one of these.'

He took a packet of *Fisherman's Friends* from the back pocket of his khaki shorts.

'Do you want one?'

'No thanks, Dad. They make me cough.'

As soon as I sat at the table, he stood and went to the sink and put the pineapple on the draining board, tried to stand it upright. When it toppled, he held its bottom and moved it round 'til he was sure it wouldn't budge.

'Thanks for the pineapple,' I said. 'Janice will love it.'

'Does she usually go out so early in the morning?'

'Sometimes,' I lied. 'She likes going for walks.'

'Is she still selling buttons?'

'No, she quit. And it wasn't buttons, it was sewing equipment …'

'I know that.'

He sat down again, but didn't pull his chair under the table. I thought he'd be leaving soon.

'How have you been?' he said. 'How are you keeping?'

'I've been well-enough, thanks, Dad. The nights are hard, but I like the quiet hours when the patients are sleeping. And the walk home is good.'

He looked at the ceiling fan.

'Is that broken?'

'Yes. The landlord's coming to fix it soon.'

He looked at the window.

'Didn't she leave you a note or anything? Didn't she tell you where she was going?'

'No, Dad. I'm not her minder.'

I sat up in the chair and put my shoulders back, tried to make my body look bigger, tried to hide my panic. But it made no difference. I was work-wrecked and nervous and he could see it. Janice was gone somewhere, and it might be for good this time.

'How about you, Dad?'

'I could use a bit more help. The locum's pretty good, but my secretary's always behind. Things are getting to be too much for us. I've been wondering if I should retire.'

We were silent then and the only sound came from the traffic in Ormond Road, the delivery trucks beeping as they reversed out of the Mornflake warehouse. He wasn't troubled by the silence, or the lack of something to do with his hands. He was tidy and ambitious and he liked his own company. Even a stranger could see it; the way he sat with his hands on the knees of his khaki shorts, the creases just as they were when he pulled them, brand new from the box.

'Maybe you need a new secretary,' I said.

'Don't be daft, son. I've spent too long training her. Anyway, the patients like her. She keeps teddy bears behind the desk for the kiddies.'

'That's good then, Dad,' I said. 'Surely the fact that the patients like your secretary's much more important than paperwork.'

'You're right, son,' he said. 'Of course, you're right.'

The baby in the flat upstairs started howling.

'It's too hot in here,' I said.

I stood and opened the back door and, as soon as it was open, the ginger cat jumped off the trampoline and ran into the kitchen and sniffed at the cupboard door under the sink, walked to the door and looked at us for a moment, then sat.

'Is that yours?' he said.

'No. It belongs to the upstairs neighbour.'

'Why does it come in here?'

'That's what cats do,' I said. 'It wants food, I suppose.'

'It stinks,' he said. 'Is it neutered? You should tell those Greeks upstairs that neutering is a relatively cheap and simple operation.'

There was no air coming through the kitchen door and the backs of my knees were sweating.

I stood up from the table.

'Listen, Dad. I might have a bit of a sleep now, if that's alright.'

'Won't you be waking up again soon?' he said. 'When Janice gets home?'

'Not necessarily. I'm a heavy sleeper.'

He stood and looked over at the pineapple on the draining board.

'I'll get out of your hair then, will I?'

We faced each other across the table, and we were breathing in unison.

'OK. Stay for a bit,' I said. 'I can sleep later. Let's go into the lounge room.'

I stopped in the hallway and told him I'd be in soon.

'I just want to open the bedroom window.'

Janice had cleared out most of her clothes. I couldn't check the bedside drawers, without my father wondering what I was doing, but I knew the drawers would be empty, too. She'd threatened leaving, but I didn't believe she would, not like this, not this suddenly, not without a final warning, not without a last chance. People didn't end marriages this way, without warning, without second chances.

I got two glasses of orange juice and brought them into the lounge. My father was standing by the window and he'd unclenched his jaw, let his mouth hang open. I saw how he might look in repose, when there was nobody else around. He'd let me see him, not as strong, and not as calm. He was thinking about my mother, and I sensed it there in his slackened mouth and, for a moment, I thought of her too, the memory that always came to me first, though I didn't want it to.

It was a few months before she left home, a winter's day, and the three of us were eating lunch in a café. She told the waitress she wanted something that wasn't on the menu. She asked for a 'large onion sandwich'. The waitress was still at our table when my father laughed at her. 'Precisely how large is a large onion?' he said.

My mother got out of her seat.

'The waitress knew what I meant,' she said. 'Everybody else knew what I meant.'

He tried to apologise, as he often did, by saying, 'Oh, pet. Don't feel that way.'

She came round to my father's side of the table. She'd hung her coat over the back of his chair and she needed him to sit forward to get at it.

'Move,' she said.

He turned round to her, put his hand on her arm, and tried to console her as best he could, as he often did, by holding onto a part of her.

'I said move,' she said, 'you slow, deaf pig! I need my coat.'

My father didn't move quickly enough. She wrenched the coat from behind his back.

'You're embarrassing me, Richard,' she said. 'Get off my bloody coat!'

I stood in the lounge room doorway and held the glasses of orange juice and looked at him, waited for him to see me.

'Oh, hi,' he said. 'I've turned on the fan for you.'

'Thanks, Dad. Here's your OJ.'

I sat down on the end of the settee and he sat in the armchair near the door. As we sat, we crossed our legs, left over right, a genetic tic, something we always did when we sat down.

'So, where do you think that young wife of yours has got to?'

'She's probably meeting a friend for coffee or something.'

He looked at his watch. 'It's very early for that.'

I said nothing, and he sat forward, moved his legs round so that his knees and feet were aimed in my direction.

'I think I'll call Janice,' I said. 'I'll ask her to bring some milk and ice back with her.'

'Alright,' he said. 'I should be heading off soon anyway.'

'OK,' I said and felt the phone warm in my hand.

He waited for me to check for messages, but there were none. She was gone.

'She's on her way home,' I said. 'She says she'll be back soon.'

'Where is she?'

'I don't know yet. But I think I'll try and get some sleep now.'

I thought he'd leave then, but he didn't. He was going to stick it out, wait with me until she came home – or didn't.

'I've been meaning to ask you,' he said. 'Have you given any more thought to taking the exam?'

He was talking about the mature-age medical school exam. He'd reminded me of it the last time we met, and the time before that.

'Not yet,' I said, 'but I will.'

'Do you think you'll work as a nurse for the rest of your life?'

'I might, Dad. I like it.'

'How's your blood-pressure been of late?'

'Normal, Dad. It's normal.'

'Do you still get those dizzy spells? Maybe while I'm here I could check your pulse?'

'I can check my own bloody pulse. There's no need.'

'You look a bit flushed. A bit iffy around the gills.'

'There's nothing wrong with me. I'm just real hot, Dad. It's just stuffy in here. I feel like I'm wearing a bear suit.'

'I see,' he said. 'You never did warm to the heat.'

He laughed at himself, like a school-boy.

'Good one,' I said. 'That's a good one.'

We were silent and he scratched his arm while looking out the window. A Mornflake truck was reversing out of the factory warehouse.

'There might be fleas in here,' he said, 'from that cat. Have you been bitten?'

'No. I haven't been bitten. It was probably a mozzie.'

'There's a lot of sand,' he said. 'In the carpet.'

We lived fifteen minutes from Bondi Beach and that's part of the reason why we paid so much rent for such a cramped, gloomy flat. I wanted to move out to the suburbs, just for a few years, and save some money for an air-conditioner and a trip back to London, but Janice couldn't stand the stench of the suburban sticks and so we stayed and bought three fans; so that made four fans, including the overhead in the kitchen that was busted.

I looked at him and jiggled my glass, swirled the juice round as though it had ice in it, and said nothing about the sand.

'You can check your mobile phone again if you want,' he said.

'I'm not worried, Dad. She'll be here in a minute.'

He stood. 'I should be going,' he said. 'I'll see myself out.'

'OK, Dad. Thanks for coming over. I'm sorry I wasn't very good company.'

'You're tired, that's all. You've never liked the heat.'

We stood in the hallway, near the front door. His hands were stuffed inside his khaki pockets and he didn't look like he was ready to go. In this in-between state, this waiting, this not coming or going, he'd usually be the one to make the first move to action. But on that morning, he stood stock still, and looked at me. I didn't want to speak, and he didn't either, so I opened the front door and stepped outside and waited for him to follow. I was in a bad state, sweating and nervous, and even though I didn't want to be left alone, I didn't know how to be this way with him watching me.

'Goodbye,' I said.

'Goodbye, son.'

I'd already turned to go back inside when he stepped back onto the porch and took hold of me. He hugged me, long enough for me to feel what went on beneath his chest, and I closed my eyes as he held me, and there was no rush from either of us to get it over with, and I held him with the same strength as he held me.

He let go first, but it wasn't to be rid of me. He wanted to say something. He took hold of my wrist.

'I hope you can find a way out of this situation, son. I wish you luck.'

And so he knew Janice had gone, and he'd probably known for a long time that she'd leave me, and maybe he hadn't come to rub my nose in it. Maybe it wasn't that at all.

'OK,' I said. 'OK, Dad.'

Saying 'OK' said nothing, and meant nothing, but as I held my breath, and watched him walk down the path, I hoped he'd realise that I wanted to say more, and that I just didn't know how to take the chance. He'd know, wouldn't he, that I was too surprised to speak? Maybe he'd have seen that I was too afraid to do anything, or say anything, that might bring my emotions to the boil. I was too busy shuddering to say anything more, and I hoped he knew that, and that he realised, that morning, I loved him.

THE GIFT

Emma Donoghue

Emma Donoghue (b. 1969) is an Irish-born playwright, literary historian and novelist. She has published seven novels, eleven plays and four collections of short stories. Her 2010 novel, *Room*, was a finalist for the Man Booker Prize.

Mrs. Sarah Bell
177 3rd Street
Jersey City

March 5, 1877

I need to put my little one with you. Her name is Lily May Bell, she is of one hundred per cent American parentage. Her father John Bell died unexpected when she was only three months old leaving me alone in the world and I cannot supply her needs tho' not for want of trying. I would work and take care of her but no one will have me and her too, some say they would if she was 2 or 3 years old. She is just from the breast, her bowels have not been right for a long time. I have cried and worried over her so much I think my milk hurt her. I boarded Lily May out for some months so I could work at dressmaking but she did not thrive, and the woman said it might be the best in the end for a fatherless mite. A neighbor told me in confidence that woman is no better than a baby farmer and doses them all stupid with syrup so I have taken Lily May out and can see no way except to throw myself on the mercy of your famous New York Society. Be kind to her for God's sake. You must not think that I neglected her. Do not be afraid of her face, it is nothing but an old ringworm. I will try hard to relieve you of her care as soon as ever can be.

Mrs. Sarah Bell
177 3rd Street
Jersey City

March 10, 1877

Thank you for your reply and for all your goodness. I hope
Lily May does not "make strange" with the nurses for long but I
suppose it is only to be expected. I do get some consolation from
knowing I have done the best for her in my straitened circumstances.
You say every child is assigned a place to sleep and a chair in the
dining room which I am glad of, except that my baby cannot sit at
table on her own yet so I hope there is someone to prop her up. I
appreciate how busy the Rev. Brace and you all must be what with
taking those unfortunates off the streets (and more swarming off
every ship it seems), but if I may I will write from time to time to
ask how mine is doing.

I am very sorry that I have nothing to send you but trust will
come a day when I shall be able to pay you for all your trouble. I
am in hopes of claiming Lily May before too long and God grant
she will not recall a bit of it.

Please find herewith the form you sent.

This is to certify that I <u>MRS. SARAH BELL</u> *am the mother and
only legal guardian of* <u>LILY MAY BELL</u>. *I hereby freely and of
my own will agree for the New York Children's Aid Society to
provide a home until* <u>she</u> *is of age or bind* <u>her</u> *out as the
Managers may judge best. I hereby promise not to interfere in
any way with the views and directions of the Managers.*

Mrs. Sarah Bell
177 3rd Street
Jersey City

April 2, 1877

I am relieved to hear about Lily May's bowels. You say a visit is
not thought advisable, well once she is more settled in it might be a

different story. I believe I could keep a hold of my feelings and not frighten her by giving way.

No one knows how awful it is to be separate from their child but a mother. You refer twice to "the orphans" but remember she is only a half, she has got one parent living. If I am spared and nothing prevents, the father of us all will permit me to have my little one back. Every night on my bended knees I pray for her.

Mrs. Sarah Bell
177 3rd Street
Jersey City

March 3, 1878

I have thought long and hard about what you say of the special trains going out west every week and the fresh air and placing out in farm homes. Institutions are confining to the young it is true and New York famously unhealthy. Do you pay these country women to take the children in? I fear that some would do it for mercerariness not kindness. Or perhaps they pay your Society, I have heard of such arrangements. But then that sounds like buying a horse at market. I am very much bewildered in my mind at the thought of my Lily May going off who knows where.

I planned by now to have put enough by to bring her back to Jersey with me but living is so dear. A home and friends is what I should wish for my little girl, at least until we can be reunited. I do recall the paper I signed last year but circumstances forced my hand. Do not take this as ingratitude, if I do not see her again I will never be worth anything on this earth. How far off do these trains go? If she is taken in by some family, do pass on my request that they will not change her name. Perhaps you will think me too particular but only consider how any mother would feel and you will excuse me.

In answer to your question there was never anything like that in my family or my husband's to my knowledge. Lily May is not two years old yet after all and my mother always said I was silent as the grave till I was three.

Mr. Bassett, Sheriff
Andes
New York

August 14, 1878

My wife and I have no children living, only one stillborn some twenty years back. Mrs. Bassett would like a girl between the ages of two and four, young enough to forget all that has gone before. No particular eye or hair color, except that if she is a foreigner she would stand out in Delaware County. So long as there is no hereditary taint we do not object to her being a foundling or illegitimate. In fact, we would prefer no relations. We do not particularly require the girl to be the student type, but want a happy-natured, responsive one and refined enough to take into our home. We would want to give her a High School education and if possible have her join the church choir.

I quite understand about no money changing hands, and signing the indenture. If a grievance arises can it be canceled?

We have gone to the hotel twice before, when orphan trains have come in, and enjoyed the songs and recitations, but never found anyone quite to our liking. There seemed a lot of older, rough-looking children. Mrs. Bassett would be afraid to take a boy, as harder to raise, and you never know. (It is not for farm work we want a child, unlike some fellow citizens we have seen squeezing boys' arms at the hotel.) I have talked to our doctor, who is on the town's Selection Committee. He said to write to the New York Society direct, and if you had a little girl who may answer our purposes, you might sew our request number right onto her hem, so she would not be given to anyone else.

Mr. Bassett, Sheriff
Andes
New York

November 3, 1878

My wife and I are so far much pleased with the child. At the
hotel we took one good look at her, and then I nodded at Mrs.
Bassett who could not speak, so I went up, and shook hands, and
said, "You are going to be our little girl." She seemed queemish at
first, but is getting used to the animals and no longer makes a face
at the milk warm from the cow. She has a funny habit of keeping
her arms on the table at meals; I suppose she learned it to prevent
any other orphan from snatching her food.

We will keep her on trial for now, just in case. But barring
serious misbehavior or disease, we mean to keep her and give her
our name, Bassett I mean. Her first will be Mabel which keeps two
of her old names – May Bell – in a hidden way as it were. She will
have her room to herself, and more bonnets than she can wear. I
can assure you we will take her to school and church and treat her
as "no different."

Mrs. Sarah Bell
347 Grove Street
Jersey City

December 7, 1878

I could not give a proper answer to your letter last month
as my heart was running over and remains the same. I am not
ungrateful for this foster couple's Christianity but I could wish
the circumstances otherwise. I write now just to inform you that I
have changed my residence to the above and to ask to be informed
the minute if anything should happen to my Lily as I have awful
dreams. In the country between dogs and barb wire and rivers
there is no knowing what could befall a little stranger.

Mr. Bassett, Sheriff
Andes
New York

February 6, 1879

Our Mabel is now one of the most content of children, and growing out of all her clothes. She has a rosy face and is most affectionate. She speaks more than before, though not quite clearly, but my wife can always make her out, so fears of feeblemindedness have been put to rest. She has quite forgotten her old name.

People here are civil, although I fear when she starts school, there will be a certain dose of meanness, as always among children. Such epithets as "bad blood" get thrown around with no thought for the hurt caused. Mrs. Bassett and I look on Mabel as quite our own, and could not love her more if she truly were. Your Agent can call on us anytime, we have nothing to hide.

I can appreciate that mothers do not like to part with their children, even to get them into much better situations. Can you assure us though that this Mrs. Bell will not be given our address? I have heard of cases where a woman abandons her child, and then lands up at the new home and makes scenes.

Mr. Bassett
Battle Creek
Iowa

November 3, 1879

Your last has, after some delay, reached us here in our new home. Please mark all future communications "Private," and do not use headed paper as nobody here knows of our connection with the Society. That in fact was one reason for our fresh start, though land and opportunity were others. It is mostly Germans round here, and no one seems to suspect Mabel is anything other than flesh of our flesh, a late gift from above. Keeping the secret we hope will shield her from the "pauper taint." She is a good girl and a talented singer, though her speech is still somewhat less plain than could be wished.

Thank you for sending the "adoption form," but on consideration we see no need for further fuss, and the risk of further publicity attendant on going through the courts. My wife holds to the principle that Mabel is our own already. We have made wills to provide for her future, all signed and sealed.

Mrs. Samuel Adams (Mrs. Sarah Bell as was)
697 2nd Avenue
Jersey City

April 23, 1880

I write to let you know of my change of fortune, as you will see from the above I am married again. We have "a good home" also (just as much as the couple who have got Lily May) and my husband Samuel who is in business is willing to welcome her into that home for which I thank God on bended knee as not every man would do the same.

If you have the slightest reservations you can send one of your Agents to ask the neighbors what you like. I will always acknowledge your kindness and what these folks on the farm did in giving refuge to my Lily in a time of calamity but that time is over. Let me know how soon she can be brought back. I will hardly know my little one now!

Mr. Bassett
Battle Creek
Iowa

May 12, 1880

It shows heart that the mother has inquired, but there is no question of return like some parcel. My wife is upset the matter has been raised so cavalierlike, and says she will defy anyone to even talk of taking our girl away when we have already adopted her "in spirit." To my mind it is the day to day that makes a family, *de facto* if not *de jure*, and since your Society thought fit to give Mabel into our care, there have passed some five hundred days. She is going on four and we are all she knows in the world.

If as you say this woman has a new husband, why can't she make the best of it? Perhaps she will have more children with him, whereas Mrs. Bassett and self are past any chance of that.

I enclose a recent photograph so you can see how pleasant looking Mabel is turning out. I am in two minds about whether you ought to show the mother the picture. It might ease her to see how well the child is getting on, but then again it might increase the longing. On second thoughts, as it has the address of the studio on it, you had best not let her look at it.

Mrs. Samuel Adams
697 2nd Avenue
Jersey City

January 18, 1884

You may recognize my name as Mrs. Sarah Bell as I was before my present marriage. Since I wrote asking for my child Lily May near to four years ago and was refused, which I took very much to heart, circumstances have gone against Mr. Adams's ventures. But things are looking up again and we have moved to the above, which if you send an Agent as I asked you last time they will see is a gracious home fit for any young person. The Lord knows I am not the first mother to have been obliged to let go of a little one in a time of trouble but now I am in a position to keep house and reclaim my own Lily May.

I think of her all the time, at seven years old what kind of life can it be in the wilds of Iowa when she was always nervous of a cat even? You say this couple treat her as "their own" but that is only make do and make believe as they must know in their heart of hearts. What is done can be undone if there is a will and a way. Surely if you pass this letter on to them so they can hear a mother's misery then they would have mercy if they are such good folks as you keep saying.

Mr. Bassett
Battle Creek
Iowa

September 24, 1885

I thank you for your two last. I apologize if mine had a "testy tone," only Mrs. Bassett was ill at the time, and sometimes it seems as if we will never be left at peace with our girl.

No, we do not think it advisable to enter into any kind of correspondence with this Adams woman (Bell as was), or encourage hopes of a visit. Is it not a queer thing for her to resume her talk of retrieving her child after all these years? I fear she has hopes of being paid off, as it is well known that the blood relations only kick up a fuss if they sniff money in it.

Mabel is so much our daughter, we look back on the time before God gave her to us, and cannot imagine how we got through the lonesome days. She goes to school and Sunday School regularly and learns quickly. She regards tardiness almost as a crime. She is largish and has good health on the whole, though hardly what you would call rugged. She has not the least notion of being an adopted. My wife and I abide by "least said soonest mended."

Mr. Bassett
Battle Creek
Iowa

May 14, 1887

Enclosed please find the form completed as per and the fee of twenty-five dollars for the attorney. We never grudged the sum, it was only that my wife stood out against the intrusion and kept saying it smacked of having to pay for our beloved. But I have prevailed, since I live in terror of the mother turning up on our doorstep some day.

> *The NEW YORK CHILDREN'S AID SOCIETY hereby adopts to* <u>Mr.</u> *and Mrs.* Bassett *an orphan* <u>named Mabel Bassett formerly Lily May Bell</u> *as our child, to keep, protect and treat as our own. We covenant with said Society to provide said orphan with suitable food, clothing, lodging and medical attendance, in health and in sickness, and to instruct* <u>her</u> *adequately in usefuless, as well as to advance and settle* <u>her</u> *in life according as circumstances may permit.*
> *Witness our hands and seals this* <u>12th</u> *day of* <u>May 1887</u>.

Mrs. Sarah Bell
214 Beckman Avenue
Jersey City

February 20, 1889

As you will see I am going by my old name again, Mrs. Sarah Bell. I have suffered a divorce since I wrote last but will likely be married again shortly to a much more worthy man. Just now I can be reached at the house of my father Mr. Joseph Prettyman, address above, if you wish to send me any word.

It seems I have known no luck in this world since the day my first husband Mr. John Bell up and died on me when Lily May my one and only was on my breast. These ties are mysterious and unbreakable, you call her "Mabel" but I will never use that name. Child stealing is what I call it, to send innocents by the trainload into the most backward parts of the country and hand them over to God knows who all, even when they have family living back East. All I asked was to take my Lily home with me and who better to love her than her own mother whose only crime was poverty?

It occurs to me now that my darling is past twelve. I wonder does she think of me at all or have her "folks" so-called kept her in the blackest ignorance of who she is.

Mrs. Sarah C. Mulkins
Davenport Center
New York

October 26, 1894

You may remember me as Mrs. Sarah Bell. I have been married again for some years to a good man called Mulkins and we have a very comfortable residence, see above. The other day I was thinking about my Lily May as I often and will always do and nothing can prevent a mother's heart from grieving, when I remembered that she comes of age next month. Surely at eighteen she should know the truth, that she has a loving mother who has never ceased from inquiring for her and never "abandoned" her as you cruelly put it, only gave her over for temporary safekeeping to preserve her from starvation. If she contacts your Society I trust you will in Christian charity give her my address, you can do that much for all your cant of "legalities." Won't you please tell me how my Lily May is and whether I will be permitted to lay eyes on her again in this lifetime?

Mr. Bassett
Sioux City
Iowa

November 30, 1897

In response to your last several letters, I will tell you that Mabel was married this October 12th to a fine young man from Cedar County. We are much obliged to the Society for its concern over these long years, but now she is a grown woman and a wife, it seems to us her file should by rights be closed and as if it never were. You ask if she is ever to know who she is, which question

Mrs. Bassett and I call impertinent, as she knows she is our beloved Mabel. We must insist that neither Mrs. Bell nor any other former connection shall ever learn anything about Mabel's whereabouts. We keep the papers locked up safe and whoever passes first, the other will burn them. We are not wealthy folk but this one gift we can leave to our girl and will.

MILLIE AND BIRD

Avril Joy

Avril Joy is a British author. In 2003 she won a Northern
Promise award from *New Writing North*. Her short story
'Millie and Bird' won the inaugural Costa Short Story
Award in 2013.

It was the kind of summer when the grass grew too long to cut and
your toes stubbed at the damp end of your trainers, the summer I
was sixteen. It rained all through May and June. It rained on my
birthday. It never let up and the weeds in the yard grew taller than
the gate post. Jonty Angel, our next-door neighbour, gave Millie
the bird that summer, a white zebra finch, and she spent all her
time coaxing it onto her shoulder, whispering to it and feeding it
titbits. He gave her a cage too and she put it in her bedroom out
of harm's way. It was the summer of Bird, it was the summer I fell
in love.

'Why the hell does she have to go round the house with that stupid
bird on her shoulder, for Christ's sake? What girl her age does that?'

'I don't know but she's only thirteen. Where's the harm?' I say.

'When I was thirteen I had better things to think of, like school for
one thing. No time for pets. No time to whisper sweet nothings at
a stupid bloody bird.'

I watch Millie walk into the yard and up through the garden. Bird
on her shoulder, its beak buried in her hair. She disappears behind
the shed. Behind the shed it's mostly overgrown with nettles.
There's an old crabapple, a sink which coats over every spring
with a skin of spawn, a rusty bike and a couple of broken cold
frames.

'Why don't I make you a cup of tea Mum? See if there's anything on the radio, a concert or something? There might be a play on.' I say.

As if she doesn't hear me she goes to the sideboard, opens the door and reaches inside to the stash she keeps behind the pile of old records we're not allowed to touch. She lifts it out like she's won a raffle, like it's a surprise, like she didn't know there was a half-full bottle of vodka there. She pours herself a mug, holds it up and smiles like she doesn't ever need to be put to bed, or ever get sick, or rant and rave about it all being our fault.

I go out into the garden and look for Millie. I won't go behind the shed into the nettles as I don't want my legs all messed up with stings. I want them silky smooth and ready for the fake tan. 'Millie, what are you doing?'

'Nothing.'

'Come over here then and sit for a bit.' I'm on the bench in front of the shed. It moves when you sit on it. The grass is shorter here on account of it having to work its way up through crazy paving and gravel. 'Come on.' I want her to come but not for her sake. I'm not worried about her getting nettle rash and besides she's got Bird. That's what she calls the bird: Bird. When I asked her why, she said it seemed for the best, that naming leads to attachment and I said where the hell did she get that idea from, and she said she read it on the internet.

Millie sits next to me. Bird is on her shoulder moving from one red foot to the other like he's stepping up and down in time to music we can't hear, clawing at her t-shirt.

He turns his head and looks at me with a black eye. I think about Otis and his smoky, black skin that smells of walnut and vanilla. 'You going out tonight?' asks Millie.

'Yes, seven o'clock, Elaine's first, we're meeting there then going into town.'

'Can I come?'

'Don't be daft, you're thirteen.'

'Well *you're* only sixteen and one week.'

'Next year maybe, anyway I don't think Bird would appreciate it, in Jelly's, with all that noise and all those people.'

Bird is still now. A cabbage white floats past and a swarm of midges hover above the long grass. I think I should do something about the grass, like ask Jonty if I can borrow his mower, though he said it needed to be cut down first. A crow flies out of the lilac tree above us and Bird jumps up onto Millie's head.

'Is it stupid or what, that bird? It'll get eaten by the crows if it's not careful.'

'He's just nervous,' says Millie and puts her hand up and grasps the bird and brings it down into her lap where she cups it in both hands. 'His heart's beating like crazy,' she says, 'feel it.'

She goes to pass the bird to me but I pull away, 'don't give it to me,' I say, 'I don't like birds.' But it's not that I don't like birds, it's that I don't want to feel its heart beating like that, not when its skin is all feathers and a puff of wind coming by could break its bones.

'What's not to like? He's beautiful, feel him, he's like silk and he smells of grass.' She holds the bird towards me.

'Don't bring it near me,' I say. 'Keep it to yourself. Come on, I'll make us tea before I go out.'

I make egg and chips because it's easy, oven chips cook themselves. It's just for us. Mum's in the front room with the telly and her bottle. Millie feeds the bird a chip. He's not normally allowed at the table. We clear away and then go upstairs to my room. Millie puts

Bird in his cage and then comes and sits on the bed and watches me get ready. We share a bottle of coke and I smoke a cigarette out of the window as best I can, but it's hard because it's raining and the cig is getting damp.

Millie does my nails with the purple varnish I bought especially. She's good at doing things like hair and nails although you wouldn't think so to look at her. 'You could be a hairdresser or a beautician,' I say, 'if you weren't so brainy.' She smiles. Millie is clever; the cleverest girl in her class, although how she's going to be anything beats me. I used to think about being a lawyer. I fancied that, but now, well I'm not sure. Jonty Angel says he might be able to get me a job in the auction house where he works. Sometimes you have to be realistic and scale things down, the kind of things you'd been hoping for. I used to pray about that kind of stuff but then your prayers they get rained on like the grass.

I like it when Millie takes my hand and then each of my fingers, one by one, and holds them while she paints the nail. She's just dipping into the thick, pearly varnish when we hear stumbling on the stairs and the bathroom door banging shut. Millie puts the brush back in the bottle and we wait. I listen hard. I'm good at listening, it comes with practice. I've got dolphin ears. Dolphins hear fourteen times better than humans. After a minute or two we start up again and one by one my nails take on a glossy purple sheen. I look at Millie, at her bitten-down nails and I think – tomorrow I'll paint them purple.

The toilet flushes and the bathroom door opens. Her bedroom door closes. 'She's gone to sleep it off,' I say. 'She'll be snoring like an old bag lady soon.' Millie stops, brush mid-way between bottle and the little finger of my left hand. I can tell she doesn't like what I've said. But I laugh and before long she laughs and then we both laugh and we roll about on the bed laughing, only not too loud and me with my hands in the air to stop my nails smudging.

'Can I wait up for you?' Millie says.

'It'll be late.'

'I'll get into your bed.'

'Not with that bird you won't.'

'I'll leave Bird in his cage. Promise.'

'All right then.'

It's gone eight when we wake in the grey light I hear the rain outside and a cheeping noise at my ear. What the hell. I told her no bird. 'Millie,' I turn. The bird hops away from my ear and onto Millie's pillow. 'I thought I said no bird.'

Millie opens her eyes. 'I couldn't leave him. Mum got up after you went out and came downstairs and said I'd got to give Bird back to Jonty or else she'd get rid of him. I was scared she'd hurt him.'

'Well put him back in his cage now or get his box or something, just get it out of the bed.' I turn over and push my head back in the pillow and replay last night's kiss, and then I hear her.

'Breakfast!' She shouts up the stairs, 'Come on, up you get.'

I turn back to Millie and raise my eyebrows in a kind of here-we-go-again way. 'Better get up,' I say. 'It's going to be one of those *happy-family days*.'

No one makes pancakes like she does and she's cut up fruit and there's syrup and sugar and lemon and a clean cloth on the table. When we finish eating, she says, 'The rain's stopped. Think it's about time we saw to the garden. There's a scythe somewhere in the shed. I'll find it. You go next door and borrow Jonty's mower.'

It's true, the rain has stopped and the sun is out and it's warm enough to be outside in a t-shirt, and I don't care that I've had less than five hours sleep, what with getting in so late, because I'm in love and, as it turns out, it is one of those *happy-family-days* and who knows when the next one might come around.

The garden looks different by the time we finish, like it's doubled its size. The sky is cloudless and we've got the old car rugs out on the lawn. Mum reads the paper. I doze on and off and think about Otis walking me home. I think about him kissing me in the lane; kissing Otis is like sucking chicken from a bone, and I think about how when I went round to his house his Mum made us a whole plate of chicken sandwiches for supper. If things carry on like today, then maybe I can invite him back, that's what I'm thinking when I hear the click of a lighter and look up to see Jonty leaning on the fence.

'All right girls? Looks a bit more like it,' he says, lighting his rollie with the Zippo flame. Jonty's got a pierced tongue and a tattoo of an eagle on the back of his neck and he's wearing a t-shirt that says *The World is Disappearing*. It's black and it's got a line of blue-green worlds across the front that get smaller and smaller until they disappear round the back. I used to think Jonty was a messenger. Well for one thing 'angel,' means messenger, Millie told me that, and for another, because of his t-shirts which said things like: *I Just Wanna Be Myself, Love Kills, No More Pain.* I used to think he was speaking to me until I realised he was the drummer in an old punk-rock band and it was his uniform. He doesn't play in the band anymore on account of him nearly losing his foot in a motorbike accident.

I wonder if Jonty is really worried about the world disappearing: the land sinking, the seas rising, polar ice caps melting. I know all about it from school and Mrs Allen in geography but I can't be worrying about it. I've got too many other things and besides it's not exactly news to me; my world's been disappearing from as far back as I can remember, mostly into the bottom of a vodka bottle. Today, just for once, I wish Jonty was wearing something to make us smile, like that t-shirt of his that says, *If You Want Breakfast in Bed, Sleep in the Kitchen*, or best of all, the red one with, *Save the Drama for Your Llama*, in big white letters across the front.

'Fancy a Barbie? I've got a few burgers in the freezer, veggie as well as meat.'

Millie's eyes light up. She likes being around Jonty, we both like being around Jonty because you can rely on him. Jonty is reliable which you have to be if you've got an aviary full of birds to look after. Millie is the only one he lets help him. Mum likes him too, she's known him since she and Dad first moved in, further back than we can remember. Sometimes they play old records together, sometimes he calls her *Blondie* and you can tell she likes that.

'Come on then before it decides to set away raining again. I'll get it lit. If you want ketchup you'll have to bring it with you.'

By the time we've eaten our burgers the sky is the colour of wet tarmac. We sit sipping coke and waiting for the rain. Nobody speaks. I'm praying it won't rain, praying for the end of the summer when rain washed the baby wood pigeons out of their nests in the plane trees and into the gutter. I think of Otis and I pray: let everyday be like today, so I can bring him home; no more sideboards and vodka, no more coming in from school and her sparked out on the sofa. I let that fantasy loose in the air around me and I wonder if we're all, in our own way, dreaming of the same kind of thing. I'm sure Millie is because she's got that faraway look and a half-smile on her face and for once she isn't petting Bird.

'We should go away on holiday,' says Mum, 'get away from this sodding, sandbag summer, somewhere hot – Greece. I went there once with your Dad.'

I hold my breath.

'Let's drink to it,' she says.

We all hold our breath. Jonty gives me a quick look then says, 'Aye, good idea, why don't I make us a cup of tea?'

Jonty brings a pot of tea and a packet of digestives on a tray with four mugs. We drink tea and listen to the birds shushing and chirruping in the aviary. The rain clouds pass and the sky turns blue again and I'm starting to think that everything seems OK and maybe I'll get out tonight, so I take my phone out of my pocket. I'll text Otis, who knows I might even go round his house for a bit. And I'm thinking how his Mum might make us chicken sandwiches again for supper, when I look up and see Millie's gone.

Don't ask me where it comes from or why but I can feel it, like a wild animal feels the coming storm, something moving on the air; it's my dolphin ears and most likely my nose too. I know something isn't right. I put my phone down. 'Where's Millie?' 'Gone to put Bird away,' says Jonty, 'she's going to give us a hand feeding that lot,' he nods in the direction of the aviary. Mum's drinking tea and smoking, her head buried in Jonty's newspaper. She doesn't look up as I get to my feet.

I call for Millie in the house but there's no reply. I walk through the garden, following my dolphin nose, down to the shed, then round the back to the nettle patch. Millie is there, squatting by the old sink with her hands in the water.

'Millie, what's up?' I say but I don't need an answer because Millie takes her hands out of the water and I can see what's up, right there, under that clear blue sky, shining in the sink, I can see it, see him: Bird, floating lifeless, his feathers slicked onto his tiny body. 'Millie, what, how …?'

'I'm going to take him out now, find something to wrap him in, then bury him.'

'But Millie, what happened?'

'Some things are too hard to bear,' says Millie laying his body on the grass. 'Some things you just couldn't bear.' She looks up at me with a look that says -*you know what I mean*, and I don't need to think about it because I do. I know exactly what she means.

I nod. 'We'll bury him,' I say. 'Then you can go and help Jonty with the aviary, and after that I'll paint your nails purple.'

Millie already has a trowel and she's digging a hole at the base of the crab apple. She takes an old crepe bandage from her pocket and wraps it around Bird. She lays him in the hole and covers him with wet leaves and soil. 'Say a prayer,' she says. And I do.

EXTENDED COPYRIGHT